SAINTS & SUSPECTS

FICTION BY JORDAN MCCOLLUM

SPY ANOTHER DAY NOVELS
I, Spy
Spy for a Spy
Tomorrow We Spy

SPY ANOTHER DAY PREQUELS
Spy Noon (novella)
Mr. Nice Spy (novella)
Spy by Night (novel)

SAINTS & SPIES SERIES
Saints & Spies

NONFICTION BY JORDAN MCCOLLUM

Character Arcs
Character Sympathy
Character Depth

SAINTS & SUSPECTS

SAINTS & SPIES SERIES
VOLUME TWO

JORDAN McCOLLUM

DURHAM CREST BOOKS

First printing, 2017

Published by Durham Crest Books
Pleasant Grove, Utah
Set in Linux Libertine

ISBN 978-1-940096-20-9

PRINTED IN THE UNITED STATES OF AMERICA

1

SURVEILLANCE. SPECIAL AGENT ZACH SAINT shifted against the gray upholstery. He'd already served in surveillance squads, but with their target's regular babysitters testifying in court, here he was again. Two hours and thirty-seven minutes of sitting in downtown Chicago, trying to seem inconspicuous in their car, staring at nothing, waiting for Irish terrorists.

Today, they weren't so much terrorists as regular people running errands.

Zach rubbed his hands together, though staying warm was a lost cause. Next to Zach, Supervisory Special Agent Xavier Mason sipped his coffee without taking his eyes off the street. "See the Bulls game?"

"Nah." College ball was more his thing. "They win?"

Xavier snorted. "Another loss."

Zach suppressed a wince. That record took him back to his own college team. He scanned the sidewalk down the block. The Canavans were still in the red brick tailor shop. Even terrorists had to shop. And eat. And bank.

For two hours and—he checked the dash clock—forty minutes.

Sometimes the hardest part of surveillance was staying awake.

Zach rubbed his eyes, refocused on the street, and continued the world's slowest conversation. "Think they'll make the playoffs?"

"Not at this rate."

Down the block, the tailor shop's wrought iron security gate swung open. Zach grabbed the binoculars from the console between the seats. A stout woman with dark auburn hair and a taller, craggy-faced man stepped out of the building. The target couple. Zach reached for the keys in the ignition. "Eyes on."

Xavier raised his camera and peered through the viewfinder,

sweeping the lens across the scene. "Wait. I've only seen pictures, but isn't that your . . . Molly?"

What? No. Last he'd heard, the FBI assigned Molly to Arizona. Zach swung the binoculars to follow Xavier's line of sight.

He spotted her in front of the bright yellow burger shack at the corner: tall, beautiful, dark curls that bounced with her springing step. Yep, definitely Molly, but she hadn't been "his" for a long time. Seeing her hit him like a no-look pass drilled straight to the gut.

Molly rounded the corner, heading toward their target. What was she doing here?

Maybe visiting her parents. Zach held his breath. If she passed the Canavans, he could imagine this hadn't happened. He wouldn't have to see or talk to her, and he could keep doing his job and pretending to forget her.

But could it be a coincidence his Irish ex-girlfriend was walking right toward Irish terrorists? Zach slid the binoculars to the target couple. Still headed Molly's direction.

Every step brought them closer together—and pulled Zach's ribs tighter. Ten steps apart. She passed the nail shop. Five. They passed Subway. Molly came even with the Canavans, and time seemed to stop.

Molly kept going. The Canavans didn't acknowledge her. Nothing. Finally they passed one another.

She was safe.

Before Zach could release a breath, Grace Canavan stopped short and turned back. And Molly did the same, turning to the target couple.

So much for the day going well. With the way things worked in the Bureau—and his life—Zach figured he might see Molly again. But he didn't think she'd be talking to suspected terrorists.

Much as he wanted to act like he'd never seen her, no way would he leave her out there, alone and unprotected. Urgency pushed him into action. Zach reached for the door handle. "You drive."

Xavier caught Zach's sleeve without taking his eyes from his camera. "Do not approach, Z."

"She's got no idea who she's dealing with." He knocked X's hand away and stepped out of the car into the sharp cold. He needed a heavier jacket. He needed a cover.

He paused at the street vendor on the corner to buy two pretzels—and buy himself one more minute to pick an identity, someone with a right to jump into their conversation, or at least something to tip Molly off that this was bad. She might've danced an Irish jig on his heart, with all the things that she wanted to do before she could think about marriage, but he couldn't leave her alone with terrorists.

The target couple was too busy chatting to notice him until he slung an arm around Molly like she'd never left. He finally settled on a cover: deep South. "Here ya go, darlin'," he drawled.

Molly looked up at him with a spark of surprise in her deep blue eyes. Did she have to be even more beautiful than he remembered? She hesitated a moment before smiling and accepting one of his pretzels. Good recovery.

Zach let go of Molly only long enough to offer the target couple his hand. "Jason Tolliver."

"Is this your man?" the stout woman gushed in a thick Ulster accent, clapping her hands over one of Zach's.

"That's me." Zach grinned and hoped he covered the flinch at "your man," although he couldn't be sure whether Molly had mentioned a boyfriend. Either that, or Grace was guessing, or maybe using the Irish equivalent of "that guy."

"Brilliant." Grace beamed at him. "You're a lucky one, aren't you?"

"I know it. Now, who're y'all?"

The woman shook his hand again, even more emphatically, her dark auburn bob bouncing from the effort. "Grace Canavan."

"Ed." The man gave a curt headshake, a standard Irish greeting, his weathered face impassive.

"We're friends of Molly's parents." Grace turned to her husband. "When did we last see the Ryans?"

Ryans? Molly's last name was Malone. Zach kept his expression unchanged, and his mind on his mission: get Molly out safe. "Great to meet y'all, but we really gotta run." He slipped his arm from Molly's shoulders to take her hand.

"Actually, Jason, we were just catchin' up," Molly said. He'd forgotten how much he loved her Dublin lilt—but not so much her talking with terrorists. "It's been—what, twenty years?"

"We did see you only a few years ago, in Dublin."

Despite her gloves muffling the sound, Molly snapped like *you've got me there.* "How could I forget?"

Zach picked up on a tiny undertone of tension in her voice and shifted closer. If she insisted on staying, the least he could do was protect her.

Down the street, the church bells of Holy Name Cathedral pealed. The place Zach had begun his FBI career in Chicago was giving him the perfect excuse. "Molly, darlin', we're gonna be late for Mass." He met her gaze, trying to urge her along without attracting the Canavans' suspicions.

"Jason." Each syllable was a prelude of practiced patience. "Surely five minutes won't hurt."

His stomach dropped an inch. If she was this set on talking to them, could she know who they were? And if so, what was going on here?

He wasn't about to be the last to know. "Hey," he said, "why don't you get their number and we all can catch up later?"

A heartbeat of silence, and mettle flashed in Molly's eyes. He'd been on the receiving end of her determination more than once—when she was the one trying to keep him safe.

Wait. That wasn't happening here. Right?

Then Molly smiled. "Sure now." She released his hand and got her phone to trade numbers with Grace. "I'll be seein' you soon, I hope?"

"Aw, sure look it," Grace said. Which didn't mean yes or no, but probably meant no if she wasn't saying yes.

"We'll give y'all a call," Zach said, like Molly hadn't tried to cut him out. "See ya." As soon as her phone slid into her purse, Zach took her hand and tugged her away. They walked to the end of the block, eating their quickly cooling, over-salted pretzels in silence.

He had to say something about what he'd done. Using a cover had to be a huge red flag. Her insistence on talking to them certainly sent him the same warning.

Of course, the things they hadn't said today were only the tip of a much bigger iceberg.

They rounded a corner, and Molly withdrew her hand from his.

She shook a few wind-whipped snowflakes from her dark curls, like that was the reason she'd pulled away.

What did he expect? She didn't want to hold hands with the guy who'd dumped her six months ago. Zach stuffed his hand into his pocket.

Molly finally spoke. "Watchin' the Canavans, are we, 'Jason'?"

"Yes, *we* are. They could have your badge for consorting with suspected terrorists."

She raised an eyebrow, but didn't look at him. "Think this is all a coincidence?"

Zach had sensed something else was going on but—"You're here on assignment."

Why hadn't anyone warned him?

"Naturally. Headin' back to the office?"

"Yep." He led her across the street and tossed the wrapper from his pretzel in a trash can.

She fished in her purse for her phone. "Let's see if my parents are ready to talk."

Could her parents be the Ryans? Though he'd known Molly for over a year, he still had a lot to learn.

But he'd already figured that out the hard way.

He walked on, pretending it made no difference that he was once again inches from the one that got away—no, the one he'd had to let go.

Grace waited until they reached their platform for the 'L' before allowing her elation to register on her face. "Imagine, Molly Ryan."

"Forgot how tall she was," Ed muttered.

"Her fella, too." Grace checked the platform. The claustrophobic waiting area was hardly more than a hallway. Whoever heard of an "elevated" train underground? "We just found our fourth," she whispered, letting the Friday afternoon hubbub drown out her observation to all but Ed.

Ed shook his head. "Not a chance."

Could the eejit never do anything right? "Are ya coddin' me? She's a *Ryan*. If she heard half what her parents must've told her, she's already politicized."

"Politicized, maybe. Big leap from there to here." He glanced around the platform, subtly holding his hand palm down, signaling Grace to keep quiet.

She lowered her voice. "Her uncle was martyred for this."

"So was Donal's."

Grace flinched at the double punch of emotion. Ed knew better than to casually mention her brother, God rest his soul. Somehow, even after British soldiers deliberately ran down his uncle during a peaceful gathering, Donal, their older son, had devolved into tepid nationalism.

She changed the subject back to her original tack. "Wouldn't it be better if we had a fourth?"

"Not someone we've hardly seen in twenty years." Ed's certain tone showed he was right and he knew it. The only reason they'd recognized her was because they'd briefly met Molly with the Ryans in Dublin seven years ago.

After all these years, the empty-headed man still knew nearly nothing. She'd have to ease him into seeing reason. "How's about we feel them out a bit?"

"Not for this job. Too late," he stated emphatically. "We haven't the time to bring them up to speed now everythin's in motion."

Grace huffed, hiding her small victory with a show of frustration. She didn't *need* Molly now, but she'd slipped the idea of her joining them into Ed's subconscious. "Fine. I still say she's our fourth."

"'Time can but make it easier to be wise.'" He motioned for them to draw closer to the blue loading line on the floor as their train approached. "Maybe next time, Grace."

A step behind him, Grace allowed herself to smile. If she was half the soldier her parents had been, Molly would make the perfect addition to their team. In four weeks, when this job was finished, she'd see that they needed her—Ireland needed her.

Only four more weeks.

By the time the Canavans had been tracked back to their apartment, Molly was waiting for her parents at the security gate of the Chicago FBI office. And Zachary had disappeared inside the building. Thankfully. Hard enough feigning calm when she was talking to terrorists, but to be faced with the man she'd loved—a man still handsome enough to take her breath away? Who could work under those conditions?

He'd broken up with her last summer because their lives were "headed in different directions." Why did those different directions have to throw them together again?

At last, she saw the familiar sight of her parents, her mum's funky purple glasses and shock of bright highlights hiding the gray in her short hair, her father towering over Mum, his narrow features and even his stylish wire-rimmed glasses weary with the world. Hopefully, now that she'd officially met the Canavans, her parents could add something to the case file.

Once they were past the security gate, Molly led her parents into a windowless conference room where an African-American agent waited. He stood and introduced himself. "Supervisory Special Agent Xavier Mason."

"Colm and Katie Malone," Molly's da said, gesturing at himself and Mum.

Molly shook Agent Mason's hand. "Special Agent Molly Malone." Her father raised an eyebrow, but because there were already Special Agents Mary Malone and Mary Margaret Malone in the Bureau, Molly had to use her nickname officially at work.

After a round of handshakes, SSA Mason gestured for the Malones to take a chair at the long faux-cherry table and did the same himself. Molly seated herself between her parents and the supervisor. This would be interesting. Though she "knew" what her parents had done until she was five or so, she'd never pressed for specifics before. Never needed to.

Agent Mason placed a photo of the Canavans in front of them.

Da looked up first—no recognition. "Sorry, can't help you."

"Colm." Her mum remained fixed on the photograph.

He turned to Mum. "We can't be talkin' about that." They stared at one another in silence, the steel in both of their eyes speaking for them.

"It's been over twenty years," Mum whispered.

"I don't recall there bein' an expiry date on 'Top Secret.' And seven's a lot less than twenty." He added a pointed glance in Molly's direction.

Molly tried not to laugh at her father. "Don't go tellin' us you're withholdin' information for my sake. The IRA's been an open secret in our family since before I was born." And the *real* nature of their involvement in the Irish Republican Army hadn't been a secret at all since they'd been whisked to the States seven years ago—after seeing the Canavans. Having her parents here was a formality for the Bureau's sake.

Mum glanced at Agent Mason across the table and back to Da. "If they're here and they have the FBI's attention—you think they called us because the Bureau wants their phone number?"

"Oh, the FBI'll spirit us away if they go bumpin' into us again?"

"If the FBI arrests them, they won't have to relocate us." Mum turned to Molly and Agent Mason.

"You know them from the IRA," Mason stated.

"We do," Mum said. "But it's not quite what you're thinkin'."

"Oh?"

"We didn't join the Provos to 'liberate' the northern counties, exactly."

Agent Mason cleared his throat. "What does that mean, *exactly*?"

Molly's parents exchanged another glance, then focused on her. Da ran a hand over his close-cropped gray hair. "Can Molly step out?"

She managed not to roll her eyes and addressed Mason. "You're familiar with the term *agent provocateur*?"

To his credit, Agent Mason didn't flinch. "MI5?"

Her da silently scoffed.

"Special Branch," Molly provided. They'd never said as much, but it didn't take a genius to deduce they hadn't spied for the British—they'd reported to a division of the same Irish police force that hired her twenty-five years later.

This time, Da dipped his chin in a single nod.

"Special Branch of what?" Agent Mason asked.

"Special Detective Unit of *An Garda Síochana.* Spyin' for the Irish."

"Ah. We've got the files, but what can you tell us about *them*?" Agent Mason tapped the photo.

Mum sighed. "More married to the cause than one another—Janey Mack, Colm, do you remember the fuss Grace made over their weddin'?"

The tiniest smile tugged at the corner of Da's mouth. "And ours?"

Mum laughed softly. "Sometimes she was more interested in gettin' married than who she married—as long as he was IRA." She pulled herself back to the topic. "We ran into them in Dublin seven years ago, and even then they were tryin' to drag us into it again."

Right. When Molly had been home on holiday, a few months after graduating from Garda College and receiving her first assignment on the force.

If the Canavans had found out she was a Garda, they could've targeted her entire family. The threat was serious enough that the Irish government had shipped Molly, her parents and her older sister's family to the United States within days.

"They're the reason we left Derry, too," her mum continued. "We'd given it up, retired, and they kept houndin' us to do this and that."

"You were the Ryans," Molly prompted for Agent Mason's benefit.

Da took a breath. "We were. Our cover."

"We're all familiar with their profile." Agent Mason steered the conversation back to the Canavans with a tap on the photo. There was a beat of silence before he pulled out another photo, this one from an hour ago—Molly talking to the Canavans. "What might they be up to now?"

Her parents stared at the photo, Mum swallowing audibly. She looked up with concern in her eyes and the V of her brow, but it was

Da who spoke. "Particularly fond of bombs. Big statements. Public displays."

Agent Mason nodded slowly. "Any ideas on a timeline? Any dates significant for them?"

"Your guess is as good as ours," Da said. "Probably better."

Mum thought a moment longer. "If they're commemoratin' somethin' personal, her brother was killed in May. Maybe the Easter Risin' if it's more political. Only speculatin'." Mum pivoted to Molly. "You know what you're gettin' yourself into, don't you?"

"I do."

Her mum's gaze grew distant, and the set of her lips seemed to say she was as satisfied with Molly's answer as if she'd given an evasive excuse for breaking curfew.

Da shook his head, defeated. "We just don't know. Never worked with them directly—more of a social relationship within the Army." He stood and helped Mum to her feet. "Sorry to waste your time."

Agent Mason gave a nod of grim understanding. Mum kissed the top of Molly's head, and Da squeezed her shoulder. "See you at rehearsal."

Molly patted his hand and stood to show them out. Agent Mason hurried to open the door for them. Mum shook Agent Mason's hand again. "You have work to do," she said.

They certainly did. Agent Mason stepped out and signaled someone over, and another agent approached. Molly turned back to collect the photos before she saw who it was.

"Colm, Katie." Though she couldn't see him, she recognized Zachary's voice addressing her parents. Molly stepped further out of sight of the door. If she could avoid him, she would. Who wanted to run into an ex at work? Especially one who still left her breathless as if she'd run a marathon?

As if she hadn't seen other attractive men since he dumped her last summer.

"Ah," Da said. "Now it makes sense."

Mum rushed to explain. "We wondered if you were secretly unemployed. You know, workin' for 'the government' and all, never anythin' specific."

Sarcasm rang in Zachary's reply. "Good to see you again, too."

"We're just leavin'," Da said. "Always a pleasure, Zach."

"Likewise."

"This agent will escort you out," Agent Mason said.

Before Molly could muster the hope that he meant Zachary, his voice carried again, softer. "Any idea on a timeline?"

"Haven't been in contact with them for years. Easter, maybe."

A beat of silence passed, but Molly wasn't moving until she was sure Zachary was gone.

He wasn't. "Did you know about Molly?"

"Are you kidding? You think I would've dragged you down there if I did?" Agent Mason paused. "I called the ASAC on my way back. He notified the regular surveillance guys this morning."

"Convenient, when they're in court all day."

Molly allowed a silent sigh. The Assistant Special Agent in Charge—who'd transferred her here for this case—should've told Agent Mason she was going in today, not just the surveillance team who normally watched Grace. That had backfired on them all.

"Don't think we won't talk about what happened," Xavier said. "I am *not* the one—"

"I know. It was stupid. But I couldn't leave her out there."

"She was on assignment." Agent Mason reiterated the point with the right balance of firmness and defense. At least someone recognized she knew what she was doing.

"Last I knew, she was *assigned* to Arizona. I thought she was here on vacation."

Agent Mason was silent a long moment. "She's our ticket in."

"Listen, I can do this, but Molly—"

"In an hour she's gotten us closer to them than we have in six weeks." Agent Mason jumped up Molly's mental list of agents she'd work with again. Respect went both ways.

Zachary didn't seem to get that. "She's not even counterterrorism."

"If you can't work with her, you can be reassigned."

"Me? Molly's practically a first office agent still. There's gotta be something less dangerous."

Less. Dangerous. Hadn't she been the one protecting Zachary from the mob when she met him undercover? Wasn't she an FBI agent now?

Molly strode to the door to face Zachary. "What were you plannin' to do? Call up Grace and say you're completely taken with these total strangers?"

Zachary grimaced. "Molly, I didn't—"

"I appreciate the vote of confidence, Agent Saint." She brushed past him, calculating how quickly she could make it to the lift without appearing to be running away.

Zachary stopped her with a hand on her arm, and she spun back. He offered a strained smile. "That's not what I meant."

"You didn't mean I can't handle this?"

His deep-set blue eyes fell. Molly ignored a quick stab of guilt. She was glad not to have to stare into those knowing eyes as if nothing had changed. Nothing was the same.

"I don't want you to get hurt," he said.

He should've been that considerate last summer. But Molly glanced at the sea of cubicles and desks stretching across the squad room and held her tongue. She wasn't about to humiliate them both by airing their personal problems in front of Zachary's entire division, not to mention his boss.

"Can you work together?" Agent Mason asked.

Molly turned to him. "The assignment was for me, on my own."

"You need the backup," Zachary stated like it was more than fact, like it was Gospel Truth.

"You realize I'm an FBI agent, don't you?"

Zachary opened his mouth and closed it, then nodded. "You got a plan?"

Molly clamped down on her rising anger. "Ring the Canavans Monday night and invite them to lunch next week."

"Paella," Agent Mason suggested.

Much as she liked the Spanish rice dish, Molly couldn't help but raise an eyebrow. An oddly specific recommendation.

"Restaurant in the Loop," Zachary clarified. "They play nice with us."

"Right." So Zachary knew one little thing she didn't. He'd worked in Chicago longer.

How long? The last she knew, he was on the fast track at headquarters. What was he doing here?

"What will you tell them about me?" Zachary asked.

"*If* they ask, I'll say it's nothin' serious." She wanted to watch his reaction, but she didn't dare. Staring into the eyes of a man that handsome, one she'd once loved? Now *that* was dangerous.

"No." Zachary flat-out rejected her story—which she was making up on the spot and doing a grand job, thank you very much—and turned to Agent Mason. "I need to stay on this case."

Agent Mason's gaze slid to Molly and back to Zachary. "She's doing okay on her own."

"X." Zachary's chin lowered, like he was leveling with his blood brother. "Keep me on the case."

Agent Mason met Zachary's eyes, and they shared some silent conversation in man-ese. Not Molly's first language—not even her fourth—but she picked up on Zachary's ridiculous over-protectiveness.

"I can manage," Molly said.

"*I* know. But . . ." Agent Mason checked with Zachary again and pressed his lips together. "Backup never hurts."

Molly set her jaw. Obviously she couldn't compete with the boys' club bond. She'd have to prove herself at Paella.

"Coordinate." Agent Mason pointed at them and checked his watch. "Before you leave today. Check in once a week." He headed for his desk.

Fine. She wheeled on Zachary. "I'll be Molly Ryan. I remember my childhood in Derry with ridiculous fondness; I cannot fathom why those evil imperialists insist on maintainin' control of land in my country."

Zachary's tone verged on patronizing. "Cool the nationalist rhetoric—don't want them to think you're too eager."

"Oh, I am eager." She smirked at him. He returned the smile without sarcasm, but with—nostalgia?

Love?

A mad buzz vibrated through her at the thought. No, definitely not that. Molly clenched her fist. This time, she'd keep her heart intact.

"Not trying to step on your toes," Zachary said. "I just . . . know how hard it is to be alone undercover."

For half a minute, Molly almost let herself believe him. Could he really be here for support, not because he doubted her abilities?

"We can work on my legend over the weekend," Zachary offered.

Seeing any man that attractive outside of work was a recipe for heartache. This had to be business, and business only. "I'm sure you can handle it."

"Okay." He paused, and when he spoke again, something about his voice was . . . gentler. "Really good to see you."

Molly nodded, barely daring to look at him. Did he have to be handsome as ever, the same knowing blue eyes, the same light brown hair, the same balance of confidence and kindness in his smile?

The same man who'd stolen her heart undercover and broken it with the truth. "Good to see you, too," she lied.

Did one of them move, or had they been standing this close the whole time—in the middle of the counterterrorism division?

She backed toward the conference room. Attraction was only natural; she'd have to manage. Wasn't as though she still had feelings for him. Now, which was the best way around Zach?

"We should catch up. You have plans tonight?"

"I do." She was grateful it wasn't a lie—but she wasn't ready to twist the knife and tell him about Nate.

"Okay." Zachary took the blow . . . not like a blow at all. "See you Monday."

"Monday."

Zachary headed for his desk, and Molly retreated to the conference room to collect the Canavans' photos. She swallowed a sigh. They had virtually nothing on the Canavans except Grace mentioning the IRA to someone who worked with her on a night janitorial staff.

This was not how Molly had imagined her first major undercover assignment—or running into Zach again. In fact, she'd tried not to imagine seeing him at all. The Bureau was big enough for the two of them to never cross paths, especially with him climbing ladders in DC and her just happy to be back in law enforcement after all those years away.

Because of the Canavans. Molly glanced down at the photo of

herself with the suspects. Seven years ago, Grace and Ed had ruined her perfect life. At twenty, Molly had been on track for her dream job with Irish intelligence. Then her family was shuttled off to Chicago, where her career had hit a brick wall, where nobody wanted an Irish citizen enforcing American law.

Where she'd met Zachary.

No. Zachary was what she'd called him when they were dating. Everyone but his mother called him Zach, and she'd follow suit as long as they had to work together.

Molly studied the Canavans' photo again. She'd bring them down for what they did to Northern Ireland and whatever they were doing now, and then she could move on from her past once and for all. Including Zachary.

Zach.

THAT NIGHT, MOLLY FOCUSED on her car window as Nate pulled into Bandera's car park.

"You've been quiet," he noted. "You okay?"

Molly looked at her boyfriend and took a deep breath. She hadn't been good company, trying to avoid all the things she couldn't say. She couldn't tell him she'd run into people she'd hardly seen since she was five; she couldn't tell him she was hunting down terrorists; she definitely couldn't tell him she'd seen Zach.

Nate didn't have the security clearance, and he wouldn't understand. Besides, he didn't know who Zach was. "I'm grand," she said. "How was your day?"

Nate gave a low whistle. "Crazy. You wouldn't believe what Carlington's like when you're trying to prove yourself."

Management consulting seemed less daunting than a job with people's lives on the line, but she let that slide.

Nate shifted the car into park, leaving the engine running. "Um, I've been thinking."

He paused, but she'd learned to let silence force someone else to speak.

"There's something I want to talk to you about."

That sounded none too good. "What's that?"

"We've been dating for a while."

She nodded and let the silence spin on, Nate growing more fidgety.

"I gotta say, things are going really, really well."

She would've agreed far more emphatically had she not just seen Zach. In fact, until that afternoon, she'd thought she was starting to fall for Nate.

Seeing Zach shouldn't change that. She'd moved on.

"Maybe," Nate finally continued, "we should think about marriage."

She blinked twice, and yet the words still didn't seem to sink into her brain. "That's, ah, a big decision."

"Not saying we'll elope tonight." Nate smoothed his chestnut pompadour, already impeccable, and laughed.

Molly joined in, though she sounded nervous to her ears. "Then what are you sayin'?"

"We should pray about it."

"Nate," she began carefully, "I have a lot to accomplish before I get married."

"Believe me, I get that. But when you find the right person, why wait?" Nate switched off the car and hurried around to get her door. Two months and he was talking marriage? Was he crazy? Did all Mormon men bring up marriage this soon?

Zach hadn't. Molly shoved that thought aside.

Nate opened the door and helped her out. Other than this rather insane notion, Nate was nearly everything she'd want in a boyfriend: considerate, sweet, chivalrous, romantic. And it wasn't as though they'd just met; they'd been friends at church while he was in business school and she was at Quantico, and he'd been there for her online and then on the phone while she adjusted to her first assignment in Arizona. Though they'd only been official for—what, eight weeks?—they'd dated for another month or two before that. He'd nearly taken a position in Phoenix when this assignment had come for Molly.

Within a week, he'd landed a job here, to be close to her. As boyfriends went, he was practically perfect, Molly reminded herself. Almost too good to be true. Nearly everything she could ask for. She took Nate's arm and he walked her into the restaurant. The low, dark ceiling and heavy wood tones blended a feel of the Old World with an intimate, modern ambiance.

"Now, this place is nice," he whispered as they followed the hostess to a table, his green eyes sparkling. "But wait until tomorrow night."

"What's tomorrow night?"

"Celebrating Valentine's day, since I'll be gone Tuesday—but more importantly, it's our second 'monthiversary.' I've been planning it for about two months."

She joined in his laughter. She wasn't much for sentimentality normally, but remembering silly occasions like that was cute.

Now if only he'd forget this talk of marriage, everything would be nearly perfect. Nearly.

In the entryway of the Irish American Heritage Center the following morning, Molly chatted with the teenagers in Scoil Síofra's Irish dance company. Didn't seem all that long ago that she'd been in their ghillies and jig shoes. Now she was their teacher. Molly's parents wove through the mingling teens, careful with their instrument cases—though Da's uilleann pipes could double as a weapon.

"Practice those bicycles and birdies!" Molly called after a pair of departing dancers. Three girls left to be picked up.

"Miss Molly," Olivia said, "what are you doing for Valentine's Day?"

Next to her, Maddi scoffed. "Going out with her boyfriend." Adding "duh" was unnecessary with that tone, as if remembering the details of Molly's personal life made her a better human being.

"Attitude, Maddi," Molly said just loudly enough for the girl to hear. "My boyfriend's plannin' a surprise." Dinner? A movie? She could only imagine what he might plan, and for a few seconds, she let herself.

A blue minivan pulled into the car park to claim the last carpool load of dancers, and Molly waved goodbye, still focused on the possibilities for her date tonight. She drifted back into the building, before she finally realized she'd been imagining the evening's possibilities with the wrong man.

Her mobile rang. A pop of panic played out in her heart, as if thinking of Zach would will him to ring her.

Ridiculous. Sure, he was attractive, but it'd been long enough. No feelings beyond knee-jerk attraction.

Fortunately, the display showed "Canavan." They were calling her twenty-four hours after they'd met. Getting in with them might be easier than they'd thought.

Molly stepped into the dance studio before she answered the call. "Hello?"

"Is this Molly?"

"Grace?"

The other woman crowed with laughter. "How's about ye?"

"You know yourself. So good to see you yesterday." Molly forced an extra note of lightness into her tone, and conveyed her nervous surge of energy into pacing the dance floor.

"You as well, dearie. Ed and I were just thinkin' how we'd like to see you again—how's about tomorrow?"

"Em . . ." Molly stalled. She wasn't even supposed to ring them until Monday, and they weren't getting together until later in the week. Though they might be able to move up the timeline, she didn't want to miss church if she could avoid it. "I'm up to ninety tomorrow." The Irish phrase about being busy felt rusty, it'd been so long since she used it.

"Monday, so? We'll have lunch."

"Sure now, that'd be fantastic." But goose flesh prickled down her back.

No. She could do this.

Grace laughed again. "Have you a preference?"

"I know a place that's just deadly." She hoped. In her small-town Arizona field office, they stuck to cheap delis and fast food. She wasn't sure about the Bureau's restaurant choice here. "I'll make us a reservation." They set a time for lunch and rang off, Grace bidding her goodbye repeatedly until she cut herself off. Another Irishism Molly had fallen out of using, that one in the last year or so.

Molly made two circuits pacing the studio. Instead of clearing her mind and her nerves, she only succeeded in stoking the embers of anxiety sparking in her stomach.

Before she even knew what she was doing, Molly dialed Zach. She'd deleted his number from her mobile long ago—but apparently not her memory.

"Molly?"

She released the tension in a shuddering sigh before speaking. "Zach."

"Hey, what's going on?"

"Grace Canavan called."

He paused a moment. "Oh. How much damage control do we need?"

"Damage—? It went grand, naturally." He expected otherwise? She might've cut her first year's assignment short to come hunt the Canavans, but she wasn't a complete rookie. "We're goin' to lunch, Monday."

He groaned. "Monday? That's so fast—"

"I'm sorry." Though she didn't feel sorry. Or sound it. "But I'm supposed to get in with them as quickly as possible, amn't I?"

He heaved a sigh. "We can do Monday. I think." He was quiet a moment. "How about we get together tonight to go over my legend? Maybe get some food?"

Dinner? Tonight? Tonight was Nate's little "monthiversary" celebration. Should she cancel on Nate for her job? He knew she was with the Bureau—unlike Zach, she wasn't a covert agent, so her job was no secret. But she certainly couldn't tell Nate she had to cancel his special dinner for an evening in with her ex. "Not tonight."

Silence. "Uh, lunch?"

"Why don't you come by my flat in an hour?" That should give her time to run home, and him time to eat and make it to her house.

"What's your address?"

She rattled it off.

"Ugh, you're a North Sider now?" Zach's distaste sounded more like teasing.

"Ah, didn't you know? I've always been a North Sider at heart."

"Too good for us, huh?"

Molly caught herself laughing. She would not flirt with him—or flirt back. "Didn't want to commute that far."

"Is there anywhere to park within a mile of your place?"

He was still codding her. "Guest parkin' in the garage below my buildin'."

"Psst!"

Molly jumped at the hiss behind her. She checked the wall of mirrors in front of her. Her mum leaned in the dance studio door. She held up an apologetic hand. "Sorry, didn't see you were on your mobile."

Mum started to duck out, but Molly motioned for her to wait. "Zach, I've got to go. See you in an hour."

Zachary—Zach agreed, and Molly ended the call.

Mum's gaze followed Molly's mobile to her pocket. "That was Zach?"

"It was."

Mum crossed the hardwood floor. "Molly, love."

She wouldn't talk about Zach—she couldn't. "Ed and Grace called."

Da stepped into the studio. "What did they want?"

"We're goin' to lunch Monday."

Her parents exchanged a wary glance. They had to be able to help. Conveying both confidence and intimacy, she moved closer. She was their daughter; of course they could trust her. Molly filled her tone with all the urgency she felt. "I need to get in with them. Can you give me a profile?"

"Only one that's decades out of date." Mum sighed. "Grace is the ideologue; Ed's the munitions expert. Both were desperate ardent when we knew them. But were it not for Grace, Ed might not have got involved."

Da's laugh echoed through the studio. "Were it not for Grace, Ed might not have a home. He'd be out on the street, tryin' to sell his poetry. Fancied himself the next Yeats."

"More like *The Pocket Quotable Yeats.*"

Molly arched an eyebrow. "Then did *he* write *The Blood-Dimmed Tide*?"

Da and Mum shook their heads in identical exasperation. The latest exposé from a pseudonymous ex-IRA/undercover operative had generated plenty of headlines since its title, borrowed from Yeats, had hit the news circuit. "Sure Ed and Grace love that one," Molly said.

"Sure." Mum drew the conversation back to the real topic. "But they're not such gobdaws that they'd ask you to enlist the first time they see you. They'll have to see that you're interested, feel you out a bit, make sure you're trustworthy. Takes time."

"We're expectin' this to be a slow burn assignment."

"Right," Da said. "But you already have an in—that's why the FBI is usin' you, isn't it?"

Molly nodded at her father's assessment. Her parents shared a silent debate.

"Go for Grace," Da counseled. "But they'll turn on you the minute they sense somethin's not right. Be careful."

"I will."

Da clamped onto Molly's shoulder. "We know this is what you want to be doin' with your life, but be careful. These two can be ruthless. Can't imagine what they'd do to someone who betrayed them."

"That's why we need to be left out of it," Mum added.

Left out? She wasn't planning on using them as backup, but she couldn't very well tell the Canavans they were in Chicago and not get together with them.

Molly looked at her parents again. Her mother's eyes carried a hint of pleading, verging on fear. Had she ever seen her mum afraid? Not even when they'd fled Ireland. "Please," Mum whispered, "don't bring us into this if you can help it. We left all this behind for a reason. Most of all, we're worried they could find Bridie and Fionn and the babies."

That didn't seem likely, but if her mum, her sister, and her family needed her, Molly would do whatever it took. "All right, Mum, Da. We'll make sure it doesn't come back to you. Keep your heads down, so, all right?"

"Thank you, love."

Molly looked at the clock. She needed to run—literally—if she wanted to beat Zach to her flat. She shuffled off her dance trainers and grabbed her running shoes beside the stereo. "I'll see you soon."

Mum and Da bid her goodbye, but at the studio door, Mum doubled back. "Molly, love, be careful with your heart, too."

"Believe me, I will."

More careful than ever.

Zach knocked on Molly's door a third time. Still no answer. He'd been here ten minutes, and he was about ready to pick this lock. What was this, some passive-aggressive ploy to avoid spending time with him?

That wasn't like her—but nothing about her seemed to be the same anymore. Yet he almost wished—

"Zach?" Molly approached from the other end of the hallway, pulling her phone from an armband carrier. She checked the screen and winced. "Sorry to keep you waitin'."

"Where have you been?"

She glanced down at her running jacket and leggings—exactly what Zach was trying not to look at. "An audience with the Pope, where do you think?"

"Hope you put in a good word for me."

Considering she'd met him while he was undercover pretending to be a priest, there wasn't much she could've said to get him into the Pope's good graces, especially not after she'd joined the LDS church.

"I was talkin' to my parents," Molly finally clarified. She dug a key from her armband and let them in.

All he had to do was get through this, keep it professional. Zach surveyed the living room. One wall of exposed brick gave a nod to the building's historic façade. Her framed black and white atmospheric photos of Ireland made the apartment feel familiar, and yet different. "Nice place."

Molly got herself something to drink in the kitchen area. "Thanks."

"Thought you hated running."

She shrugged. "Quantico will do that to you."

He didn't even want to think about how many miles he and every other FBI trainee had run over those Virginia hills.

"Besides," she continued, "easier than findin' parkin'." Her tone seemed to conceal a laugh. Was she teasing him, playing on what he'd said earlier?

"Water?" she offered.

"No thanks." He sat on her couch. She had the same modern gray couch—at least one thing she hadn't completely changed about her life in the last year. That, and the huge collection of spy fiction on her bookshelves. She might even still have the books he'd given her.

Zach shook off the thought. They were here to work. "What's Molly Ryan's job?"

"Nursin' assistant; I work three nights a week—freein' me up for anythin'."

"Good cover."

"Thanks." Molly settled into the chair by the couch, smiling modestly. "How long do I have to get in with the Canavans?"

"Faster is better. We think they're in the early planning stages—but, again, you don't want to seem eager."

"I know." She bit her lips before she spoke. "This could be a long-term assignment."

Trepidation filled her expression. Exactly how he must've looked when the Bureau asked him to go undercover indefinitely—though his assignment had been 24/7, instead of the two-hours-a-week kind.

And yet it still had to feel like a life sentence. She didn't know the half of it—how used to her assumed identity she'd get; how close she could come to losing herself; how strange it would feel to just be herself again when it was over, as if half of her was suddenly gone.

How terrifying it would be to deal with people who might kill her if they knew the truth; how close they might come to discovering her. The sudden panic when any word resembling her real name crossed their lips.

Was Molly really ready for this assignment after less than a year? He hadn't been with quadruple the experience. No wonder he'd been so worried about her: purely professional concern.

As professional as that overpowering drive to protect her.

Zach stared into her deep blue eyes a long time, but the future wasn't written there, much as he'd wished it had been. "Think you can do it?"

The trepidation in her face hardened into steel. "I do. Where is Paella?"

He gave her the address. "Reservations under Ryan." Molly programmed the address into her phone, and it dictated the first direction.

He quizzed her on her legend for twenty more minutes—the depth a casual conversation might go in an hour. Finally, Molly stood and shook out her long legs to refill her glass. Zach looked anywhere but at her. Was it him or was it suddenly warm in here? He shrugged out of his jacket and searched for a distraction in the conversation. "How about your parents?"

"I'm sayin' they're still in Ireland."

Zach frowned. "They're not helping?"

"Not if we can avoid it." She returned to her chair. "They've protected me my whole life; it's my turn."

"Right." But couldn't they tell she needed all the help she could get?

At his silence, Molly focused the interrogation on him. "How'd we meet, Jason?"

"Mutual friend. His party."

She flashed a smile. He knew her well enough to see the calculated charm—it'd worked on him, hadn't it? "Andy does throw quite the party, doesn't he?"

"Yeah." Zach returned the smile, though his was probably more wistful. He turned away. "I work in logistics for Arbor Haynes, I'm from Georgia, moved here for college and stayed."

"Grand." Her gaze shifted to the table in front of them, and she tapped each finger against her thumb in turn. "Logistics, Arbor Haynes, Georgia, moved here for college," she murmured, coordinating a fact with each tap. After five rounds, she folded her hands, finished.

"Familiar with the equipment?" he asked.

"Basic Bluetooth earpiece? Our table will be miked? I have it, yes."

"We'll be listening and watching. We won't let anything happen to you."

"What, the waiter forgettin' to put my dressin' on the side?"

Zach wagged a finger in mock solemnity. "Heads will roll if your dressing isn't fat-free."

Molly laughed. "Then I've nothin' to fear."

Man, he'd missed her laugh.

She settled into her chair, getting comfortable. "Your turn. What's your middle name?"

"Um . . ."

"What's your favorite thing to do on a Saturday?"

Zach chewed his lip, thinking. He hadn't had a chance to work on his legend, and an hour from the time Molly called wasn't enough to work out every detail.

"What's your favorite date?"

"Anythang with you," he drawled, pasting on puppy dog eyes.

Molly countered with an expression both patient and sarcastic. "We need to know these things about each other if we're goin' to be workin' together, Zach. Unless you'd rather me tell Grace we broke up."

Yeah, they'd broken up. And she'd never called him Zach when they were dating.

They were light years from dating.

"You need the backup, Molly."

She pressed her lips together until they turned white. "Sure now."

"They won't ask for my life history on our first meeting."

Her attention had strayed to the clock on the wall, but his last words pulled her back. "*My* first meetin'."

"Sure."

"I love that I 'need backup,' but your legend isn't even half done. If they ask me somethin' I don't know about you, how am I to sell this? Just as easy for me to say our relationship died a quick death."

That it had. Zach shifted on the couch. "Can't you steer the conversation?"

A muscle flexed in her jaw. "Once again, appreciate the vote of confidence."

Did everything he said have to make her angry? Zach lifted his hands in a placating gesture. "Don't take it the wrong way."

"Is there a right way to take that?"

He mentally replayed his words. "Okay, maybe not. Just . . . say whatever you think works. I'll roll with it."

Molly stared him down for two seconds before she nodded. He

was practically giving her the reins to the whole op, and that was the thanks he got?

He'd really screwed this up. But dumping someone did put a damper on the relationship.

So did insisting you "had a lot to do" before you'd even think about getting married.

"Anythin' else?" Molly sounded like she'd measured out the perfect amount of patience, and then skimped a drop.

He mentally grasped at something—anything—to get back into her good graces. And he failed. "Then I'll see you Monday," she said. "Well, I suppose I won't." She gestured for the front door, and he obeyed. She didn't walk him the five feet out.

Light years.

Perfect. He'd keep it professional, calculated, cold, like her. If she didn't feel anything seeing him again, he certainly didn't, either. They'd work side by side and then part ways. No future here, just like she'd always wanted. No matter what he'd hoped for.

The sooner this lunch—this assignment—was over, the better.

MOLLY HAD ONLY BEEN to the Adler Planetarium once—and it certainly wasn't like this. She and Nate were the only ones there after hours on a Saturday evening, alone in the glassed-in café. From the planetarium's peninsula in the lake, Chicago's city lights provided the perfect backdrop. Inside, the café had been cleared, leaving a single table set for two.

A far cry from the afternoon at the Sky Theater with Zach a year ago, on one of the few weekends he'd bothered to visit.

No more comparing. Nate had outdone himself this time and he knew it, judging by his satisfied smile.

He pulled out a chair. "This is fantastic," she said for the third time, taking the offered seat. "How did you do this?"

He shrugged, then pushed her chair up to the table. "Carlington's a big donor. But if you hear anything, hit the deck." He waited a full second before laughing at his joke—and reassuring Molly their visit was aboveboard.

"All this for our 'monthiversary'?"

"Valentine's day, too—but this is just the beginning." Nate dished up the dinner from Styrofoam containers. The instant the garlic and herbs from the lamb chops hit her, she knew it had to be from Sapori, Nate's favorite Italian trattoria. He served her half the lamb rack, then a generous portion of the risotto with porcini mushrooms she loved. He filled his own plate, lit the candles and took his place across the table from her.

Nate regaled her with tales of childhood mishaps—the man was lucky to be alive, it seemed—but Molly didn't have much to share. Right now, her childhood, albeit semi-fictionalized, was a tool to target the Canavans. Sharing even the real parts here, among the stars and city lights and candles, felt almost profane.

Once their plates were empty, Nate brought out a smaller container. Dessert. Molly hoped for the chocolate hazelnut panna cotta she'd been dying to try, but Nate had probably chosen his usual rich chocolate raspberry cake. He paused before opening the dessert. "You really are beautiful, Molly. Especially tonight."

"Thank you."

"I know, I said no Valentine gifts, but this is a monthiversary present." Nate rounded the table to stand next to her and pulled out a small velvet box—and Molly's lungs froze.

No. Nate wouldn't propose the night after mentioning it for the first time. Besides, that was too big for a ring box. Right?

Nate remained standing. Not kneeling. A good sign. Molly tamped down her errant nerves. He opened the lid, revealing a beautiful pair of creamy pearl earrings. "Molly, I love you. Happy anniversary."

"Thank you so much—they're lovely." She accepted the box and gestured around the room. "Everythin' is."

Nate leaned down and kissed her. Molly kissed him back, but two thoughts drummed in her brain.

He'd said he loved her. And she hadn't said it back.

Nate didn't seem to notice. He stepped back and opened the cake. "I wanted everything to be perfect."

And it was. Nearly.

Molly shifted on their booth's padded bench at Paella Monday afternoon and inhaled the restaurant's aroma of saffron, butter and lime. Her bright yellow rice was about all she'd managed to get out of the meeting so far. Twenty minutes with the Canavans, and she wished she'd had another hour to prepare. Or to practice injecting herself into a monologue.

Unless the FBI was maintaining radio silence for a reason, Grace's incessant chatter wasn't her only problem. If she didn't focus, play her cover and hunt for her angles, she'd get burned.

Grace's constant stream of conversation had meandered to the weather, as if Molly needed catching up on missed meteorological reports from her homeland. "Oh, did you hear about Hurricane Katia?"

"Sounds fierce. How—"

"Desperate fierce." Grace plowed over her. "Enough to put the heart crossways in ye."

Molly took another bite of saffron and shrimp rice. She hadn't had a chance to say two words, let alone paint herself as a potential IRA acolyte.

Worse, the biggest threat to Ireland Grace had mentioned so far was El Niño. Last Molly knew, El Niño affected the Pacific far more than the North Atlantic.

"And the wind." Grace clasped at an imaginary strand of pearls. "You wouldn't believe—over a hundred KPH!"

Ed interrupted again. "Let the girl speak, woman."

"Whisht," Grace barked at her husband. Her scowl softened when she turned to Molly. "What're you up to these days, dearie?"

"Ah, tearin' away." Molly hesitated to be sure Grace would allow a real answer. "I'm a nursin' assistant."

"Brilliant. Always knew you'd make somethin' of yourself. And your fella?"

Her heart stalled a split second. She didn't remember, and no helpful voice prompted her from her earpiece. She stalled with a drink of water, then hid her hand beneath the table, tapping each finger on her thumb, as if the meaningless gesture would help her remember.

She wanted to prove herself to Zach and the rest of the team, but they couldn't be this quiet because she'd impressed them.

She had to cover this somehow. "I don't really know what he does, you know yourself. It's complicated."

"Can't be that complicated." Ed grunted. "Didn't strike me as a nuclear—" His insult was cut off by a groan. He rubbed his side and glared at Grace.

Finally the memory clicked into place. "He works at Arbor

Haynes." Molly hoped her relief didn't show in her voice. "But I'm no good at explainin' what he does."

Grace bought it. "No matter."

"What do you do?" Molly asked.

"I clean. Odd hours, but it's honest work for decent pay. Can't complain." She waved a hand. "Ed, the skiver, hunts for work."

Ed frowned over his gazpacho, the folds of his cheeks carving deeper. "'All thy toilin' only breeds new dreams, new dreams.'"

Molly didn't know the quote. She checked Grace's reaction and thought she saw the other woman roll her eyes. Still nothing from her radio support. Now would be the perfect time. An Internet search for that line could build rapport with Ed. Or some weather fun facts for Grace. Or anything. This silence couldn't be normal.

Though Molly had only drunk a quarter of her glass, a new server in the yellow and black restaurant uniform appeared, offering water. Ed and Grace took refills, but Molly declined.

"Please? You'll thank me later," the server chirped.

Molly held out a hand in acquiescence although she murmured it wasn't necessary. The server lifted her glass—and sloshed the ice water over the edge into Molly's lap.

"Oh, sorry!"

Molly grabbed the soaked napkin out of her lap before the water reached her slacks, but the server leapt forward to help, too, dumping the rest of the glass onto Molly's legs.

"I am so, so sorry!" The server tried to mop Molly's lap with her apron, but it was little help. First the cold, then the water itself crept through the material now clinging to her legs. "Let me help you clean up in the restroom."

"That's all right," Molly said. She'd done more than enough already.

"Really," the server protested a touch too much. "My manager would *insist*."

The Bureau had to pour cold water on her to get a message through? Something was seriously wrong. Molly shrugged an apology to the Canavans and followed the server to the unisex restroom far from the Canavans' line of sight.

"Sorry about that."

She expected the words—but not that voice echoing through the room. She shot Zach a glower where he stood, leaning against the black tile wall. "Is this *your* joke?"

"No, X is pulling the strings. I don't give people cold showers as a joke."

Molly bet his sister would be willing to differ on that one. The server yanked out a fistful of paper towels to scrub at Molly's slacks. "My earpiece is banjaxed."

Zach smiled at the Irishism. "Sounds like you've spent too much time with them already. We just tested it; I don't know what's up." He pushed off the wall and offered her a new receiver.

Molly tried not to let her frustration show, switching out the earpieces. "Better?" came SSA Mason's voice in her ear.

Molly flashed Zach a thumbs up. "We're good," he said.

She raised an eyebrow, and he pointed to the top button of his collared shirt, sticking out above his gray sweater. "Anyone have any global warmin' statistics?" Molly asked his button.

Agent Mason laughed. "I'll Google it."

"Need anything from me?" Zach offered.

Molly shook her head. "Doin' all right on my own."

Whatever response she'd anticipated, it didn't come. By the time he finally, half-heartedly agreed, his hesitation had conveyed all the doubt she didn't need. "Logistics," he said. All he had to say to highlight her mistake: forgetting his stupid, made-up job.

He directed her to the hand dryer—as if that would help her trousers—and ducked out through the door facing away from the Canavans. Molly waved the server/special agent away and punched the button.

She could do this. She *would*—and she'd show Zach while she was at it.

"Focus," she chanted to herself as the dryer's noise drowned out the radio chatter. Focus. Focus.

Zach slipped out the restaurant's back door and jogged toward the gray surveillance van in the alley. She was doing all right. Holding her own.

Still, she needed his help. With the earpiece. And remembering what Jason Tolliver did.

He reached the van where X waited, observing. Zach opened the door and took one look at Xavier. With that expression, Zach didn't need to hear the bad news aloud.

"Trouble," X said anyway. "Ed Canavan thinks it's 'deadly strange' Molly doesn't know what you do. Tell me that came up in there."

"Yeah." But coming back from the bathroom suddenly knowing the answer to the question didn't seem any less suspicious. Her cover hadn't been half-bad.

The microphone at the table inside picked up Ed's voice. "Are we about finished? I'm ready to head."

Xavier added context. "He's been trying to convince Grace to forget her 'plans.'"

Not the first time internal strife took down terrorists before the Bureau could. "And that's a bad thing?"

X swiveled on his stool to face Zach. "Her 'plans' for Molly. And the server's packing up their leftovers."

That was trouble, whether Ed succeeded or failed in persuading Grace. Could Zach let Molly handle them alone?

Hadn't he already answered that question?

"X," he started, "I need to go in."

"I don't know."

"Somebody's gotta take charge of the conversation. We can't let Ed win that argument."

Xavier studied Zach a moment, then glanced back at the equipment panel. Ed was whining about leaving again. Molly still hadn't made it back from the bathroom.

Finally, he nodded. "Go in."

"We need to keep their interest long-term." Zach grabbed the bin of earpieces—empty. "Where'd these go?"

"Inouye," Xavier muttered. "He did the inventory in here last."

He'd be flying blind. "I'll explain how I turned up here to the

Canavans; you find a way to keep me there."

"I'll figure it out." Xavier turned back to the broadcast microphone. "We always do," he added before pushing the button. "Molly?" he said. "Incoming. Going off script. Roll with it."

Zach strode back through the service entrance, rehearsing his cover, setting aside who he really was to *be* Jason Tolliver. Georgia. Logistics at Arbor Haynes. Meeting them here because . . . ?

Twenty feet ahead of him, Molly returned to the Canavans' booth. Zach rerouted to approach from behind the Canavans, giving Molly the small advantage of seeing him first.

See him she did, in a double take. The alarm in her expression shifted to surprise, though her smile was kind of forced. "Jason?" she called.

He reached their booth and grinned. "Hey! How y'all doin'?"

"What a surprise," Grace exclaimed.

"What're you doin' here?" Molly asked, her eyes narrowing in real suspicion.

Hadn't she gotten Xavier's message?

Zach's mind danced as fast as possible. Fortunately, it was much better than his feet. "Well," he drawled the word into two syllables, "Molly's gone on and on 'bout y'all all weekend, and I wanted to get to know y'all too. 'Sides," he said, taking the seat next to Molly, "usually I'm the one takin' Molly here on Mondays."

"Oh." Grace held a hand over her heart as if a weekly lunch date was up there with rescuing princesses. "You should've told us, Molly. We hate to ruin your time with your fella."

"No big deal." Zach wrapped his arm around Molly, where she still fit perfectly. "Now we're all here."

"Ah, but you've missed lunch." Molly pointed to the Styrofoam holding her meal. Played-up puppy admiration glowed in her face, but her tone said something like *sucks to be you.*

"That's all right." But he had to draw this out or he wouldn't have a conversation to control at all. "You know I'm always up for dessert." He picked up the little dessert menu display off the table. "I'm fixin' to try the Catalan cream."

Molly leaned closer to him to read the menu. "Like crème brûlée? You'd like that, so."

Zach drew in a breath—and realized his mistake too late. She still smelled like those flowers strangling the oaks in his parents' backyard. Like home.

His heart stuttered, and those compartmentalized walls cracked. He hadn't anticipated the biggest challenge: being close to Molly. They needed distance, now.

Zach released her to flag down a waitress—a real one—and order four Catalan creams. "My treat," he said over Grace's alternating protests and mutterings about the poor, oppressed Catalan people. Exactly. He fought back an inward smile. Their fight for independence had a lot more to do with his dessert choice than burned sugar on custard.

"What do you do?" Ed asked. "Molly doesn't know."

Zach patted Molly's hand. "I work for Arbor Haynes."

"She said that," Grace said. "What do you there?"

"I'm in logistics."

Ed still didn't get it. "So, what do you actually do?"

"I logisticate." He grinned at his joke. Molly rolled her eyes in a patronizing gesture, but the Canavans appeared mystified as ever. Ed shot Molly an almost sympathetic look, even with his perpetual scowl.

"Say, for example," Molly jumped in, "you're organizin' a talent show."

Did she have to bring up something they'd really organized together?

Compartmentalize. "Then it's my job," Zach continued, "to see everythang's exactly how you need it: make sure the stage's ready, microphones, lightin', performers, costumes."

"Ah." Finally Grace and Ed understood, nodding in unison. However, they weren't as intrigued as he'd hoped—he'd selected logistics to seem like a one-man support team, the perfect asset to any terrorist assault.

"Bit like a weddin' planner, are you, so?" Grace asked.

"Sure; a weddin' planner for transportation and aerospace."

"Ah," Ed piped up. "What kind of fuel do your machines use?"

Zach had researched the answer—or as much as he could get through their government contracts that morning—but before he responded, the waitress returned with dessert. She distributed the plates, then set a small box by Zach's plate with a quick wink.

A ring box.

Suddenly it didn't matter he'd skipped lunch. His stomach shrank so much he wouldn't eat for a week.

"What . . . is that?" Molly breathed. Was it his imagination, or did she sound angry?

That made two of them. He'd kill Xavier.

Zach glanced at Molly. The color drained from her cheeks. He had to play this straight. He had to do this. He had to *be* Jason. Every eye at their booth—no, the whole restaurant—was on him and that little mahogany ring box.

If he were working with anyone else—anyone—this wouldn't be a problem. But she had to be Molly.

He would seriously kill Xavier.

Zach gave a nervous laugh, fighting to strain out the anger in his tone. Sheepish. Embarrassed make something this personal public. He had to shoot for that.

He slid off the bench and slid the box off the table. Zach forced air into his lungs, but he couldn't force the right words into his brain. Taking a knee, he prayed his hesitation seemed like he was collecting himself—and that they bought it. And he'd know what to say.

The last request, however, fell through fast. Zach swallowed and looked up from the still-closed ring box. Molly's deep blue eyes were frozen wide open. But as she met his gaze, the deer-in-the-headlights expression receded into something more like . . . hope?

If she could muster that look, maybe she didn't need his help after all.

But now he was stuck.

His heartbeat echoed in his ears. Zach opened the ring box, but didn't bother glancing at whatever the Bureau conjured up on short notice. They were out of earpieces but had an engagement ring handy? Priorities.

Still no words—and if he didn't speak up, Grace would do it for him.

"Molly." Why couldn't she use a different name? His voice came out as an embarrassing whisper, so he cleared his throat and tried again. "Molly." Deep breath. "I love you."

Tears glistened in her eyes. He felt like crying, too, but he wasn't about to do that here. Not in front of Molly, not now, not with the way his pulse was still pounding. He just had to choke something out and it'd be over. Anything but the words he'd tried so hard to get right, the words he'd tried so hard to remember, the words he'd tried so hard to forget.

The words came anyway. So much for compartmentalizing.

"You're my whole world. If I ever let you go, my life would never be complete. Marry me, Molly?"

Molly blinked to clear her tears, but two fell down her cheeks anyway. She covered her mouth with her hands, saying nothing.

"Please?" he finally added, again no more than a whisper for the single syllable.

She nodded and the restaurant erupted into applause, led by Grace.

He should kiss her. But no matter how good his legend, how good her cover, how much they wanted the Canavans, that was too much. Too dangerous.

Instead, Zach caught Molly in a hug aimed to hide his next move. "You'll pay for this, X," he said for his microphone.

One of them definitely would.

ZACH PULLED BACK and wiped Molly's tears again. This was beyond cruel—even more for him than her. He. Would. Kill. Xavier. Though X couldn't know the real reason he'd broken up with Molly. For now, Zach had to to take this moment to—what, apologize? Tell her this wasn't his idea?

Not in so many words. "Sorry for doin' it like this," he murmured. "Wasn't quite how I planned."

"How did you plan it?" Something flashed through Molly's eyes—definitely not good.

"What a holy show." Ed's grumbling about making a spectacle wasn't directed at anyone, though Zach kind of agreed.

"When's the weddin'?" Grace cut in, wiping away a tear herself.

If Grace was interested in wedding planning, maybe a short deadline would get her even more involved. "We were thinkin' May eighth." Shouldn't be too hard to remember: Molly's birthday.

The date drew a reaction from the taciturn Ed. "Less than three months away." He focused a scowl on Molly. "Not up the pole, are ye?"

"Ed." Grace turned his name into a reprimand.

"Of course not!" Molly kept her dismissal light.

Zach shot a silent question her way, pretending the Irish phrase confused him.

"He means pregnant," she said.

"Oh, no, sir," Zach said. "I want her to say 'I do' before she realizes she should say 'I don't'!"

Their laughter dissolved the tension, and Grace mopped more tears with her napkin.

"Aw, ma'am, don't go cryin'."

Grace waved away his concern. "It's only so lovely to see the two of youse happy together."

Yeah, that. Zach reminded himself to smile at Molly and squeeze her hand. Compartmentalized.

"Let's see the ring," Grace cut in again. Zach found the box where he'd set it between their plates and gave it to Grace.

"On her, ya dense bogtrotter," she teased.

Zach finally checked out the ring—showy, blinged out, and almost criminally ugly—and took it from the box. Not Molly's style. He willed himself not to remember as he slid the ring on her finger. A little too big—well, the band was. The rocks on the thing were a lot too big.

Molly showed it to Grace and hid it as quickly as possible. She always was a smart girl.

Grace started on her Catalan cream. "What's next in your weddin' plannin'?"

Zach filled his mouth with creamy custard. He looked to Molly to answer, though five minutes ago, neither of them were planning a wedding.

She took a bite to stall as well. "We have a lot of things to be doin'—ah, find a reception hall—and hopefully that'll take care of food and music, too—the cake, the flowers."

Time for the logisticater. What did he remember from his older siblings' weddings? "Invitations," Zach added, but his list stalled after the first item.

Molly nodded to his meager contribution. He decided to stick to eating.

"When are your mam and da gettin' in?" Grace asked.

"They're lookin' for tickets at least a week beforehand."

Grace gasped, horrified. "A week? Oh, dearie, who'll shop for your gown?"

"Em, I don't know." Molly reflected Grace's dismay toward Zach.

"Jason can't be helpin' you with that—but I could, if you'd like."

Molly beamed, though Zach knew her too well to miss the shadow of uncertainty in her smile. "Would you really, Grace?"

"I'd love to!"

Good way for Molly to get in with Grace, if she followed through.

Zach picked up the planning slack. "Now, darlin', weren't you sayin' you wanted to do that Saturday afternoon?"

"Was I?"

"Uh, yeah." Zach raised his eyebrows, trying to convey that this was more than a suggestion. "You said you couldn't go to the game."

"I'm free Saturday," Grace offered.

Molly took his "hint." "Fantastic. Four o'clock all right?"

"Wonderful." Grace grinned back.

Perfect. They'd gotten the next appointment, he was done with his dessert, and now it was time to get out of there before either of them messed anything up.

"Well, I hate to break up the shindig, y'all, but we should get goin'." Zach grabbed his wallet and fished out a twenty to cover the desserts.

"You have to get back to work, don't you?" Molly smiled pityingly. "I'm free a little longer, so why don't you head on? I'll see you tonight."

Oh, he'd stepped right into that. She wasn't even done with her dessert. He couldn't backtrack without seeming suspicious. He gave Molly the money and stood. "I'll let you know when I'll be home."

"All right." Molly tilted her chin up.

His stomach plummeted like an air ball. He couldn't compartmentalize his ex-girlfriend sitting there waiting for her kiss goodbye. Like they did this all the time. How could he get away without kissing her? He had to make a move quickly or it'd look strange.

She'd moved on enough that this didn't bother her, and he . . . was good undercover. "Bye, darlin'." With a conscious effort not to take a breath of her curl cream, he kissed her on the cheek.

"Love you." Again, she was unfazed by the gesture.

Then he'd have to be unfazed, too. "You too. Good seein' y'all," he bid the Canavans.

Zach left the restaurant, gave the sidewalk a cool glance, and circled round to the back alley and the gray van. The first sunny day in a week, and he was stuck here again.

"Congratulations," Xavier murmured once Zach closed the door behind him.

"You're dead."

X didn't acknowledge him. "At this rate, the Canavans will give Molly away at your wedding."

"ASAC Saenz might prefer it if we, y'know, arrested them, but he'll be thrilled as long as you're my best man. Unless that wasn't what you meant by sending a ring to the table?"

"It's a secret decoder ring. I was sending a message with your post-dessert drinks."

Zach glared at Xavier and settled onto the stool next to him.

Xavier didn't care. "Molly's parents said Grace is obsessed with weddings. You were the one who said we needed to keep them interested."

He'd had done a bang-up job of that. Zach reminded himself not to murder his boss.

"We had a mutual friend, and he introduced us at a party," Molly was saying. Speaking loud and clear for the microphone hidden under their table.

"Seems you've made the right choice. He's pure class."

"Thank you. I think so, too."

"Though I should remind you," Grace continued, "marry in May, rue the day."

"Need to be headin'," Ed grumbled.

"Will we get the bill?" Grace offering to pay—perfect, since Molly wouldn't have credit cards or checks under the name Molly Ryan for another hour or two.

"Are you sure?"

Zach leaned toward Xavier. "Tell her not to argue with them."

X didn't move.

"Naturally," Grace said.

"At least let us cover dessert."

"Sure, look it." Grace's standard Irish non-answer could be a yes or a no. If no, Zach wanted his twenty bucks back.

Oh. Right. Molly could've paid cash.

"Thank you," Molly said. "And thank you for goin' shoppin' Saturday. I really appreciate it. Wouldn't have anyone to go with otherwise."

Zach settled back, the stool beneath him creaking like a warning buzzer. She had to be careful—she shouldn't be too effusive about anything. Then again, if she were really a blushing bride, maybe she would be that grateful for a shopping partner.

And maybe she would've done just fine on her own.

Once Grace and Ed had bid Molly goodbye, Grace knew she had to raise the issue. She could barely wait until they'd boarded the next train, half-empty. "Someone workin' in logistics would be helpful in the future, too."

"All right." Ed's tone carried the finality of a royal decree in a whisper. "That's where I draw the line. No Yank could ever understand our cause."

"Ed, ya eejit, didn't you see the way her fella goggled at her? He'd do anythin' for her."

He simply shook his head.

Could he be more dense? "The Americans fought for freedom from them, too."

"Not in that boyo's lifetime." He grunted. "His idea of independence from the Brits features Mel Gibson in a wig."

Grace slumped back in her seat. "Granted, he doesn't seem a great student of history. But he does have a useful skill set."

"Can't trust these Yanks—if he catches wind of what we're doin', he'll run right to the police or the FBI."

She paused to take in his argument. Could they trust Molly if she was marrying an American? And even if he didn't participate directly, might Jason suss them out and tell?

"What say we keep feelin' both of 'em out. On the off chance that we can trust him."

"'All is changed, changed utterly.'" Ed sighed. "All right. But hold your whisht until after this job."

Fine. She could wait four weeks. Twenty-six days.

The whole drive back to her flat, Molly managed to keep calm. Stony, deadly calm. Aside from the pitcher of water spilled in her lap, Molly thought she'd done rather well on her own. Well enough she didn't deserve to have Zach foisted on her.

And a ring? As if seeing him again weren't hard enough. As if her personal life could not crash into her job more. As if anyone deserved that much torture.

How could Zach do that to her?

Molly parked in her building's garage and took the lift up to her flat. Sure, Mum had mentioned Grace's passion for weddings, but Molly would've found something to make sure she saw them again.

Fortunately, she'd kept Zach away from their next appointment. He couldn't barge in on wedding dress shopping. Her heart could hardly take it.

Molly let herself into her apartment and leaned against the door a long moment, pressing a fist to her lips. She was supposed to be professional—to be over him. To protect her heart. And now?

She held out her hand to examine the gaudy bauble on her finger. Molly yanked off the ring and—well, she couldn't throw it; she needed it for the Canavans. She balled it in her fist and stood there, the stones and setting digging into her palm. Pinpoints of pain kept her centered, kept her grounded, kept her from drowning in the past.

She was dating Nate. She was over Zach. She had to be. This was simple attraction. Attraction stronger than any magnetic pull.

Or was that the memories they shared?

No. Nate. She was with Nate. She pictured Nate's face and took a deep breath.

She'd barely calmed down when the knock came. Molly checked the peephole. She wasn't expecting Zach, but after the restaurant, nothing he did could surprise her.

"What were you thinkin'?" she demanded once the door closed.

His defenses flew up. "I'm sorry—"

"How long have you been plannin' that?"

"I didn't." His protest came a beat too quickly. "X was pulling the strings. I was just as surprised as you."

Hardly. He'd at least had something to say. She'd had to cover her silence with tears.

Four days of being in contact with Zach again, and she was already crying over him.

"What were you even doin' there? You thought I couldn't handle myself?"

"Hey, I never said that."

Molly scrutinized him. He'd said it in actions today. He'd said it in words Friday. He'd said it in the utter shock and disbelief in his voice when she'd told him she'd got "The Call" into the FBI.

He didn't think she could do this.

Well, she'd been doing it for over nine months, and she hadn't got herself killed yet. In fact, she had an excellent record with a commendation. She didn't have to stand for this. She moved for the door.

"Molly," Zach said, reproach in his tone. "It wasn't my decision."

She wheeled on him. "Then how was I doin' before you swooped in to save the day?"

He shrugged one shoulder. "Not bad." But his tone was non-committal, as if that was the most praise he could allow.

"Not bad?" She hadn't been perfect, but his tone made it sound like she'd flubbed far more than his job title. Molly folded her arms across her chest, against the heat beginning to build there. "I was flyin' blind in there. I was freakin' brilliant."

"Sure," he said. But his eyes were far too amused.

She scoffed. "Sorry, but which of us set up the next meetin'?"

"As I recall, *I* made sure you took her up on the offer."

Molly threw up her hands, fully incredulous. "Fantastic—will you be the one strippin' down in the fittin' room Saturday, then?"

"Molly." He laughed—even his laugh was condescending—and backed up onto her green area rug. "I'm not one-upping you."

"No?"

"Just saying you did a good job, for being straight out of Quantico."

"I've been in the field as long as I was in trainin'." She pinned a glare on him. Had he ever believed in her? "You just watch Saturday, Agent Saint."

"The stripping down? Better stick to listening." He grinned.

Did he think he was being clever? The anger simmering in her belly turned to ice. Molly slowly arched an eyebrow. Zach met her gaze, but after a minute, looked away, fidgeting. How had she ever found his obnoxious smugness charming?

Before he picked up the attitude again, her mobile rang. For a split second, her ribs tightened. Could it be Nate? Molly crossed the room to her handbag sitting on her sofa and fumbled for her mobile. Not Nate—Kent. She groaned inwardly. She liked the fella, but the man had to learn to do his job on his own. "Special Agent Malone," she answered the call.

"Malone." He was already breathless. "Can't find those 302s."

Her paperwork from observing Kent's fruitless interviews. "Which case?"

The frantic clacking of a computer keyboard carried over the line. "Moskovitz."

She didn't want to insult him, but she had to start with the obvious answer. "Did you check that folder?"

"Yeah, not in there."

Molly nodded toward the door, signaling Zach to leave, and followed him out. "Did you check under Relyea?"

"Why would it be there?"

Because he was the other suspect—but Molly reined in her impatience with a measured breath. "I'll be there in fifteen."

"Thank you." Kent's voice carried a rush of relief. She wasn't sure how he'd managed before she transferred here, because the man was barely competent even with her help.

She and Zach rode the elevator down in silence until they reached the ground floor and Zach stepped off.

"'Not bad.' I'll be showin' you 'not bad.'" Molly hit the button to close the doors between them. If only she could cut off this partnership that easily.

Zach was still reeling by the time he reached Xavier in the elevator lobby of the FBI office. If X had called ten minutes sooner, Zach could've caught a ride with Molly—but he wouldn't have asked with the mood she was in.

What did she want him to say? She was the best agent he'd ever seen?

Zach shook his head. If she was this mad today, breaking up with her was probably for the best. Right?

"Who's sitting the kids?" Zach hit the up button. The Canavans were almost never without surveillance these days. The elevator arrived.

"Inouye and Roberts." Xavier waited until they were on the elevator to continue. "Debriefing go okay?"

"Yeah, no."

X grimaced. "Sorry again."

"Yeah. What did you need?"

Xavier stepped off the elevator. "You know Deisinger on the task force? CPD?"

"No." He didn't work with the Chicago Police or the Joint Terrorism Task Force as directly as X did.

Xavier gestured at an unfamiliar face waiting near Zach's desk. "He's got something I need you to look into."

Zach started for the waiting detective, X trailing behind.

"How's it going?" the cop asked.

"To be honest," Zach said, "I've had better days."

"Z, this is Detective Deisinger. Dice, Special Agent Saint. You can call him Z," Xavier added. He turned to the cop. "Z is our resident specialist on Ireland."

"What, you've got an Irish grandma?" Dice asked.

No, ex-girlfriend. "I lived there for a couple years." With in-country experience and his position in the counterterrorism division, that must've made him the go-to guy for every Irish threat in the

Chicagoland area. All both of them.

X gestured for Zach to take over the conversation and headed for his office. Like Zach needed another cue to think X just didn't want to handle the case. "What've you got, Dice?"

"A source who says one of his coworkers might be shorting the company of blasting caps and C-4."

Enough for Zach. He motioned for Dice to pull up a chair, and they huddled around his desk. "You send the file?"

"Yep."

Zach refreshed his email. There it was. He skimmed the perfunctory information on the suspect.

When it rained, it poured—to hijack the Irish phrase—a shower of savages. "What else do we know about this guy?"

"Where he hangs out after work." Dice flipped open his notebook and slid it across the desk to Zach.

"Every day?"

"We tried to catch him a coupla two three times," Dice said, his Chicago accent showing, "but he made us."

An undercover challenge—one that didn't involve Molly? Oh yeah, he was down. He grinned at Dice. "How soon do we start?"

JUST BEFORE MOLLY LEFT Tuesday afternoon, Kent approached her desk, balancing a thick stack of papers. "Oh, hey, Malone, having a tough time cross-referencing these cases. Any idea how to start?"

Her gaze jumped between the stack and the earnestness in his eyes. They'd sat in the same classes at Quantico—at the exact same time. Why did he always come to her for the most mundane tasks? "Start with the interviews closest to the time of the crime, and go from there. Unusual for a witness to recall somethin' later. At least not reliably."

"Good idea." He ran a thumb down the folders' tabs. "Guess I should put these in chronological order, huh? Or maybe subject's last name?"

What order had he put them in? Subject's favorite color? "Just use the standard system. It should all be in the computer." Molly pointed at his desk, then mentally winced. Kent could find his own computer. She didn't need to insult him.

He looked at his desk, then to her again. "Could you help? I'm trying to put together all the mentions of foreign sales across the interviews."

"I thought you did that last week."

"I started, but . . ." He frowned at the stack.

"Maybe tomorrow." She stood, gathering her purse a few minutes sooner than planned. "I'm afraid I can't now." Tonight she had to teach dance—and then hope her parents had remembered something useful.

Molly stopped by their house for a late dinner after dance. The familiar kitchen with its mismatched chairs, all painted cream, and the table's comfortably worn dark wood didn't feel so comfortable tonight, waiting for them to tell her more.

"Would you like an ice cream?" Da offered.

"Naturally!"

Da served the ice creams, but still, neither he nor Mum alluded to the subject.

Leaving it to Molly. She kept her tone businesslike. "How did you come to be in the IRA for Special Branch?"

Mum and Da telegraphed a silent caution, but Mum began to answer. "I suppose it started after I graduated university and came back to Derry." She bowed her head, her glasses' thick purple frames hiding her eyes at that angle. "When Teague was killed."

"Sorry—killed?" The story she'd always heard was that Mum's younger brother died in Lough Foyle at age seventeen.

Mum kneaded her fingers against the table as if to rub the woven flowers out of the pastel damask. "He didn't drown. Got himself blown up by an IRA *amadán* who didn't know how to build a proper bomb. The first time someone in our neighborhood had died that way." She pulled her fingers into a fist.

Da placed his hand over Mum's. "I was already talkin' to Special Branch when I heard about Teague, and I went to the funeral to see your mum."

"I was so angry." Mum stared down at her blue bowl and her white knuckles. "I didn't expect Teague to know better—teenager, furious with the world after our parents died, thought he knew everythin'. That fool with the bomb, though, he was an adult. Any eejit could see violence wouldn't help the political situation—if anythin', their efforts hurt the cause of Irish independence."

"And turned people who might've been more sympathetic against the movement altogether." Da took Mum's bowl and started brewing the coffee. "The Gardaí tried a few undercover agents, but it was a long slog. We happened to have better connections." He traded a conspiratorial look with Mum. "Once I recruited your mum."

"How'd you become the Ryans?" Molly asked.

"We didn't have to." Da finished with the coffeepot and joined them at the table. "I was born a Ryan."

"Ah—your da." Even Molly sometimes forgot her father's father had died just before he was born.

He nodded. "He was a Ryan, and everyone knew me as a Ryan. I didn't take my stepfather's name until we were in Dublin, before I left for university."

"We had to be so careful." Mum spoke gingerly, as though even now, she measured and weighed each word before releasing it. "Northern Ireland's like a village—everyone knows one another—and we knew we'd have to get out one day. We wanted a clean break." Mum smiled. "He had Ryan church records and everythin'."

He wouldn't be the only one: when she'd met Zach, he was undercover as her parish priest, complete with fabricated records of his own. But, as her parents didn't know that about Zach, Molly declined to bring up the parallel.

The aroma of roasted coffee began to fill the kitchen. Da got up from the table, the chair creaking under his wiry frame. "When we got married," he added, "we had to elope to Dublin. Your grandparents wouldn't have even been invited if they hadn't already moved to Dublin."

"Then we went back to Derry for our fake weddin' there—and a good eighty percent of the guests were Provos from our battalion."

"And Grace was the world's first neurotic weddin' planner." Da suppressed a grin, but only just, before turning to rummage through the pantry.

"You know, she's why you're called Molly."

That wasn't the story they'd always told. "I thought Bridie couldn't say Mary."

"She said it 'Mah-wee.' Grace decided she was tryin' to say 'Molly,' and there's no song called 'Molly Ryan' to raise an objection."

Da returned from the pantry with brown sugar. "Then it stuck. It fitted you."

"Have you any stories I might know—somethin' I can use to build rapport with them?"

Mum chewed her lip and looked to Da, checking the coffeepot. "Can't think of anythin'."

"Could you email them to reminisce?"

Mum sighed. "Afraid that'd arouse their suspicions."

Probably right. "What was it like, workin' with them?"

"Have you read *The Blood-Dimmed Tide*?" Da asked. "It was like that."

Mum and Da exchanged a nostalgic smile, apparently finished. Da collected their empty bowls and deposited them in the sink, then ducked out.

Mum kept her gaze on the woven poppy in front of her. "How's it workin' with Zachary?"

Moments from yesterday flashed through her mind: Zach horning in on her assignment, him arguing with her at her flat, the acute torture of getting engaged to Zach-but-not-Zachary. She couldn't lie to her mum—and no American English word expressed the true depth of the awfulness. "Wojus."

"Aw." Mum leaned around the table to slide a comforting arm around Molly. "Have you considered askin' him why you broke up?"

"'Our lives are headed in different directions' was pretty clear." Even Zach couldn't explain it better. Talking wouldn't change anything.

Mum clucked over her. "At least you have Nate, right?"

Right. Nate the Nearly Perfect. So why didn't that make her resent Zach less? Zach had blindsided her with a breakup before and second-guessed her now. Nate loved her and wanted to marry her.

At this rate, she'd end up pretending to be married to Zach.

"Mum," Molly began tentatively, "did you marry Da for the assignment?"

"Of course not. We wouldn't have bothered with goin' to Dublin for all that." Mum grew contemplative. "But part of me wondered if we shouldn't wait until things were more settled."

"Why didn't you?"

Mum met her eyes. "Would've meant puttin' it off too long. Because I loved your da."

Speaking of the devil, Da returned, and Mum gave Molly's shoulders a squeeze before sliding back to her seat. "Hazelnut creamer in your coffee, Molly?"

She drew an inward sigh. The sacrifice still wasn't easy. "No coffee for me, thank you."

"Oh, that's right, your church. Sorry, love." Da busied himself pouring and doctoring their mugs.

"Did you accomplish your objective?" Molly picked up the conversation where they'd tried to end it.

Da's usual terseness returned as he gave Mum her favorite purple mug. "Somewhat. Shut down operations, laid the groundwork with supergrasses."

The IRA turncoats' testimony was only a vague memory from Molly's history lessons—but she had a stronger recollection of the convictions that were later overturned.

"When they started releasin' the prisoners again, we knew it was time to get out." Mum began worrying the tablecloth again. "We had you girls, and it wasn't how we wanted you two to grow up. We tried to retire in Derry and relocated to another neighborhood."

"But Ed and Grace found us," Da murmured. "So we moved house down to Dublin."

Even that only lasted fifteen years. "I remember that part—and I remember how they showed up in Dublin right before we had to leave Ireland." Days after Molly had met the Canavans again, she and her family were in Chicago.

Mum took a long pull of her coffee. "We could've come alone, but we couldn't leave you or Bridie and Fionn, either. Special Branch worked out the details while we put Ed and Grace off. We did it for you," her mum concluded softly, her fingernails rasping against the damask threads.

What? She'd spent her first two years in the States resenting her parents for dragging her here. How was ripping her away from the life she loved for *her*? "We emigrated for my sake?"

Her da nodded, fixed on his gray mug. "We knew if they found you—the real you, Garda Malone—you'd be in danger."

"They were no great friends to any police officers," Mum said.

No, the IRA never was, even in the Republic. Molly could list a dozen IRA offenses against the Gardaí. "I thought we left because they were tryin' to recruit you."

Mum shifted uncomfortably, and Molly finally recognized the expression she'd seen from her a few times tonight: she'd been caught in a lie. "They tried. But if they realized we weren't who we said we were, I could see them exactin' revenge on our Garda daughter."

The unspoken conclusion hung in the air, trailing a chill down Molly's back. If they ever saw through her cover, the Canavans would do the same to Special Agent Malone.

Wednesday evening, Zach finished the last interview summary from the fringe militia group he was investigating and stood, but Xavier drifted to a stop in front of Zach's desk before he could leave.

"What do the Canavans drive?" X asked over the top of the paper he was reading.

"Mostly they take the bus or the 'L.'"

"They have a car, right?"

Zach riffled through his mental Canavan file. "Mid-eighties Mercedes."

"Diesel?"

His memory came up empty. He hit up his computer. "Eighty-seven Mercedes-Benz S300D."

Xavier screwed up his mouth like he was thinking. "Diesel." He placed his paper on Zach's desk. Yesterday's log of the Canavans' activities. "Surveillance saw her buying diesel last night."

Zach leaned down to read the line X indicated. "What's off-road diesel?"

"It's for tractors. Doesn't have the same taxes, so it's cheaper—but it's illegal to use in your tank."

Gasoline was always more likely to burn than explode. Zach ticked off the possibilities on his fingers. "Arson, Molotov cocktails, . . . BLEVE?"

"They're boiling the diesel?" Xavier repeated the suggestion, incredulous, then circled back to more viable ideas. "How much beer are they drinking?"

"Probably enough to collect plenty of bottles."

"Let's search their recycling. And rule out illegal diesel in their tank." X walked away, leaving Zach to relay the message to the usual surveillance guys, Dantzler and Garrido. He finished up and made sure he'd saved his file on the fringe militia group, but he had a feeling they weren't the most immediate threat in his caseload.

That worry nagged him the whole drive home—Molly was right about the commute to the South Side—and to his sister's apartment. Lucy let him in, and he held out her birthday gift. "How's everything at St. Adelaide School for Wayward Teens?"

Lucy took the present. "You know it's not like that anymore. Father Gus cracked down on the dress code, sent kids home—finally got through to parents."

"Father Gus must be a vast improvement over the last two priests." He grinned. Undercover, he'd been one of those priests for the Catholic church and school where Lucy worked. Then he'd arrested the other priest and a raft of mobsters from the congregation. Not the parish's finest hour.

And the reigning gossip queen loved to complain to Lucy. "I bet Kathleen's relieved."

Lucy's gaze wandered to the side. "You have no idea." Her tone implied there was more to that story, but Lucy didn't give him time to ask. She unwrapped the book and broke into a smile. "*To Know as We Are Known*—ooh, by the same guy as *The Courage to Teach*. Thanks, Zach. I loved that book."

"I heard. Eight thousand times." She'd hardly shut up about it for the last two months. "Happy birthday."

"Thanks." Lucy led him to the coffee table and a flotilla of cupcakes shellacked together into a misshapen heart. She glanced at the clock nestled between their family photos and a print of Jesus Christ on her floating shelves, then extracted a cupcake for Zach.

He examined the dessert. Seemed okay, but . . . "What's that supposed to be?"

"Internet joke—Cake Wrecks?"

Uh, sure. Zach took a bite. Mostly tasted like sugar, but he wasn't complaining.

"My friend Brittany made it. From upstairs." Lucy looked her watch.

"Well, the cake's good."

Lucy's tone turned sing-song. "You should take her out."

This was getting old. "Same one you've been trying to set me up with for three months?"

"She's really nice, Zach. I think you'd like her."

"Because she makes ugly cakes?"

Lucy shot him a sarcastic smirk. "Because she runs her own company—"

"So she'll try to sell me essential oils all night?"

"You don't know JingleJangle makeup?" She looked at him like everyone with a pulse and half a brain knew this company.

"How could I forget my favorite eyeshadow?"

"She's got a whole Internet empire."

Whoa. Zach let his reaction show and Lucy pressed on. "She's funny and pretty, and the kind of girl you'd be dating if you actually went out. Remember how hard it is to get married if you don't date?"

She'd never let him live down that moment of weakness when he'd admitted he was tired of the single "scene" and ready to move on. Usually he'd feed her a line about being too busy for a blind date—but usually he wasn't spending work hours around Molly. He had to do something to get his mind off her. Discussing that situation with Lucy would do anything but help. "Fine, Luce."

"Really?" She whipped back from checking her clock to beam at him. "When—is this week too soon?"

Zach nodded. "Working this weekend."

"How about next week? Paul and I could double with you Friday."

He folded his arms. Lucy's boyfriend still acted strange around Zach. Considering they'd met when Paul was in Catholic seminary, and Zach undercover as Father Tim, he couldn't blame the guy too much. "Sounds *super* fun. A blind date doubling with a guy that still sees me as a priest and my sister, who loves to make me look bad. Good way to guarantee our first date will be our last. Plus, I still need to punch him."

"Why? Because we had a fight?"

Zach leveled her with a get-serious expression. Sniping at one another didn't quite constitute a fight, but he'd have to be blind, deaf and stupid not to see his sister's relationship imploding.

"Fine, go out with her alone." Lucy glanced at her watch. "If you're so set against hanging out with him, you'd better go. He'll be here in ten."

Zach grumbled. "I'm not the one with a problem. It's been, like, eighteen months. He's gotta get over this."

"Guess we all have our hang-ups." Lucy opened the door.

"Happy birthday, Lucy."

"Thanks, bro. See you Sunday." She hugged him, then practically shoved him out.

Grace wasn't an expert at corporate espionage, but when her support was as dense as Ed and Pearse, she'd do whatever necessary to pick up the slack. Wednesday night, that meant arriving to clean O'Connell Publishing before her coworkers.

As part of the staff for the office park, she could've easily entered their offices during business hours—but she'd be sure to arouse suspicion if she riffled through the company's filing cabinets. Far easier to start her regular shift a few minutes early.

If only her job included cleaning the warehouse, or even access to it. But the doors were locked tight, and she'd tried every key in the place.

Tonight would be different. She ran the extension cord for her vacuum cleaner to the lobby outlet, indicating to any other early crew member that she was already hard at work inside the generic offices. Apart from no one else taking the initiative to come early, her only other stroke of luck was that the filing cabinets weren't the locking kind.

After half an hour of searching, however, even that seemed a small victory. Finally, in the very last drawer, she found what she wanted. Grace pulled the single-leaf form from its file, turning the folder on its side to mark its place.

DONTRAIN PARADE FLOATS, the block letterhead read. She snapped a picture of the rental receipt with her mobile. She groaned at the cheesy slogan beneath the company name: *Use DontRain on Your Parade.*

She dropped her mobile into her handbag and replaced the receipt with plenty of time to spare before any other custodians arrived. One more piece she needed.

Over Nate's objections, Molly let herself into Lucy's flat. The living room was empty, but Lucy poked her head out of the back hallway. "Hey! Paul called—he's running late."

For some reason, Molly's heart sank. She definitely wasn't that disappointed Lucy's boyfriend wasn't here yet.

No, no, she wasn't disappointed. She couldn't be. Sure, she'd almost expected to find Zach here for his sister's birthday, but she didn't *want* to see him. Wanting to see him would mean more than simple, reflexive attraction.

Until last week, Molly hadn't known he was in Chicago, so hanging out with his sister again—who'd been her friend since before she'd known Zach for who he was—wasn't awkward. She wouldn't let him steal her best friend. Lucy had never brought him up, and Molly wasn't about to violate their tacit agreement, especially not with Nate here. This assignment would only take a couple hours a week. No reason to make Lucy worry.

"Want your present now or later?" Molly asked.

"Might as well, while we're waiting."

Molly gave her the wrapped package, and Lucy tore into it. "Another—I mean, a book. *Poetry That Sustains the Courage to Teach.* Awesome; thank you!"

"You were worried she wouldn't like it." Nate slipped an arm around Molly's waist.

"No, I love it." A secret seemed to light Lucy's smile. Or Molly had spent too much time interpreting and reanalyzing everything everyone said, from the Canavans to Zach to Lucy. "Have some cake, guys."

On the coffee table, cupcakes had been frosted together to form a bulbous . . . heart? It seemed one cupcake was missing.

Nate grabbed a cupcake for each of them, and Molly sampled hers. Fortunately, it tasted better than it looked.

A knock came at the door. Molly jumped inwardly. No, that couldn't be Zach. Lucy opened the door for Paul, and her boyfriend gave her a quick kiss. "Happy birthday, Lucy."

"Thanks, babe."

Paul handed Lucy a small box—a ring box. Molly's stomach turned. She was not enduring this again this week.

Molly glanced at Nate. He simply grinned back at her, planting a kiss on her forehead, as if witnessing a proposal was only natural. As if watching someone else's romantic moment was romantic because they'd follow in their footsteps eventually.

But she didn't feel romanced. She felt sick. Did her nightmares from work have to chase her into real life?

Lucy opened the box—a ring. She gasped. "Wow, Paul. I can't—I mean, it's beautiful."

An invisible grip tightened around Molly's chest, but Paul was oblivious. He took the ring out of the box and slipped it onto Lucy's finger. She admired it for a minute before smiling up at him. "Thank you."

"You're welcome." He gave her a long kiss, leaving Molly and Nate to smile at one another awkwardly.

Was that it? At least Zach had asked *something* when he fake-proposed.

"Happy birthday," Paul said again. "Let's get cooking." He helped Lucy with her coat.

Molly and Nate joined them at the door. "Let's see it, so," Molly said.

Lucy held out her hand—her right hand—to show off an amethyst in sculpted silver. Not an engagement ring, merely Molly's overactive imagination after the week's trauma. "Lovely," she said. "Fair play to you, Paul."

He raised an eyebrow.

"That is, well done. Very tasteful." Unlike the ring Zach had given her—Molly caught a gasp in her throat and checked her left ring finger with her thumb.

No, she'd taken the tacky thing off as soon as she could Monday. That was a relief.

"What are we doing tonight?" Lucy asked.

Paul grinned. "Couples' cooking class. Sushi."

"No actual cooking? Whew." Nate took Molly's hand, and they headed for the car. That had been close. She'd had one too many engagements for one week.

6

THURSDAY MORNING, Grace took her handbag from its spot on the rickety bookshelf by the door. She retrieved her mobile and paged through the photos to find the parade float rental receipt. Grace turned to her grown son. "Pearse, the other mobile." They might not need him at work when Precision Demolition was between jobs, but having the eejit around the flat was driving Grace mad. Pearse stayed glued to the telly while he tossed her the cheap, untraceable cell phone.

She caught it. "Turn it down."

Ed grumbled from behind his newspaper, and Pearse rolled his eyes, but obeyed. With a deep breath, Grace wheeled away from the two skivers lounging in their ancient furniture and dialed the parade company. After giving the receptionist the order number, she was transferred to the sales manager handling the prestigious O'Connell Publishing parade float account. She introduced herself as Colleen O'Dea, a new secretary to the company, and the manager accepted that without question.

"How can I help you?"

"We're hopin' to have the chance to inspect the float before the parade this year."

"Um—"

Grace pressed on before he could continue hemming. "We're mainly concerned our float will be too similar to others. How many floats is your company runnin' this year?"

"Ma'am, I promise, we're working on the exact float you designed—and it's truly unique, different from everything else."

She frowned. Talking her way into the warehouse should be the easy part; the hard part was supposed to be sneaking in Ed and

Pearse to plant the bomb. Grace tried again. "We'd like to verify that ourselves."

"Of course—isn't that why Mr. O'Connell's coming down next week?"

Grace floundered in silence. "We appreciate all you've done for us. I'll see he gets there." The words tumbled out on top of one another. She ended the call, hoping the manager hadn't sensed something amiss. She found herself pacing in the narrow, outdated kitchen that forever smelled of mushrooms.

She wandered back to the parlor and scratched oak coffee table. Ed hadn't looked up from his newspaper, but Pearse was staring at her.

"Not goin' well, Mam?" Pearse asked.

She fixed him with a glare. If he were capable of doing his part, everything would be grand. "Not easy bein' the entire brains of this outfit. How's your end holdin' up?"

"Slow." He shifted under the heat of her laser gaze. The burnt orange sofa protested beneath him. "My supervisor's real close with the Semtex. Maybe if I could find another source or a way to use det. cord—"

"Can't use det. cord without a secondary explosive." In the brown and orange lounger by the sofa, Ed still perused the paper.

"What if we added more fuel oil?"

Ed shook his head. "Have to switch to nitromethane to overcome the stability issue. Too easy to trace."

"And my boss's Semtex isn't?"

Grace held up her hands. "Won't do us any good if we can't get to the floats in the first place." If she had to listen to one more discussion on the exact composition of this bomb—as if that mattered—

"What're we goin' to do?"

"Which one of youse will see about gettin' a job with a parade float company?"

Pearse and his father exchanged a sarcastic expression. "Isn't it your turn for that, Grace?" Ed asked.

She pursed her lips. "I suppose I do want this done right." She looked back at the DontRain Parades receipt. Maybe they could find another way in.

Zach headed down to the counterintel division Friday afternoon. X was busy meeting with the DOJ, so Zach was on his own for this status meeting with Molly. If this was anything like the debrief Monday, though, it wouldn't be pretty. He steeled himself for the fight. Ten minutes and they'd both be free.

Seeing her used to be the best part of his day. Now?

Honestly, he still looked forward to seeing her. Pathetic.

He found Molly at her computer. "Ready to go over your objectives?" he asked.

She stopped typing to acknowledge him. "Just have to send this email."

Zach waited another minute before a few final keystrokes concluded and sent her email. "Sorry. Here to brief me on the latest weddin' fashions?"

"I understand ruffles and lace are hot, and white is always in."

She smirked—maybe the closest she'd come to joking with him.

Zach shifted away from her. "Mostly the usual reminders: don't seem too eager, be careful."

"Appreciate your concern." Clearly, he was supposed to take that as a dismissal.

And clearly, Molly was forgetting she was new on the job. She might not like it, but Zach had to help her prep for tomorrow, especially since X wasn't here.

Zach relaxed his stance like he was making himself comfortable. "I guess these places usually assign helpers—she'll be an agent. Her name's Claire. Her mom owns the store." He gave Molly a paper with the address for Gail's Gowns. She read it over and set it on her desk.

"Anythin' else you wanted to remind me of?"

Zach ignored her sarcasm and ticked off the mission goals on his fingers. "Objectives: get a feel for her schedule so we can tell if they have a deadline soon, figure out if they have any partners in the area—" Especially any explosives experts named Patrick, but he didn't need her help. "—and leverage your relationship to build their trust."

Molly's expression seemed to ask if he could possibly be any more boring. "And you'll be listenin'?"

"No. I'm backup on another case. Claire will be yours."

Molly sighed, propping one elbow on her desk to rest her forehead on her hand. Exasperated or intimidated?

Their real relationship hadn't ended well—wasn't exactly going great now—but he wouldn't abandon her if she needed him. "I can come, if you want."

She straightened in her chair. "Thank you, no. Believe it or not, I can handle myself."

"I know," he said quickly. Obviously she'd think that. But looking at those deep blue eyes again took him back to when he was undercover, protecting her. Not enough had changed.

Everything had changed. Molly was ticking off the goals on her imaginary, interminable "To Do Before I Get Married" list, and here he was, still sadly single.

He pulled himself back to the present, but Molly's gaze had shifted to the middle distance too. When she focused on him, her lips twisted and her eyes held dread.

"Everything okay?" he asked.

"Are we goin' through with this fake weddin'—fake marriage?"

The question landed like a slap. Just pretending to be married to him made her visibly nauseated. Zach fought for a blank expression. "We'll push the wedding back. You know how these things can drag out. The place you want is booked, the caterer's too busy." He shrugged.

"An expert on plannin' a weddin', are we?"

"You forget." He slipped into Jason's drawl. "I logisticate."

Molly smiled, the fear gone. Zach handed her the folder and headed out.

If he'd wondered if she would've said yes if he'd proposed, despite her endless to-do list, he didn't have to now.

An hour, a change of clothes and a drive to the Northwest Side later, Zach tried to brush off the afternoon. He checked his slicked-back hair in the rearview mirror. Undercover. No distractions. He had to be desperate, with his sanity on its last legs.

He rubbed his hand over his five o'clock stubble. Should he have skipped shaving this morning?

Nah, this would do. He hurried through the cold into the bar. A quick recon while he took off his coat showed his target nursing a beer at the bar. Even if he hadn't seen pictures, Zach would've spotted Patrick, quintessentially Irish with dark hair and small, deep-set eyes. He could've passed for a younger Pierce Brosnan who'd lost a boxing match or two.

With a nod in the other man's direction, Zach took the stool two seats down and ordered a tonic and lime in an undertone. He subtly mimicked Patrick's posture, elbows on the polished oak bar, one thumb pressed against the bridge of his nose instead of two.

The bartender placed his glass in front of him. Zach took a sip and cringed. He'd forgotten how bitter that was. He loosened his tie and undid his collar button, activating the tiny recorder hidden in his shirt collar.

In his peripheral vision, Zach caught Patrick glancing at him. Zach's ribs constricted. What would he have to do to attract this guy's attention without raising his suspicions?

After twenty minutes of mirroring his movements without being too obvious, Zach was ready to take the lead for an unwitting Patrick. He reached for the bowl of nuts on the far side of the bar, away from Patrick. He dragged the bowl closer and started cracking them open.

His stomach seemed to hover like a basketball circling the rim. Had he made the shot?

Half a minute later, Patrick reached over and grabbed a handful of nuts.

Bingo. Groundwork he could build on. Zach downed the rest of his tumbler and accepted the bartender's offer of a refill. He took one sip, then plunked the new glass back on the bar with a low groan.

"Rough day, mate?" Patrick asked.

"Rough life." Zach took another drink, but Patrick didn't take the bait from his statement. "Got laid off today," he volunteered.

"Brutal." Patrick shook his head in sympathy.

"No, what's brutal is I got a kid, two months old. *That's* why I've been late—that's why they fired me."

"Go 'way outta that." Patrick leaned closer. "Hate to be buttin' in, but you should be at home, shouldn't you?"

Zach snorted, sliding his glass from one hand to the other. "Why? Christy moved into her mom's place yesterday."

Patrick grimaced at his plight. "Desperate. This should be illegal."

"Tell me about it." Zach huddled over his drink, but instantly straightened. "And you know they won't give me a good recommendation. If I can even get an interview."

"You could switch careers."

"To what? I don't have a degree—lucky to get this job."

Patrick shrugged one shoulder. "Construction. Myself, I work in demolition."

"What kind of demolition?"

"Explosives, det. cord, bringin' down buildin's."

Zach turned back to his glass. "I know one building I'd like to bring down," he muttered.

Patrick studied him a moment, then shifted a seat closer and offered his hand. "Pádraig."

Zach picked up on the throaty consonants of the Irish version of Patrick in the split second before he shook his hand. "Allen O'Kelly."

"You're Irish? Or Irish-American?"

"My grandparents were from Sligo." Zach was careful to say the name properly to sell the role. Also, at least one little old lady in County Mayo would throttle him if he didn't.

"Fair play to you." Pádraig raised his drink. "But heaven help the company what hires the likes of you—you've a head on ya like a bag of spuds."

The man was slagging a guy who lost his wife and his job in the same day. Of course, the national sport of Ireland was giving people a hard time, good-naturedly, so this might be a good sign.

"Aw, go ask my granny," Zach replied.

Pádraig laughed out loud. And the hook was set—almost.

After an hour of bemoaning his unfair life and exchanging friendly barbs, Zach set his third empty glass on the bar. He'd made sure his anger at his former employer carried some dark overtones, but that was as far as he'd go in their first meeting. "Well," Zach said,

"I gotta eat, and nothing here sounds good. Good to meet you, though, Pádraig."

"You as well, Allen."

Zach tossed some bills on the bar and started for the door. If Pádraig didn't take the bait and follow him, the whole night would be wasted. If "Allen" came moping back again, Pádraig's sympathy might not hold.

Nobody called for Allen. Zach gritted his teeth as he pulled on his coat, taking as long as he could without making it obvious he was stalling. He stretched out the tension in his neck. A glance back at the bar would be too telling, so he kept his back to Pádraig.

When a hand fell on his shoulder, he startled a little more than necessary. If this was his target, he had to act like he wasn't expecting this.

"Sorry," Pádraig said.

"That's okay." Zach turned back to him. "What's up? You hungry?"

"I amn't." Pádraig held out a piece of paper. Zach took it—a napkin with a phone number scrawled in blue ink. "On the chance you're serious about bringin' a certain buildin' down."

Inside, Zach celebrated like he'd sunk the tourney-winning shot. Outside, he simply looked from the napkin to Pádraig and back, walking the fine line between stunned and intrigued. But if he pounced on this, he'd seem like too much of a liability to work with. "I'll let you know." He held up the napkin. "Thanks, Pádraig."

Pádraig's lips thinned, almost like he was trying to smile. "Call me Paddy."

Now the hook was set, and this really was groundwork he could build on.

If only his other partnerships worked this smoothly.

Friday night, Molly tried to put her conversation with Zach and her appointment with Grace out of her mind tofocus on Nate. He flashed her a grin and pulled into a parking space in front of Lucy's. He switched off the car, but made no move to get out. "Molly?"

"Hm?"

"Have you thought about what we discussed last week?"

Heat pressed in on her lungs. Molly fought off the panic and took a deep breath. "Gettin' married?"

"Yeah."

She'd been trying to avoid thinking of weddings since the minute the waitress dropped off a ring box at lunch Monday—but she couldn't tell Nate that.

"I've had a busy week," she managed. It was partially true. Aside from the Canavans' case, she'd barely been able to keep up with Kent's requests for help. The man had nailed the desperate, helpless puppy look.

With gown shopping with Grace tomorrow, her work week was far from over, as was the wedding hysteria.

Nate patted her arm. "It's okay. I was just thinking." He winked, then got out and opened her door for her. If she were looking to marry, she could certainly do worse than Nate. Didn't Zach prove that every time they spoke?

Paul answered Lucy's door. His frown seemed more worried than Molly had seen him in years. He silently admitted them into Lucy's flat. Lucy bore a similarly troubled expression, but offered a forced smile that did nothing to dispel the lingering tension.

The uneasy feeling set Molly's nerves on edge, and she wrung her hands. Even Nate sensed something was wrong, shifting from foot to foot. "What did you guys want to do tonight?"

Paul and Lucy glanced at one another; Paul shrugged. "We could see *White Roses.*"

"Isn't that rated R?" Nate asked.

"No, no." Molly waved the objection aside. "It's in a series with *Righteous Among Nations.*"

"Yeah, this one's about some college students' anti-Nazi propaganda campaign." Paul's uncharacteristic monotone made the intriguing description ring flat.

"And it's really violent." Nate folded his arms, delivering a verdict. "They both are."

"It really happened." Annoyance crept into Paul's voice.

"I bet Molly wants to see *The Woman from AUNTIE.*" Lucy knew her too well.

Nate rolled his eyes. "That movie sounds ridiculous."

Now it was Molly's turn to get her hackles up. "It's a spy spoof; that's the point." And this pair could use some humor.

"I was thinking," Nate continued, "skating and this hot chocolate bar I've heard about."

"Sounds romantic," Lucy said. Paul nodded absently.

Nate stared at Paul and Lucy in the awkward silence. "Great," he said slowly. "Let's go."

As they trudged out to Nate's Lexus, Molly fell behind Nate and Paul to walk with Lucy. "Everythin' all right?"

Lucy shrugged. "The inevitable's catching up with us."

She wasn't sure what Lucy meant, but it certainly didn't sound good. Molly wrapped her friend in a consoling side-hug. "It'll all work out for the best, right?"

"I guess. But it hurts now."

Molly squeezed her shoulders. She knew the feeling all too well.

The perfect beginning for a romantic evening.

Molly was the only one who spent more time on skates than off. Lucy was fine until a child ran into her, knocking her flat on her back. She spent the next half hour on the sidelines with Paul holding an icepack to the back of her skull. Both of them insisted Nate and Molly keep skating, but Nate needed a break every five minutes, and, like Paul and Lucy, he insisted she not sit out. When the rink closed for resurfacing, Molly was the first to suggest that they leave.

It was an excellent choice. Blocky dark wood furniture made the hot chocolate bar feel rustic and cozy. The aroma of cocoa with a hint of a dozen other tantalizing scents from amaretto to wintergreen filled the restaurant—and seemed to relieve the stress hanging over them.

Once they were nestled into a booth, they discussed the myriad choices for cocoa while waiting for the waitress. She arrived and took down Nate's order of iced Chocolat de Menthe, Molly's Heavenly Hazelnut Hot Cocoa with steamed caramel almond milk, and Lucy's

White-Hot Chocolate Raspberry.

Paul glanced up from the menu. "Is the CinnaMochaCocoa or the MochaChocoLatte-Ya-Ya better?"

"The CinnaMochaCocoa is hot chocolate and espresso with cinnamon." She sighed as if bored—and paid no attention to the exaggerated discomfort from Nate's corner of the booth. "The MochaChocoLatte-Ya-Ya is orange syrup, hot chocolate and espresso."

Had Paul ever ordered coffee in front of them? Molly watched Lucy. Something behind her eyes shifted, defeated.

Paul made his decision. "I'll have the CinnaMochaCocoa."

Nate barely waited until the waitress left. "Really, dude?"

Molly didn't bother hiding the sharp elbow she sent into his ribs. Paul and Lucy shot him matching glares.

"I know he's not Mormon." Protest rose in Nate's voice. Molly had never seen him that upset. He turned to Paul. "Way to respect your girlfriend's beliefs, man."

Paul stared swords at Nate a moment longer, then turned to Lucy. "Is that a problem for you?"

"Least of our problems," she muttered.

"Shall we make this to go?" Molly suggested.

The ride home was quiet, as if drinking their cocoa precluded conversation. Once they'd dropped Lucy and Paul off, the unease of the evening lingered. Molly would have to talk to Lucy later—without Paul or Nate around.

Should she talk to Nate about what he'd done? He'd stuck up for her best friend, but the way he did it left a bitter taste with Molly.

"What would you say if I got you a ring for your birthday?" Nate glanced at Molly. Despite the teasing tone, Molly had a feeling he was serious.

Her hot cocoa grew cold in her stomach. She held her seatbelt to take pressure off her rib cage. "Lovely gift, wasn't it?"

Nate wasn't falling for that. "Nice straight answer."

She stared out the window.

"I don't want to seem pushy about this. Really, I'm not in any hurry."

"It's not that I'm hesitant, Nate. It's just—" That she was hesitant.

"I have a lot I want to accomplish," she finally finished.

"I know. I love that about you." He reached over to pat her knee. "We can take it slow. But just think about it: do you have to be single to do all those things?"

Of course she did. Pretending to be engaged was an advantage at work, but she couldn't possibly reach her goals if she let herself get distracted by Nearly Perfect Nate.

And the same went for Zach.

A very good thing neither of them would be within ten miles of her and Grace tomorrow.

MOLLY TAPPED HER FOOT in front of Gail's Gowns. She focused on the rain hitting her umbrella, the weather that almost qualified as warm in February, the shop's window display, anything except the nerves humming in her system.

Nervous? Not really. Anxious, yes. A lot might be riding on this appointment, from Molly's career and pride to Grace's potential victims.

Molly mentally recited her objectives. Get a feel for Grace's schedule. See if she'd recruited—or imported—any allies. Build a relationship of trust. She could do this.

But her parents' warning flashed through her mind. If Grace ever found out—

She wouldn't find out. Molly would see to it. She just had to *be* Molly Ryan, marrying Jason Tolliver. Not Special Agent Malone, not Garda Malone and especially not Molly Malone, ex-girlfriend of Zach Saint.

Molly spotted Grace's car and braced herself. She needed to be Molly Ryan, but she needed to protect her heart. Good thing neither Jason Tolliver nor Zach Saint was invited today. She could stuff her real life in a box in the corner of her mind and be a blushing bride.

Maybe.

Grace hailed Molly across the car park and ran up to her, launching headlong into the day's wedding plans while still twenty feet away. "What colors did you want for your bridesmaids?"

A safe start. Molly slid into her cover. "Haven't totally decided—but I'd like get Bridie back for the fuchsia and lime green number I had to wear in her weddin'."

Grace cringed. "Sounds desperate attractive, *mar dhea*."

She finally reached Molly and directed her to the shop doors. To add a level of difficulty to the mission, she had to tie in dress shopping to Molly Ryan's Irish nationalist roots. "I'm definitely wantin' shamrock green," Molly said.

"Then let's do orange as well. If you can't go to Ireland for your weddin', you should bring Ireland to you. Now, orange flowers." Grace rattled off orange and green flowers from the bells of Ireland to tiger lilies, two solid minutes of her personal Parade of Roses.

"You certainly know a lot about flowers."

"I worked as a florist in Derry." Grace took Molly's umbrella and stuffed it into the canvas tote on her arm. "Come to think of it, I have some contacts in the area. I could get you a good deal."

Contacts? The Venn diagram of Chicago florists and IRA terrorists couldn't overlap much. Molly opened the shop's glass door. "Thank you—you're doin' so much for us."

"Haven't done anythin' yet." Grace nodded toward an approaching attendant and turned back to shake off her umbrella on the doormat instead of the mauve carpeting.

"Hi," said the shop assistant. "I'm Claire."

Grace jumped in before Molly introduced herself. "I'm Grace and this is Molly. She's the bride."

Claire noted that. "Is this your mother?"

"No, friend of the family slash weddin' planner," Grace supplied, though Molly hadn't agreed to that. Molly held her tongue and again said a prayer of thanks that Grace was taking the bait and Ingratiating herself . . . and Grace was not actually her mother.

Grace turned to her. "Have you a budget for your dress?"

One detail they hadn't discussed in the briefing. So much for Zach's vast wealth of knowledge and experience and superiority.

"We've at least two thousand to work with, right?" Grace almost pleaded.

Molly flinched, but managed to smile and nod. "Wouldn't be the most expensive dress I've bought."

That caught both Grace's and Claire's curiosity.

"Solo dresses—the fancy ones in Irish dance—are expensive." She didn't want to admit how much her family had spent on the ones she'd worn at Worlds as a teen.

"Oh, you danced?" Grace sighed, her hands clasped over her heart. "Do you still?"

"I do." Molly could build on that, too. "I teach for Scoil Síofra at the Irish American Heritage Center." Where her parents accompanied the dance company. "From time to time," she added.

Hopefully Grace would never look the school up.

Claire took over, launching into whirlwind tour of gowns, an overwhelming array of silhouettes, necklines, sleeve styles, train lengths, fabrics, colors and price choices.

Molly nodded as if she understood and cared about all that. "Seems the only option you're missin' is nuclear armaments."

"Why on earth would we be needin' somethin' like that?" Grace's voice jumped up an octave in a fevered tone. "That's patently ridiculous."

"I was only jokin'." Molly couldn't tell if Grace was angry or defensive, but either way, that was a misstep. She'd have to watch herself.

After a moment of awkward silence, Claire stepped in. "Have you started shopping?"

"I haven't." Molly had been involved in three weddings in her life—her sister's and two friends'—and all were high stress affairs. One shopping trip had ended with the even-tempered bride in tears. She didn't want to bring that upon herself any sooner than she had to.

"That's all right. Anything in particular you want?"

Grace took this opportunity to jump in. "I'd love to see you in somethin' like this." She hoisted a thick three-ring binder from her bag and flipped it open. The top page was a picture of Audrey Hepburn in *Sabrina*: white strapless dress, full skirt, black floral decorations.

"I'm no Audrey Hepburn." Molly had a completely different body type.

"You want to be the center of attention at your weddin', don't you?"

Molly had already had that happen once, and it wasn't an experience she wanted to repeat. "Bridie's fuchsia and lime green bridesmaid dress? Strapless—and let's just say walkin' in the procession coined the term 'wardrobe malfunction.'"

Claire laughed. "Okay, not strapless. Anything else?"

"White?"

"I know!" Grace thumbed to another section in her notebook.

Could she have a binder for whatever she was planning? Where might she keep it? Could Molly get into her house with time to snoop around?

"Have you anythin' along these lines?" Grace held up the notebook for Claire at an angle to shield her next suggestion from Molly. Was that light in Claire's eyes more eager or evil?

Molly suppressed an internal groan. She was not looking forward to the rest of this afternoon.

Claire took Molly's dress size and led them to wait by the fitting rooms a moment.

"I'm sure a strapless dress wouldn't be a problem again," Grace murmured while they waited. Most likely, whatever she'd shown Claire was strapless.

"Perhaps not. I just don't want to spend the day worryin' about it."

Grace clucked sympathetically. "You'll have enough to worry about, I'm sure. Will you be gettin' married in your parish?"

Fortunately, Molly Ryan hadn't left the Catholic church, but Molly Malone didn't know if the Bureau would forge church records again. Even more fortunately, Molly Malone had worked in a parish office long enough to know exactly what excuse to use. "Ah, well, the archdiocese requires counselin', and our parish is booked out through June."

"Might you try one of those weekend counselin' retreats? I'd go with you."

To a couples pre-marriage counseling retreat? "We might get married in his church. Or somewhere else."

"Oh." Grace was quiet for a moment, giving Molly enough time to build to a panic. Would Grace not accept that? They might be able to get a church if they needed. Definitely not St. Adelaide, but there were plenty of other parishes where she might call in a favor—

Grace brightened. "You'll have to find an officiant, so." She browsed through the tabs in her notebook, then opened to another section.

Molly closed her eyes to hide a wince.

Claire returned to let Molly into the fitting room. "Can I help, dearie?" Grace offered.

In the changing room? Molly gaped at her for a full second before Claire saved her. "We're great, thanks."

While Molly changed into the store's foundation garments, Claire popped out to fetch a chair so she could lift the dresses over Molly. Molly reviewed her unmet objectives—figure out Grace's calendar, search for co-conspirators, build on common ground.

"Molly?" Grace called from outside the fitting room. "I've the store's color card, and clover's the best shade of green. Would you say tangerine or pumpkin is closer to the right orange?"

Shouldn't Molly be the one picking the green?

Didn't matter. Molly checked the spare, narrow changing room, but there was no color card for her reference. "Hard to say from here, but if I had to guess, pumpkin?"

"All right. Should I go fetch a few bridesmaid dresses?" Grace's retreating footsteps gave an answer before Molly could.

Claire returned to the fitting room dragging a chair. She gathered up the dress, hopped onto the chair and slipped the dress over Molly. "Hope it's long enough."

Claire zipped up the dress and fiddled with something in the back. She jumped down walked around Molly, brushing and making minor adjustments. She finally admitted defeat. "Too short." She fetched a veil, hopped back on the chair and forced the comb into Molly's curls.

Molly flinched at the slice of pain across her scalp. "Sorry," Claire said. She jumped down and got the door. "Time for the big reveal!"

But Grace wasn't there. Molly followed Claire to the green carpeted platform in front of a three-way mirror. A brief glimpse showed the dress was gorgeous. Before she got a full view of herself, Claire gave her a tiara, nearly as sparkly as the ones Molly had worn on the Irish dance stage. Molly worked the headpiece into her hair under the comb for the veil.

As Molly stepped onto a riser, Grace returned to deposit an armload of orange and green dresses in a nearby chair. "All right, I think we have the bridesmaid dress in here, and then we have to—oh, Molly! Look at you!"

She turned to the mirror and instinctively inhaled.

There was a bride.

A bride with revoltingly gaudy taste. No, she should probably like this. Molly Malone might've had her fill of everything that glittered, but the thousands of crystals flashing in the dress matched Molly Ryan's over-the-top ring.

Her ring. Molly's stomach clenched, and her fingers flew into a fist. Whew. Still there. Still a bit too big—ring size and stone size—but the little ball of Scotch tape held for now.

Claire smiled at Molly's frowning reflection. "The crystal silk chiffon overlay gives the gown this fluid, shimmery motion." She plucked at the skirt to show off the fabric's movement.

"I like that," Grace interjected. "Do you think we should tie your colors in to your invitations—and are you puttin' photos in with them?"

Molly's shrug sent a ripple flowing down the dress. "I think so."

"We need to have you register, too," Grace said.

"Let me tell you about the dress so you can decide what you like." Claire traced an outline of Molly's figure in the mirror. "This dress is cut in a fit-and-flare or trumpet silhouette—it's fitted through the bodice and hips and flares out at the knees, which shows off your figure and balances your height nicely."

Molly scrutinized her reflection—it was too fitted if she wanted to walk in it—but Grace agreed. "That it does. Oh, have you any ideas for the centerpieces—and how many people are you invitin'?"

"We haven't decided." And there was an opening. "Any other family friends in the area?"

"I don't know, you know yourself."

Fantastic. Claire pressed on in her dress description, gesturing at each feature. "The horizontal pleats on this panel accentuate your narrow waist, and the vertical ones on the bodice and the sweetheart neckline draw the focus up."

"Is that quite white?" Grace squinted at the dress.

"This shade is champagne magnolia. Oh, I compromised on the sleeves: sleeves and straps for extra stability." Two centimeters of ruffled organza at Molly's shoulder and a centimeter-wide strap hardly seemed strong enough to keep the dress up.

"Will you be wearin' your hair up or down?"

"Hadn't really thought about it," Molly murmured, fighting the tension tightening her shoulders. Or was it the restrictive undergarments?

Claire arranged the veil. "With these curls, you'll be gorgeous either way. This tiara and veil are by the same designer. Champagne pearls and enameled gold and silver flowers. The veil is silk tulle with a silk charmeuse ribbon edging."

"Have you memorized the entire catalogue?" Grace asked with a smirk.

Claire smiled patiently. "It *is* my job."

Right. She was Molly's backup, and everything from her insincere smile to this soliloquy of silk had to be her trying to sell the role.

Grace turned back to Molly. "Have you any jewelry, or do we need to get some?"

"I might have some." The pearl earrings Nate had given her last week would match the tiara. But she could use that opening for the case, too. "Wish I could borrow Mum's emeralds, but she won't fly with them."

"Emeralds would be perfect." Grace didn't seem to read anything more into it.

All right, it *was* a rather weak attempt.

"Here." Claire took Molly by the elbow and rotated her 180 degrees. "Let's see the back, with these gorgeous organdy flowers accenting the half-bow sash."

Could this dress be any more ridiculous? Even the flourishes had flourishes.

Grace walked around Molly to examine the fabric flowers at the small of her back. "Will we have a dinner or just refreshments? Have you thought about your cake?"

"I haven't—what's your schedule like the next fortnight?" Molly cringed mentally at the less-than-subtle segue. At least it was more likely to work than the last ploy.

She waved that away. "Don't worry about me, dearie. Happy to make time for you."

Claire knelt to pull the little train to its full length, though the skirt was too short. "This is a sweep train, but the designer offers an attachable semi-cathedral train to take this from semi-formal to a more church-ready option."

Each word fell on her all-too-bare shoulders, adding more and more weight. How was an imaginary wedding causing her this much stress?

"I don't want to seem pushy about this, but we're in a bit of a hurry." Grace's words echoed back to what Nate's last night. Now *that* was a reason for stress.

"What kind of ring does Jason want?" Grace asked. "And what will Jason be wearin'—suit or tuxedo?"

In a flash, Molly remembered Zach in a tuxedo, when he took her to a concert at the Kennedy Center. The event warranted a presidential appearance, but that wasn't what made that day special. Zach took the time to familiarize her with the artists and their works and significance beforehand—under the cherry blossoms by the river, and by the reflecting city lights from the Kennedy Center terrace during intermission—so she could understand and enjoy something he loved so much. *That* made the evening unforgettable.

If she hadn't already fallen for him, she would've that night, with the way that he looked at her like she was his whole world.

That old cavern cracked open in her chest, first etched there when he'd dumped her. She had loved him more than air.

She refocused on her reflection. Could she walk down the aisle in this dress, toward Zach looking the way he had that night?

The bride in the mirror began to blur. Molly blinked furiously, trying to allay the tears.

She wasn't quick enough. "Dearie, you all right?"

Molly didn't dare speak. She couldn't risk losing Grace because of her inconvenient emotions. Grace took her hand. "Come, dear heart, let's get you down off there."

She stepped off the riser, allowing Grace to lead her to the only chairs not covered with orange and green dresses.

"What is it, dearie? Don't try tellin' me these are tears of joy."

Molly cursed her stupid tears—over Zach, no less. So much for putting her real life into a box. Or protecting her heart.

Then she saw the opportunity. She drew in a ragged breath and wiped an errant tear with the back of her wrist. "I don't know, just the stress of it all. So much to do and no time."

"When you're on such a tight schedule, this is bound to happen." Grace patted her arm. "You'll have to pick the most important things and focus on those. And if that's impossible, then you might consider pushin' the weddin' back."

She swiped at another tear. This could be her chance to get out of this dress, this appointment, and perhaps even the partnership with Zach.

More than that, it was her chance to get away from marriage for more pertinent topics. "I don't know if I'm up for this today. Maybe if we just . . . talked."

"Of course, dearie." Grace nodded emphatically, her bobbed hair bouncing in time. "Why don't you get dressed and we'll go get some bridal magazines and start on some priorities for your weddin'? All right?"

Not what she meant by talk, but close enough. "All right. Thank you." She'd get another shot at her objectives while they were talking.

Had her goal been finding the perfect dress that day, the afternoon would've been a failure. But it seemed she'd accomplished her real mission of earning Grace's trust in record time.

It'd only taken a little heartbreak.

Zach double-checked the van back in the garage Saturday afternoon and made sure there were plenty of earpieces. They'd finished earlier than expected—their guy had been very convincing to the rest of the fringe militiamen.

Was Molly doing as well at convincing Grace?

"Hey, man," Xavier called as Zach climbed out of the van. "Anything I need to put in the notes?"

Zach quick-scanned his notes. Without visual contact, they didn't have many observations to add. "Remember his tone here?" Zach pointed to one quote from the militia leader about the future of democracy.

Xavier noted the sarcasm. "You busy now?"

"Not if we're done with notes." Though he could go see how Molly—no, she was fine. Maybe.

"There's a free Thelonious Monk tribute concert at the Cultural Center. Want to come?"

Free jazz? Zach looked at the time on his phone. If he changed into the extra slacks that were hopefully still folded in his trunk, they could make it. "Let's do it."

Besides, Molly didn't want his help.

Zach regretted his choice the minute he and Xavier walked through the Chicago Cultural Center's ornamented archways—and met X's girlfriend, Lila, and her sister Nia.

The sister Zach had already said he didn't want to go out with again.

"You haven't put me through enough this week?" Zach muttered to the guy who was supposed to be his friend.

"You need to get out more," X said. "And you need to get over Molly."

"I *am* over her." Enough to not be subjected to this. But X was his friend—and his boss—so he'd grin and bear it. Mostly bear it, if Nia's manners were as bad as the last time they'd been set up. She'd talked loud enough for the performers to hear at their last concert.

Pretty much the opposite of Molly. When she'd come to DC and he dragged her to a jazz concert, she'd at least pretended to be interested as he probably bored her all day with too much information about the Duke and Lady Ella and Billie Holladay. She'd even had perfect performance etiquette. Like he needed another reason to love her.

Of course, she'd shown up for the Kennedy Center curls pinned up, long white dress—and he'd gotten Ideas. Stupid, painful Ideas that left him wide open, bleeding and raw.

Okay, maybe he wasn't as over her as he thought. He could endure a blind date if it helped him move on. And people could change. Zach forced on a smile and walked over to Nia.

Whatever it took to get over Molly.

In the queue at the closest Barnes and Noble, Molly accepted a chocolate croissant from Grace and glanced down at the top-most wedding magazine. Couldn't they talk about anything else? "Not sure this is where I should focus. There's so much."

Grace patted the magazines. "Bound to be a checklist in these. Perhaps even a list if you only have ninety days to plan your weddin'."

"It's only eleven weeks from today."

Grace sighed. "How do you take your coffee?"

Molly took in a lungful of burned coffee. She still missed it. Molly read the menu boards: seven panels listing coffees and teas. Only four drinks without caffeine. "You know, I can't have coffee after noon. I'll be up all night."

"Didn't realize you were so sensitive."

"Caffeine, you know yourself. I'll just have the hazelnut cocoa."

Grace took a magazine from Molly's stack. "Maybe you should talk to Jason about movin' the weddin' back," Grace suggested again. "To get everythin' in order."

"Knowin' Jason, he'd worry I was backin' out."

"You've got to let him know how stressful this is. The next eleven weeks will be a nightmare for you both if you don't discuss these things—not to mention the rest of your lives."

Molly couldn't agree more. Especially not as Molly Ryan, blushing bride.

"Dearie, you sure you're makin' the right choice? Jason's pure class, but . . ."

But marriage was so . . . final.

Without the wedding, she could lose Grace's interest altogether. "I'm sure," she said, her tone decisive.

"All right, then." The barrista rang them up, and Molly paid for the magazines. They took a seat at a high table and spread out the magazines between them. Grace pulled out her binder again and flipped to a section filled with lined paper. "How many people are you thinkin' of havin'?"

"Not sure, but we'd like to keep it small, especially if we're doin' it this fast."

Grace seemed to be fighting whatever expression was trying to show itself. "Are you not pushin' it back?"

"I'll have to talk to Jason; I can't go makin' that decision without him."

"Sure." Grace clicked her pen. "So how small?"

Molly tore a bite off her chocolate croissant and ate it to stall. What was considered small? "Fifty people?"

Grace wrote that down. No, she wrote down *150.*

"Oh, I said fifty."

"Nonsense," Grace said. "You'll barely have your families with that."

An opening. "Who else should we invite? Do you have family friends' addresses in Derry?"

"Sure I do."

"Not many of them will make it, I'm sure." Molly took another bite of croissant, pretending to ponder. "Know of anyone else in the States?"

"Off the top of my head, I don't." Grace set aside her pen. "I'm sure you've been dreamin' about this day since you were a girl—so what have you always wanted?"

Molly used last bites of the croissant to buy herself one minute. She hadn't dreamed of her wedding since she was young enough to play with dolls, and she doubted play acting decades ago would help. "I don't know, Grace. I haven't kept a Pinterest board of weddin' ideas."

"What's a Pinterest?"

"A website—never mind."

"Well, we have to start somewhere, dearie. You want a ceremony, yeah?"

"Obviously."

"Then you'll need an officiant and a place—and if you don't care about bein' married in a church, then you might look for one venue for your ceremony and reception."

"Good idea." Better idea: pressing her objectives. "But are you sure you'd have time to help us with all that?"

"And if you choose a place that's done it enough," Grace pressed on without acknowledging Molly, "they can take care of the decorations and music and food, too. Maybe even the photography. Then the only other things you have to worry about are dressin' the weddin' party, the invitations and maybe the cake."

Molly waited for Grace to finish writing her list before she spoke. "And rings and the honeymoon. And logistics."

"Jason should handle the rings and the honeymoon—and I'm sure he'll be in charge of the logistics, once we get the other details hammered out."

"We really can't ask this of you, Grace." Molly geared up for another attempt at Grace's schedule. "I'm sure you're up to ninety."

"Nonsense. You're like a niece to me, Molly. I'm happy to help. Might be busy for the next little bit, but we'll be workin' as fast as we can."

Did Grace mean only she'd be busy—and with what?—or they all would, with wedding planning?

Grace turned back to her notebook. "The top priorities are findin' your dress in time for alterations and reservin' a venue. Difficult on short notice. Naturally, I'll take care of the flowers."

Molly again waited for Grace to finish writing. "Let's see the list, so."

Grace passed her the paper. Molly silently vowed to search the Internet for each of those things and tell Grace she'd got whatever came up first on the search engine. She couldn't possibly go through with the ceremony anyway. Time to bite the bullet and lie.

"How soon can we start?" Molly asked. Anything to get at the schedule. "What's your schedule like?"

"I've got more time today, but I'll need to ring 'round to find a reception site with an openin'. How's about next weekend?"

"Don't have anythin' planned."

"I know: I'll give my florist friend a ring and find some fantastic full-service reception sites, and the four of us will do a tour."

Four? Jason, right. Molly guessed he had to be invited. Unless he could be "busy."

Didn't help that she'd just broken down over him. Fine, she could admit it: maybe she did still have feelings for him. But he'd obviously moved on, so she'd have to deal with those feelings. Like the professional she was.

Grace dug in her tote and came up with a smaller notebook—a day planner. Was it too much to hope for a glimpse, and that she'd marked the "red letter day"?

Grace stayed on the page for the upcoming week. All Molly could see were her work hours. "We're free Friday afternoon, if that helps," Grace offered.

Only if she testified in Doyle Murphy's case as scheduled Thursday. "Mightn't the evenin' be better?"

"We'll get more individual attention durin' the day, dearie."

"Is that best for you?" Molly tried to slide the datebook over, but Grace held it fast.

"It is. You need my datebook for somethin'?" she teased.

"Just thinkin' I'll probably need somethin' similar."

"Good idea." Grace snapped it up and tossed it back in her tote. "So, your reception?" She began a new list without waiting for Molly's response. "Dinner, dancin', cuttin' the cake, of course, greetin' your guests—and let's settle on Jason's attire."

Molly sighed. At least she didn't have to fill in the details herself—or confer with Zach about their imaginary wedding for another week.

AFTER THE SECOND-TO-LAST REHEARSAL for their stake young men chorus Sunday night, Zach and his sister stayed behind with the last young man in the church building. Parker was too shy to hold up a conversation. Lucy flopped into a paisley armchair and drummed her fingers on the arm, refusing to acknowledge Zach. Obviously she wasn't going to help pass the time. Zach slowly paced the gray carpet, trying to keep his mind from wandering yet again to Molly's assignment yesterday.

If it was as bad as sitting through a concert with never-stop-talking Nia, he would've already heard. He'd get the details soon enough.

Tonight he had only two problems: whether the young men chorus was ready, and calling Paddy once he got home.

Zach attacked his first objective. "How were the soli tonight?"

"Lorenzo's really good." She shifted in the chair, further away from Zach. "But Andy's not practicing, I can tell."

Teenagers. "Remind them we're performing next week with a General Authority sitting two feet away."

"I did." She bit her thumb, cradling her elbow with her other arm.

Closed body language went well with the I-don't-want-to-talk mood she'd been in all night. Conversation killer. Fortunately, Zach's phone spared them further discomfort when it rang. He checked the number: Molly. He wasn't about to discuss her with Lucy anyway. Zach turned away from his sister and wandered through the wooden doors to the darkened chapel to answer. "Hello?"

"Zach—are you free Friday?"

Was she asking him out? Zach bit his lip to hold back a grin. "What time?"

"Afternoon. Grace's takin' us to reception and ceremony sites."

His shoulders fell, and Zach took a moment to let his disappointment dissipate. Didn't matter anyway. Even if Molly wanted to date, their relationship would end the same way it had last year. He focused on the case. "She's really getting into this wedding planning."

"That she is. So, can you?"

Zach took a mental glance at his calendar. Doyle Murphy's trial was underway, and he knew Molly hadn't testified. He'd have to risk calling the Assistant US Attorney prosecuting the case—when she wasn't after a second date—to see when Molly was on the schedule. "I'll make it work."

"Fantastic."

Now was his chance to ask. "How'd yesterday go?"

Molly hesitated. "Not quite how I anticipated, but pretty well. Very glad I'm not really gettin' married, though."

Zach didn't trust himself to say anything.

"That is, she picked out my colors. She tried to force me into a strapless dress."

"Physically?" Zach teased.

Molly seemed to appreciate the joke. "Silly. She asked how many people I wanted to invite and then tripled the headcount."

"Sounds fun. For her. Is she inviting more IRA people?"

"Couldn't pin her down to it."

But she'd thought to try? Good. His vision had adjusted to the dark enough to head down an aisle between the pews.

"What's my budget, by the way?" Molly asked.

"I'll have to check with X."

"Holdin' the purse strings for you, is he?"

Zach sniffed in fake indignation. "I have my pin money, thank you very much."

Molly laughed, and Zach stopped for a second to listen. He still loved that sound.

She moved on, oblivious, as always. "What're you plannin' to wear with that pin money?"

"I dunno. A tux, I guess?"

Silence on the line. Silence that meant something. "Remember the

Kennedy Center?"

"And the concert? Just thinking about it yesterday."

Again, a pause. "You were?"

She didn't believe him? "Yeah. You wore that white dress." Maybe she'd believe him now, but that was as far as he could go with the memory. "It was a great night." A great night that had led to a lot of pain.

"And a great day," Molly said softly. "Anyway, Grace and I decided Jason isn't the tux type."

"Grace and you, or just Grace?"

"You've caught the gist of how the day went. Knowin' Grace, this Friday could be a marathon appointment, too."

Lucy had set up his blind date for Friday. "'Kay. I'll clear my schedule for that evening." He slipped into his cover's drawl to add, "Anythang for you. Even weddin' plannin'."

"You liar." She bid him goodbye with an undercurrent of teasing. Zach stared at his phone. He'd actually joked with Molly again—and she didn't sound angry. Almost like . . .

It was nice. Civil. That was all. He wasn't interested in treading water in the dating pool anymore, and she wasn't interested in getting married, so he didn't have much choice.

He left the shadowed chapel to find his sister in the foyer again, but he definitely didn't want to discuss who he'd been talking with. "Hey, Luce, can your friend reschedule? Something came up. Work."

Lucy's shrug held no suspicion, but she was probably too wrapped up in her problems to care about his call. "I'll see."

"Here's my mom," Parker piped up. "See you later." The fourteen-year-old jogged out of the foyer. Zach and Lucy pulled their jackets tighter and followed into the snow.

"What's wrong, Lucy?"

"Paul." Had any syllable sounded so sad ever?

Lucy climbed in Zach's Subaru and waited until Zach got in to continue. "We're at a place in our relationship where we're ready to . . . go on, but we both feel really strongly that we can't marry outside our churches—and obviously we can't just change." She sighed a cloud of condensation. "Feels like the end, and the death throes are painful."

"Yeah, the quick death's easier. You know, so you can run into him at work six months later." He started the car.

Lucy snorted. "Thanks for all two-point-four seconds of your sympathy." Silence settled for a beat. "Are you really working with Molly?"

"Yep. Have you known she was in town this whole time?"

She tugged at her blonde ponytail. "It's only been a few weeks."

He groaned and finally started the heater. "Lucy."

"I promised not to tell. I kept the same promise to you, remember? Twice, actually."

"I remember—but that was an issue of national security."

"The first time." Lucy rolled her eyes, then looked out the window. "Still don't understand why you broke up."

"She's got too much to accomplish before she wants to get married." He glanced at Lucy, AKA Molly's BFF. "Right?"

Lucy's gaze fell, and she nodded.

No point torturing himself. "So, you and Paul?"

She was silent a long time, and finally moaned. "We've seen this coming—sometimes it feels like our whole relationship has built to this. Or maybe dissolved into this. We've ignored all the issues so long, but any of them' is enough to kill the relationship."

"The elephants in the room."

Lucy laughed bitterly. "Elephants just waiting to stampede."

"Have you two talked about this?"

"Duh. We both know we're grinding the relationship into dust, but we just don't want to let go. Friday night we went out with . . . some friends, and Paul's always really nice about the Word of Wisdom thing in front of other members. But not this time, and the other guy made it this big issue, so then Paul and I fought, but he said it didn't make a difference anymore."

Zach accelerated to merge onto the freeway, chewing his lip. He wasn't totally following, but how could he solve this problem?

No—living near Lucy had trained him on one thing: she wanted someone to listen, not fix her life. "What do you think?"

"I don't know. Maybe it doesn't make a difference—maybe it never did. But I never asked him to do that. He just did it. I loved that he respected my beliefs so much, that he wouldn't even let it be an issue. We love each other too much to ask the other to give up God." She fidgeted with her fingernails. "But maybe we were only fooling ourselves, ever thinking it could work out."

His sister's thoughts were beginning to sound too familiar.

Lucy hugged her arms around herself. "Guess it all works out according to God's plan."

Had God led him back to Molly—and if so, why? To prove he needed to move on?

"Why do these 'learning experiences' have to be so painful?" Lucy murmured, her voice thick like she was about to cry.

"Aw, Lucy." Zach slid his arm around her shoulders and gave her the best side hug he could while driving. "Wish there was something I could do."

But he couldn't help thinking Lucy wasn't the only one in for a painful learning experience.

Tuesday night's dance classes were a first for Molly—someone she knew showed up for the last session, Irish dance aerobics. Lucy kept to the back, but managed to pick up everything but the sevens step. Molly spared her learning leap-two-threes her first time.

The other students bid her goodbye and filed out, but Lucy approached Molly packing up at the mirror. "Hey," Lucy puffed.

"Have fun?"

"Oh yeah." Lucy's smile dimmed a watt after a second. "Got a minute?"

Molly stuffed her dance trainers into her bag and stood. "Sure now."

Lucy tugged at her T-shirt's hem, her gaze level with Molly's shoulder. "It's about Zach."

Molly drew in a silent breath. Lucy couldn't know Molly still had feelings for Zach. Molly had barely acknowledged it herself. And she was working on them.

"He said he ran into you at work," Lucy finished.

"Oh." She'd hoped to avoid this conversation. She didn't want to face Zach, but even more, she couldn't put her best friend in the middle of their fake engagement. Molly tried for a reassuring grin. "We're workin' a case together."

Lucy grimaced. "I didn't say anything. I mean, about you being town."

That'd been obvious.

"Or about Nate."

"Ah." Molly nodded. "Probably for the best."

"But, um, I think you need to tell him."

Although her body language had been evasive, now Lucy held her gaze. The pain in her eyes seemed to say this was something Lucy didn't want to say, something Molly didn't want to hear, something that needed to be said. "You didn't see him after you broke up. Believe it or not, it was rough on him, too, and none of us want a repeat."

Had he told her about their cover? Wait—dumping her was rough on *him*? "Did he say somethin'?"

"Nothing specific, but he thinks you hate him."

Molly searched for the words. "I don't *hate* him. I . . ." Part of her hated that she still cared. But she couldn't say that aloud. "I don't know."

Lucy waved her off. "It's okay; I'm not playing telephone for you guys. I just can't watch that again. I mean, my personal life is imploding enough as it is, and one of us needs to be emotionally stable." Her laugh segued into a sigh. Molly could've asked a dozen questions now that the subject they couldn't talk about was before them, but not while Lucy was hurting.

Molly hugged her. "You'll make it. I did."

Lucy pulled back, blinking away tears. "Now you've got Nate. And that's . . . great."

Better than great. Nearly perfect. Suddenly sour, Molly focused on her stocking feet in the mirror.

"Molly?" her da called from the front of the studio.

"I better go." Lucy waved goodbye and headed for the door, and Molly walked to where her parents were packing up.

Mum watched Lucy leave, then stuck her bow her violin case.

"We're worried about you," she said.

"Why's that?"

"We understand that you're doin' this for your job—we've been there. But do you understand who you're dealin' with?"

What would they do, give her a copy of *The Blood-Dimmed Tide*? She'd studied the Troubles; she had the basics.

"They go beyond bein' only trigger happy." Da clipped the case of his uilleann pipes shut. "When they were at their peak, they were . . . bloodthirsty."

"Da." Molly gave him a stern look. "Thirty-five hundred people died in the Troubles."

"You sound like that's nothin'." He straightened, folding his arms as though about to lay out the law to teenage Molly. "Percentage-wise, that'd be like killin' half a million Americans."

"That's not my point. I'm tryin' to ask what made the Canavans unique."

Mum accepted the challenge. "The IRA and its splinter groups were violent, sure, but their goal was to bring attention to the cause, not just murder civilians. Bad enough to make a statement with a bomb. Another thing entirely to make a statement with someone else's blood."

Da took the next volley. "Remember Omagh?"

"Of course." Even after nearly two decades, who could forget the deadliest incident of the Troubles, one that took place after the IRA's cease-fire?

Mum shut her violin case and pulled a music folder from the outside pocket. She handed it to Molly. Molly opened the folder to a school portrait of a teenage boy with a quiet smile.

"Alan Radford, sixteen. He was Mormon. The IRA tried to murder his father years before." Her mum flipped to the next picture, another stranger. "His uncle was murdered by the IRA in the eighties." She turned to another picture, a woman with straight blonde hair and glasses.

"I went to primary school with her fiancé," Da said.

Another picture, and another, and another. Grandmothers, school children, teenagers. "They killed twenty-nine people that day."

"Thirty-one if you count Avril Monaghan's unborn twins," Da

added.

Mum opened to the last page. A toddler with a shock of black curls stared at the camera. "Maura was their sister. She was eighteen months old."

The chill creeping down Molly's arms wasn't just because of the little girl's tragic end. That chubby-cheeked child looked exactly like Molly at that age. Mum flipped to the next photo, a devastated street with survivors staggering off. "Two hundred others were injured," Da said.

"The IRA usually called in bomb threats to minimize the civilian toll, but this time, the threats actually herded people toward the bombs." Mum shut the folder. "Bloodshed for the sake of bloodshed."

She let her words echo through the empty studio.

Molly rolled the facts over in her mind. "If you had any evidence, you should've—"

"We hadn't," her da cut her off. "Nothin' concrete. But we thought Omagh had their names all over it. No one else was ever convicted."

"And it'd been so long since we'd got out of the country," Mum added. "We really didn't know. The Real IRA claimed responsibility for Omagh, and I think the Canavans ended up with that splinter group, but who knows now? They might be RIRA, or maybe they've gone off on their own."

No one could accuse anarchists of marching in lockstep with their leaders. "Are you tellin' me I shouldn't be doin' this?" Molly asked. She'd had about enough of that.

"Not at all, love," Mum said. "We don't want you to stop you. We want you to stop *them*."

Da patted her shoulder. "You've got to keep your country safe. Just make sure you stay that way, too—change your routines every day."

Tension started to turn in her stomach, but her da wasn't done.

"Never take the same route to work. Don't let them see your car, if you can avoid it."

She frowned. She'd driven Grace to the book shop over the weekend.

Da mirrored her frown. "Always check your car before gettin' in."

"I'll be careful, Da."

He pushed his wire-rimmed glasses up his narrow nose and leaned forward to lock onto her eyes. "Be careful or be killed. Remember."

"I will." Though she'd known the Canavans had been involved in violence during the Troubles, seeing people whose lives they'd taken—putting a face to the abstraction—that little girl . . . She'd been upset the Canavans had effectively exiled her from Ireland, but obviously they could do far worse.

Molly walked to her car and stooped to scan the undercarriage. *Be careful or be killed.* A standard every day for an FBI agent—but this case suddenly felt different, as though a sharp electric current flowed around her, and any wrong step could kill.

She was not looking forward to Friday. With them.

GRACE BARELY LOOKED UP from her pot when Pearse bounded through the door—until he proclaimed, "Got it, Mam!"

He'd got it? Grace dropped her spoon, and Ed abandoned his newspaper to gather around their son. Had the gowl actually done it?

Beaming, Pearse produced a golf ball–sized lump of off-white putty from one pocket and from the other, a thin silver cylinder with wires dangling from the end. Semtex and a blasting cap.

Grace basked in the victory. One step closer.

"Fair play, son." Ed cracked a smile. "I'll get on the electronics end." They both pivoted to Grace. "Have you found work at the parade float place?"

She turned on him. "That was your responsibility, ya skiver."

Ed scowled back. "I've been lookin', and I haven't seen anythin'. They must've already hired their extra help."

The surprise complication doused her enthusiasm. DontRain wasn't hiring? They had to get in there. What else could she do? Grace paced back to the stove and stirred the stew. How could they get in?

"Maybe somethin'll happen to one of their valuable employees," Grace said. "Give it a few more days. I'll see to the other components, if you can look after the trigger, Pearse."

He saluted.

"And get more as soon as possible."

"Sure, Mam. No one saw me. I should be able to manage."

She clapped his shoulder. Maybe she'd sold him short. With one last obstacle and just under three weeks to go, things were on the cusp of falling into place.

By six fifteen Wednesday evening, Molly had almost finished plowing through the paperwork Kent had begged her to help with. Surely it was time to take the stabilizers off the bicycle for the poor man. But with her best friend in the midst of an excruciating breakup, and her boyfriend working in Hawaii—*Hawaii*, the lucky fella—Molly didn't have much else to do.

Molly stretched her neck. Across the room, she caught a glimpse of a very tall, very attractive man coming her direction. She knew him—obviously she did—and yet her fingers and mind stopped working at the sight. Between his slicked back hair and a suit that was clearly expensive, Zach appeared different enough to remind her just how handsome he was.

"Giving up on me, Malone?" Uncertainty drew the end of Kent's question up even more. "I really need your help."

Zach eyed Kent as he reached their desks. "How's it going?"

"Grand. Why else would I be here at this hour?" She made sure not to glance at Kent. Not that staring at Zach was much safer.

After all, they'd fallen in love while he visited her desk daily.

"Where's that file on Claes?" Kent muttered half to himself. He looked to Molly. "Hey, should we follow up with him?"

"Yes, you should." Molly hoped he'd take the hint. She stood and pointed to his desk. "Your file's probably there."

"Right, yeah." He wandered away to check.

Molly turned back to Zach. "All set for Friday, meetin' downtown at one. Lunch first."

"Great." A slow smile spread across his face.

Did he have to look so good in a suit?

"Wait," Kent interrupted. Molly realized she'd started leaning into Zach and jerked back.

"You won't be here Friday?" Kent's eyes grew round like a child realizing he was lost.

Through great force of will, she did not groan aloud. "I have to do my job, too, Kent."

Zach scrutinized Kent, who seemed to be collecting his thoughts. "Okay. Yeah." Kent's gaze focused on something between them.

"Anyway," Zach said, "I was thinking you might want to practice your cover."

Molly pulled back a bit further. "I think I have it."

"Malone?" Kent said, and she turned to him, but he was addressing Zach. "Did you just ask Special Agent Malone if she needed practice?" He laughed, a high double-step of incredulousness. "Obviously she's good."

A flash of satisfaction splashed in her chest, and Molly found herself sitting up a centimeter straighter.

"Yeah." Zach trailed off, absolutely unconvinced. He looked in the direction he'd come—the elevators, and Xavier waiting there.

"Oh, hey," Kent began again. This time he *was* talking to Molly. She flinched at the phrase she'd heard too many times, always prefacing a favor, or an obvious question. So much for satisfaction.

"Can you help me with—"

"Can I walk you out?" Zach cut him off.

Not likely. Obviously she shouldn't trust herself to walk out with him—but moreover, she didn't need his rescuing with Kent any more than she did with Grace.

She gestured to Kent. "Thank you, but I'm needed here."

Zach looked from Kent back to her again. "Obviously." His lips scrunched together as though he had a lot to ponder, then pivoted to walk out.

"Okay, so," Kent launched into his question. Molly tore her gaze from Zach. At least one person recognized she could do her job, even if he thought she needed to do his as well.

Zach reached the elevators and Xavier, but his mind was still on Molly. He glanced back at her desk again. Thinking.

Why on earth should he feel like he needed to protect Molly? Wasn't like her pet was a threat.

He wasn't jealous, was he?

"Worried?" Xavier asked. "Something happen?"

"No, an agent on Molly's squad." Zach chose to keep it vague.

"What'd he do, shush her repeatedly?"

Zach tried not to react on the outside. X was still on his case about the date with Nia—who talked all through the concert Saturday. He'd been raised better than that.

Or he was being ridiculously picky.

"Listen," Zach said, "sorry things didn't work out."

"You're the reason I've been in the doghouse all week."

"I didn't mean to . . ." He sighed. "What do you want me to do, take her to dinner to make up for it?"

X grunted. "So I can work my way back into Lila's good graces again?"

"Then drop it."

The elevator chimed, and the doors slid open to reveal the Special Agent in Charge. Though Zach had gotten to know the guy some through church, facing the man in charge of the entire field office was always unnerving.

SAC Evans nodded a greeting. Zach and Xavier boarded the elevator.

"Night on the town, Saint?" Evans gestured at Zach, and Zach looked down. His suit—right. He was already dressed for his meeting with Paddy.

"Working late, sir."

"Don't have too much fun."

"You know me, President Evans. Still keeping the mission schedule." Up at six, home by nine? Right.

Evans laughed, then snapped his fingers as if remembering something. "Are you free next Friday? My niece is coming to town, and I was thinking you could show her the Chicago sights."

Man, he hoped his personal life wasn't such a legendary sob story around the Bureau that this was another pity set-up. "The fifth?"

"Yeah—that work for you?"

"Sure. Looking forward to it."

The elevator stopped, and they let Evans off first.

"Friendly with the SAC, aren't we? Taking his niece out? 'President Evans'?"

Zach rolled his eyes to cover the flinch—he hated using church titles at work. "He's a member of my church. We're working on a project together." If the stake young men president assigning him to organize a chorus of the teenagers qualified as "working together."

"As long as I can ride your coattails. Make sure I get a cushy office when you're ASAC."

"Don't worry, I'll remember everyone I stepped on to make it to the top."

Xavier pointed at him. "As long I get a *really* nice chair."

"You got it."

X saluted and peeled off for his car, and Zach was on his own for his meeting tonight. The familiar pre-op nerves sang to a crescendo. Zach took a steadying breath.

Everything would go fine. Paddy would see what he wanted to see—a guy on his last threads of sanity, ready for revenge on the people who'd hurt him.

Zach strolled into the low-key bar. He surveyed the cluttered décor and found Paddy in a corner booth. He joined him, ready to walk the fine line between trust-me-I'm-not-too-crazy and I'm-just-crazy-enough-to-do-this.

"All prettied up for me?" Paddy cast his suit a meaningful look.

He'd come with a reason for unemployed Allen to be dressed up again, and pile onto his grievances with his ex-employer/target. "Interview today. Went great until they mentioned they'd call my last job to check me out."

Paddy grimaced and gestured to the seat across from him. Small talk came first, but once the chili cheese fries arrived, they turned to business.

"Sure you want to be doin' this, now?" Paddy asked. "Can't take this back."

"Oh yeah," Zach said, working on a defiant set to his jaw around a mouthful of French fries.

"Understand what I mean by an 'explosive' message?"

"I want them to get my point."

Paddy scrutinized him a heartbeat too long. “What might that point be, exactly?”

His pulse revved in his throat. Was this testing his commitment, or his cover? “They can’t use people. They can’t use *me.* They took the last ten years of my life—my marriage fell apart because I was busting my hump seventy hours a week for them. Every *day* grinding me down, and then I get home and—” What was his imaginary wife’s name?

After a burst of panic, he saw how to finish. “And she’s gone.”

Paddy’s deep-set brown eyes stared through him. “Worth their blood?”

An explosives dealer with a conscience. “Every. Drop.”

Paddy gave a curt nod. “Done. I take it you’re targetin’ your superiors?”

“Yeah. Simon—”

“Don’t need names. For a personal target, we can’t use a timer or a behavioral trigger—openin’ the box, for example, might hurt the wrong person.”

He got the feeling indiscriminate violence wasn’t what Paddy wanted in a buyer, so Zach nodded. “So a remote control?”

“Remote control,” Paddy repeated, sneering. “Bit more sophisticated, boyo.” He pulled out a cheap flip phone that looked anything but sophisticated. “Here’s your trigger.”

Zach reached for the phone, but Paddy moved it away. “You’ll be usin’ your own,” he said.

“Fine. How’s it work?”

“Wire the phone to the trigger circuit. Give her a ring, and—boom.”

Zach examined the phone again. How long had this guy been on the streets of Chicago—and how much blood had he already shed?

He could find out. Zach pushed away his fries. “I hate to ask, but—I mean, I don’t know how this works. Can I talk to somebody you’ve worked with before—?”

“What, *references*? What are you, a peeler?”

Zach tried to place the Irish term, but came up empty. “What?”

“Police.”

“What’re you talking about, man? Do cops want to blow people up?"

"Where I come from, you don't need 'user reviews' for squibs—you need proof."

Zach settled back in his seat. Paddy was making this too easy. "Great," Zach said. "When can I get that?"

"When you ring your man." Paddy wagged the flip phone again.

Zach leaned across the table. "You think we'll get more than one shot at this? If it doesn't work the first time, we're both in trouble."

"Speak for your—"

"I need a demonstration."

Paddy folded his arms. "Semtex doesn't grow on trees, Allen. I'll not be buildin' two bombs for you."

"Then why am I paying you?"

The other man rubbed his hand over his mouth, hard. "Tell you what: you bring me the Semtex—C-4, whatever—for your bomb, and we'll have a demonstration. Otherwise, one bomb, no demonstrations."

Zach ran his tongue over his teeth. "Fine. I'll find the stuff. Demonstration Saturday."

"If you're wantin' a demonstration, *I'll* be tellin' *you* when."

He didn't like that one bit—but from the way the guy was staring him down and biting his lip like Zach's head was next, this might be one thing he could give on. "Fine. You know the number."

Zach left half his fries and a ten on the table. Not nearly as tough as Dice made it out to be.

The next day, Zach and Xavier sat in X's office going over one last file for his afternoon with the Department of Justice. Zach, on the other hand, was trying *not* to think too much about the DOJ case he was keeping tabs on: Doyle Murphy's, and Molly's impending testimony.

Xavier finished the file and closed it. "You're seeing the Canavans tomorrow." He reviewed the docket. "We'll need to reschedule our check-in meeting."

"I'll catch up with Molly and figure out a time." Wow. His brain was automatically making up excuses to see Molly. Maybe he deserved all the pity set-ups he was getting.

Xavier stood and Zach followed suit, but before they left, his cell rang. "Hello?"

"Agent Saint? AUSA Jill Hardt."

The Assistant US Attorney on Murphy's case. "I was just leaving—"

"Actually, cross is taking longer than we thought. The other agent won't be on the stand until tomorrow."

Hopefully Molly was taking the witness stand freeze-out okay. "Thanks for letting me know."

"Though if you wanted to come down, we could get a bite to eat."

Not for the first time, Zach mentally kicked himself for buying her lunch a couple months ago while they were working on prosecution strategy. Yeah, he was tired of the dating treadmill, but seeing a prosecutor felt wrong. He held his phone to his chest. "X, go on without me." He picked up the call again as Xavier walked away. "Sorry, I'm really busy. See you tomorrow."

"All right." She didn't hide the disappointment in her voice.

"Thanks." Zach hung up and skimmed his files, loosening his tie. Before he picked one, Xavier walked back to his desk again, on his phone.

He finished the call with a "Hope you have better luck" and turned to Zach. "You busy?"

Not too busy for his supervisor. "What's up?"

"Garrido just broke his arm stepping—tripping—off a curb. Dantzler's taking him to the ER, but they were supposed to be the Canavans' surveillance today."

"I got it."

"This time," Xavier said with more than a hint of sarcasm, "do. Not. Approach. She gets off work at the Paltec building in an hour. Take whoever you want."

A second set of eyes was useful, but the real advantage of bringing a partner was staving off the more immediate threat of death by boredom. Plus, he'd promised to get up with Molly, and her afternoon just opened up.

Molly was leaning back in her chair, her chin in one hand, listening to her one-man fan club. Kent rubbed at his blond stubble, looking around like he was lost. He had to be desperate for help if he was asking the least experienced person on their squad.

"Who do you tell if you're 'accidentally' sellin' sensitive matériel to terrorist front companies?" Molly prompted Kent as Zach came in range.

"Nobody, if you've got half a brain."

Molly held out ta-da hands, as if the conclusion was equally obvious if you had half a brain. Zach bit back a smile. Seeing her fight back was good—and with someone else for a change. But from the edge in her voice, he'd bet she was ready for a break.

Maybe she didn't need protection from the fan boy—but she might appreciate it. At least Zach could save her from . . . boredom.

He dropped the keys to a surveillance sedan on the file in front of Molly. She looked up in surprise.

"Let's roll."

She picked up the keys. "Am I drivin'?"

"Uh, no. You don't even know where we're going."

"What makes you think I'm comin' if you don't tell me?"

Zach dangled the bait. "Gotta see what Grace Canavan's up to."

"Wait." Kent's face filled with alarm. "You can't steal her from me again this week."

Zach eyed him. "Hernandez is your supervisor, right?"

Kent nodded.

"Cleared it with her."

"Oh." With that, Kent's sails flagged, and he turned away.

Molly didn't watch his retreating figure as she collected her jacket. "Are we sittin' outside Grace's job and starin' at the door in case she walks out, so?"

Sounded like she'd done her time in surveillance too. "She's off after two."

"No wonder she has time to plan a practical stranger's weddin'. I *am* drivin', right?"

"Nope." Zach held out his hand for the keys. "I want to get there in one piece."

Molly scoffed. "If you want safety, better let me drive. If nothin' else, my car's a tank compared to your little two-door."

"My little two-door's a little totaled."

"What happened?"

That subject would lead directly to dangerous territory for him. "Accident. A while ago." The reply came out too monotone. He shouldn't have said anything. Zach mentally fenced off that topic and motioned for the keys again. "We're using a bureau car."

"All right." She dragged out the words, like that would make him fill in the blanks.

Nope. She gave him the keys. In his peripheral vision, he caught Molly studying him, but he didn't acknowledge it.

He'd made it through that one safe. Hopefully they could watch Grace without any more close calls.

GRACE LAUGHED AT KIM'S JOKE and sipped her coffee at the counter of her friend's florist shop. Still two shoppers in the place. After half an hour recounting Molly and Jason's engagement and sketchy-at-best wedding plans, she was tired of biding her time.

But she couldn't afford any witnesses beyond Kim, who'd never consider her old friend a suspect if she were ever questioned.

Grace tsked. "Can't believe they expect to have all this done in eleven weeks—ten, so."

The bell on the door rang. Grace checked—one of the shoppers had left.

Kim slid onto her stool behind the glass counter. "Kids these days. Nice of you to help them out."

Grace shrugged off the compliment, half her attention on the last customer in the shop, amid the seed packets. "Her mam's in Ireland, and like I said, they're needin' the help."

"Beginning of May." Kim pulled a calendar from under the counter. "Should be able to do it. What are their colors?"

"Orange and green."

Kim wrinkled her nose, and Grace struggled not to purse her lips. Would Kim object to a red, white and blue wedding? She thought not.

"I was thinkin' we could do a calla lily in orange—maybe three per bridesmaid. They'll be in season then, won't they?"

"I'm sure we can find some." Kim got up to refresh her coffee, then joined Grace at the counter again. "Any ideas for a green flower, or should we go with foliage?"

"Maybe bells of Ireland, with orange geraniums or bush lilies. Or the bridesmaids may carry bells of Ireland. Havin' trouble pinnin' her down to anythin' when she won't answer half my texts."

Kim snorted. "Even better. If she can't make decisions, how'd she say yes to him?"

Grace set her mug on the counter. She pondered Kim's half-serious question, half an eye on the customer browsing the bulbs. Molly had dissolved into tears after one dress, and she hadn't been able to express even a single sensible preference afterwards. She seemed more interested in Grace's day planner than the wedding magazines, and she'd practically forced Grace to decide on specifics.

"I honestly don't know," Grace concluded. "I've only seen them together a few minutes, but it seemed like there was this . . . distance between them."

"Things'll get real expensive if she doesn't figure it out quick."

"That they will." Grace shook her head. The customer had moved on to the books and magazines. What was he trying to do, memorize each one?

She wasn't sure how much more chitchat she could drum up before it seemed odd. And coming back again could arouse Kim's suspicions.

She had to get it today—without witnesses. Grace asked for a refill on coffee and shoved the conversation along. "We're lookin' for a full-service venue this week. Any suggestions?"

Molly stared at the florist shop, warming her hands on the last of her hot cocoa. Zach had insisted they stop on the way—and he'd remembered hazelnut was her favorite. They'd reached Grace's job in time to follow her to the suburbs, to a strip mall, to a florist.

Then they'd sat there for half an hour. After catching up on their families—Molly wasn't sure whether to be proud or chagrined she still knew all his nieces' and nephews' names—Zach allowed the conversation to lapse, gazing through the flurries at the flower shop.

Why had she agreed to this? Sure, forcing herself to work with him *might* help her get over him, but . . . it was more that he'd finally shown her some little measure of professional respect. Of all the people he could've brought with him today, he'd chosen her.

How could she turn that down?

Zach set aside his empty cup. "Glad we're keeping tabs on our wedding plans. What kind of flowers mean 'subversive'?"

"Don't know, but they'd better be orange or green."

He smiled, and silence settled over them like snowflakes. It was . . . comfortable.

In fact, it was the best moment they'd had since she'd returned to Chicago.

"Oh, hey," Zach said.

Molly tensed at the phrasing: he'd captured Kent's intonation perfectly.

"What's up with your fan boy?"

"Sorry?"

"Kent. He worships you. What's the deal?"

Molly concentrated on the street and keeping her sarcasm to a minimum. "Not everyone has a colossal superiority complex." She pressed forward without checking his reaction. "Kent and I were in the same class at Quantico."

Zach raised an eyebrow, focused on the florist again. "Okay, you two go back almost a year. So why are you practically working his cases?"

She'd asked herself that more often than she'd like to admit. Anyone else, and she would've quickly and carefully minimized contact. But Kent wasn't doing it to get out of his own work. Perhaps he did worship her a little.

And for her part? "Honestly, I feel bad for him."

"You pity him," he stated.

"Thank you, Dr. Zach. An Oprah endorsement and your career will be all set."

"Too bad she had to go Hollywood on us."

"'Us'?" Oprah had left her Chicago studios years ago. "How long have you been in Chicago?"

"A while."

First about totaling his car, and now again with the evasion? "I thought you were on the fast track in DC."

Zach shrugged one shoulder. "Something came up."

She rubbed her thumb and middle finger together. Her law enforcement "spidey" sense was tingling. What wasn't he saying?

He changed the subject. "Think we should move closer? We might be able to see into the store from the street."

"To make sure she's not purchasin' illicit floral arrangements or other crimes against nature?"

"Or interior decorating." He cast her a teasing glare. "Do you want the world's tackiest fake wedding?"

Molly joined his light laughter. After a few minutes of silence, another customer strolled into the shop. Molly nodded at the woman, who was at least eighty. "Clearly a den of underground insurgents."

Zach grinned. He grabbed his mobile, sent a text message and set it aside again. "You go to church on the North Side now?"

She was not so naïve to not see the underlying question: if he hadn't seen her at meetings, was she still part of the Church? "I do."

"North Sider." He sounded offended, but she imagined that was fake. "What do they have you doing?"

"Sunday school teacher. You?"

"Family Home Evening group leader with Lucy. The committee thinks it's hilarious to call us 'Ma and Pa Saint.'"

Molly cringed. "Hilarious or disgustin'?"

"Exactly."

Speaking of Lucy. "Have you talked to her lately?" Her solemn hush carried enough of the context to convey the real question: do you know how things are between her and Paul?

"Still hanging on." Zach shook his head, more pitying than judgmental. "Wish they'd just face it: they're never getting married." His conclusion carried an extra note of bitterness.

Molly studied him studying the street a moment, but couldn't decipher a reason for that feeling. "Better to figure that out now, before doin' somethin' so . . ." She swallowed the last dregs of her cocoa, cold and silty and bitter with cocoa powder. "I don't know. Final, I suppose."

"Final," Zach repeated. He turned to her, his expression more serious than it'd been all afternoon. Before he spoke, his mobile rang.

He frowned and checked the caller, then answered. "Hi, X. You not get my text message?"

Molly concentrated on the shop instead of Zach's call, but his voice seemed not just business-like, but tense.

"She's here with me," Zach said. "Want to do it now?"

Zach set his mobile on the armrest between them, cuing the speakerphone. "Status meeting," he murmured.

"How's it going, Molly?"

"Xavier," she acknowledged him, still focusing on the street.

Zach made a cutting motion across his throat.

"Sorry," she said quickly, "Supervisory Special Agent Mason."

Xavier laughed. "Zach giving you a hard time? He means don't call me Ex-Xavier. You don't say Ex-Xerox do you?"

"Suppose not."

"Call me Xavier."

"Or X," Zach added.

"And he calls you 'Z.'" She tried to cover her grin. "Should I call you 'Zed'?"

"No." Zach fought a smile of his own.

"Only fair," she protested. "'Zed' is the last letter of the alphabet everywhere but the United States," she added for Xavier's benefit.

Xavier disagreed. "Zed's a character on *Men in Black*."

"That wouldn't cross your mind, would it, Zed?"

Zach leveled a scowl with feigned venom at her. "Never, M."

She couldn't share a nickname with the fictional head of MI6, even if Dame Judi Dench had played a gender-reversed version of the spymaster. "Point taken. Speakin' of spy movies, you see *Enemy of the State* is on Netflix?"

"Good one," Xavier remarked.

Molly checked Zach's reaction, but his expression was blank. "Haven't seen it. I mean, I know what it's about—"

"Oh," she said. "Like I'm familiar with *Star Wars*, but I've never watched it."

Zach gaped at her. "You've never seen *Star Wars*?"

"I haven't, but—"

"Not even the new ones?"

"No." She tried to concentrate on their surveillance target, but

Grace's car offered no distractions, still parked by the shop.

Zach wasn't done. "You sure you're American?"

Molly pursed her lips in a half-mocking protest. "*I* took a test to become a citizen; what did *you* do?"

"Sorry to break this up," Xavier said over their laughter. Break up? Break up what?

"What has our friend been up to?" Xavier asked.

"The florist," Zach said.

"Arrangements for our weddin'." Molly sighed.

Xavier grunted. "It's what, two months away?"

"Just over ten weeks," Molly corrected him.

"Keeping track?" Zach sounded . . . triumphant.

"You would, too, if you had to act excited or stressed about it in front of her—or just put up with her. You know she's texted me four times about wearin' a strapless dress? And don't get me started on the flowers."

"Seems like you're handling it well," Xavier said.

Molly watched Zach's reaction to that statement. He was fixed on the street, but she picked up a small but certain nod. The closest thing he'd given her to praise, unqualified, unconditioned, unstipulated. Her heart seemed to puff up a bit at that pinch of progress.

"How was Saturday?" Xavier asked.

Molly gave him the run-down of her last meeting with Grace, skipping over the tears and the heartbreak, and Xavier approved it. "Anything else to report?" Xavier asked.

"We're meetin' with her tomorrow," Molly said. "Huntin' for weddin' venues—oh, and are you free for lunch, Zed?"

"Sure," Zach said.

"Romantic." Xavier almost sounded amused. "I'd better let you get back to your previously scheduled programming." Xavier seemed to be saying that was more than watching Grace Canavan.

Nothing more was going on. Not with the man who'd dumped her six months ago. Not even if she did still have feelings for him.

Molly's mobile chimed for a text message. Zach was on surveillance again, so she took the opportunity to read it.

Nate. *Guess who caught an earlier flight! I brought you a present from Hawaii.*

Naturally. She was happy to see him. Wasn't she?

Grace gripped her mug and tried to keep her posture casual when the last customer finally shuffled out of the shop. Selecting Molly's wedding flowers wasn't her biggest goal today. "I should head—but before I go, I wanted a couple flats of strawberries and some fertilizer. Nitrogen, you know yourself."

Kim frowned in thought. "Isn't that a little early?"

Grace's fingers tightened around the mug handle. "I've got a greenhouse on the roof."

"Oh, gotcha. How much do you need?"

"You know, I'll just take a whole bag." She released her mug to wave a hand casually. "I'm lookin' to put up preserves."

"All right," Kim said slowly. Suspiciously?

Grace tried to fight off the sick tide rising in her stomach. Kim couldn't know—

"You know to be careful with this stuff, right?"

"My landlord would have a mickey fit if we damaged his roof shed." She laughed and Kim joined in. She rang up the purchase, and Grace paid in cash. To her knowledge, the state had no reason to be monitoring their accounts, but caution couldn't hurt. Though buying it from Kim meant that anyone investigating later would be able to find out her name, odds were Kim wouldn't think to mention her old friend if anyone came asking around about a bomb.

"I'll have to get it from out back. Why don't you pull around to pick it up?"

"Grand," Grace said. "Cheers."

Objective accomplished. Now she only needed a job for Ed at DontRain and the rest of the matériel from Pearse.

ZACH KNOCKED ON THE DOOR to the apartment above Lucy's, bouncing on his heels with excess energy. He definitely wasn't this excited for a blind date.

Normally, after hours of surveillance where nothing happened, he would've been drained. Though Grace had only meandered around downtown a while and gone home, Zach'd been charged up ever since.

Definitely not because he'd had fun with Molly—though seriously, that was the best time he'd ever had on surveillance.

But now he had another job: Lucy's blind date. Lucy's friend answered the door. She beamed and flipped her blonde hair. "Zach?"

"Brittany?"

"That's me," she chirped. Seriously, the woman chirped. "Come in! I'm almost ready."

Zach followed her into her well-decorated apartment—where his sister was waiting amid the black couch's throw pillows. Brittany disappeared into the bedrooms, and Zach arched an eyebrow at Lucy. "Why are you here?"

"Helping Brittany."

Help prepping for a date? "Obviously a girl thing."

Lucy sniffed in his direction. "Guess we should be grateful you showered. Yesterday."

"Today, thank you." After another minute, Zach turned back to his sister. "How are things with Paul? Any better?"

She frowned, sulking. "Still working with Molly?"

"Today, tomorrow, for the foreseeable future."

Lucy furrowed her brow, and before she spoke, he knew why. His answer should've come in a tone of grim determination, like a life sentence. It hadn't.

"You're okay with that?" she asked.

Saving him from answering, Brittany returned from the back—with a little girl in tow.

A little girl? Nobody mentioned a kid. Brittany leaned down to talk to the girl. "Alyssa, you listen to Lucy, okay?"

Alyssa nodded, jostling her blonde curls, and bounded over to Lucy. "I kept my Pollys the same as last time," the little girl said, her eyes wide with the seriousness of Polly Pockets.

Zach raced through the mental math. If Brittany was about his age, and the little girl looked the same size as his Polly Pocket-obsessed niece, this wasn't her sister.

He shot Lucy a pointed glare. She never said Brittany had a child—something kinda pertinent to a potential date.

"Alyssa," Lucy said, "meet my brother Zach."

The little girl spun back on him, squinting in an expression shrewd beyond her years. "Be nice to my mom."

"Planning on it. Be good for my sister."

"Okay!" Alyssa grabbed Lucy's hand and tugged her to her feet.

"Ready?" Brittany retrieved a coat from the closet.

"Yep." He helped her into her jacket and opened the door. Brittany stepped out, and behind her back, Zach shot another sharp look at his sister. They'd definitely be discussing what he should know *before* agreeing to a blind date. He wouldn't have said no—Lucy didn't give him much of a choice anyway—but he should've at least known.

Lucy faked innocence with a mystified shrug before allowing Alyssa to tow her down the hall. Zach finally followed Brittany. "Alyssa's cute."

"Thanks." Brittany smiled. "Most guys freak out, but Lucy said you love kids."

"Yep." He did, he reminded himself. Not that big a deal. Just not information he wanted to be ambushed with.

"I'll drive," Brittany said. "Lucy said we should go bowling."

"Did she?" Bowling? Seriously? This setup must be an attempt to get under his skin.

"Actually, she said you'd rather go to shooting. Has she always been that funny?"

Zach forced himself to laugh, though Lucy was right. Maybe his sister wasn't trying to sabotage this date. And neither should he.

They reached Brittany's car, and Zach got her door. "Bob—my ex—loved bowling," Brittany continued once they were in the car. "He was league champion."

What was he supposed to say?

She started the car and whipped out of her parking spot. "But, Bob was always at the alley, so yeah."

"Right." Zach searched for something to change the subject. "Must be—"

"It was like he wanted to be there more than home with us. I don't know; I mean, Bob's a good dad and all, but you gotta put in the time, you know?"

"That's tough." What else was he supposed to say?

"Then Bob bought a boat." Brittany launched into traffic and another story about her ex.

Maybe he didn't need Lucy's meddling to ruin a date.

After the constant crashing of the bowling alley and Brittany's retellings of Bob's jokes, Zach had never been so ready for a date to end. He actually missed the afternoon's surveillance assignment. With Molly. His ex.

Definitely healthy.

His headache had sharpened enough to whittle away at his patience by the time they reached Brittany's apartment. She turned to face him and again he made himself smile. "Hope you had a good time."

"Mm hm."

Zach raised his arms for the obligatory hug, but Brittany stuck out one hand.

A doorstep handshake? Wait, what had *he* done wrong? He shook her hand. "Say hi to Lucy. Good night."

"'Night." Brittany didn't even pause in the doorway, though she stopped short of slamming it in his face.

What just happened? Lucy would have some serious 'splaining to do. He texted her as much and jogged down the stairs to break into—er, wait in her apartment. With her deadbolt nearly dead itself, picking the lock was hardly a challenge.

Before he reached her door, Lucy texted back. *Later. Brittany woke Alyssa up and I'm settling her. Could take a while.*

Fine. Zach rerouted for his car. Somehow the part of the day that was supposed to be fun was the opposite. And somehow, he wished he was still back in the car, staring at a boring street.

Yep. Healthy.

At home that night, Molly finished her notes and tucked her notebook into her handbag. An hour brainstorming new leads on a Belgian case hadn't yielded much. In fact, she'd doodled a web about Zach, as if he were a suspect. By the time she'd drawn out the subjects he'd avoided with her, her strongest hunch was that Zach was keeping something from her.

He'd been vague about simple facts: what had happened to his car, when he'd transferred to Chicago, and why. Why the evasion?

If she wanted facts, Zach wasn't her only source. She picked up her mobile, but before she started a text message, it rang—"I Only Have Eyes for You," the ringtone Nate had chosen for himself. "Hello, Nate."

"Hey, babe. You get my text earlier?"

His text? Oh, right—he was back early, but she'd been with Zach at the time. "Sorry, I was workin'."

"That's okay. You busy now? A movie just came to Netflix that I bet you'll like."

She'd meant to watch *Enemy of the State*, but Molly had a feeling that wasn't what Nate had planned. "Sure now. Finished your talk for Sunday, haven't you?"

"Yep, so let's celebrate that. Have you eaten? I could pick something up."

"That'd be grand, thank you." Molly hoped that didn't mean they'd go picnic somewhere romantic or something. She definitely wasn't up for his usual grand gestures.

They finished the call, and her mobile returned to the texting screen. She typed out her message to Lucy and sent it before she could think better of it. *When did Zach move here?*

Nate arrived at her apartment in record time. Had he planned something big or simple? Molly gave him a once-over: his favorite George Mason University sweatshirt and a Wendy's bag. Perfect: she needed a quiet night in.

"Got here faster than I thought. I always forget traffic's not quite as bad as DC." He gave her a quick kiss on the cheek before unwrapping their food on the coffee table: a baked potato for her and a hamburger for him. "Oh, man—I forgot your present from Hawaii."

"That's all right."

"Can I talk to you?"

"Sure now." She paid her potato more attention than it warranted, even if she wanted to watch the butter.

"You have a lot to accomplish before you get married, right?"

"I do."

"Like what?"

Did they have to discuss this? Molly hunted for a salt packet in the takeout bag. "Well." The FBI had been a goal, but obviously that wasn't a "to do" anymore. Neither was the Gardaí or earning her masters or traveling. Other than that . . . "I don't really have a specific list, Nate. I'm only—" She couldn't finish the sentence aloud: not ready to get married.

"Just thought I'd ask." He picked up the remote control. "I saw this movie was on and just knew it'd be perfect for you."

Unless it was *Enemy of the State*, she just knew it wasn't. Molly busied herself in the kitchen, hunting down condiments while the movie loaded. When the movie that Nate was so excited to watch with her started, she didn't have to turn around to identify it. Tom Cruise's Irish accent was that unforgettable—and that wasn't a compliment.

Molly strolled back to the sofa and the confirmation she didn't need. "*Far and Away*," she said.

"Do you like it?"

Molly could only commit to a shrug. "I suppose it's my equivalent of a spaghetti Western—it's got a lot of clichés and flat-out mistakes, you know yourself. A little insultin', really."

Nate's smile slipped a centimeter. "Really?"

"What if every movie you saw had all the American characters sayin', 'Duuude, that wave was righteous'?" Her surfer accent wasn't great, but it was enough to amuse Nate.

"If you want to watch something else—"

"I was plannin' to watch *Enemy of the State.*"

"Oh." His good humor slipped away again. "Doesn't that have a lot of language and violence?"

Molly contemplated her potato. "You know I've seen R-rated movies before, don't you?"

"Guess I hadn't thought about it." Nate bit his lip for a moment—and she could almost read his thoughts: what else had she done before she joined the Church?

He was as horrified as if she were covered in visible filth. She rubbed her arm, as if that could take away the stain, her heart shrinking a centimeter in her chest.

He seemed to shake off the thought, too terrible to contemplate. "But that doesn't mean you should do it now, now that you know better."

Nate wasn't the only LDS man she'd dated, but she'd never been made to feel as though she came from a squalid past. Zach was far from her biggest cheerleader, but he was practically breaking out the pom-poms compared to how Nate just looked at her. They focused on the television, eating in silence—a silence that was less comfortable than sitting in the car by Zach.

She'd spent—enjoyed—hours one-on-one with Zach today. Was time alone with an ex-boyfriend like that fair to Nate? She was his girlfriend, and even if the Bureau had tasked her to work with Zach, today hadn't been part of the assignment. She had to be careful.

Very careful.

Nate paused the movie and turned to Molly. "If you want to watch your show, I'm sure we can find one of those rental services where they clean it up for you."

Not with their legal battles. "I should get some work done." Molly folded her baked potato's container. "Thank you for dinner."

"See you tomorrow."

Tomorrow, when she'd be pretending to be engaged to Zach all afternoon, possibly into the evening. "I'm workin' late tomorrow. Sorry."

Nate nodded, hesitant. "Okay."

"But you can come by Saturday, and we'll do somethin' then."

He relaxed, as if this suggestion had finally put him at ease, and kissed her. "See ya."

Molly locked the door behind him. She needed to distract herself from that awkward situation. Work. She needed to work—to prepare for tomorrow. She fetched Grace's stack of wedding magazines from her closet and spread them across the coffee table.

After a few minutes of studying, her mobile chimed with a text message. From Lucy. *Sorry, babysitting. Z moved in June. What are you up to?*

A cold chill crept across her shoulders. While she was at Quantico, frustrated because he never visited her—he'd transferred to her hometown?

Did that make a difference? He knew odds were a thousand to one the FBI would assign her here. Though he might've started the transfer before she'd got "The Call."

Molly tried to shake off the chill. No, that made no difference. She texted Lucy back about dinner with Nate.

Have you told him about Z?

Of course not—but Lucy didn't know the full reasons why. Molly just texted back a *No.*

Have you told Z about him yet?

Molly frowned at her phone. It'd only been two days since Lucy had told her to talk to Zach. *Do I really have to?*

You know the answer.

Her heart foundered. She did know.

Zach had dumped her. She should be happy to show him she'd moved on. Even throwing it in his face. Instead, she'd kept that from him and didn't want to tell him the truth.

Now she'd have to tell him while they pretended to be engaged in front of terrorists.

Late Friday morning, Grace knelt at her battered coffee table with Pearse. With her appointment with Molly this afternoon, she'd almost not bothered to see what Pearse was so eager about, but he'd actually done a fair job this time. She made a final check of the design, from the little she knew, and helped replace the banker's box lid. "That'll do, Pearse."

Pearse's lips pressed into his version of a smile.

"When's your demonstration?"

"Tomorrow night." He ran a hand across the top of the box, his first solo squib.

The flat's door swung open. Grace's heart leapt. She shifted to hide the bomb, despite its camouflage.

Ed marched into the flat.

"Where have you been?" Grace demanded. "We're meetin' Molly in a few minutes."

Ed ignored her. "What's this, so?" He peered around her. "Not the squib, is it?"

"It is." Pearse lifted his chin and his voice in defiance.

"Can't go buildin' it this early. It'll go damp in seven days. Worthless."

Pearse rounded the coffee table to confront his father. "You think I don't know that? That I'm a total eejit?" He stuck his nose in the air. If he wanted the best way to draw his father's ire, he'd found it. "I've a client."

Ed half-scoffed, half-laughed. "A client, have you? And you've gone and built this yourself? Did you get your mix right?"

"Straight Semtex, Da. No mixin' required. Personal target."

Ed made that incredulous sound again. "Where were you gettin' the Semtex?"

Pearse looked at Grace. The answer was too obvious—he'd used their supply. Ed had to be baiting him. "Cop on, Ed," she snapped. "We need the money. Fundin' for phase two."

"You're so worried about the next phase—won't *be* a next phase if we don't finish the first."

"I'll get more Semtex, Da," Pearse said, his tone placating.

"Are you coddin' me, boyo? You've nearly got caught how many times? Too risky. You're bound to get sacked."

"I won't lose my job."

Ed threw a hand in the air. "Sure, your brute strength's far too valuable in this economy." He whirled on Grace. "I didn't like sellin' off the bits and bobs before, but now you're cuttin' into *our* stash for your 'fundraisin'.'"

The man was unbelievable. "We're only usin' a little." Plus the finished squib for Pearse's client. Grace declined to mention that. "We'll have enough."

"What if we don't? Wait until next year?"

Grace planted her hands on her hips and her feet on the floor, drawing her line in the green shag carpeting. "Things have changed—Americans are still too scared after 9/11 to be helpin' their oppressed brothers. This is the only way we'll be gettin' the money."

Ed set his jaw and focused on the wall.

"He's be bringin' me more C-4, Da," Pearse added.

"Could you at least call it Semtex?"

"Da, it's the same thing."

"Nearly." His father sighed. "'Though now it seems impossible, and so all that you need is patience.'"

Again with useless poetry. Grace forced herself not to roll her eyes. Pearse furrowed his eyebrows at the Yeats quote and looked to his mother. Grace nodded. They'd won—as long as Pearse's client delivered the money and plastic explosives.

"Grab your jacket, Ed," she called. "We've an appointment to keep."

Zach had never hated defense lawyers quite like today. He shifted on the bench and tried not to scratch at his wig. As the covert agent who'd brought Doyle Murphy down, he shouldn't be here. His few turns at the witness stand in the past had been nothing like this.

Murphy's lawyer spun on his heel for another attack on Molly. "But you had no problem living in the apartment Mr. Murphy provided?"

"I wasn't aware he owned the apartment." She kept her voice even, professional. "I was told the parish was providin' it."

"Uh huh." Murphy's lawyer was applying another Murphy's law to the prosecution's case. "But you did live in an apartment owned by someone you believed to be a criminal?"

"I wasn't aware—" Molly began again, bordering on patronizing.

"And now you're an FBI agent?" The lawyer wheeled toward the jury, and Zach glimpsed his practiced smirk.

As if the badge on the lapel of her blazer wasn't evidence enough. "I am."

"Does the FBI often hire people who've lived in apartments owned by 'criminals'?"

AUSA Jill Hardt—no, wait, was it Jean?—spoke up. "Objection."

The defense waved away his question like a cobweb. "No further questions."

Jean stood. "Redirect."

The rail-thin judge nodded. Zach checked the time on his phone. They were supposed to meet the Canavans ten minutes ago.

He couldn't meet them by himself. His cover wouldn't be a problem, but Molly not showing up to plan her own wedding? They'd never buy it.

Before the AUSA started, Zach's phone vibrated in his palm. Paddy. He swallowed a groan and stood, shuffling past another spectator to reach the aisle. Just before he turned away, Zach caught Molly's gaze. Despite the red wig and horn-rimmed glasses he wore, something flashed in her eyes: recognition—and anger.

Not good. But they couldn't talk about it now. He barely reached the hall in time to answer. "Allen O'Kelly."

"It's ready."

"The demonstration, right?"

"No, the Queen of England. What do you think? Tomorrow

night."

"I don't have the stuff yet." That was actually the truth.

Paddy grunted. "What d'you mean? You're the one wantin' to meet tomorrow."

"I'm meeting with a guy to get it Sunday." Although what he was really waiting on was the paperwork for the FBI's inert C-4.

And they'd told him Tuesday. Why hadn't he said Tuesday?

"Monday, then," Paddy said. "Squib's ready, and these things lose potency over time."

Zach checked the courtroom doors. Nothing. "I'm seeing my kid Monday, first time since her mom took her. Tuesday."

"Don't go soft on me."

"No way. Tuesday night. I know just the place." Zach rattled off the address and ended the call.

He turned back to the courtroom, but the spectators he'd sat beside were already streaming out. Great, he'd missed her redirect.

Zach ducked into a bathroom to change out of his disguise unnoticed. They had to hurry to catch up to the Canavans.

BY THE TIME ZACH HAD TOSSED his wig and glasses, checked his real hair and made it out, Molly was already down the hall, waiting for the elevator. With the size of the lunchtime crowd between them, no way could he make it to her before the next elevator.

Shouldering through the flow of foot traffic, Zach tugged on his coat. Across the sea of people, the elevator arrived and Molly stepped on. He needed a faster way. Zach craned his neck, surveying the high-ceilinged hall until he found a stairwell door. He ducked through the door—and so did that Assistant US Attorney. Jean—right?—Hardt.

"Hey, Agent Saint." The AUSA stayed close to him like they had to crowd together on the stairs. "Star prosecution witness in another case today?"

He didn't make eye contact. "Nope, here to support a friend." Something Jean hadn't done for Molly very well.

"Thoughtful of you."

"Thanks." Zach reached the first landing and rounded the corner.

"Hey." Jean kept up with him to touch his arm. Awkwardly. "The Murphy case is going good, thanks to you."

"Were we in the same courtroom?"

Surprise flitted across her face, and Zach realized he hadn't said what case he'd been watching—or who his friend was. Jean's satisfied smile showed exactly who she thought he meant: her. Though he hadn't exactly complimented her prosecution skills.

She seemed nice enough, but he couldn't bring himself to date a lawyer—even if she was prosecution. Just . . . no.

"Tell me you brought up the priest's rent payments on the

apartment," Zach said.

"Of course."

They reached the ground floor and charged back into the hallway. Zach rushed more than he needed to, to put distance between him and Jean and catch up with Molly. A quick scan of the elevators and hall didn't help. He pulled out his phone and dialed Molly.

Jean came even with him again. "The case is a slam dunk." She placed a hand on his back. "Thanks to you."

Zach pressed his phone to his ear. "Thanks. Again." He hurried out of the courthouse doors, already inventing reasons Jason Tolliver might've made Molly Ryan this late without texting. Minor crisis with a supplier? Last-minute travel arrangements for an important client?

"Where are you?" Molly answered.

"Sorry, darlin'," he replied in his Southern drawl. "I was just—"

"Sorry I'm late," Molly said. "Are you with them?"

"No." He dropped the accent. Obviously she hadn't found the Canavans yet.

Half a beat of silence. "You're not?"

Did she not believe him? He cleared the shadow of the awning overhang and stopped at the top of the stairs. "I'm on the courthouse steps."

"Stay there."

"Hey, Zach?" Jean called after him as soon as he tapped the button to end the call. "Why don't we go grab lunch?"

Zach turned back to her. "Listen, Jean—"

She frowned. "Um, Jill?"

"Sorry, Jill, I—" A hard double poke to his arm cut him off, and he turned to find Molly. "There you are," he said.

"Here *I* am?" Molly nailed him with a look of *are you serious?* She paused to acknowledge Jean—no, idiot, *Jill* Hardt. The women nodded to each other, wary.

"You did a good job," Jill told Molly.

"Thank you."

Was it Zach's imagination, or were they sizing one another up like rivals? He decided not to clarify his relationship with Molly, stepping very close to her before addressing Jill. "Sorry, we have to go. But thanks."

Jill backed off a step with a nod of understanding—showing enough grace to make Zach feel bad for not quite telling the truth.

Almost. Zach slid his arm around Molly's shoulders and leaned closer to whisper, "Thanks. You saved me from an uncomfortable situation."

"Did I?" Stress strained her syllables. She retrieved her phone from her purse. "Four missed calls," she muttered. "And they texted." She shrugged off his arm and started down the street, tapping on her screen.

Zach kept in step with her. "Can we catch up with them?"

"They had trouble parkin' and then gettin' a table. They're still waitin' to be seated." She kept her pace and her tone brisk.

Was she mad? What had he done? They walked a block in silence, and not the comfortable quiet of yesterday. Finally, Zach ventured to speak. "Do you have your ring?"

"Naturally." She held up her left hand, sparkly as ever.

"Where are you parked?"

Molly glanced over her shoulder. "At work."

"Then where are we going?"

She pointed down Michigan Avenue. "Said we'd meet them at the restaurant once we found a spot." She stopped abruptly—red light.

Zach leaned in front of her to catch her gaze. "How are you doing?"

"Fantastic." Her voice came out totally flat. "You?"

"Great." But his tone didn't match his response either. Something was definitely up. With the case or with him? "The Canavans will see you're mad at me."

"Fine." She stopped and whirled on him. "Why did you leave the courtroom?"

"Phone call for another case."

The fire in Molly's glare died down. "You weren't leavin' to get to the Canavans?"

"Not without you."

She looked him up and down, like she was calculating how much he meant that. Whatever her verdict, she turned and started walking again. The uneasy silence still hung over them.

"How much farther?" Zach asked.

"Two more blocks."

"Perfect." He jogged a couple feet ahead to spin around and face her, walking backward. "Just enough time to tell me what's bothering you."

"Nothin's botherin' me."

"Yeah, right." They might be physically closer today walking down the street, but he'd have to be pretty dense not to notice the frigid gulf between them—one that wasn't there yesterday.

He waited another block before trying again. "Come on, this will throw us both off with them."

She didn't slow down, but she bit her lip and looked away for a few seconds. "Fine." She stopped. "I need to tell you somethin'."

"There you are!" Grace Canavan crowed, not ten feet away.

"Sorry 'bout that," Zach drawled. Obviously the real Molly didn't want him cuddling up, but they had to sell this to the Canavans. He slid an arm around Molly's waist and rotated her toward Grace. "You know how crazy it is 'round here Friday afternoons. Had to park halfway to Detroit."

Grace nodded sympathetically. "Apparently there's some big event, so parkin's terrible all over city center. The place is heavin', but Ed's got a table."

"Fantastic." Molly smiled—but Zach could still see the remnants of whatever was bothering her lurking behind her eyes.

Whatever she had to tell him wasn't good, and he'd get to spend the rest of the day wondering what that might be.

Like Grace said, the restaurant was packed. Once they joined Ed in their booth, Grace gave the menu a perfunctory glance. "I hear their fish 'n' chips are the best in Chicago."

"Not sayin' much," Ed grumbled. "Better have brown sauce."

"We'll have to see, won't we?" She shot Ed a scowl to squelch any further criticisms before turning to Zach. "Do you like fish 'n' chips, Jason?"

"I'm Southern, ma'am—I'll eat just about anythang battered 'n' fried."

"Fittin' in with the family already."

Zach checked on Molly, absorbed in studying the menu. "You

ain't gon' get the fish 'n' chips, Moll?"

"I am."

Ed dropped the lunch menu for the miniature booklet of alcoholic beverages. "What d'ya drink, Jason?"

Oh boy. "Water."

Ed stared at him like he said he'd prefer gasoline. "What kind of man drinks water?"

"If I'm eatin' somethang double battered and deep fried, I gotta make up for it somewhere."

"Jason's very health conscious," Molly backed him up.

Ed gave an incredulous cough. "Hm." Once again, an awkward silence settled over them. When the waitress arrived, Ed ordered a glass of Irish whiskey and a bottle of Belgian beer to go with the Canavans' fish and chips. "And this cute hoor here," he gestured at Zach, "will be havin' water."

Zach didn't bat an eye at the Irish insult—he'd been called worse than "suspiciously resourceful"—but the waitress aimed an appreciative smile at him, as if Ed's phrase actually made him "cute." He laid his hand on the table, open and waiting for Molly's. She obliged him without looking up from her menu, letting Zach angle her fingers to show off the gaudy ring. Good thing she'd remembered.

"We'll have fish 'n' chips, too. And water, like he said."

"Great." The waitress collected the menus, completely businesslike.

Molly kept staring at the silverware. Zach leaned over to whisper in Molly's ear, but kept his accent. "At least pretend you're havin' a good time."

"I am." Molly smiled at him and almost seemed sincere.

"Good." He squeezed her shoulders, but Molly leaned forward, pulling out of his grasp.

"Molly," Grace said. "Why are you so dressed up?"

Zach waited for her answer, racing through possible covers for her.

"Funeral this mornin'." Molly kept her gaze lowered and extracted her hand from his to fold them in her lap. "A patient."

Pretty decent cover, and now her serious mood made sense. Had she planned that? Maybe she'd just been getting into character.

"So sorry," Grace said.

"He lived a good life, but we'll miss him."

Zach slid an arm around her again for a comforting squeeze. Molly didn't fully meet his eyes, then moved out of the hug. Again.

And maybe she did still have something to tell him. He shifted to make not touching Molly seem more natural.

"'We have naught for death but toys,'" Ed said. What was he talking about?

Grace silenced any further commentary with a swift elbow to her husband's ribs. "Hope we're not tearin' you away from anythin' important, Jason."

"Nah. I've been workin' extra hours all week to make sure I'd be free." Zach flashed Molly a smile. "I'm all yours for the rest of the day."

"Grand," Molly murmured.

Yeah, whatever was bothering her definitely wasn't good. He almost wished he could get rid of the Canavans as fast as possible—or delay Molly's message for him as long as he could.

Grace quickly made it clear he wouldn't have a choice about the day's agenda. "Once we've eaten, I've a few places for us to visit. Remind me how many people you're invitin'?"

Zach and Molly were saved by the arrival of the food. If only he could get out of everything that easily. Especially whatever Molly needed to tell him.

He had to fix this, to get back to how easy things were yesterday. For the case. What could he do?

Molly took one last bite of the Blackstone Hotel's appetizer platter. After the fish and chips, and then sampling the full menu of the hotel venue, she'd had all she could take—of waiting to tell Zach. Her full stomach took a little dip at the thought.

Why did they have to continue this charade? Sure, Grace loved weddings, but couldn't Molly Ryan just profess her love for the IRA instead of Jason Tolliver?

The hotel event manager, Mr. Maggio, reviewed the appetizer and meal options, which included a dozen specialty foods she'd never even heard of. Zach kept shooting her silly looks, poking fun at the all-too-trendy menus.

Mr. Maggio turned to Molly, expecting an answer. She hadn't heard the question with Zach's distraction.

"Given us a lot to think about," Zach drawled.

"Certainly. Now for the best part." Mr. Maggio stood and led them through the hallways. Molly followed along, still silent. Zach rotated his wrist, subtly offering her his hand.

No. She couldn't.

She had to. They needed to portray the happy couple, no matter how much the truth weighed on her. She slid her fingers between his. It was . . . perfect. Exactly why it was awful.

She had to tell Zach. And he'd ask why she hadn't told him—and she still didn't know the answer.

Molly fought the feelings back into the corner of her brain. She was a professional. An officer of the law. That was the only reason this would work. She was Molly Ryan, and he was Jason Tolliver.

Mr. Maggio paused in front of a pair of glass doors. "This is our Crystal Ballroom. We have a few other rooms to see, but this is really the premier wedding venue in the area. I'd go on—" He paused dramatically and grabbed the door handle. "—but the space speaks for itself."

He threw open the doors, and Molly and Zach entered the cavernous room. Mirrored French doors adorned every luminous white wall of the room; above them, a balcony wrapped around a second level of arched French doors. An enormous red flower, its petals gilded with golden yellow, blossomed across the carpet of the entire room.

Zach took another step forward, and Molly took the opportunity to release his hand. He gave a low whistle, slowly spinning to take in the space. "Quite a place you got here."

"Indeed, Mr. Tolliver. The ballroom seats three hundred forty-five. The daylight is stunning, as you can see, and at night we have beautiful city views. It's also a historic landmark, since it's been the place for Chicago's elite social gatherings since 1910."

"What about dancin'?" Grace asked. As an afterthought, she turned to Zach and Molly. "Were you wantin' dancin'?"

Molly managed not to purse her lips at Grace making the decisions for them—again. Zach saved Molly from answering. "I can't dance a lick, but I know Molly loves it." He turned to Mr. Maggio. "Are the acoustics good enough for music?"

"The acoustics, Mr. Tolliver, are excellent. We often have live music for weddings."

"Oh, do you have bands or DJs you recommend?" Grace asked.

Mr. Maggio nodded. "A few. Looking for a particular style?"

"We're celebratin' Molly's Irish heritage," Grace said decisively.

"Oh?" Zach raised an eyebrow. Hadn't she told him?

"Her dress will have Celtic knot embroidery."

They'd never discussed that.

"The colors are orange and green," Grace pushed on, "and the flowers are goin' to be the bells of Ireland, shamrocks and whatever orange flowers are in full bloom."

Zach's eyebrow crept higher. "Orange and green. My mama ain't gon' be very happy."

Grace lifted her chin, standing up for Molly, who hadn't said anything. "Your mam doesn't have a say."

"That's fine." Zach raised his hands defensively. "But I'm bettin' Mr. Maggio doesn't have an Irish group on tap."

"Well, not an Irish group per se, but I'm sure—"

Grace waved a hand. "Doesn't have to be Irish, but they should know a few Irish standards, definitely."

"Like what?" Zach gave Grace an impish grin and launched into "Danny Boy" in a frighteningly accurate imitation of Daniel O'Donnell, the iconic Irish singer she and Zach always snickered about. Wayne Newton's popularity, Garth Brooks's personality, and Lawrence Welk–worthy pipes—but a beloved favorite of any woman of Grace's generation.

Sure enough, Grace's jaw dropped and her eyes lit up.

"Jason." Molly made her murmur a subtle warning.

This time he shot a smile at Molly and switched to "Molly

Malone."

"Jason," she said more sharply. The Canavans couldn't suspect her surname was anything other than Ryan.

"Sorry, Molly."

She fixed him with a deathly glare.

"Oh, but your singin's heavenly." Grace's hands flew to her heart. "Do you know any other Irish songs?"

Zach said nothing. Molly started toward the door—until he started the next tune.

"*'Sí Moll Dubh a' Ghleanna í.*"

The world froze, stopping Molly's heart with it. "Moll Dubh"—"Dark Molly." His song for her.

"*'Sí Moll Dubh an Earraigh í.*"

She's Dark Molly of the valley, she's Dark Molly of the spring. Molly, with her dark curls, was the subject of the song, and everyone, other than Mr. Maggio, had to know.

She wheeled around. Zach continued with the next line. *She's Dark Molly more ruddy than the red rose.*

Zach met her eyes: that was love. Nate's expression from last night flashed through her mind. He said he loved her, but the judgment in his face made her feel . . . subhuman. Zachary had never made her feel that way, even when he dumped her.

And this song was how Zachary had first told her he loved her, and the way he looked at her—his song stopped.

"Go on!" Grace prodded. "Haven't heard that since I was a girl."

He held Molly's gaze. Heat crept up her neck, but she couldn't tear herself away. Would he sing the next lines—*And if I had to choose from the young maids of the world, Dark Molly of the glen would be my fancy*?

If he did, could it mean he still—

Zach broke their gaze and looked to the flowered carpet. Molly stumbled back a step.

"I forget the rest of the words," he muttered. Why couldn't he forget all of them?

Molly said nothing. Zach came to stand by her, and Mr. Maggio and Grace extolled his singing. "Where'd you learn that one?" Grace asked, practically fawning.

"I taught it to him," Molly volunteered, seizing the opportunity to make their escape. She turned to Mr. Maggio. "Thank you very much for seein' us on short notice, but we need to be goin'."

"Yes, loads more to do!" Grace lugged out that blasted blue binder and flipped it open. The contents had doubled during the week. "Thank you, Mr. Maggio. We'll be in touch."

Mr. Maggio led them out, but leaving the room wasn't enough to escape the echo of Zach's song.

No, he was Jason now. Not Zach.

The same chill from the night before stole across her shoulders. She had to stop. Searching for meaning in these things was setting herself up for heartbreak.

13

HALFWAY BETWEEN THE BLACKSTONE HOTEL and the next stop, Grace checked behind her. Jason and Molly had fallen even farther behind. She stopped to wait. "Ed," she whispered. "Does somethin' seem off tonight?"

"I'm here, doin' this?" he grumbled.

"Eejit. I meant Molly and Jason. Just look at them."

Molly focused on the ground, huddled into her coat. Jason kept perfect pace with her, but didn't offer his hand or his arm. As Grace watched, Jason glanced at the street, then turned a concerned eye on Molly.

"Maybe she didn't like him showin' off, either."

"Whisht." Grace flapped one hand at him to silence his blather, but it did seem Molly veered toward melancholy after the singing.

"'Too long a sacrifice can make a stone of the heart,'" Ed tried again, in low tones.

Grace rubbed her mittens together. "If he hurts her," she vowed, "he's the first to go." She raised her voice to call to them. "Hurry along—but it's icy." She lowered her volume to a threat. "Watch your step."

Molly and Zach caught up to the Canavans and stayed close while Grace shuttled them to an upscale pâtisserie. Grace's logic behind the bakery choice was quickly obvious. One five-tiered round wedding cake in the window display featured irregular shards of white chocolate forming a turret around each tier, with the top of each layer filled with deep red raspberries, the bottom layer of the cake tied with an ornate red bow.

The other window, however, held a five-tier square wedding cake, with each layer turned diagonal to the one below. The middle tier bore an elaborate monogram, and the exposed corners of each layer were piled with delicate, perfect shamrocks.

Grace nodded at the clover-adorned cake. "Are they real?"

"I wouldn't think so, but . . . they certainly look it."

"We could go a bit less subtle and just use the Irish flag."

Molly's pulse picked up. There it was, the opportunity she'd waited all day for: time to bring up the "republican fight." "Better the Starry Plough," she murmured, referencing the lesser known flag of the IRA.

Grace cast her a sidelong smile. Molly returned it, reveling in a splash of success. If this brought her closer to the Canavans and whatever they were planning, then the night was worth it.

Now she'd celebrate with cake. Ed opened the door for them. The rich aroma of sugar, flour and butter filled the shop. "Sorry." Grace greeted the shopkeeper with an apology, another Irish habit Molly had recently lost. "We're needin' a weddin' cake."

"That's okay, we do wedding cakes." The shop assistant closed the glass display case. "I'll grab a sample plate." He ducked into the back, leaving the four of them alone.

"Did you see the shamrocks?" Molly asked Zach.

"Prettier 'n a speckled pup. You should ask if they're edible."

The assistant returned as Zach finished his sentence. "If what's edible?"

"The shamrocks on that cake out front."

"I wouldn't, but you could. They're sugar paste, hand painted for that realistic effect."

Molly craned her neck as if she could see the window. "They're amazin'."

"Thanks. Just wait until you've tasted the cake." He placed a platter of two dozen sample petit fours in neat rows onto the counter. "We have twelve signature combinations of cake, filling, and frosting."

"They're just lovely," Grace gushed. "But what if we can't agree on a flavor?"

Molly flashed a glance at Zach, and he caught her eye—and her message. '*We*'?

"Each tier of the cake can have a different flavor. Popular choice, actually."

Molly swept her hand over the plate, a go-right-ahead invitation.

"Oh!" Grace clapped, and Molly braced herself for another brilliant idea. "Can you guess what the other would choose?"

"Ah, why don't we—"

"Choose for one another and see if you can pick their favorite. Let's see how well you *really* know one another."

Was this a test of their cover? Better go along, just in case. Zach picked up the menu card. "Think it's gon' be hard to go wrong, Molly." He handed her the card. If she'd hoped he'd give her some more explicit hint, she would've been disappointed.

"Ready if you are." He grinned.

"All right, which one?" Molly flipped the menu back to him, waiting for him to indicate his choice for her.

"No, no." Grace held up her hands as if stopping traffic. "You must practice feedin' one another cake. Wouldn't want your weddin' day to be terribly awkward."

"Can't have that," Zach murmured.

They were supposed to be madly in love, and madly in love people would play along. They'd play their covers to the bitter end. "Grand."

Molly reached for the sample plate, but Grace again interrupted—and this time, there was more steel than fun in her voice. "Close your eyes, Jason—not fair if you see what she's choosin'."

"Grace, we're gettin' ridiculous here," Zach protested.

Grace pinned him with a look Molly had never seen from her, one that carried an edge of a threat.

Zach rolled his eyes, but he obeyed. Molly scanned the sample plate and settled on the "Red Velvet": red velvet buttermilk cake and cream cheese icing with raspberry cream filling.

Molly frowned at the sample cake cube. At that size, there was no good way to stuff it in someone's mouth. She gingerly plucked the square from the platter and turned to Zach, still waiting.

"Feedin' you's difficult if you don't open your mouth."

Zach pursed his lips a second, but capitulated and opened his mouth.

Now she'd have to feed him. Grand. No wonder Grace insisted they practice. The task *was* unwieldy.

Especially when she was trying to forget the first time he'd sung "Moll Dubh" to her.

Not the best thing to think of at that moment. Her heart was already beginning to pound a fast hornpipe rhythm.

She needed to do this without emotion. No, not without emotion—with enough emotion that Grace would buy it. Molly had to *be* his fiancée.

But she had to protect her heart, too.

Then she could be Jason's fiancée. Molly carefully grazed the sample square against his lower lip. Zach opened his mouth wider and leaned forward to take the petit four with his teeth. She pushed the cake the rest of the way into his mouth, her fingers brushing against his lips as she withdrew them.

Zach opened his eyes and instantly met her gaze. It took everything she had not to relive their kisses.

"Wow," he said once he'd swallowed. "What was it?"

"Red velvet."

"Shoulda guessed." He cupped her chin is his hand. "You know me better'n I know myself."

Grace clapped again. "Nicely done. Aren't you glad you've practiced?"

"I am." Molly stared at the counter. "More difficult than you'd think."

And more difficult than Grace could ever know.

Grace turned on Zach. "Your go, Jason." At least she wouldn't be the only one tortured.

Zach picked up a petit four before Molly could close her eyes. He held out the sample square for her, and Molly looked into his eyes.

Had Nate ever looked at her that way?

No, that admiration and happiness and love was fake. Part of the cover. He was Jason Tolliver. Her fiancé. But all she saw when she stared into those knowing blue eyes was Zachary Saint.

He wasn't supposed to be the danger, and her heart was never supposed to be in peril on this assignment. Molly couldn't tear her gaze away from his. She instinctively licked her lips before taking a bite from the cake square—and this time, she couldn't hold back the memory of their first kiss.

A kiss she'd thought they'd never share, from a man she loved but believed she'd never have. A kiss that was still the single most electrifying moment of her life. A kiss that the very memory still made the back of her neck tingle.

A kiss that, if she were truly honest, she'd trade almost anything to have again.

Molly drew in a breath. Could he know—no. Zachary was no mind reader.

She finally remembered to chew the bite of cake. Chocolate and hazelnut. If he knew her that well, maybe he already knew what she'd been thinking.

She turned away. As soon as she could, she thanked the shop assistant and led them off to Grace's next stop.

As interminable as the wedding planning parade felt, the night still held something far more difficult for her.

With the Canavans a couple feet ahead of them after bidding goodbye, Zach held Molly's hand the whole way back to the garage. He tried not to dwell on the point of contact.

Instead, he kept replaying the sweet, torturous seconds of feeding Molly her cake.

Zach should've made her close her eyes, instead of locking onto them as she took a bite.

That look had nothing to do with cake.

They bid the Canavans goodbye and headed into the parking

garage. Normally, that would signal the end of the op, and they both could relax and be themselves again.

But tonight the tangible tension lingered after the Canavans' departure—just like Molly's hand lingered in his. Zach realized the rushing sound in his ears was his pulse.

And Molly had to talk to him about something.

Maybe it was good, and she just thought it was bad. If she was still in love with him, and she'd changed her mind about marriage, maybe she was afraid he didn't return her feelings. Or maybe she'd tell him what made her think he wasn't worth marrying.

Whatever it was, he'd change.

Had he always been this desperate? But even as he asked himself, Zach knew the answer: only when it came to Molly. What wouldn't he give for a second chance?

It had to be something good with the way she'd looked at him in the bakery.

Didn't it? A wave of ice swept through him.

"Can I give you a ride back to your car?" he asked, hardly a tremor in his voice.

Molly stopped and lifted her eyes to meet his. "Can I ask you somethin', Zachary?"

When did she start calling him that again? "Sure."

"When we were datin', did you ever think—" Molly lowered her eyes, plunging him into sheer panic a second until she met his gaze again. "Did I tell you I used to smoke?"

Not what he expected. Zach recovered fast enough to nod. "Kathleen helped you quit."

She focused on his feet. "Did you wish I'd grown up Mormon? That is, did you ever think differently of me?"

What brought that on? "No. Your experiences made you who you are."

She still stared at the ground.

Zach tilted her chin up toward him. "Molly, I loved you. Nothing else mattered."

"Nothin'," she repeated in a whisper. Those beautiful blue eyes searched his, every bit as intense as when he fed her that cake—or when he'd kissed her for the first time. Then her gaze flicked to his lips and back.

He traced his fingertips along her jaw, waiting for her silent consent.

Her lips parted and she moved a fraction of an inch closer. This was happening. He cradled the back of her neck and leaned down.

Was it possible? He was really going to kiss Molly again. All the blunted feelings he'd buried fired to life, heat pouring through his veins. She was his again.

Just as Zach closed his eyes, her hand hit his chest. Stopping him. His eyes snapped open—she'd turned away. Her face was stone.

Zach pulled back. "What is it?"

"I'm seein' someone."

A visceral pain ripped through his body, made it impossible to breathe. He swallowed against a dry mouth. "Oh."

"That's what I was wantin' to tell you today."

Zach nodded, reeling a minute. He took a step back and shoved his hands into his coat pockets. "Sorry about . . . this." He took another step back. "Guess I always let my covers go to my head when it comes to you."

Molly finally met his gaze again, and her eyes held hurt.

What had he ever done to *her*? She already had someone else; what did it matter to *her* if she was stomping on his heart all over again?

"That's what this was?" she asked. "Your cover goin' to your head?"

Zach shrugged. "I just—after the bakery, I was—"

Molly reached for him, but abruptly retreated into a fist. "I didn't want to hurt you, Zachary."

Yeah, that'd worked. He gave a small laugh.

Her gaze fell. "I'll take the 'L' back to my car."

He had to veto that. "No, we're adults. That's okay."

She backed up three steps. "I'll be grand."

"Molly—" He caught her hand, but she jerked away.

"You can't go doin' that to me." She studied his face like it hurt to look at him. "Apparently we should've had this conversation sooner."

"What conversation?" He couldn't keep the dread out of his voice.

"Boundaries." Molly outlined a box around herself. She lowered her voice. "Let's face it: our lives are headed the same directions they were last summer."

He closed his eyes to hide the pain. Yes, he'd broken up with her because their lives were headed in different directions.

And that hadn't changed.

"I can take care of myself." She strode off before he could stop her, and when he followed she shot him a look sharp enough to sever a limb.

"I'm. Fine."

"Okay," he said slowly. "Later, then." Hopefully *much* later. He definitely couldn't face her for a few days.

In his last glimpse of Molly before she pivoted away, Zach could've sworn he saw something glint on her cheek. A tear? Nice gesture. Because this was all so easy on him.

After all this—two weeks of working together, of planning a wedding, of realizing how much he still cared—Molly was seeing someone. And Zach was still stuck on the case with her.

He needed this: a good, hard smack of reality. Nothing. Had. Changed. She probably still had a lot to do before marriage—things that were way more important than he was. So important she didn't even know what they were.

Of all the times he'd snuck into Lucy's apartment, did he have to overhear *that* conversation?

No, that conversation had saved him from a lot of pain. Until today.

Duh, she didn't want to get married. Duh, she didn't want to date him. That was how it worked when you dumped someone.

Despite the heat lamps at the 'L' station, and the heater on the train, Molly was still thoroughly chilled by the time she sank into her driver's seat at the FBI parking lot. She stared out the windscreen at the concrete wall of the parking garage.

Not. Fair. It wasn't fair to him, and it wasn't fair to her.

Zachary's face—she'd tried not to check, but she couldn't help it—his pain was so clear that she almost took it back. She almost lied to him just to make it better.

Had he always cared that much? If there was some chance it wasn't too late, did she dare try? To risk getting hurt that badly again?

No. She was right to establish boundaries. They had to be professional if they were working together. If she wanted to get over these stupid feelings.

Molly let her head fall back against the headrest. How could she have let Zachary walk away tonight? She should ring him, stop him—

No. She was dating Nate, and she'd already come too close to crossing a line. The cover relationship was one thing, but the Canavans weren't the reason she'd been centimeters away from kissing Zachary again. Exactly why they needed boundaries.

That wasn't fair to Nate—and that was her fault, too.

Molly started her car, but after a few seconds, she switched it off. She wasn't ready to drive home. Going home would mean the night was over, that she'd go back to her real life. To Nate. At least Nearly Perfect, Skin Deep Nate was real—more real than Jason Tolliver.

She wasn't in love with Jason Tolliver. And she wasn't in love with Nate O'Shaughnessy.

"Feelings"? For a week now, she'd let herself belief she only had "feelings" for Zachary.

She loved him. Still.

Now she'd told Zachary the truth about Nate. And she'd have to do the same for Nate. Molly pulled her mobile from her handbag. Nate was might still be free tonight.

A text message was waiting. From Nate. *Work emergency in Toronto. Be back late tomorrow night. Good thing you made me finish my talk early!*

She could have the decency to wait to do this in person. Unlike Zachary. Molly tossed the mobile back into her handbag and started her car. She'd have to wait, so.

And prolong this for them all.

14

MOLLY MARCHED INTO the Irish American Heritage Center's dance studio for the second time that Saturday. With Scoil Síofra's other teachers prepping the dance companies for the St. Patrick's Day parade, only Molly was left to teach the afternoon Irish dance aerobics session. Exactly what she needed to work out last night's lingering stress.

She monitored the adults filing in, some of them familiar from the last time she'd substituted here. And then came a face she knew well: Lucy.

Molly wasn't sure whether to be relieved or worried to see Zachary's sister. Lucy smiled and waved—apparently she hadn't spoken to her brother yet. As if he'd ever tell her about that. He'd always been good about not letting their relationship affect his sister, and vice versa.

Molly tied her ghillies and picked out a CD for the warm up. Aerobics was the one Saturday class her parents didn't play for, so she always came prepared.

Just as she walked to the front to start the class, one last participant wandered in. In Molly's peripheral vision, she glimpsed a woman who was short, heavyset and redheaded.

She turned and tried not to jump—Grace Canavan.

Hadn't she had enough of wedding planning for one weekend? But there was a bigger worry—Grace hadn't come looking for Molly and found her parents here, had she?

No, she would've heard about that. Better warn her parents.

Better warn everyone. Who knew her last name here? Molly scanned the class. The other ladies only called her Molly. Just Lucy knew her as Malone.

Yet another reason to keep them apart.

"Don't mind me," Grace called loudly, waving for Molly to continue. "Only watchin'." She took a position at the edge of the group.

"Oh, if you're watchin', you certainly don't want to stand the whole time." Molly escorted her to the far corner bench and moved her dance bag to make room for Grace. "I have to warn you, though, it won't be very entertainin'. This class is more about gettin' exercise than perfect form."

"Ah." Grace waved a hand. "I just needed to make sure you're all right after last night. You seemed . . . sad."

Molly mentally kicked herself. She hadn't meant to sulk yesterday, and now she'd drawn Grace's attention. "I'm grand, you know yourself."

"Good to hear. I was just worried there might be a problem with you and Jason?" The up-turn in Grace's voice made it sound almost like hope.

She forced herself not to look in Lucy's direction to see if she was listening. "Oh no, no problem at all."

"Grand—oh, dearie, where's your ring?"

Molly's heart jumped nearly out of her ribs. She clenched her fist, but it was too late to hide. She'd worked so hard to remember to put it on and take it off, and now she'd be caught not wearing it on purpose.

Her mind danced faster than a double reel. "Can't wear jewelry when I'm teachin'. Wouldn't want to hurt anyone." And the stones on that hideous thing could do definite damage.

They already were.

Molly derailed that train of thought, hurrying to the mirror at the front again. She tried to slide into the aerobics instructor persona she'd developed. Grace, for her part, sat quietly in the corner.

The corner closest to Lucy.

And this day had almost been going well.

Molly clapped for attention. She had to find a way to move Lucy somewhere else in the room. "All right, folks, we're tryin' somethin' new today for our warm up." Her instructor's enthusiasm sounded awfully contrived. "We'll practice each of our standard steps around the room in a circle." She grabbed the remote next to the stereo and started a slower song, then led the warm up by jogging around the room.

After practicing skip-two-threes, side sevens and anything else Molly could think of to get their heart rates up—though she didn't need any help with that—she stopped the circle with Lucy at the front of the room to start class.

Halfway through the first step of an easy reel, Lucy started edging toward the back of the room. Toward Grace.

Molly quickly revised her plan for class. "Let's practice what we've got so far. This is a two-hand reel," she lied, "so partner up." She beckoned to Lucy.

Lucy's eyes widened, and she backed away a step. Honestly, it wasn't a perfect plan—she was so much taller than Lucy they'd appear rather ridiculous—but Molly wanted Lucy far from Grace as possible.

She waved for Lucy to come up again, and this time she obeyed. Molly demonstrated holding a partner's hand, with an extra lesson on what to do if your partner was a different height. She scanned the class. One girl in the middle row, Andrea, had no partner. Molly sent Lucy to dance with her. On the opposite side of the room from Grace.

Molly managed to focus the rest of the class and almost had fun, though it wasn't the stress relief she needed. After class, she bid her students goodbye and ushered them out. Once the class dispersed in the car park, Molly gathered her things. She turned to leave herself, only to find two people waiting for her at the Heritage Center doors: Grace Canavan and Lucy.

The two of them together. Exactly what she'd spent the last hour trying to avoid.

Lucy, standing closer, approached first. "Molly, about what I said on Thursday."

"It's all right," Molly tried to cut her off, though she didn't know what she meant.

"No, I'm sorry. I shouldn't have told you to tell Zach. I'm sure you'll tell him whenever you need to—if you actually need to."

Molly's mind couldn't juggle her personal life and that of her cover at the same time. Had Grace heard Zachary's real name, and would she suspect?

Grace moved forward. "Who's this, so?"

The muscles in Molly's shoulders tightened. "Grace, this is my friend." No name. She introduced Lucy. "This is Grace Canavan. An old family friend." She silently prayed that would suffice as an introduction.

Of course it didn't. "I'm helpin' Molly plan her weddin'," Grace said with a smug little tilt to her head.

Oh no. Molly did her best not to let any reaction show.

Lucy, however, startled. "What?"

"Haven't I told you?" Molly forced a bright note into her tone. "I'm so sorry! It's been a bit . . . sudden."

Lucy slowly nodded. Had she picked up on the subtext? "Okay, call me later."

Grace turned to look at Lucy go. "Aren't you close?" Grace murmured.

"Not really." Would that be enough to satisfy Grace? "She's breakin' up with her boyfriend, and she doesn't like Jason, so I hadn't told her yet."

"She doesn't like Jason. . . ." Grace frowned after Lucy. "Can't have a friend like that, can we?" Grace watched Lucy get into her gold sedan. Molly drew a quick breath. She'd spared telling Grace her name, but letting Grace—the noted bomber—see Lucy's car? A fat lot of good Molly's caution during class had been.

"This was lovely. Thank you." Grace started toward her car.

Molly had to give Lucy time to get away. "Isn't there somethin' you needed to talk about?" There was always wedding minutiae.

"No, dearie, I only wanted to see you dance. Fierce lovely!" She didn't even pause, tossing the words over her shoulder as she walked.

Molly hurried to keep up. "But Grace, can't we talk about my dress?"

"I have a shop in mind." She paused at her car door. "I'll make an appointment. Next weekend?"

Lucy was still sitting there. Why hadn't she pulled out yet? "Next weekend," Molly told Grace. "But the afternoon's better on Saturday. I won't be teachin' next week."

"Saturday afternoon it is. Shall I come collect you?"

"That'd be grand."

Lucy's reverse lights finally glowed, and Molly exhaled. But Grace took that split second to slip into her car. She cracked her window. "Bye, dearie!" she shouted to Molly as she started the car.

What could Molly do? Stand in Grace's way until Lucy was out of sight? Worth a chance. She lingered behind the old Mercedes until Lucy left her parking spot—and Grace tooted her horn at Molly.

She stepped aside, waving to Grace. Molly didn't dare to breathe, watching them go. Grace pulled up behind Lucy in the queue to leave the car park. Lucy turned.

And Grace pursued her.

Molly's stomach took a bounce. She fetched her mobile from her bag and hopped in her car. As Molly left the lot after them, Lucy's number rang and rang—voicemail. She could barely see Grace, now a block ahead of her. Molly tried to ring Lucy twice more with the same result.

She had no other choice. She rang Zachary.

When he saw who was calling, Zach almost didn't answer. Molly couldn't have anything to say to change last night. Or reality. Not that sitting around his place and watching old spy movies on PBS were helping him forget either.

But that wasn't the only reason she might need him. "Molly?" he finally answered, his tone full of caution.

"It's Grace." Molly jumped into the conversation, breathless.

He flinched and shifted to the edge of the couch, ready to spring into action. "Are you okay?"

"Me?" She sounded taken aback. "*Lucy* just met Grace, and she might be followin' her."

"Wait—Grace might be following Lucy?" Fight-or-flight energy surged into his system, and he was on his feet before he even finished the question. "Where are they?"

"Northwest Side. Just left the Irish American Heritage Center."

He didn't know exactly where that was. "Have you called Lucy?"

"I tried. Voicemail."

"Keep trying. I'll text her. Was she going home?" Zach grabbed his keys and wallet.

"No idea. Keep me updated. I'm in pursuit."

Zach tapped out the text message on the way to his car: *Mercedes behind you? Evasive maneuvers.*

A one-man search of the Chicagoland area wouldn't help Lucy. Molly was behind her, so Zach had to attack this from the other end, where Lucy was headed. Probably her place.

If Grace was following Lucy, Zach couldn't exactly meet them in her parking lot. He parked and pulled his lock picks from the glove box, though he hardly needed them to get into Lucy's apartment with her deadbolt broken.

Once he checked her place—safe—he got a bag of pretzels from her table, flipped on PBS for the last few minutes of his movie as background noise, and knelt on the couch to watch the parking lot through the blinds.

The end credits rolled on *Our Man in Havana*, the Alec Guinness spy flick he'd started at home, and the spy spectacular continued with *I See a Dark Stranger*. He'd never heard of it.

He checked the time. How long would Lucy take to get here? When should he start worrying?

When the movie's dialogue started a few minutes later, he almost fell off his couch perch. A woman in a Hollywood Irish accent ranting about a guy because he was English? Not the background noise he needed.

His phone vibrated. Molly. "Got her?" His voice betrayed more stress than he wanted to admit.

"No, and I lost Grace as well."

Crud. "I'm at her place. I'll let you know when she gets in. Keep trying."

The minutes ticked by, and Zach grew more and more tense, alternating between peering at the parking lot and pacing. And dialing Lucy. And pacing.

Molly had called around three. With construction downtown,

Lucy should take a good forty-five minutes to get home from the Northwest Side. Already after four.

But she could be running errands. Or lost, knowing Lucy.

Or Grace.

The Irishwoman on TV had long ago been rejected by the IRA and recruited as a Nazi spy by the time Lucy's car finally pulled into the lot around four thirty. Zach concentrated on the street—no Mercedes in sight. Was there anywhere she might hide to watch Lucy come home?

Nothing he could see. The only pedestrian on the sidewalk had a dog, and he doubted Grace could commandeer one of those on short notice.

By the time Lucy made her way to her door, Zach was sure of it: Lucy was safe. He released the pent-up stress with a deep breath.

He needed to let Molly know. Zach grabbed his phone and typed a text, but before he hit Send, his phone vibrated with an incoming call. Not Molly—Lucy. "Hello?" he answered.

"Zach?"

His sister's panicked whisper instantly set him on edge. Had she already had a brush with Grace? "What's wrong?"

"I think someone's in my place—I hear voices."

Zach walked to her front door. "Someone *is* in your apartment." He opened the door to find Lucy on the other side. "Me," he finished.

"Zach! Are you trying to give me a heart attack?" Lucy swung a wide arc, aiming a right hook at his shoulder. Zach sidestepped and caught her fist, then used that to tug her into the apartment, closing the door behind him.

"If I were trying to give you a heart attack, I'd be on the other side of the door with seven hundred cutesy paper hearts. Remember that time—"

"You foiled my visiting teachers?" She pushed past him into her living room. "Thanks again for not shooting them. Who else is here?" Lucy asked. "Or are you talking to yourself?"

Zach fixed her with a mock-scowl and pointed to the TV, then switched off the black-and-white movie. "Why didn't you answer your phone?"

Lucy glanced at the phone in her non-punching hand. "It was on silent for . . . class."

"Heard you made a new friend."

She narrowed her eyes. "What are you talking about?"

"Afterwards? With Molly?"

"Oh, that lady." She frowned at the carpet.

Not good. "You're not getting together with her anytime soon?"

"Molly or the lady?"

"The lady." Why would he mean Molly?

Lucy grimaced. "It was pretty obviously an A-B conversation."

"Wow, taking it back to the sixth grade." But hopefully that meant she hadn't engaged with Grace.

She strode to the kitchen and filled a glass with water. When she returned, her attitude kicked up a notch. "So you broke in to discuss my social life?"

"Basically. But listen, if you ever see 'that lady' again, get out of there."

Lucy fastened him with a scanning stare. "You need to talk to Molly."

She knew. Obviously. "Oh, I did. Last night. How long have you known?"

"I just found out, actually. I'm kinda mad, too—"

"That Molly's seeing someone?"

"'Seeing' someone," she repeated. "That's what she told you."

Lucy had made it clear she was Molly's friend first, and Zach's sister a distant second, but that tone definitely didn't sound right. He angled his head to scrutinize her from the corner of his eye. "You had to know that already."

She turned to toss her gym bag into the front closet. "I—I mean, yeah, I knew."

"You said you didn't."

Lucy's gaze dropped to her tennis shoes again. "I did? I thought you meant something else. I went to her dance class, and I found out how incredibly hard that is. I've been before, but, man, that's tough. I feel as coordinated as an octopus on roller skates, and I'm totally gross now. Have you ever tried it?"

"Ramble much?" Zach picked up the pretzels and headed for the pantry. "What did you think I meant?"

"Your date with Brittany. We haven't talked about that, either."

Still in the pantry, he winced. "Can we not?" he said, returning to the living room.

"You don't want to know what she said?"

"Don't know what she could say about three hours of talking about her ex with another man."

"She thought you were really handsome," Lucy singsonged.

What were they, six years old? "I guess she's pretty." Listening to anyone rant for three hours had a way of making them a lot less attractive.

"And really funny and charming." Lucy paced a circle around him.

Had he said one remotely funny thing the entire night?

"And incredibly sage."

"Okay, I'm not sure you talked to the woman I went out with."

"Yeah, me neither—none of those words describe my brother."

Zach rolled his eyes. "If you've put this much analysis into it, she probably told you every single thing I said to her. Twice."

"I think she did. What did you guys do for the other two hours?" Lucy wriggled her eyebrows in mock insinuation.

"Uh, no. She did all the talking."

Lucy's shoulders fell, and she retreated to the couch. "Worth a shot."

"What, pestering me to go out with her for three months?"

"No, setting you two up. But I guess some people really are hopeless." She tossed a blue pillow at him.

He caught it. Right, *he* was the hopeless one.

"Too bad," Lucy continued. "She probably would've gone out with you again."

Wait, what? "Probably?"

She cringed. "She said you were a great listener and really seemed to get her, but you're pretty hung up on your ex, so she wouldn't go out with you again until you're over her."

His jaw dropped. "What? I said one thing about Molly, and I was only agreeing with Brittany! I spent three hours listening to Bob-this and Bob-that and bob-tail and bob-cat." He raked a hand through his hair. "She's seriously obsessed, Lucy. And *someone* conveniently forgot to include that she'd been married in the pre-set-up résumé. Or that she had a little—no, a medium-sized child."

"Hey, you love kids."

"Still something you should tell me *before* bullying me into taking her out. And the divorced part."

Lucy sighed, tucking her feet under her on the couch cushion. "Fine. Next time I set you up with a divorced mom, I'll warn you."

"Just what I need, more setups." He threw the pillow back at her. "How long have you known?"

She blocked the shot. "What? Brittany's divorced?"

He pursed his lips. "Abrupt subject change. That Molly's seeing someone."

"Um . . . since they started dating."

Zach gaped at her. "What? Never once crossed your mind to tell me?"

"Of course, but she wouldn't want me to. She wasn't doing it to hurt you." She trailed off.

He snorted. "That worked."

"How'd you find out?"

"She told me. It . . . wasn't good."

Lucy grimaced. "I'm sorry, Zach."

"Yeah, well, better get home." He got his coat and hesitated—he should ask how things were with Paul. Though he hardly wanted to know the obvious answer. "How're you holding up?"

Lucy looked down and retrieved the pillow he'd thrown. "Not great."

"Can I do anything?" Wait, no, she'd want him to listen. "You want to talk?"

"No." She hugged the pillow and seemed to shrink into the couch, as if she could get any smaller.

Why did he bring that up? "'Kay. Call me if you do. See you in the morning." Zach let himself out. Not telling him about Brittany—making him go out with her in the first place—*and* not telling him Molly was dating someone? Maybe Lucy secretly did hate him.

If she did, she could join the club.

Saturday night, Grace and Pearse sat in her car outside a set of rundown rowhouses. The streetlight two poles down cycled off. Perfect.

Grace got out of the car and opened the boot of their Mercedes. She found the case of bottled water and loaded her coat pockets. Pearse followed suit.

"Sure we have the right flat?" He peered up at the townhome, which appeared even shabbier in the streetlight's glare.

Did he think she was an eejit? "Not that difficult to tail someone when they don't expect surveillance." They sat in silence, watching the clock until the next streetlamp fired back to life. The light above them went dark. Suddenly, she was very supportive of energy conservation. She pulled out a small broom and closed the boot.

They crossed the quiet street to wait under a tree. As soon as Grace stopped walking, the cold crept through her coat. "Everythin' ready for your man Tuesday?"

Pearse nodded. The streetlamp in front of their target shut off. Without a word, they started down the street together, both unscrewing their first water bottles.

They reached their target's solid concrete stoop, and Grace knelt to sweep away the rock salt leftover from the last hard freeze. A bucket of the stuff stood at the top of the steps. Grace moved it to the foot of the stairs.

Pearse poured his first bottle on the steps, and they observed the water flow. Whoever built these steps had done them a great favor—the water pooled in several spots. She signaled Pearse, and together they emptied a half dozen bottles.

"We'll be back for a second coat at midnight." Grace pushed the bucket of rock salt over onto the sidewalk at the base of the stairs as if it had fallen. "That'll be the first thing your man sees," she whispered. "When he goes for it—" She swept one hand across the other, mimicking someone slipping. "DontRain will be hirin'."

15

MOLLY WASN'T SO HEARTLESS that she'd break up with a man before he had to speak to thousands of people in a regional church conference. She took the end of a pew while Nate found his place on the stand. He winked at her; she smiled back but looked away quickly as she could.

At least she wouldn't have to face Zachary until tomorrow at the earliest. And then, despite what she'd told him Friday night, she wouldn't be dating anyone.

Did that change anything between them?

She couldn't contemplate that, not until she'd told Nate the truth. Part of the truth.

Guilt twisted in her stomach.

The prelude started, beautiful piano music Molly didn't recognize. A hand landed on her shoulder, and she jumped. Lucy stood by her. "Hey," Lucy said. She gave the stand a so-glad-I-amn't-you grin. "Guess they roped him into playing."

Molly followed Lucy's gaze. Zachary was at the piano. Fantastic.

"He tried to get me to do it, actually, but I threw pepper in his eyes and ran away."

Molly scooted down the pew to give Lucy room. Once she was seated, Lucy turned to her, her expression drawn. "You know you're my best friend, right?"

Molly grabbed her hand and gave it a squeeze. "You're mine as well."

"And even after everything that happened with Zach, I want you to be happy."

This speech was turning strange. "Em, thank you."

"And you can tell me anything."

What was she getting at? Before Molly could review her last few conversations with Lucy, Zachary concluded the prelude, and the meeting began. Molly turned her attention to the podium. Zachary made his way to a seat on the stand. A seat behind Nate, where there would be no way for Molly to glance at one without seeing the other.

As if the nightmare could've grown worse—and more surreal—the man conducting the meeting thanked Zachary, and Nate perked up. He half-leaned, half-turned to Zachary behind him. It didn't take a lip reader to understand Nate's warm greeting, like seeing an old friend.

Zachary shook Nate's offered hand. Even at this distance, she could tell Zachary's energetic nod wasn't just accepting a compliment.

With each breath, Molly's lungs seemed to shrink. Nate had earned his MBA at George Mason, outside DC. Zachary worked for the Bureau at Headquarters. In DC. Of course they knew one another. Of course the two men she wanted to keep separate in her mind and the real world already knew one another.

"Did you know they were friends?" she asked Lucy, her whisper harsher than she'd intended.

Lucy shook her head, the horror in her eyes almost as severe as what Molly felt. "Nate moved here from DC, right? Small world when you're Mormon."

Indeed. Molly pretended note-taking occupied her full attention for the first two talks, but in reality, she could hardly focus on the speakers. The little she did catch was all about marriage. Before closing, the elderly man bore his testimony of eternal marriage.

Just what she needed to hear before Nate took the microphone. She fixed her gaze on him and hoped Zachary hadn't spotted her in the congregation. She had to offer one little measure of support to the poor fella. An assignment like this was one of her personal nightmares.

That, and pretending to be Zachary's fiancée. Her mind sank into the memory of Friday night, feeding one another cake, the love in his eyes, the pain on his face. And then further back: strolling through Grant Park together. Lounging under the cherry blossoms. The way his hand fit so well with hers. His daily text check-ins.

The first time he'd said he loved her. That first perfectly electrifying kiss.

Nate closed his talk, and Molly joined the murmured chorus of amens. Had she spent his entire talk looking straight at Zachary? Guilt tugged on her heart. Again.

Luckily, neither man had seen her staring. Zachary nodded his compliments to Nate before he sat down. Molly smiled at Nate, though her smile would've been a bit brighter were it not for the memories of Zachary—and the man himself not four feet behind Nate.

Was she was trading a good man who loved her for one who'd broken up with her six months ago? Because he'd let his cover go to his head, she was supposed to chance it and admit she still loved him, months after he'd dumped her? That sounded brilliantly stupid.

She forced herself to focus on Nate. She shouldn't even be thinking like this until she handled things with him. Straightforward. Honest. No reason for the guilt eating at her insides like acid.

The stake president announced a special musical number by a young men chorus, led by Zachary Saint. Then he wouldn't be standing at the podium. She wouldn't have to worry about keeping her eyes *off* him.

Molly whispered an excuse to Lucy and retreated to listen to the rest of the meeting from the foyer. As every day since she'd run into him again, today was not going well.

Grace jolted awake when Ed poked her. They were in the car. Right. Setting up the DontRain employee. No wonder she'd fallen asleep, after freezing his steps repeatedly throughout the night. If only she had someone competent enough to trust with this crucial task. She checked her watch—half past ten. "How long—"

Ed shushed her, staring past her out the window. She whipped around to see the target's door open. The Sunday paper and the overturned salt bucket sat at the foot of the stairs, where she'd left them. Dallas Hermann stood at the door in a bathrobe.

Had he been up half an hour ago when she polished the surface of his steps? Grace held her breath.

Dallas lowered one slippered foot a cautious step, then another. Four stairs later, he'd reached the pavement, no problem. Grace groaned. What would it take to track another DontRain employee home and make sure harm would befall him? They hadn't the time to cover the tracks from a car bomb.

Dallas collected his newspaper and his bucket and started back up his stairs. Grace reached for the keys in the ignition.

But Ed tapped her arm, and she turned in time to see Dallas land on the steps, his bathrobe flying as wide as his splayed limbs. He slowly rolled onto one side. Even from here, they could hear the scream.

Grace tried not to gloat. "That's the glorious sound of a position openin' up."

"'A terrible beauty is born.'" As much celebration as she'd hope for from him.

The young men chorus got the tricky passages right, and the soloists nailed their parts. Zach's excitement at the performance lasted through the rest of the meeting, bolstered by Elder Wood's excellent talk. Together with running into Nate O'Shaughnessy, his Sunday morning was the best part of his weekend.

Nate grabbed him after the closing prayer. "What're you doing in Chicago?"

"Transferred here for work. You?"

"Work, too. Heard from Petersen lately?"

"Not since his wedding, the loser."

They laughed and joined the crowd trudging down the chapel aisle.

"Still can't believe I'd run into you here." Nate gave a soft whistle.

"Small world."

"I know." They reached the end of the pews, and Nate lowered his voice. "What made you come back to church?"

Zach pulled back. "What?"

"I mean, we never saw you in DC. What made you come back?"

He blinked in silence for a second. Nate thought he'd been less active? "I traveled for work a lot, and then I moved to a different ward."

"Oh." Nate processed that a second. "Hey, you should meet my girlfriend." He craned his neck over the churchgoers gathering coats and umbrellas in the foyer. He found her to the left, and checked to make sure Zach followed.

He saw her a second before Nate reached her—long enough to desperately hope she wasn't the one. Nate slipped his arm around Molly's shoulders. A vise grip slid around Zach's chest.

"Molly, you won't believe this," Nate said. "This is Zach Saint. We're friends from DC—my roommate was his mission buddy."

Molly studied her shoes.

"So he served in Ireland." Nate turned to Zach. "She's from Ireland."

Zach gave a half-smile, half-grimace.

"We've got to hang out—who knows, maybe Petersen's around, too. Then you three could talk about Ireland. Isn't it great to meet someone who loves it like you do?"

"We've met before," Molly clipped off.

Yes, wonderful. She could spill their whole personal life in front of a thousand strangers. Might as well pry open his ribs and yank out his heart too.

Nate did a double take, grabbing Zach's shoulder too. "Really?"

She looked at Zach, and he braced himself for the blow. Hearing reality from her was even worse than living it.

"He's Lucy's brother," Molly said at last.

"No way! Lucy's a Saint? Guess I didn't even know her last name."

"Yeah." Zach tried to focus on the sweet relief and not the bitter disappointment of this whole moment. At least she wouldn't drag the past out for everybody here.

But that was all he was to her. Her friend's brother. No matter what he thought he saw in the bakery.

"What a small world," Nate marveled.

"Yeah, it is when you're Mormon." Zach glanced around for an escape. Finding out the woman he loved was dating someone else *and* that someone else was an old friend was enough torture for one weekend. "I gotta go. We'll catch up later."

"Cool, man." Nate let go of Molly to slap Zach on the back. "Good to see you."

"Yeah." He didn't even force himself to return the sentiment before walking away.

Two minutes ago, this meeting was the highlight of his weekend. Now, Sunday fit right in with the theme of the last three days: pain, suffering and humiliation.

Apart from complimenting Nate's talk, Molly didn't say much on the drive to her place.

She knew Nate had attended business school in DC, and she knew Zachary had lived there. Had she just been in denial that they might have known one another?

No. Until two weeks ago, she thought Zachary still lived in DC. And she'd been careful never mention Zachary by name or that she'd dated Lucy's brother—who liked to hear about their predecessor?

Molly shook her head. Common backgrounds or not, she should've seen this coming.

Nate was too excited to take notice of her silence. Fortunately, he was oblivious enough not to marvel aloud at his chance meeting with Zachary.

They reached her flat, and Molly steeled herself, a soldier preparing for battle. Time for the hard part.

She unlocked the door and stepped into her flat, but Nate stopped in the doorway.

"I need to run home and grab something. Back in a bit, okay?"

"Grand." Or the opposite.

Nate kissed her on the forehead, and Molly shut the door.

Did she really need the extra time to second-guess this decision? She cared about Nate—of course she did. She couldn't hurt him like this, dumping him out of the blue.

No. She had to break up with him. It wasn't fair to stay in this relationship when she felt this way about . . . about a man who'd trampled on her heart six months ago.

She gathered her courage again. Zachary or no, she had to do this now.

By the time Nate returned in a sweatshirt and jeans, Molly had run her thoughts in circles until she was dizzy.

"I brought your present from Hawaii," Nate announced as soon as she let him in.

"Oh?"

He produced a small, white box. A ring box.

Her heart shuddered to a stop. She'd seen more than enough of those lately, but she hadn't expected this from him. Not after the way he'd looked at her Thursday.

Nate opened the box to reveal a ring made of beautiful gold flowers, bordered with black enamel. "It's a Hawaiian heirloom."

Not an engagement ring? Molly couldn't hide her relief. "My goodness, thank you."

He pulled the ring from the box and held it out, obviously expecting her to let him slide it on her finger. Instead, she took the ring. It was lovely, but she couldn't make herself wear his ring, not with what she had to do.

Cold dread seeped into her chest.

"Did you get the cheesecake I sent last night?" Nate asked

"I did." As soon as she got home from the scare with Grace and Lucy. The perfect thing to recover from the rest of the weekend.

Until she remembered making a cheesecake with Zachary on one of his visits, and the outcome, disastrous and sweet. She'd dropped it on the floor in front of a church group. Zachary had not only comforted her in front of everyone without making it awkward, but he'd convinced everyone to eat the dessert despite the incident.

Molly focused on Nate. "Would you like a slice?" Maybe the rich dessert would soften the blow.

He kissed her on the cheek. "Thanks, babe." He walked back to the living room and flopped on her sofa.

"I should be thankin' you." She set the ring on the counter and pulled the cheesecake from the fridge.

"I don't have long, though," Nate called from the living area. "I have to be at the airport in an hour. California this week."

No pressure to get this breakup right, then. Best to hurry with the cheesecake. Molly set it on the table and served a slice onto a plate.

"Molly," Nate began after a moment, "I think we need to talk."

This might be her best opening. "We do." She grabbed a fork and brought it all over to Nate on her sofa—where he sat with a stack of wedding magazines.

Her wedding magazines, ones Grace had bought for her. Hadn't she put those away?

"Where did you find those?"

Nate pointed to the end table and tossed the magazines underneath again. He accepted the plate of cheesecake and set it on the coffee table. He stood and took her hands.

He gazed into her eyes with genuine, pure affection. "I love you, Molly."

Before she could respond or even muster a stricken expression, her mobile rang. Molly took the excuse to pull away from Nate and retrieve her mobile from her handbag, which she'd conveniently left by the door.

It was Lucy. "Hello?"

"Could you come over?" Her voice trembled—was she fighting tears?

Couldn't have anything to do with Grace, could it? Molly glanced at Nate. "I'll be there as fast as I can."

Lucy hung up before Molly could say goodbye.

"What's the matter?" Nate asked.

"I don't know. Lucy was upset, though."

Nate gave her a cross between a smile and a sympathetic frown. "Guess you should go be with her, then."

"I should." Molly gave Nate his slice of cheesecake, ushering him out.

She hoped she wasn't just taking any excuse not to break up with him right then. But there was no time to worry over that. Lucy needed her.

WHEN LUCY ANSWERED THE DOOR, she was exactly as Zach had feared—her whole face red and puffy from crying. She sniffled and let him in. "I didn't mean for you to come over."

"Of course I came. Misery loves company. I would've brought ice cream or something, but I figured you had some."

"Yeah." Lucy closed the door and leaned against it.

Zach held out his arms to her. She complied, burying her face in his chest. "Want to tell me what happened?" he asked after a moment.

She shrugged and pulled back. "Same argument we've been postponing for months. A year. That actually made it worse."

"Usually does. Why don't you sit down? I'll scoop."

Lucy sank into the couch, tugging one of their grandmother's plaid afghans around her. "It shouldn't be this hard, you know? Intellectually, I've always known it'd come to this. I mean, I guess I shouldn't have let it get serious. I just . . . couldn't help it."

He headed to the kitchen. Good thing she didn't expect him to fix this. He had no clue how to even start.

Zach got the ice cream from the freezer. "You couldn't control it."

"I guess. Didn't a prophet say you could fall in love with the wrong person?"

"More like you could fall in love with someone you shouldn't marry."

"Same thing." Lucy sighed. "A bird may love a fish, but where would they live?"

Okay, now she protested too much. Zach glanced back between scoops—she was wiping away more tears. Did he dare point out she was trying to guilt herself into feeling better?

"But I still loved him," she murmured.

"I know." He finished scooping the ice cream and put the carton away before bringing Lucy her bowl.

Zach joined her on the couch. Lucy stared at the ice cream for a long time before she took a bite. "My whole life, I thought I was smarter than this. I mean, I know you marry who you date, and when I went out with guys who weren't Mormon before, I knew it would never go anywhere."

Zach nodded sympathetically.

"But when I went out with LDS guys, especially after I moved here, I knew it'd never go anywhere, either. My dates with Mormon guys were ridiculous compared to my dates with Paul." She laughed with a touch of bitterness.

"Don't you think there was a reason for you to date Paul? You wouldn't have done it if you ever felt like you shouldn't, right?"

Lucy pondered for a long moment. "Sometimes I don't know. Maybe I just didn't want to listen."

"But you did listen. You made a hard choice."

She took two slow bites of her ice cream. "I should've known better. I put myself between a rock and a hard place."

"No, Peter's the rock," Zach joked. "Paul was—"

Lucy cut him off with a jab to his shoulder—but she did manage a small smile before sinking back into her sadness. "I'll never find someone like him again, you know? If I made a list of what I wanted in a husband, he would've checked off every box but one—and I've lost it."

"And you'll always know what you're missing." Zach cut himself off, but the memories still surfaced. He knew exactly how she felt: he'd been in the same place after he'd broken up with Molly, for the same reason: he loved her, but they couldn't get married.

On some level, he'd never left that place. How could he have thought two weeks of a pretend engagement could change everything?

Zach turned back to his sister, physically and mentally. "Do you believe God has a plan for your life?"

"Of course." Lucy nailed him with a *duh* glare and popped a spoonful of ice cream into her mouth.

"And as far as you remember, He never said, 'Stop dating Paul,' right?"

She nodded.

"Then maybe it was what Heavenly Father wanted. An experience He needs you to have."

Lucy rubbed her bleary eyes. "Are you fixing the problem?"

"No."

"Good, because that solution sucked."

A knock at the door made them both look up.

"Think he changed his mind?" Zach stood. "And how hard do you want me to hit him?"

Lucy sniffled. "Don't break anything."

He grabbed the doorknob. "Have it your way."

It shouldn't have been that big of a surprise, but Molly nearly dropped the cheesecake—again—when Zachary opened the door to Lucy's flat.

Molly rebalanced the cheesecake and caught her breath. She had to tell Zachary how she felt—but she hadn't broken up with Nate. Lucy had apparently broken up with Paul. Was Zachary's timing always this awful?

He stared at her, his expression completely blank, for several seconds. At last, he reached out and took the cheesecake box from her. Mechanically, he let her in and shut the door.

Right. She was here to support Lucy. Molly turned to her. "Are you all right?" she asked gently.

Lucy fought back tears for a moment, and Zachary took her empty bowl into the kitchen. "Paul and I," she choked out.

Molly took the seat next to her friend on the sofa. "How did it happen?"

"He said it was time to stop fighting with one another, and I said we were really fighting what we knew was coming. So—" She paused with emotion a moment. "—it's over."

Lucy was again overcome, and Molly hugged her. "I'm so sorry."

Zachary returned with a slice of cheesecake on a plate.

"I brought that for Lucy," Molly informed him. And to have one less reason to feel guilty.

"What kind of a monster do you think I am?" Zachary gave the plate to his sister, who scrubbed at her tears with one hand and accepted the plate from him with the other. "Molly brought you a cheesecake. Probably isn't floor flavored this time."

Molly hoped he'd drop the subject of their cheesecake misadventures and retreat back to the kitchen.

He only did one. "Paul *was* right, you know."

Lucy sighed and picked up her fork. Zachary dropped onto the couch on Lucy's other side. "I know how much this sucks," he said. "But we can't control other people's choices."

"Duh," Lucy croaked through her tears and her cheesecake.

"I'm just saying it's not your fault that things didn't work out. That your paths took you different directions."

Molly gawked at him, but Zachary wasn't looking at his sister—he was looking at Molly.

Her stomach soured and her heartbeat slowed. He was talking about them and their "different directions."

Two minutes ago, she'd almost considered confessing her feelings. Obviously her feelings didn't matter.

Finally, he broke their gaze and focused on Lucy. "Maybe you can do grad school at BYU."

Lucy elbowed Zachary, then finished her cheesecake. He carried her plate back to the kitchen.

How could he drag their relationship into this, when they should be there for Lucy? Molly patted Lucy's arm before following Zachary. Although Lucy's kitchen opened into her living room, the distance afforded them a thin veil of privacy.

"Want another piece, Luce?" Zachary shouted back to his sister.

"Sure." She sighed. "If I eat myself sick, I'll forget about Paul."

He was laying another slice onto her plate when Molly reached him. She stood shoulder-to-shoulder with him and leaned in—and didn't dare meet his eyes in such close quarters.

"You should be leavin'," she said under her breath.

"I'm her brother—"

"And you're not helpin'." Molly stepped back to a safe distance. She focused all her determination on him. Zachary met her gaze with equal steel, ready to continue the silent argument, but his jaw hardened, and he shoved the plate into Molly's hands.

Zachary returned to the living room and sat by Lucy again. "I get the feeling 'girl time' will help you more than me."

"Thanks for trying."

Zachary hugged his sister. "You did the right thing. It'll be okay. One day."

"Really?"

"So they keep telling me." He shrugged and got up from the sofa. "See you later."

Lucy waved before he left. Molly finally crossed the room and brought Lucy her second slice of cheesecake.

"You didn't have to do that," Lucy said.

"You wanted another piece."

"I mean you didn't have to tell him to leave. I'm depressed, not deaf."

Of course she'd done that for Lucy. Not because she couldn't look at him after that slap in the face. Molly turned back to the kitchen and got herself a piece of cheesecake.

She returned to the sofa and poked at her dessert. "He wasn't bein' very supportive."

"I think that was him trying."

Sure, and fixed on her while he spoke. Molly stared at her cheesecake in silence.

"I didn't ask him to come," Lucy stated. "After I called you, he texted to invite me and Paul for dinner. So I told him, and he came over all by himself. So don't go throwing me and Paul together as payback."

"Wouldn't dream of it." They fell into silence for a moment, focusing on their food. "Did Paul come over, or did he call?"

Lucy sighed yet again. "I couldn't break up with him over the phone. That's too . . ." She shuddered.

Once again, guilt landed in Molly's gut. Nate had to be at the airport, and he'd be gone all week. Lucy was right; breaking up over the phone was low. Practically cowardly.

Lucy pressed on. "I can't believe I fell for someone when I just *knew* it could never end well." She took another bite. "Maybe I've been lying to myself this whole time, you know?"

Molly nodded slowly.

"I think the hardest part was when he said—" Emotion choked her off, and she tried again. "He said he understood I was putting God first, and he loved that." She paused and sniffled. "He'd always loved that—but at the same time, it hurt so much. I just—I wanted to have both. Have my cheesecake and eat it too." She speared another bite and popped it in her mouth. "Marry him and marry in the temple."

"Were you thinkin' of gettin' married?" Molly asked gently.

Lucy shifted back and forth, arguing both sides with herself. "We never talked about it, but . . . I mean, we knew we wanted to get married in our churches, and the other one wouldn't convert, so it wouldn't have done us any good to talk about it." She focused on her plate a long moment. "But I think we both wanted it, even if we couldn't bring ourselves to say it. I kind of thought that's why he gave me that ring, actually. Like we were playing pretend proposal."

Lucy held out her right hand, rubbing at that amethyst ring again. She didn't take it off, though. Molly willed herself not to think of the gold ring Nate had given her, sitting on her counter. "I'm so sorry, Lucy. This is always hard."

"Um," Lucy began, "not to change the subject, but taking break from the screaming agony of my life—why's that Grace lady planning your wedding?" She checked Molly's response with caution, as if anticipating bad news.

Good heavens, was that what Lucy was getting at this morning? "It's complicated."

"Are you engaged to Nate?"

Molly took a bite to keep her expression neutral. "Grace is a work project."

"Good. No offense, but I *so* don't want to hear about marriage. Maybe I should just give up and start collecting cats."

Molly laughed softly. "You're not that bad yet."

"Yeah, I am. I don't know how it is on the North Side, but do you remember what the prospects are like down here?"

"There now—you're doin' better already if you're thinkin' in those terms."

Lucy shook her head. "Definitely not ready to think about moving on. I'm actually physically hurting." She set down her fork and pushed her fingers against her sternum, as if direct pressure could relieve her pain.

"But you know it'll get better, don't you?"

Lucy took two deep breaths. "I guess. Just feels like I'll never find someone like him—and even if I did, I wouldn't want that guy because he wouldn't be *Paul.*"

Molly set aside their plates and hugged Lucy, who dissolved into sobs. Molly was careful not to let herself do the same, though she'd felt the same way seven months ago.

And now.

After a long day working to develop an asset, Molly had only intended to stop by the office long enough to write up notes. But then Kent spotted her, and one question had led to another. She was pretty much filling out his FD-302s and showing him which way to go with his case when their supervisor slowed to a stop at her desk.

"Malone, can I talk to you?" Supervisory Special Agent Hernandez asked.

Was this good? "Certainly, ma'am."

Hernandez laughed quietly and shook her head, as she did every time Molly called her that. Old habits.

Molly followed Agent Hernandez to her office, trying to focus on Hernandez's dark hair swept back into an elaborate bun rather than the nerves gathering in her stomach. They reached the office, and Agent Hernandez closed the door behind them. "Molly, thanks for working with Kent."

She gave a quick nod.

"Got an interesting phone call today. Do you know ASAC Scott Chin in Phoenix?"

Molly combed her memory. She'd only spent a little while in the main Arizona office before she'd ended up in a tiny town hours away, working on the Navajo reservation. "Don't recall him."

"Well, he knows you. He mentioned your work on a cold case on the rez."

Now, *that* she remembered.

"He wanted you to know your arrest led directly to the arrest of Roberto Salinas Favera a week ago."

She remembered him, too—hard to forget a name and a face she'd studied every day on her tiny field office's old school "Arizona's Most Wanted" board. "Really?"

Hernandez grinned. "Yep. He wants to get you back to Phoenix as soon as your special assignment here is over."

"As in the Phoenix office?" A big step up from the resident agency she'd been at.

Hernandez's grin doubled. "Obviously, I want you here, but I know Chicago in March is a hard sell compared to Phoenix."

Molly laughed along with her boss. ASAC Chin wanted her back that badly? Putting away a long-wanted criminal *and* being recognized for her efforts felt almost too good to be true.

"He would've called you directly," Agent Hernandez continued, "but he wanted to make sure you weren't absolutely vital here—which you are, of course, but, like I told Chin, I could never stand in the way of another woman's career."

"Thank you."

"You've got time to think, depending on how your current assignment goes, but I thought you should know."

Molly turned over the possibilities. Her parents lived here, sure, but when she was assigned to Arizona, they'd talked of moving west to be with her and her sister in California. The weather was certainly better there in March. July wouldn't be pleasant either place.

And Zachary was here. The man she still loved. The man who was still headed in a different direction.

"Well," Hernandez broke into Molly's thoughts. Molly pulled herself to the present, finding her gaze focused on a shelf with a photograph. Agent Hernandez with a Hispanic man and two teenage boys trying to look cool, posing together in the snow.

"I don't mean to keep you." Hernandez opened her office door again, dismissing Molly.

"Thank you. I'll definitely think about that."

Agent Hernandez gave her elbow a squeeze as Molly passed.

What should she do?

Close the Canavans' case.

How? Molly slowed to a stop. Time to circle back to the beginning. Within an hour, Molly was in her parents' kitchen, settling across the dark wood table from them. Mum's gaze had drifted to the window's lace ruffles, wistful. Da frowned over his coffee and pushed his wire-rimmed glasses up his nose.

"C'mere to me," she began, starting with a familiar Irish common ground. "I've rung the Police Service and the Gardaí. They've got nothin'. The longer I spend gettin' to know the Canavans, the longer they have to find out the truth."

Mum nodded. "I'm sorry, love. We want to help, but—"

"We know they're plannin' somethin'. I can't let another Omagh happen. Another Maura Monaghan."

They both flinched at the slain toddler's name.

"We don't know anythin' about what they're doin'." Mum shifted her coffee mug to her other hand.

"I know, but anythin' might help."

"We really didn't work together long."

"Oh?" Molly suppressed a scoff. "They seem to think you were fast friends."

Mum rolled her eyes, sipping her coffee. "They've always thought we were closer than we really were because they had sons the same age as you girls. We sometimes joked you two would marry their two."

"Grace never mentioned any children." Her parents protecting her sister made sense, but why would Grace hide her sons?

"Donal and Pearse," Da spoke up. "Donal's a year older than Bridie and Pearse is about the same to you."

"Where are they?"

Mum shrugged. "Perhaps still in Ireland. I'm honestly surprised Ed and Grace are here, even without immigration issues."

Da took his mug to the sink. "Maybe they got asylum, like your man—"

"You didn't work with them long?" Molly cut off the subject change.

"Different battalions. Knew each other more socially."

Da thought a moment, leaning against the counter. "After we left, I think they ended up with a splinter group. Whichever one was the most radical and violent. Maybe INLA—the socialist one."

She'd learned about the socialist one at Garda College . . . "Oh, the ones that kidnapped your man and cut off his fingers—and the shootouts with the Gardaí?"

Da nodded. "And the disco in Ballykelly."

"No, no, no," Mum said. "The kidnappin' was by an INLA dissident. The Canavans were RIRA."

Da acknowledged Mum's point with a *touché* gesture. "Right. Omagh, and—"

"Those British soldiers," Molly finished. A few months after their family had moved to Chicago, the "Real" IRA claimed responsibility for killing two soldiers in the North. Technically, it hadn't even happened in her country, and yet it'd been torture for her, newly minted as an *ex*-Garda. She was supposed to protect people, and she'd ended up half a world away when violence struck.

What had that been like for her parents?

Her mum answered her unspoken question in a low tone, fixed on the damask tablecloth. "After the other murder that week, it seemed everythin' was startin' again. I wanted to be there to stop it—and I was so glad we got out when we did."

"But other than those murders," Da said, "they've mostly kept to minor injuries and failed bombs."

"Don't forget their turn to vigilante justice. Murderin' child molesters, drug dealers and gang bangers." Mum offered a grim smirk and took a draught of her coffee.

Molly had never imagined her parents showing such sang-froid in discussing violent murders, high crimes and the rest of the Troubles. They were supposed to cluck and shake their heads and frown. They were supposed to lament the lives lost. They were supposed to wish for a united Ireland but condemn violence, as everyone else did, as they had all their lives.

But they were probably quite used to putting on a front when it came to Irish republicanism.

Now it was Molly's turn to take up the family tradition. "So what *did* the Canavans do? You've told me Ed's good with munitions, and Grace's a planner, and Omagh—but that doesn't tell me where we should be lookin' for them to act now. I want to close this case as fast as I can." So she could take the job in Phoenix. And never have to face the man who didn't love her back.

Mum raised her eyebrows in Da's direction, shooting him a silent, coded message.

"I have somethin' for you," he announced. "It'll take a minute to find it." He left for the bedrooms. What was that about?

"Molly," Mum began. "I've been wantin' to talk to you."

Why did this sound like an intervention?

"How are things with your Nate?"

Molly sighed, letting her shoulders drop. Was she that transparent? "Terrible. He wants to get married." And he thought she felt the same.

Mum set aside her coffee. "That's terrible?"

"I have a lot to do before I get married. You know that."

Mum gave her a thoughtful frown, and even to Molly's ears, the standard excuse was wearing thin. "How do you feel when you're with him?" Mum asked.

She remembered the disdain in his face when she'd "confessed" to watching R-rated movies. Part of her life, her past—not a character flaw. Romantic dates and heirloom jewelry couldn't compensate for the pity and contempt under that perfect veneer.

Mum perched on the arm of Molly's chair and threw her arms around her. "All this time I've been worryin' about protectin' your heart at work, and you should've been defendin' yourself on the other front."

Molly leaned against her mum's arm. "I've had enough assault-proposals to last a lifetime."

Mum startled and nearly fell off the arm of the chair. "Proposals?

He's already asked you?"

"He hasn't. Zachary and I are havin' Grace plan our weddin'. To build a relationship of trust."

"Clever, that is." Mum's gaze grew distant and she smiled, but her smile faded. "But I didn't mean defendin' yourself from a proposal. If that's how you look just thinkin' of how you feel when you're together, you've no business datin' Nate."

For the millionth time, Mum was right, and Molly knew it.

"Molly," she began again, but before she could continue, Da returned, carrying a book. Mum stood, and Da passed the book to Molly. The cover featured an armed man in a balaclava in front of a map of Ireland, with the northern counties splashed with blood. *The Blood-Dimmed Tide* by someone writing under the pseudonym Seán Martin.

"The characters are composites, accordin' to the author's note, but some of it sounds familiar," Mum said.

"Like the time the author's dragged out and beaten by RUCs." Bitterness tinged Da's tone. "Hard to be abused by the people you're riskin' your life to protect." Had that happened to him?

Could *he* be Seán Martin?

Mum patted the cover. "We've highlighted the passages that sound like the Canavans to us."

"This is the most complete profile we could give you." Da placed one hand on Mum's shoulder and the other on Molly's. "Sorry it took us so long."

"Also, I've a friend whose husband was with the Independent Monitorin' Commission. I've finally found his email." Mum patted Molly's arm. "We know this is difficult—we've been there. But you can do it."

Certainly her parents' assignment had been at least as hard as hers. But they'd had each other, instead of trying to constantly fight through old feelings and old wounds.

Hopefully this book and Mum's commissioner friend would bring them closer to the end of this case and her involvement with Zachary.

GRACE GLANCED AT THE CLOCK on the range Tuesday evening. Fifteen minutes until the end of business. The last chance to ring them today. Every day that Ed waited, someone else might take that vacancy she'd worked so hard to create. Only eleven days left.

She poked Ed's elbow. "Do it."

He frowned at her—as usual—and hit the Call button, then put it on speaker phone.

"DontRain Parade Floats. Can I help you?"

"Yes, are you hiring?" Ed put on an impressive American accent. When had he picked that up?

"No, we're fully staffed." A muffled sound came from the background. "Hang on," said the secretary.

The modulated hold music blared with heavy distortion. "Where'd you learn an American accent?" Grace asked.

"Telly."

So that was what he'd done with himself the last few months. Would explain why the skiver hadn't got a job yet. "Plannin' on usin' that if you get hired on?"

"I am."

The hold music cut off. "You still there?"

"I am," Ed repeated, back to the American accent.

"Seems one of our seasonal workers broke his arm this week. How soon can you interview?"

He cast Grace a triumphant smirk. "I'm ready when you are."

The last roadblock was crumbling.

Zach was happy for Molly and Nate. Yep. So happy he'd thought long and hard about the many ways the US government could make life difficult for Nate O'Shaughnessy.

Zach caught himself plotting again Tuesday afternoon and shook off the thought. He refreshed his email, and a new message popped up. From Molly.

Yeah, that'd help.

He braced himself and clicked.

> Talked to Mum and Da yesterday. They said the Canavans are in *The Blood-Dimmed Tide.* Gave me a highlighted copy. You should see this.

Work. Zach blew out the breath he'd been holding. That was safe.

He had to face her sometime. Work was fine, right? He headed for the elevators.

When Zach reached Molly's desk, she was on a phone call that seemed important, judging by the way she clenched her cell, her free hand pressed to her forehead. "Sorry," she said, tension making her voice taut. "But I can't be doin' that for you. You need to step up. I won't pull your weight anymore."

Yikes. Zach didn't let himself hope Nate was on the other end.

Okay, he kind of did.

"Grand. It'll be here waitin' for you." Molly hung up and tossed her cell onto her desk.

"Hey," Zach said. Molly jumped and looked up at him. "Trouble?"

"Only with my fan club."

She said that to Kent? Go, Molly. She shook off that issue and focused on him. "Did you get my emails, so?"

"That's why I'm here—wait, more than one?"

"The second one said my mum knows the wife of a commissioner that used to monitor paramilitary activities. She sent me his email this mornin', and I've written him."

"Nice."

Molly downplayed the compliment with a shrug. "Somewhere to start. But the commission disbanded years ago. They may not know anythin' about the Canavans now."

Zach frowned and scratched the back of his neck. What if the Canavans weren't a threat at all?

Yeah, right.

Zach's phone rang, but he didn't recognize the number. He sent the call to voicemail.

"And this." Molly brought out a hardback copy of *The Blood-Dimmed Tide.*

He hadn't read it, but he knew the author claimed to be an informer who'd infiltrated the IRA. "Did your parents know 'Seán Martin' too?"

Molly glanced up at him. "I'm wonderin' if he isn't my da."

Her dad . . . was an informer?

She flipped open to a bookmark. Both pages were bracketed with yellow highlighter. Zach leaned over her, resting one hand on her desk to skim the passage. "Edna and Gene O'Callahan" proposed a car bomb, set in city center, with bomb threats phoned in to strategically herd civilians closer. When other IRA soldiers objected at the target, the O'Callahans replied, "The only way to win this war is to take it home to every Irishman, to make the complacent stand up and act. Ireland will never be free until every person in Ireland—Britain—*the world* will stand up against their oppression."

"'The world,'" Zach echoed. He raised an eyebrow and turned to Molly—really, really close to Molly. She didn't pull back.

"They carried out that plan eighteen years ago." Molly opened a website filled with pictures of a city street that looked like a battleground. "Thirty-one killed, two hundred-some injured."

His heart constricted for a beat. He knew this story. "Omagh." He'd lived in the city for three months as a missionary. "I knew these two guys there, brothers. One lost a leg and the other lost a hand that day. I was there for the tenth anniversary, when they put up a monument. Even for the people moving on with life, there's a hole, still. Not in the street." He tapped his chest, trying to express something words couldn't. Life had continued for the survivors, and the city had recovered, but Omagh carried an ache that would never go away.

That ache could strike their country next.

"We need to talk to CPD about bomb threats," Molly said. "Still hopin' Mum's commissioner knows somethin' that might help. Somethin' more recent."

He maintained eye contact and stayed close to Molly, though they were done with the computer. "Hope so."

They started to slide into silence. Zach gestured toward the empty desk across from her. "How'd your fan club take the man-up talk?"

She wasn't pulling away either. "Em, there might've been tears. But now he's off takin' his car into the shop." She tipped her chin up with an air of meditation. "You never did tell me what happened to your car."

For a good reason. "When did I tell you about that?" he didn't quite answer.

"Thursday, before we left for surveillance."

Zach pulled back a few inches, dancing around the truth. "Hit a telephone pole."

She winced. "What were you tryin' to do, kill yourself?"

"Fell asleep at the wheel." He didn't have to admit he'd lost sleep over dumping her for weeks before it came to that. He tried to play it off. "Got a new car out of it."

"Hardly seems worth the trouble."

"Oh, but I loved taking the sobriety tests—and when I told the officer how inaccurate the walk-the-line test was, they made me do the breathalyzer."

Molly pursed her lips. "Must you go antagonizin' the police *again*?"

She remembered that? "Not like last time. That was the highlight of my life. How often do you get out of a ticket because the SAC is behind you?"

"You're forgettin' the ticket in DC."

Did she have to remember that, too? He laughed and she joined in, leaning closer.

But their laughter quickly subsided, and Molly's gaze shifted past him—and past the distraction of that memory. "Were you hurt?"

"Compound leg fracture, and they still made me walk in a straight line."

Molly didn't laugh at that joke.

The truth, then. "Only my ego. And my insurance premiums."

As if on cue, her computer chimed. They turned to her computer monitor to see a popup notification for a new email. "Here's your man the commissioner." She double clicked the notification, opening the email, and Zach shamelessly read over her shoulder. He didn't catch much before she closed it, but he definitely saw Nate's picture and his final question: *How about the Oakland temple?*

Pain seared the words into his brain. Zach jerked back as if he'd been suckerpunched.

Molly quickly clicked away from the window. Hopefully she hadn't seen him peering at the screen.

"Not him. Anythin' you wanted to ask the commissioner when I do hear from him?" She stared past Zach again, with the same distant look as a minute before. Did she think he pulled away before or after he'd read it?

"Uh." Zach blinked, trying to focus on the assignment. "I guess ask if there's anything the FBI might want to be informed of, and if they know of any potential actions set stateside. And the Canavans, obviously. But don't let on about how much—or how little—we know." He hoped his disjointed answer made some sense.

Molly didn't make eye contact. "I'll BCC you."

"Great." He pushed off her desk and staggered back, still reeling from the blow. His entire chest felt sore and bruised. He steadied himself and headed for his floor.

Could she be that serious with Nate after the way she'd laughed with him today, and the way she'd looked at him Friday?

On the other hand, he couldn't imagine Nate randomly emailing her about visiting a temple in California, or jumping to that level without Molly onboard. They were deciding where to get married. Not if, not when. Where. Those other details must be in place.

The elevator arrived, and he stepped into the meager shelter, finally out of Molly's line of sight. The doors slid closed. He was alone.

Totally alone.

For half a second—okay, maybe a little longer—part of him wanted to curl up in the elevator corner and die.

No, he couldn't do that. He wouldn't. His phone vibrated, and he pulled it out, grateful for something to anchor him in the present, distract him from . . . reality.

Molly had too much to do to marry him.

No, it was worse. She wanted to marry Nate. Not him. She wanted boundaries with him.

He shook off the thoughts and checked the notification on his phone. A voicemail. He hit the play icon. "Mr. Saint? This is Duncan Jewelers, about the piece you had on consignment. Please give us a call as soon as you can." The guy left the number, and the message ended.

Zach stood in stunned silence until the elevator opened. He thought he'd never forget that—and yet he had, for weeks. He started toward his desk and tapped the icon to redial the number. Once the clerk answered, Zach explained who he was.

"Oh, yes. We had someone in who was interested in your piece, but their offer was below your threshold. It's our policy that we talk to you before accepting."

Yeah. Sure. *Now* he'd get the first offer on Molly's ring.

Not Molly's. A ring he still owned. She'd never seen it. Didn't even know it existed.

And she didn't care. She was dating Nate, no matter what he thought he saw Friday—Molly's eyes from that night flashed through his mind. Feeding her the cake, leaning down to kiss her. Living the memory again was more than déjà vu—it was just like the first time they'd nearly kissed. Both times, she wanted him to kiss her. Even if she'd stopped him. This time because of Nate.

Nate? He liked the guy, but could he seriously let *Nate* stand in his way? Maybe Nate had gotten her used to the idea of marriage. But if Molly looked at Zach that way, she had no business marrying someone else. No way would Zach roll over and let Nate take that from them both.

"Mr. Saint?" the man on the phone ventured. "Do you know what you want to do?"

"Yep," he said, a smile rising to his lips. "I do."

Time to fight.

Zach was looking forward to blowing something up by the time he rolled up to his meeting with Paddy that night. Zach had picked the spot, a warehouse they'd seized from Doyle Murphy after they cracked his latest round of creative accounting. If Paddy knew how to look it up, he'd never trace the property back to the FBI.

Paddy was there waiting in the drizzle, apparently alone. No bomb in sight. No good tactical positions in the open lot if that became necessary. Zach rolled to a stop thirty feet from Paddy, parking between him and the exit.

Zach climbed from the Bureau sedan and took two steps toward Paddy, but stopped there. "Let's do this!" he shouted across the lot.

"Don't you want to see it?"

"All right." Zach followed Paddy to a cardboard banker's box near the half-demolished warehouse next door. "A little obvious, don't you think?"

"This is only proof of concept." He lifted off the lid of the box, angling it to keep the rain off the bomb. "Here's your explosive, mostly Semtex. We could bump it up if you're hopin' to make more of a statement."

Zach pretended to ponder. "Not in the market for collateral damage."

"All right, so. We'd want to cover this up with papers." He pointed to the flip phone wired to the end cap of the pipe. "There's your receiver. We've the option for a contact plate—but that's probably not ideal for you."

Zach raised an eyebrow. "Oh?"

"Imagine if the secretary picked up the box before your man got to it. Plus with the mobile, you can be far enough away to be safe, but still get a front-row seat to the destruction. That's where I'd be, myself."

"Looks good, I guess. But does it work?"

Paddy scoffed. "Does it work? What, did you think I'd drag you here for nothin'? I promised you a demonstration, and a demonstration you'll be gettin'." He replaced the lid and started away from the bomb. Zach was careful to follow close behind him.

Once they were out of the blast zone, Paddy turned back and took another phone from his pocket again. "Then you give your mate a ring." He tapped a button on his phone.

Instantly, the bomb detonated. Zach jerked back before the smoke ball dissipated. Paddy squinted at the blast zone. "Anythin' look like it's damaged?"

Didn't look like anything was *left*. "Not that I see."

A slow grimace-smile spread across Paddy's face. "Well?"

Zach mirrored the smile. "Oh yeah."

"When I put yours together, I can adjust the size of the blast."

Zach glanced back at the smoking remnants of the bomb. "Okay, when can I get it?"

"Ah, but first we have to talk specifics. Have you the stuff?"

"Wasn't easy." Zach pulled the brick of fake C-4 from his jacket pocket. The Bureau had long ago come up with a clay-like substitute made with something inert instead of the explosive RDX—plus a chemical additive for tracing. The consistency and smell seemed perfect. But Zach didn't work with the stuff every day, and Paddy did. He mentally crossed his fingers as he handed over the plastic-wrapped block.

Paddy scanned it and his gaze flicked back to Zach. "And the money?"

"Money?"

Paddy's eyes grew wide. "We agreed on a price—Semtex and cash."

"Are you kidding? I just got laid off. How much more cash do you think I have after getting that?" Zach nodded at the C-4.

"I need the money. Blastin' caps and mobiles aren't free!" Paddy advanced on him, and Zach tensed but didn't reach for his gun. Yet. Paddy gritted his teeth. "You think you're the big show here?"

His hackles jumped to full alert. Zach Saint needed to know what the big show was—but Allen O'Kelly didn't. Did he? He took a breath and a chance. "What do you mean, the big show?"

"Mind your own house," Paddy said, carefully enunciating each word. "And you get me the money." He named his price.

"I'll need time."

Paddy crossed his arms. "You won't be gettin' your squib until we get our money."

Zach Saint's priorities won out. "We? Who am I dealing with here?"

That caught him off guard. Paddy backed up. Even in the shadows, Zach could see the color draining from his face. Zach advanced, trying to spin this into something Allen might feel.

"You aren't using me for something, are you?" Zach ground out his next words with all of Allen's pent-up rage. "I'm not gonna be somebody else's pawn." He reached for the block of C-4 in Paddy's hand.

Paddy snatched the plastic explosives away. "Nothin' to do with you."

"Prove it."

"I—I've another client. A big order."

"For what?" Zach lowered his voice and put an edge on it, leaning in to tower over Paddy.

Paddy cringed, but then straightened. "I don't see where it concerns you."

"If you get in trouble, I need to know you won't turn on me."

Paddy straightened his jacket. "I won't be gettin' in trouble, but if ever I did, the best way to keep me from turnin' tout on you is to make sure we both end this happy."

Sensing the upper hand slipping away, Zach stared at Paddy's squinty eyes. "Tell me what you've got planned," Zach demanded.

"You're not buyin' details." Paddy lifted his chin and his price. "Next Sunday. The fourteenth. I'll have it for you then."

"Seriously? That's like two weeks!"

"I'm up to ninety until then. That's the soonest you'll get it."

Zach thought it over, a hand on his hip. "Fine. Cash. Here. Nine o'clock."

Paddy gave a short nod. And then stood there.

Zach would have to leave first. He didn't even know where Paddy had parked. Zach braced himself, turned his back and walked to his car. Whatever else Paddy was up to, it wasn't good.

What were the odds the Canavans knew Paddy?

Nah, that was confirmation bias talking, plain and simple. Just because he had one set of Irish terrorists didn't mean his other cases were related, even if there was an Irish guy involved. And why would the Canavans need another bomb builder?

Still, Zach made a mental note in his file. Keep an extra eye on Paddy.

Grace shot from their tacky orange sofa to her feet. "What do you mean, he didn't have the money?"

"He thought I said Semtex for payment—I swear I didn't, Mam."

She glowered at him. "You better not have, ya cute hoor."

Ed stormed in from the kitchen. "Did you not get the Semtex?"

"No, I got the Semtex, just not the money."

"We needed them both!" Grace rounded the coffee table, clasping her hands in a pleading gesture. "This is what I get, dependin' on the likes of you two for somethin' this important—"

"Hold your whisht, woman," Ed barked. "It was your own idea to be sellin' off the bits and bobs, and now how much have we got?"

Pearse pulled a brick of Semtex from his worn coat and plopped it on the dining table.

Ed turned on Grace again. "That's only enough to get us started."

"Then I'll get more," Pearse said.

"You've used up all the Semtex we had on this—this—lark! How much more can you take before they notice?"

Pearse took his father's challenge. "I've got it down to a system. You sign out ten pounds of explosive and place eight or nine. A few centimeters of det. cord here, a blastin' cap there. They haven't caught on yet."

Grace cut off the argument. "Focus. When will he be gettin' you the money?"

"When he takes delivery."

"When's that?"

"I said not before next Sunday."

Ed marched up to their son. "Don't go mentionin' timelines."

"Da, Allen isn't—"

Grace cut him off again by holding up a hand. "We're not gettin' into this. Pearse may not have two wits to rub together, but I'm sure he didn't tell him *why* he couldn't do it before then. We'll wait until then to decide whether we'll be upset."

"Mam, once we set this, we'll get the money, with or without Allen."

Grace arched an eyebrow. Pearse was gettin' ahead of himself; she certainly wouldn't make the same mistake.

"'Be secret and take defeat from any brazen throat.'" Ed strode from the room.

"What's that mean?" Pearse demanded of his father's shadow.

How was she supposed to know? Grace shot him a sharp glare. "You see about gettin' the rest of the Semtex."

This was what she got for relying on the likes of Ed and Pearse.

18

Zach hadn't been the one to call Lucy Wednesday night, but for the first ten minutes, he was the one doing all the talking. He kicked his feet up on his brown couch, settling into the perfect spot, the plate with the last of his dinner balanced on chest. "Anything interesting going on at Saint Adelaide?"

"Not as interesting as when you were there." Her murmur was vague, distracted. "Did I loan you *The Courage to Teach*?"

"I gave it to you, remember?"

She hemmed. "Sorry. I was hoping you had it, but I think I gave it to Paul."

There was the real reason she must've called. She was probably moping around her place, half-heartedly trying to distract herself with work or a book until her mind wandered off to Paul.

Yeah, he'd been there.

"You have to get out of your apartment." Zach shook his head, though his sister couldn't see the gesture. "You'll go crazy cooped up in there."

"I'll go out this weekend."

Zach polished off his smoked gouda panini. "Sure you will."

"I will—I even have a date."

"You do?" He made room on his cluttered coffee table for his plate. Time to do dishes or buy more plates.

Lucy groaned. "Apparently word's out I'm single now—thanks—"

"I didn't say anything."

"Right. Anyway, DeShondra's setting me up with her brother Friday."

DeShondra from church? "Her brother's seventeen."

"The other one, just back from his mission. He's taking me to

Holy Karaoke. The Northwest Side."

"He must like you already if he's willing to drive you that far." Although she probably deserved some terrible blind dates after the last one she'd sent him on, Zach wasn't about to repay the favor. Yet. Before he could say that, his phone beeped. He glanced at the screen. Molly had texted.

Zach sat up so fast his head spun. "Can we talk later?"

"Meh. I have to catch up on grading. Thanks for listening."

"Any time." Zach ended the call and opened Molly's text. *Confirmed for Saturday with Grace.*

This was his opening: time to fight. He tapped the phone icon to call her.

"Zachary?" He wasn't sure whether that was surprise or caution in her voice.

"Hey, what are you up to?"

"Did you get my text?"

"Yeah, you're all set for Saturday. You talked to Grace?" He hopped up to pace his narrow living room.

"She's scheduled the next stop on the grand tour of gettin' married."

"Where are we going now?" Zach paused at his bookshelf, his gaze landing on the jazz trivia game she'd gotten him at the Kennedy Center.

"'We'? Ah, but you'd look good in a weddin' gown, I'm sure."

He'd see her sarcasm and raise her. "I do have the legs for it."

Molly said nothing for a minute. "Loath as I am to disabuse you of that notion, I'm afraid you don't. And she might find that odd, don't you think?"

"I'll grant you that."

She got back to business before he continued the banter. "We're goin' Saturday at three, which makes my third weddin' appointment with her. Remind me again what Jason's bringin' to this relationship?"

Zach stopped short in the middle of his worn beige rug. Molly's voice carried a double edge of teasing and steel, but she wasn't wrong. He couldn't let her do all the work. "Maybe he'll come up with a romantic plan to whisk Molly Ryan away from the torture of dress shopping."

"Zachary, I'll try on every weddin' gown in the state if it means savin' lives. Any day could be another Omagh."

For a second, he was thrown back to when he first met Molly. She'd done everything in her power to protect him from the mob in the parish. The mob he was investigating, so it wasn't the most helpful thing, but even as a civilian, she'd lived for this.

"You're lucky Grace hasn't roped *you* into a fittin' room," Molly said.

"Aw, Molly, you know." Zach slipped into Jason's drawl. "I can logisticate my way out of anythang."

"That so? Then we'll have to find some equivalent sufferin' for you."

Zach wandered into his kitchen and started a slow circuit around the table. He was supposed to fight for her, wasn't he? "Maybe she'll make us practice our first married couple kiss."

"This isn't *The Weddin' Singer.*" Molly's tone turned terse.

Man, she was right, completely cliché. "Hasn't stopped Grace so far."

Molly fell silent. Had he escalated too quickly? Better back off. "So, your backup. Do you want me?" He let the question end there, hoping she'd read into it.

"I talked to X. He said I don't need backup anymore."

He had to convince her he should be there. "Did he? I dunno, Molly. I mean, you've done okay, but look how it almost turned out last time."

She was quiet for a long time. "I'll be grand. She didn't tell me the shop's name anyway. I'll let you know how it goes."

Molly quickly ended the call. But she'd joked with him. Progress. Right?

Definitely groundwork he could build on.

Grace fidgeted on that stupid, ugly sofa Thursday night, unable to stop her foot's bouncing. She uncrossed her ankles and shifted in her seat. Pearse was late. Later than he'd ever been at the pub.

What if Allen wasn't some poor sap? What if he were a sleeveen, even working for the police?

No. Impossible. How could Pearse have come to the police's attention? He wasn't even living under his own name.

Ed flipped on the television. "Can't make him appear by worryin'."

"I know that," Grace snapped.

"Tried callin'?"

"Three times."

Ed shifted on the couch to change the channel. "He's grand."

She said nothing, but recrossed her ankles, her foot taking to bouncing again.

A key sounded in the lock, and the door swung open slowly—not Pearse's usual lead-laden entry. Grace managed to not jump up. "Where have you been?"

Pearse slammed the door and stalked to the kitchen. "Where's that boxty?"

"Fridge." Grace clasped her hands until her son returned with a cold potato pancake. "Where in the thirty-two counties have you been?"

"Pub." Pearse sank onto the sofa and kicked his feet onto the battered coffee table. His gaze stayed on his food.

"Pearse, you look at me and tell me what took you so long."

He obeyed. "I got sacked."

The world tilted on its side. The words seemed to go together, but Grace couldn't parse them at first. Pearse, sacked? From his job? Grace forced air into her clenched lungs. This couldn't happen. They needed that job—for the money, the matériel.

"Sacked?" Ed demanded. "What've you done?"

"Someone noticed we were shortin' them."

Ed smacked his forehead. "Ya buck eejit, ye! We haven't got enough since *you*—" He pointed at Grace. "—insisted we sell off the bits, and you—" He pointed at Pearse. "—used what we had!"

Grace cut him off. "Did you at least bring more home?"

Pearse set his jaw and narrowed his eyes at his dinner. "They were waitin' for me me as soon as I walked in."

Grace sank into Ed's recliner, cradling her head in her hands. Her heart seemed to crumple in her chest. She never should've trusted this to Pearse.

"We don't have enough for your client and our squib." Ed's pronouncement was laden with the finality of the door slamming on all their plans.

Grace looked up. "We'll get it."

They had to. There was no alternative.

Friday afternoon, Molly plowed through the last of her week's paperwork—and thought of anything but Nate or Zachary.

She'd tried to mentally avoid Nate all week, since she couldn't very well dump him via mobile. If only she'd avoided Zachary's call a couple of days ago.

Okay? She'd done okay? *Look how it almost turned out last time?* She'd torn her own heart out in front of Grace, twice. She'd directly led to the capture of one of Arizona's most wanted criminals. She had a standing job offer from another major field office. Was Zachary's "okay" supposed to be a compliment?

She'd show him "okay."

Her computer chimed with a new email. Molly clicked on the notification, opening the commissioner's reply. She leaned forward.

> Dear Special Agent Malone,
>
> I hope your parents are well. I apologize that this has taken so long; I've been on holiday.
>
> I haven't any record of any Canavans, and I've taken the liberty of checking with the Police Service too. Naturally, members of active paramilitaries strive to maintain low profiles.

> Dealing with individuals within these movements is like dealing with anarchists: it's hard to keep them in line dogmatically because they thrive on disorder.
>
> Wish I were of more assistance.
>
> Raymond Hassan

Molly read the email twice before letting disappointment sink in. She didn't think Hassan was still cataloguing violent paramilitaries, but she'd hoped he had one small lead. She'd already checked with Irish law enforcement as well: nothing.

Before she could sigh, her mobile rang. She checked: Zachary. She almost didn't answer—but this was work, and they were on the same side, weren't they? "Hello?"

"Hey, I wanted to talk about tomorrow. Now a good time?"

"Perfect. Commissioner Hassan just emailed."

"I'll be right—"

"I'll read it to you," Molly cut him off.

He was silent for a beat. "Go for it."

She read the message over the telephone. "Disappointin'," she confessed once she'd finished, rocking back in her chair.

"Not much to go on. Guess we could double-check with the Guards—I mean, your parents said they saw them in Dublin, didn't they?"

"They did, and I've already contacted the Gardaí. They had nothin' as well. I think Hassan's right—I doubt they'd make trouble in Dublin after lyin' low so long in the North, especially if their objective was clear passage here." Molly clicked to file the email on her computer.

"You're just trying to get out of dress shopping tomorrow, aren't you?"

"You know I amn't." Molly shifted the phone to her other ear. "But don't you remember how much 'fun' weddin' plannin' with Grace is?"

"I can't forget. Let's just say I'm glad to be in the office this afternoon."

Of course. A week ago, Grace had been parading them down Michigan Avenue on her relentless wedding quest.

Including a pâtisserie. And a garage with an event Grace hadn't planned.

She had to stop this train of thought. She clicked on the search bar of her web browser and entered *Phoenix apartments for rent.*

Zachary did her the favor of changing the subject abruptly. "*The Fourth Protocol*'s on tonight—Michael Caine, Pierce Brosnan, double agents?"

"Always liked that one." But she needed to end this conversation before she forgot her self-control. "I'll give you a ring after we're done tomorrow."

"Great. I was thinking we could take a look at the reception rooms at the Irish American Heritage Center, too, if we need something else to do."

"Too many people know the real Molly Malone there."

"Okay. I'll keep thinking. Good luck findin' the perfect dress," he drawled. "'Cause it wouldn't be a weddin' without the star of the show in a ridiculously expensive dress."

How much did wedding gowns cost? She hadn't looked last time. Molly opened another tab on her browser to check. "If that's what we're goin' for, I have a few Irish dance dresses we could use. That'd guarantee every eye was on me."

Zachary didn't laugh. "You never have to worry about that, Molly."

Her heart hit a speed hump.

"What you should be worried about," he finished, "is backup."

"Are you this much of a control freak about weddin' dresses?"

"Just trying to help."

She folded her free arm across her chest. "A cold case I solved helped put away one of Arizona's most wanted criminals, Zachary. Did I need your help then?"

"I—really?"

"The Phoenix field office has offered to transfer me back once we've finished with the Canavans, and honestly, I'd rather work with people who trust I can do my job." Not to mention people she wasn't hopelessly in love with—who didn't love her back.

She waited three seconds for Zachary to respond, to correct her, to say he did believe in her. But he didn't. She ended the call and turned back to her paperwork.

Flying solo tomorrow was definitely a good thing. In fact, it was probably a good thing forever.

ZACH KNOCKED ON THE EVANSES' DOOR and shoved his hands in his pockets Friday night. His third blind date in as many weeks. Tonight would be just like the last two: utter disaster.

Had he secretly always been such a loser?

Enough of a loser to try to steal a friend's girlfriend. But tonight, he was just doing the SAC a favor. All he had to do was make sure this date didn't go as badly as the last few. Or so well that he might lead her on. But that didn't seem like much of a threat.

A woman answered the door. Brunette, tall, pretty—and she didn't look crazy.

"Zach?" She stepped out onto the stoop, pulling her coat on. "I'm Tessa."

They shook hands. "Any Chicago sites you'd like to see? Special requests?"

"Actually, a friend suggested a place that sounds fun. Let me see." She took out an iPhone and tapped the screen before turning the phone to him. "Heard of it?"

Zach skimmed the emailed review—O'Hooligans, an Irish-themed restaurant on the Northwest Side with classic Chicagoan cuisine. "Nope, sorry."

"Do you mind? She thought I'd like it."

"Sure. It'll take us a little while to get there, though."

Tessa turned back to her phone. "That's okay. I'll get directions."

He nodded and started for the car, and Tessa followed. If their date went as bad as his last few, at least he wouldn't have to blame himself with her glued to the phone.

Once they were in the car, though, the conversation picked up when they discovered their shared love—for college basketball. They debated the merits of the current AP and coaches' poll rankings between Tessa's navigation.

They broke the conversation only to get Zach's name on the restaurant's waiting list. He barely had time to notice the tacky pseudo-Irish décor: shamrocks, green top hats, Guinness harps, farm tools. Maybe it was supposed to be tongue-in-cheek.

"Why aren't you home watching a conference championship tonight?" Tessa teased.

He made a show of sighing. "Brings back too many bad memories."

"Your alma mater not fare so well?"

"We were lucky to make it to the second round in the conference tourney."

"'We'?" She scrutinized him. "Most people would call their losing team 'they.' Do you take everything this personally, or did you play?"

Zach looked away. "We were so bad I don't like to admit it, but yeah."

"I understand, believe me." Tessa wore a sad, sympathetic smile. "I would've settled for a winning season."

"No joke."

She eyed him a moment. "Bet my team was worse."

"You're on."

"We've only been to the NCAAs once, when I was, like, two."

Zach sucked his teeth to express how much he sympathized. "My team has the honor of never making it to the show."

Tessa visibly startled. "Is that even possible?" She laughed and Zach joined in—until he saw a familiar couple across the vestibule.

His heart rate hiked higher. The Canavans. Just when it seemed like he might have a normal—even enjoyable—date. If they saw him with Tessa, if they heard his real name and saw him respond—

His pulse spiked again. They had to leave.

"Tessa?" He turned his back on the Canavans and tried to keep his tone casual. "How attached are you to eating here?"

She furrowed her brow. "I guess we could go somewhere else. Why?"

"Just saw somebody I need to avoid."

"Ex-girlfriend?"

"Worse, if you can imagine."

Tessa leaned over to look behind him. Not very discreet. "Your parents?"

If she could ID them that easily, either she should be with the Bureau or—Zach checked. The Canavans were walking toward him.

He quickly turned back to Tessa. "Please, go along with whatever I say and don't ask questions. Or say my name."

"Okay," she said slowly.

"Jason?" Grace called from behind him.

Zach whirled around. "Hey, Grace, Ed. How y'all doin'?"

"Grand." Though she addressed Zach, Grace was staring at Tessa.

"Come here often?" Zach joked, trying to keep the conversation from veering in Tessa's direction.

"Should think not." Ed glanced around at the kitschy faux Irish decorations. "Let's hope the taste they spared in the décor they put into the food."

Zach did not raise an eyebrow at the longest sentence he'd ever heard from Ed. He needed to get out of this conversation without making it obvious that he was trying to escape. "Y'all might want to stick to The Fifth Province down at the Irish Center."

"Who's your *wan*?" Grace finally asked, nodding toward her.

Great. "This is an old friend, Tessa. Tessa, Grace and Ed Canavan."

Tessa smiled at them, as uneasy as Grace. "Hi."

Grace shook her head—a typical Irish greeting rather than the negative sign it seemed, Zach reminded himself—and addressed Zach. "Does Molly know you're out? Together?"

"Oh, yeah, 'course. She'd be here too if she wasn't workin'."

"Oh." Grace laughed, thin and nervous.

Time to go. Zach turned to Tessa, who'd brought out her phone again. "They musta lost our reservation, and I bet the wait's a coon's age now. Y'all enjoy your meal," he told the Canavans. "I'll tell Molly 'hey' for ya." He placed a hopefully platonic-looking hand on Tessa's shoulder and led her out of O'Hooligans.

"Sorry about that," Zach said once they were on the street.

Tessa stayed fixed on her phone. "It's okay; I know you work with Uncle Rod. There's a place pretty close that's got really great reviews, but—let me ask you something."

Zach held in a breath. He'd said no questions, but that was asking a lot. Being called Jason, talking about Molly, suddenly acquiring a Southern accent, and losing it just as fast? This date had to be over.

"Do you do karaoke?" Tessa asked.

He grinned. "Oh, I'll give it a shot."

"We could probably walk to this place." She showed him her phone. A map placed them only two blocks away from a karaoke bar with four stars from over a hundred reviews: Holy Karaoke. Somewhere the Canavans definitely wouldn't follow. Zach checked over his shoulder: all clear.

Oh—Lucy's date, here on the Northwest Side. "I think I know someone who's supposed to be there tonight."

Tessa's eyebrows jumped higher. "Another 'friend'?"

"No. Not like—" He jerked a thumb at the restaurant they'd left.

He hoped seeing Lucy wouldn't end up as bad as that last encounter could have. Lucy sometimes brought out the claws at the worst times—like when he had the boss's niece on a date. But if he could keep running into the Canavans as the only disaster tonight, they might actually have a good time.

Molly's mobile rang, and though it wasn't Nate's chosen song, her stomach still tensed for the confrontation. She was almost relieved when she saw it was the Canavans. What could Grace want? "Hello?"

"Dearie, are you busy with work now?" Grace's concern was audible.

Her eyes searched her flat like she'd left herself a clue. What was she supposed to be again? Right, a nursing assistant. "No, just finished with rounds."

"Did you . . . know?"

"What?" Molly leaned back against her gray couch, rolling her eyes toward the ceiling.

"About Jason's friend—what was her name? Teresa? Tessie?"

What was she talking about? "I'm sorry?"

"Oh, we just ran into Jason at a restaurant with his friend—I was so worried. That is, I'm sure your fella's faithful and all, but you weren't there, and she was so pretty."

A twinge of jealousy struck her chest. Zachary might not want to date her, but she hadn't let herself imagine the man who'd been inches from rekindling their relationship last week moving on that quickly. Molly stood to pace a circuit around the couch, working through the emotional whiplash.

"I—I was worried," Grace concluded.

"Of course he told me. I'd have been there too if I hadn't had work."

"So Jason said." She didn't seem convinced.

"Thanks for your concern, Grace, but you needn't worry about Jason. I've seen the two of them together loads. They're practically family."

Reassured, Grace bid her the customary Irish chorus of goodbyes, ending the call mid-"bye." Molly lowered her mobile, staring at her photos on the exposed brick wall.

So Zachary was out with someone else. So she was pretty. So it was only days since he'd nearly kissed her—that was just his cover going to his head. It meant nothing.

Molly lifted her mobile and pulled up what was becoming her favorite search term: *Phoenix apartments for rent.* She already knew she had to get over Zachary. Him being over her wasn't news. It just stung like a new wound.

The wound would heal. Someday.

Three hours later, Zach pulled up in front of the Evanses' house, still laughing at Tessa's last joke. When their laughter subsided, Tessa smiled at him. "It was really nice of you to do that for your sister."

"Nice of you to play along." Lucy had been pretty closed off—not the makings of a great date—but when Zach secretly convinced Tessa and Lucy's date Tyrone to each sign up for duets with Lucy, it'd taken her mind off her problems long enough for some stage banter.

Until Lucy changed the lyrics of "The Boy is Mine" to something closer to "Take My Brother—Please!" and their one-upmanship ended up with Tessa's jaw-dropping, three-octave improvisation over the third chorus.

Lucy had handled it well, clapping for Tessa, but he'd probably get it later. He got out of the car and got Tessa's door.

"Wait a second," Tessa said. She walked down the drive and into the garage, returning with a basketball.

What was she, crazy? Zach didn't hate the cold, but he didn't want an excuse to spend more time outside. Had to be below freezing.

Tessa shot off a quick pass that Zach caught handily. He didn't check the ball back to her, tucking it under his arm instead. She couldn't change the subject that easily. "What's it like being the most talented person in the room?" he asked.

"I bet I don't have to tell you."

He shot her a skeptical look, and then shot the ball without looking at the basketball standard beside the driveway. The ball sailed through the hoop in a graceful arc. Zach struggled against a smile—but whether that smile would've been more satisfaction or surprise, he couldn't say.

Tessa slow-clapped and made no move to retrieve the ball bouncing off the driveway. "I thought you were terrible at basketball."

"My *team* was terrible." He crossed the distance between them, joining Tessa walking up to the front porch.

"It's a good thing Molly's not a real person. She'd be right to be jealous. And keep you under lock and key."

How did she—oh, the Canavans. He'd almost forgotten about the strangest part of the evening. "Molly's a real person, but she's not jealous."

Molly had never been the jealous type, but now she probably couldn't muster that much feeling for him. She was transferring to

Phoenix. Was he wasting his time fighting for her?

"Zach?" Tessa broke into his thoughts. "You okay?"

"Yeah, sorry."

Here was a beautiful, intelligent, talented—interested?—woman in front of him, and Molly was marrying Nate.

For the last eight months, he'd tried to move on. He'd looked for other girls. He'd gone on every blind date. Honestly, this was the first time it was even close to being worthwhile. And now Molly was back in his life.

Chasing Molly was stupid. Really, really stupid. Opening himself up to her again, falling in love with her again, getting burned again—bouncing back would take even longer the second time around. If he ever recovered.

And women like Tessa would slip through his burned fingers.

Was he willing to give up a not-bad prospect with Tessa, or anyone else, on the off chance he could convince Molly he was worth another shot?

One split second of a memory replayed in his mind, sitting with Molly under the cherry blossoms, her laugh rising and falling on the warm spring breeze. The day he knew he had to marry her.

What *wouldn't* he give for another chance?

"Awesome meeting you, Tessa. I had a lot of fun."

"Me too. Thanks again." She hugged Zach before heading in the house.

If this was what he was giving up for one more chance with Molly, he couldn't afford to lose.

MOLLY MET GRACE outside an apartment building in the Northwest Side. Molly tamped down her nerves while Grace drove them to the bridal shop and filled the time with chatter. The ride was short enough that it didn't seem terribly odd that Molly didn't say anything in the two miles from her cover's address to their destination.

Only a couple blocks from Nate's building. Of course.

Grace found a parking spot down the street. "Have you talked to Jason about changin' the date?"

"No, I don't think he wants to."

Grace grumbled under her breath. "And I don't think he knows what we're up against. You realize you're gettin' married in nine weeks, don't you?"

"Of course."

"What did he say about everythin' we saw last week?"

Molly sighed. "He doesn't have a preference. He's leavin' it all up to me."

"Desperate lot to heap on one poor girl." Grace switched off the car with extra torque. "Hardly fair, if you ask me."

She hadn't asked Grace, but Molly bit her tongue. Her objective wasn't planning her dream wedding. She was here to befriend Grace, so she could stop Grace.

"You know, Molly." Grace's voice took on a gentle turn. "If this isn't what you really want, you only need say."

Molly peered through the falling snowflakes at the shops across the street. "Why wouldn't this shop be what I really want?"

"I mean marryin' Jason."

She whipped back to Grace. Was she doubting their cover? Grace kept her gaze on her folded hands. "After the way you looked, I've been worried. I know you said you were grand, but . . ." She looked up with something like real maternal concern, as if Molly were her own daughter. "If you can say, in your heart, you want to marry him, I'll drop the subject. But if you can't—think about what you're doin'."

Suddenly Grace reminded Molly of her real mum. What Molly wanted in her heart? She hadn't allowed herself to contemplate that in . . . eight months.

But Molly Ryan could have no doubts. Molly filled her voice with confidence. "Grace, I would marry Jason tomorrow in a track suit. He's the only part I do care about."

"All right, dearie. If you're sure."

"I am." Now she needed an explanation for her melancholy last weekend.

Then it hit her: her golden opportunity. "Last Friday after we left the hotel, I realized it was my uncle's birthday." She watched Grace's reaction. Nothing. "My Uncle Teague."

Molly held her breath, counting heartbeats. One, two, three. This was a lie more bald-faced than any she'd attempted. Five beats. Molly prayed Grace didn't know Teague's real birthday, whenever that was. Seven beats.

Grace's concern faded into nostalgia and sympathy. "You must've heard a lot about him."

"Loads. I feel as though I know him." Her mum hated to speak of Teague—the hurt was still fresh—but Molly took the leap and threw herself into the lie. "Growin' up where he did, seein' what he saw, the oppression. I'm proud to share his blood."

"You should be." Grace's whisper grew fierce, and tears shone in her eyes. "If only my Donal—" She held up a hand and shook off the sentiment, steeling herself with a deep breath. "Not what we're about today, right?"

"Suppose not." Molly turned away to hide her disappointment. She'd been so close. Could she get away with steering the topic back to Teague and his "heroism" again?

But Grace was already out of the car. Molly joined her in the gently falling snow, and Grace pointed out the boutique across the street and halfway down the block. When Molly followed Grace's indicating finger, the display windows' wedding dresses barely registered in Molly's mind. Instead she focused on someone just in front of them, someone she needed to see, but not here and not like this.

Nate. Back from California.

Her lungs seemed to fill with a sudden snowdrift. When had he arrived? How had he guessed she'd be here?

"Molly?" Grace asked. Did she have to say it so loudly? "Have you any quarters?"

Molly had to refrain from shushing her, but rushed closer so she'd have no reason to raise her voice or look behind them where Nate was.

"Sure I do." Molly dug in her handbag.

Grace pivoted to scan the street—toward Nate.

She had to distract her. "Why'd you choose this shop?" Molly asked.

Grace launched into her explanation, and Molly peered over her shoulder. Nate passed the bridal shop and the photography shop next door and the teachers' supply shop. Finally, he went into a storefront.

A jewelry shop.

Oh no. No, no. Not only was he twenty feet away and sure to blow her cover if he saw her, but ring shopping?

Molly looked back at Grace, who waited with one eyebrow raised. "Sorry." Molly pulled out her wallet and the change. "Here we are."

"You all right?" Grace asked.

"I am, I—I thought I saw someone I want to avoid." Especially in a jewelry shop. But she needed to deflect any suspicion from Nate, on the chance Grace had seen him. "But it wasn't her," she finished. Molly made herself smile, and they finally crossed the street and walked into the shop. But suddenly, planning a wedding made her stomach turn more than normal.

Not the kind of challenge she'd anticipated today.

Grace opened the shop door, and Molly checked the display windows. The mannequins left plenty of room to see into the shop, straight back to the dressing area and mirrors.

All Nate had to do was walk by.

They stepped into the mint and ivory interior, and a well-dressed woman—Chella, according to her gold name badge—approached them. "May I help you?"

"We're needin' a weddin' dress," Grace supplied, gesturing to Molly. Molly nodded, numb. She had to get out of here, make sure Nate didn't see her. How?

A vast blank—nothing came to mind. Chella showed them around the shop, and Grace worked through her notebook of dresses to try. Keeping her back to the front window and forcing herself to breathe was all Molly could do. He couldn't see her.

"Where are your fittin' rooms?" Molly asked at the first opportunity.

"Here." Chella led them to a set of doors.

"Why don't I get into the foundation garments while you collect the gowns?"

"Sounds like you're a pro." Chella unlocked a room, and Molly tried not to dive in.

Finally, she was safe. Until she had to step out again. Wearing a wedding dress, in plain sight of the huge front windows.

Interference. She needed someone to run interference for Nate or Grace, just to be sure. Much as she hated to admit it, she needed backup.

Zachary would know who to send. Molly grabbed her mobile from her handbag and texted him, glad they'd memorized the APCO Ten Codes as an inside joke. *10-78* was all she needed to write—request for assistance.

Chella returned to the changing room with an armload of dresses just before Zachary's reply came: *20?* Location.

Molly answered with the address of the shop and put away her mobile. Chella helped her into the foundation garments, which were less complex but just as restrictive as the last ones she'd worn. As Chella lifted the dress over Molly's head, she realized she hadn't said anything about her preferences. No telling what Grace had foisted upon her.

Chella tugged the skirt into place and began lacing up the back: the dress was strapless. No doubt Grace would gloat about winning Molly over on that point. Once Chella finished, they walked out onto the viewing stage in front of five angled mirrors—once again, Grace was busying herself elsewhere in the shop. Molly frowned at herself in the mirror while Chella fluffed the shimmering folds of the skirt. "This is taffeta, so the fabric's almost iridescent." However, instead of a rambling description as Claire had given, Chella stopped there and admired Molly's reflection.

Molly scrutinized the dress. Iridescent off-white beads covered the bodice from the sweetheart neckline to the waistband. The bottom half of the full skirt was gathered in spots. She wasn't sure how a bride should feel, but this made her feel more like a wedding cake.

"What do you think of the dress?" Chella ventured.

Molly narrowed her eyes. "I don't think I like it."

"Don't worry about offending me; my job's making you happy."

Before they made it back to the fitting room, Grace reappeared with an armload of more thick three-ring binders—the shop's formal-wear catalogues. "That dress is nice."

"Sure now." Molly returned to the changing room to wrestle another gown on.

Once she was presentable again, Molly found Grace on a settee, flipping through the catalogues. She smiled. "Lovely."

On the viewing stage, Molly surveyed the second choice, a white spaghetti-strap gown. Satin ribbon trimmed the top of the dress and empire waist; a chiffon overlay split down the skirt's front.

A much simpler dress all around, but still not . . . right. Perhaps it was too plain? Too summery? Or too . . . bridal?

Was it that she wasn't really getting married—and had just reaffirmed that by seeing Nate—or were the dresses themselves all wrong?

"I don't think this one's for you either," Chella offered. Molly led the way back into the fitting room.

She needed to get her head in the game, Zachary would tell her. What could she draw on from their conversation about Teague? What had Grace stopped herself from saying? *If only my Donal—*

"Grace," Molly called once Chella had gotten the second dress off. "My mum was askin' about your boys—um, Donal and . . . ?"

"Pearse," Grace returned. "They're in Dublin. Pearse is a tradesman, and Donal's workin' with Fine Gael."

Chella set aside the second dress and gathered the third one into her arms. "Who's Feena Gail?" she whispered to Molly.

Molly couldn't quite identify what made Chella's pronunciation not quite right, but it was close enough. "An Irish political party, one of the largest."

Chella slipped the next dress over Molly's head. Molly waited until Chella was working on the buttons before she raised her voice to carry to Grace. "You must be proud."

"Aw, sure look it." Grace wasn't a convincing liar, or she wasn't trying. Not that Molly was surprised that Grace disagreed with her son's politics. Fine Gael wasn't against a united Ireland—but they were officially opposed to violence.

"Done," Chella proclaimed. Molly looked down at what she'd gotten herself into. The shoulder straps were wide enough Molly needn't worry about a repeat of the fiasco at Bridie's wedding, and the fabric was white, but that was all she could assess from here. Molly stepped out onto the viewing stage.

This time, the only comment Grace could manage was an audible gasp. Molly dared to check the mirror.

It was perfect. The ruched wrap bodice tucked into a waistband with a beaded filigree. Below the curving design, glossy satin flowed to the floor.

"Do you like it?" Chella asked.

"I do," Molly breathed. A perfect mix of formal and understated, but more than that, it made her feel . . . flawless.

"Good news," Chella announced. "It's on sale this week, and we only have one left of this dress in your size."

Though Molly knew that last point was probably an attempt to push her into buying it, it was still working.

The Bureau had this in the budget, right?

"Hold on." Chella left for a moment.

"That's the dress." Grace nodded to herself. "And you know it, don't you?"

She didn't dare say it out loud. Molly brushed the smooth fabric of the skirt.

Grace nodded again. "You know it as sure as you know your fella's the one for you. No track suit required."

Again, Molly didn't reply. Falling in love with a dress was one thing, but she wasn't so sentimental to think getting married was as sappy as fairy tales made it seem.

Grace craned her neck, squinting at the dress's neckline. "I must say that necklace is perfect with it. I hadn't noticed it before."

"Thank you. It was a gift. From Jason." Molly had only worn the pendant, a marquise emerald in a silver Celtic knot setting, because it fitted an Irish-themed wedding. She'd hardly touched it since Zachary had given it to her, for her birthday.

This year he'd given her a fake wedding.

"Here we go." Chella returned with a veil and headpiece. Embroidery in a similar filigree pattern to the one at her waist decorated the edge of the two-layered veil, speckled with beads.

"Perfect." Molly leaned down to let Chella push the veil's comb into her hair, then Chella showed her the headband—delicate brushed silver flowers set among white and red rhinestones.

"We can replace the red rhinestones with your colors."

"Green and orange," Grace interjected.

Chella only hesitated a second. "Very nice." Molly again bowed her head to allow Chella to put the headpiece on.

Checking the mirror, Molly caught just a glimpse of a familiar face over her reflection's shoulder. For one terrified, skipped heartbeat, she thought it might be Nate.

She whirled around. Zachary stood behind her, brushing snow from his hair. Obviously Zachary would come to her rescue himself. He really was the best agent for the job: if he saw Nate, he'd know to keep him away.

"Wow, Molly." He used his Southern drawl, but from the warmth in his eyes, the sentiment was sincere. "You sure are—"

"Jason!" Grace leapt from her sofa and pushed Molly toward her fitting room. "You can't be seein' Molly in a weddin' dress."

"Grace," Molly chided. But the other woman was practically shielding Molly with her own body like a Secret Service agent protecting the president, so Molly obliged and ducked into her changing room.

"Aw, Grace, I ain't superstitious, and I didn't come down to get a peek at her dress—though I'm sure glad I did. Does she look that beautiful in all these dresses?"

Molly knew better than to take anything in that accent seriously, but somehow that little compliment made her feel more beautiful than the dress did.

Grace ignored his question. "How'd you know she was here?" she demanded.

Zachary handled that easily. "Molly has a GPS app on her cell. I logged in remotely and triangulated her." Was he using jargon on purpose?

Grace hemmed uncertainly. Molly opened the door for Chella and craned her neck to glimpse Grace's befuddled expression—but her gaze locked on Zachary's. He winked at her.

"Is that your fiancé?"

"He is." Oh, she should be smiling—but when she tried to make her face comply, she realized she already wore a silly grin.

"He'd be killer in a tuxedo."

Molly converted her smile into a smirk at the upsell.

Chella didn't press it further. "Want to get dressed or try on this last dress?"

With Zachary here to run interference, why not maximize her time with Grace? "Let's try that last one."

Molly wouldn't have agreed if she'd seen the dress beforehand. Thick floral lace covered the champagne pink dress from its asymmetrical neckline to its tight, straight skirt with a slanted hem. As if that weren't enough, a rhinestone and crystal . . . mass encrusted the gown's belly, just where every bride wanted a focal point.

By the time Molly was ready for the reveal, Zachary was sitting next to Grace, thumbing through a catalogue. He glanced up as soon as she stepped out, and for a moment all pretense slipped away. His mouth fell open, then his same old disarming smile flashed into place. But it was his eyes . . . Zachary looked at her the same way he had when he'd given her that necklace a year ago—and when he'd nearly kissed her a week ago.

But he caught himself and turned back to his catalogue. Molly checked herself, too.

Grace hadn't noticed her yet, still poring over the catalogue photos with Zachary. "Did you enjoy your dinner with Teresa last night?" Grace asked in a suspiciously blithe tone.

"Tessa? Yeah, we ended up eatin' somewhere else."

Molly cleared her throat before Zachary could go on about his date.

"Oh." Grace sounded pleasantly surprised. Or amused. "Now that one's fancy." Somehow, Molly didn't think she meant that as a compliment.

Zachary lifted a sarcastic eyebrow. "Goes with your ring like collard greens and ham hocks."

"What?" Molly checked the mirrors. The gown was more overdone than she'd feared: she looked like a cheap Vegas act. She shook her head decisively. "It's the last one."

"I told you, you'll know as sure as you know your fella's the one." Grace nodded sagely.

Molly tried not to check Zachary's reaction, but she glimpsed the hint of a frown in his reflection. "Let's get dressed then." She turned back to the changing room. All these wardrobe switches were not helping her talk to Grace.

"Just a minute." Zachary stood. "One more thang we gotta check on these dresses." He joined her on the viewing platform and held out a hand. She studied him a moment, but accepted it. Zachary drew her closer, and she drew in a silent breath.

He paused a moment, his eyes flicking down and then back to hers. "You gonna wear that necklace?"

Suddenly, she felt more exposed than she had falling down the aisle in Bridie's procession—as if Zachary could see through any other reason she might've worn his necklace than her own feelings.

No. She had to stay in cover. Why wouldn't Molly Ryan wear Jason's gift? She added a teasing twist to her reply. "Thinkin' of it."

She could practically see the memories in his mind. His free hand slid around to the small of her back. Molly reached for it, but he guided her hand onto his shoulder.

"What're you doin'?" she asked, though it was already dawning on her.

"Dancin'."

She'd hardly noticed the background music in the shop, but now the slow instrumentals filled her ears. Zachary fell in time with the music. Obviously he had rhythm enough with his musical background, but—"Thought you couldn't dance," she murmured.

"I can't. Just shufflin' my feet." But then he raised their hands for her to turn. Out of habit, she spun out to arms' length, then back, wrapping their arms around her until Zachary shifted to catch her, her back against his chest. She looked up at him; he locked onto her gaze.

She didn't remember this move ending up with the dancers this close. Her pulse rushed, and she tilted her chin up. They were madly in love, weren't they? They had to sell that role.

Although right now, Molly Malone wasn't objecting either.

Zachary leaned down, inching closer until—

He jerked backwards, tugging her down to tumble after him. She landed with her elbow in his stomach, and Zachary grunted.

"First step's a doozy," he half-said, half-coughed, his Southern accent firmly in place.

If he hadn't fallen, would she have—wait, had he fallen on purpose? Had he been leading her on only to interrupt? Teasing her with what she wanted to snatch it away? Anger blazed through her, and Molly scrambled to her feet.

"Z—" She choked on his name. But she needed to say *something* now. "Xavier!"

Zachary sat up too fast and glanced around, then scowled at her.

She hadn't blown their covers. Had she? Her face burned, and not because of the fall. She covered her cheeks and hurried into the fitting room.

"Told y'all I can't dance," Zachary called through the door.

"Who's Xavier?" Grace asked. Even from here, Molly could hear the edge in her voice. Molly tried to jam her mental gears back into place, to get through the anger and back into her cover. She had to fix this.

But Zachary was already fixing it. "Molly's ex-boyfriend." He grew louder. "She knows I hate it when she gets us confused."

"Oh," Grace said. Molly perked up. She bought that? "You could take dancin' lessons, you know yourself."

"Pretty obvious I'm beyond help."

He wasn't the only one. Was she seriously considering kissing him? And less as Molly Ryan and more as Molly Malone? That was one line they hadn't approached undercover, a line she needed to stay well away from.

Zachary had made sure of that. She shouldn't be angry—she should be grateful—but heat still simmered behind her heart.

He'd made it clear they were still headed different directions. So why couldn't he let her be? Why did he keep messing with her head? Or was he just playing the cover too well?

Molly took two calming breaths before Chella popped in and closed the changing room door. "You okay?"

"I am, I am." Molly spoke quickly and vehemently. "Sorry. Hope I didn't hurt the dress."

Chella brushed aside the concern. "It happens; it's a sample. But the last gown was definitely your dress. I've never seen it so becoming on a bride before."

"Thank you." Molly half-smiled. Chella helped her out of the overdone dress, and Molly's pulse began to return to normal. "Though I'm sure you say that to everyone."

Chella chuckled. "Maybe I do, but this time I mean it. Like I said, that dress is on sale—forty percent off—and it's the last one in your size." Chella quoted the sale price, and while it was less than that final solo dress, it also sounded like more than a nursing assistant would have in her budget.

"I'll have to talk to Jason," she said at length. Chella ducked out for Molly to change back into her Aran sweater and jeans.

She left the fitting room and Zachary set aside his catalogues, standing. "See, Grace? Told you it wasn't the gowns makin' her beautiful: it's the other way 'round. Ready to go?"

"I am," she replied without making eye contact. "Sorry about the names."

Zachary leaned down to catch her gaze. She'd loved that charming little gesture since they'd first met. "That's all right. Ain't you forgettin' somethang, darlin'?"

Molly glanced at Grace, who was still engrossed in a catalogue, before whispering to Zachary. "You don't even know what it cost. I'm only a nursin' assistant, love."

"I don't care. We'll make it work." He lowered his voice for a second to add, "You know it's the one you really want."

She nodded slowly, her eyes on his. Why didn't it feel like he meant the dress?

He returned to full volume. "Anythang for you, Molly."

"Thank you, Jason."

He pulled out his wallet to hand her a credit card. She checked the card: Jason Tolliver. They followed a beaming Chella to the cash stand and gave her the credit card.

"I'm sorry," Chella said while she rang them up. "I have to ask—are you Irish?"

Molly smiled. "I am."

"Happy Saint Patrick's Day."

"Thank you."

Grace perked up. "Have you two been to the Saint Patrick's parade here?"

Molly watched Zachary; his reaction was nearly imperceptible. "Which one?" he drawled casually. "There's the South Side Irish Parade, the one here on the Northwest Side, and then the main city one."

"My Irish dance girls march in that one," Molly added.

"Three Saint Patrick's Day parades?" Grace raised both eyebrows, but something about her surprise seemed too practiced.

"Chicago's probably the best city in the world to be Irish." She could turn this to her advantage, too. "Other than Dublin or Derry, of course."

Grace laughed without humor. "I wouldn't class Derry or anywhere else in the North as a good place to be Irish."

And there it was: the opportunity she'd waited for. If she could respond correctly, it would seal her connection with Grace. She took a deep breath—and a big chance.

"*An Sasanach. Imeacht gan teacht orthu.*" *The English. May they leave and never return.* Molly's heart beat double time against the agonizing silent seconds. Grace hadn't grown up focusing on her Irish lessons so she could join the Gardaí as Molly had—if Grace had had Irish lessons at all. Would using her Irish backfire?

A slow smile suffused Grace's features. "*Tá!*" she agreed.

A flush of victory bloomed in Molly's chest. At last, she was making headway.

"Y'all talkin' 'bout me again?" Zachary joked, cutting off Molly's mental celebration.

"That we are," Grace said.

Chella handed him back his card. Zachary signed the receipt "Jason Tolliver" without hesitation, Chella scheduled a fitting with Molly, and they left the shop.

She'd just bought a wedding dress. Well, the FBI had bought it for her.

What was she, crazy?

"Oh, not snowin' anymore," Grace remarked once they reached the pavement. She tucked her umbrella under her arm and turned to Molly. "We should have you over to dinner soon."

"We'd love that." Molly grinned. Could it really be working? Was she finally getting in with them? And if so—now what? She still couldn't appear too eager. "Give us a ring and we'll set it up."

"We will."

"Then we'll see y'all soon." Zachary spoke up before she could press her objectives again. He took Molly's elbow, silently signaling that the shopping trip was good and over, and he'd be the one driving her home.

No, she wasn't done yet. But could happily engaged Molly Ryan tell her fiancé to leave?

Grace moved closer to Zachary, and his hand on Molly's elbow tensed. Was it her imagination, or was he positioning himself as a shield to her?

"Now you listen to me, Jason Tolliver." Grace jabbed his chest. "Don't you go givin' out to Molly because she called you by some other man's name. You flustered her."

"I know, ma'am."

"You." She held up a warning finger, a threatening storm that barely reached Zachary's sternum. "Be good to her, or you won't like the consequences."

"Always, ma'am. Skin me alive if I don't."

Grace's eyes held more steel than a machine gun. "Not quite what I had in mind. But it might do."

The threat seemed awfully sincere. Molly found herself gripping

Zachary's hand on her arm; Zachary took a step backwards on the pavement, edging out a nervous laugh. They bid Grace goodbye, and he led Molly down the street. "Creepy," he muttered once they were out of earshot.

"Very." Molly watched Grace get in her car and drive off in the opposite direction from them.

"Changed your mind about backup, huh?" Zachary drew her attention back to him.

"The backup wasn't to deal with Grace." They walked past the jewelry shop Nate had gone in. Molly scanned the store through the display windows.

"What, you want to look at wedding bands?"

Molly backhanded Zachary's stomach. "I rang you because I saw Nate."

"Ah." Zachary nodded, then slid into his accent. "You ain't told him 'bout us, darlin'?"

"Are you dense or daft?"

They rounded the corner and reached his car. Molly realized she hadn't let go of his arm—even when she'd hit him, she'd taken hold of him again. He opened the door for her and then got in his side.

She'd finally made progress with. Or started to, until Zachary cut her off. Molly turned from her window. "Why'd you interrupt me?"

"When?"

"When I spoke Irish to Grace."

His tone sounded like she was testing his patience. "I told you, you can't come off too eager."

"How would you know if I seemed eager? All I said was 'May the English leave and never return.'"

"She shouldn't suspect you know she's still involved in militant republicanism."

"I wasn't anywhere near that—not that you had any way of knowin'."

"No." Zachary shifted in his seat. "But if you're too eager, she might—"

"One little sentence isn't too eager."

"It could be."

Molly realized she was clenching the seatbelt and ordered her fingers to relax. "You really believe I might've ruined everythin' if you hadn't stopped me when you did."

"One sentence could—"

"I cannot win with you. Either I've no experience or I do *too* much."

He pulled up to her building. "I'm just saying we have to be careful."

"And me doubly so? Because I don't know how to do this?"

He didn't answer the question, his mouth opening and closing twice. Because she was right.

Next he'd tell her she was doing "not bad."

Molly climbed from the car without a word. Zachary didn't look at her either.

Grand. She was still in love with him, but *he* was the one off in a different direction. And obviously that direction couldn't include her as an FBI agent. She slammed the car door and headed into her building. She'd be willing to bet he'd cut off her conversation with Grace less because he was worried she'd mess things up and more because speaking Irish meant he wasn't in control.

Which hurt more? Zachary dumping her or not believing in her?

SUNDAY MORNING, Molly braced herself and knocked on Nate's door. He'd know something was up; she was an hour early for church. But it was well past time to do this.

Molly didn't try to hide her somber mood when he opened the door, dressed in a sweatshirt and shorts, his chestnut hair still mussed from sleep. "Hey! I missed you so much!"

Oh, this would hurt.

Nate stepped out to embrace her in the hall. "You get my email?"

She swallowed and closed her eyes. Did she have to crush him?

Nate realized she wasn't hugging him back and held her at arm's length. "What's wrong?"

"Can I come in?"

Instantly wary, Nate moved aside to admit her to his flat. Molly glanced at the expensive TV, mahogany coffee table, cocoa leather sectional, all pristine as on the showroom floor. She gestured toward the sofa. He took a seat. Molly perched on the chaise. No point getting comfortable. He wouldn't want her here long.

Caution filled his face. "What's up?"

"We need to talk."

Nate fought to keep a neutral expression at those famous last words, but a muscle in his jaw tightened. "Okay."

He deserved honesty, not to drag this out. "This isn't workin'."

He turned to stare straight ahead, his mouth practically glued shut. The brushed silver clock on the wall ticked out silent seconds. "That's it, huh?" he said at last.

Molly flinched at the anger in his voice, but absorbed the blow. If she'd done this when she should have, she could've spared him some pain.

"I thought you wanted to get married. Or do you collect wedding magazines?"

She sighed. "Sort of." He deserved an explanation, one she couldn't give without telling him too much about Grace. But marriage or no, that wasn't the reason she was breaking up with him. "Can I ask you somethin'?"

Nate waved for her to go on, a sharp flick of his wrist.

"Why did you bring up marriage?"

"Molly." He threw up his hands. "What kind of—"

"Just tell me."

He ran his fingers through his hair, but it remained mussed. "I mean, we've been close for a while, and things were going well."

Molly's heart sank an inch. Did he not see it? "Was that all?"

"All? I love you, Molly. What else is there?"

She let his words hang there. Could he hear how hollow they sounded? Or did she not hear the emotion behind them because she didn't return it? "Or was it just 'time' to say that, too?"

Nate inhaled loudly and pressed one finger to his temple.

She looked down at her hands, but she wasn't even fidgeting. "I don't want to hurt you."

"Too late. Sounds like you've decided for both of us."

"Have I?" She waited until he met her gaze before she continued. "Remember how I've watched R-rated movies?"

He shifted, and his lips twitched.

"I used to smoke cigarettes, you know."

Nate looked away, his discomfort growing.

"I miss drinkin' coffee. And alcohol."

"Molly," he cut her off. "Okay, so you've got some issues."

"Nathan O'Shaughnessy, not bein' raised Mormon isn't an 'issue.' Let's be honest: the person you want to marry could never say any of those things."

His gaze slowly fell, and he sank back into the cocoa leather behind him. After another long minute of silence, Nate stood. "I'm sure you can find your way to church."

"Nate," she reproached gently. He strode past her and Molly reached for him, but he pulled away and stalked to the door. She collected herself and walked out of his apartment for the last time. At least he didn't slam the door behind her.

Molly maintained her calm exterior until she reached her car. She dropped into the driver's seat. She shouldn't have waited so long—but should she have broken up with him on the telephone? Hardly. She knew how awful that was.

On the other hand, she hadn't had to watch Zachary walk out of her life, pretending her world wasn't crumbling when he said their lives were headed in different directions.

Her entire identity wasn't tied up in being Zachary's girlfriend. She had the Bureau and dance and her family and all the things that made her Molly. But by the time they'd been dating a month, when she'd pictured her future, she'd pictured it with Zachary.

And apparently he hadn't.

And that still hurt.

Didn't seem to hurt Zachary. If anything he was surer than ever, judging by his date this weekend and the "comfort" he'd offered his sister after her breakup. Different directions.

He wasn't in cover that day. Neither of them were. There was nothing to confuse him. Friday night in that parking garage was exactly what he'd said—his cover going to his head. Now his cover had to mess with hers too? To think, she'd been glad to see him at the bridal shop yesterday.

Molly started her car and switched the heater on full blast. Did she love Zachary? Yes. But could she stand him? How could she, when he constantly belittled her?

She'd have to work with him until they cleared this case. Doable, if she was careful. She'd keep her distance when they weren't undercover. She'd finish this case fast as possible. She'd accept the offer from ASAC Chin.

How soon could she ring the Canavans to arrange their dinner? The sooner she rang them, the sooner she'd be free from the ever-confusing influence of Zachary Saint.

Mum was right. She needed to protect her heart—no, she needed to invest in coronary Kevlar.

Grace observed the evening cleaning crew filing into the DontRain warehouse in silence. She'd taken the precaution of leaving their flat the back way that night with Pearse driving, more out of the habit of secrecy during a clandestine assignment than a fear anyone was surveilling them.

"What're we lookin' for?" Pearse murmured.

"Whisht." She studied the workers, tapping a finger on her mouth. Difficult to profile someone from crossing ten meters of a dimly-lit car park.

She waited until they entered the building to answer her son's question. "Never seen a cleanin' crew what didn't do somethin' to compromise the security—forget to turn the alarm back on, leave a door open, somethin'."

Pearse shifted in his seat as if to watch the doors better. "I thought Da was our way in."

Grace impaled him with a glare. "Aren't you the one goin' on and on about 'redundancy'?"

Pearse didn't answer, but pointed back at the warehouse. Grace spun around. The side door was propped open, a lone custodian wheeling a trash bin across the car park. He took the rubbish around the back of the warehouse.

The door was completely unguarded. Grace peered through the binoculars. Though the angle wasn't the best, no one appeared to be watching from within the building. The south side of the building was lit by a single fixture above the door. Without that light, they could easily hide in the shadows and enter the building undetected.

"Do you see it?" Grace asked.

Pearse nodded. "Should we take care of that light?"

"We should."

"A gun would attract notice."

Amateur. Grace brushed aside the concern. "You'd be amazed what you can get away with in a uniform."

They both fell into silence. The custodian returned with his empty trash bin and closed the door behind him.

"What uniform?"

"Repairman coveralls. Show up with a ladder, unscrew the bulbs—if someone asks what you're doin', say you're with the landlord. You'll be away before they check. But it's unlikely you'll run into anyone; we'd have you do it the day of, after business hours."

"What about the alarm? Oughtn't the cleanin' crew switch it on?"

Grace bit her lip in thought. "I'll take care of that." Just like everything else, it would fall to her. Being the only capable member of the team was a burden she'd shoulder again. Gladly.

Zach jabbed the elevator button to leave work Monday. After the way Molly had stormed out of his car Saturday, he'd been careful to give her space all day. He wanted to win her, not smother her.

Xavier joined Zach waiting for the elevator. "How was your date with the SAC's niece?"

He'd almost forgotten Tessa—and the beginning of their evening. "Parts were good."

X raised an eyebrow.

"We went to a karaoke bar and ran into my sister."

"The one that just got dumped?"

Zach nodded. "That was the good part."

"Okay, you've got my attention." Xavier tapped the still-lit elevator button.

He grimaced. "We also ran into the Canavans."

Xavier gaped at him. "Some guys have all the luck."

"You know it. I'm assuming your weekend wasn't nearly that interesting."

"Nope. You really gotta keep your work life and your personal life separate."

While working with his ex? Zach laughed. "How, exactly, am I supposed to do that?"

"Do what I do." Xavier pulled out his car keys. "Spend every other weekend as far away as possible. This weekend we went to visit Lila's family in Michigan."

"I've met her family. I'd rather work."

X folded his arms, his keys jangling in one hand. Before he unleashed whatever response was coming, the elevator arrived. Xavier dropped his stance, and they boarded the elevator. X turned to Zach. "Did we ever hear back on CPD testing the Canavans' tank for off-road diesel dye?"

Good. Work. "Don't think so."

X frowned. "Still thinking arson?"

Gasoline burned better than it exploded, but plain old fire wasn't the IRA's style. "Blowing something up, more likely." Zach returned Xavier's frown, and the next pertinent question hung in the air—blowing up what? "Enough for a warrant yet?"

"Unfortunately, no. We gonna search everybody who buys diesel?"

"Everybody that used to blow stuff up, yeah."

"Great." The elevator doors slid open at their floor, and Xavier started out. "Give me something better than a co-conspirator to prove the Canavans did that."

Zach set his jaw and let Xavier outpace him. The Malones were only co-conspirators by a defense attorney's definition. But X was right. Even Northern Ireland couldn't come up with anything on them. Definitely not enough to convince a judge for a warrant. They needed more evidence: a target, a timeline, anything.

Now he needed to talk to Molly. For the case.

AT THE END OF WORK MONDAY, once Kent had headed for the elevators, Molly massaged her brow to assuage a headache. Beyond ridiculous. She couldn't possibly hold his hand through every step of an investigation. The man had to be capable of an original, investigative thought. Didn't he?

Phoenix looked better every day.

"Molly?"

"What?" she bit off. When Kent didn't respond, she looked up to find Zachary standing at her desk, as he had a hundred times when he was undercover.

When she'd fallen in love with him.

The biggest reason to take Phoenix's offer.

"Hard day with Kathleen, Moll?"

She had to chuckle—Kathleen was the coworker who'd made her life miserable at that same old desk. "You wouldn't believe me if I told you, Father."

Zachary wrinkled his nose. "That's weird now."

"It was weird then, too."

Zachary's smile faded, and he leaned closer. "Listen, we need something to get us a warrant or *anything* better than suspicions. What can we do?"

Was he seriously asking her? She sat up straighter. "An invitation to their apartment."

Before Zachary agreed, Molly had her mobile out, dialing. Zachary moved around her desk to crouch by her, his ear close to her phone. His face close to hers.

She noticed her foot bouncing and stilled it. She had to get this right, no matter how close Zachary was.

"Molly, dearie?" Grace answered.

"How's about ye?" Molly went straight for Irish phraseology. "Any luck linin' up venues this weekend?"

"This weekend?" Grace hesitated. "Em, Ed's feelin' neglected—"

Molly shot Zachary a look aimed to express skepticism and sarcasm. The man hardly seemed to tolerate Grace.

"—so we're plannin' a daytrip Saturday. A staycation? Whatever they call it."

Work with this. She had to work with this. "Sounds massive," Molly said. "In fact, it's perfect. Jason and I could use some stress relief."

Wait, she wasn't inviting them along on their weekend excursion. She looked to Zachary again. He nodded for her to continue.

"Why don't we get together for dinner?" Molly suggested. "No plannin', no weddin's, just a quiet night in."

Grace mulled over the bait. "How's about next Friday?"

"The seventeenth? Let me check with Jason." She lowered her mobile.

Zachary chewed his bottom lip. "Can we get in sooner?"

"Yes, let's invite ourselves over tomorrow. That isn't suspicious at all."

He held up both hands, accepting her point, and she raised her phone again. "Sounds grand."

"Are you or Jason hostin'?"

Molly swallowed a groan. Hadn't Grace invited them over last week?

She could make sure Grace hosted. "Hang on—what?" She held the phone away from her mouth again and covered the microphone. "Say somethin'," she murmured to Zachary.

"Like what?"

"Just speak. Don't whisper."

"Not sure where this is going," he said in full voice.

Good enough. She lifted the phone. "Sorry, Jason forgot his apartment's bein' fumigated next week." Did that take a whole week? Grace wouldn't know. "And my flat's a studio, so I haven't room to host."

"Oh." Again, Grace let that roll over in her mind. "We could find another day—"

"That's the only evenin' we'll both be free for another fortnight, with our work schedules. Then we won't have time to relax, with weddin' plannin' and all."

Molly held her breath. If she had to try to convince Grace again, she'd sound suspect.

"I suppose we could host you," Grace said. The least enthusiastic invitation they'd gotten from her, but Molly would take it.

"Thank you," she gushed. "I'm already lookin' forward to it."

"Us as well, dearie. Let me do you a favor for your weddin' too: I'll find a venue available for your dates this week, and then we'll go from there. Right, so?"

"Sure."

"Have to be headin'. See you next Friday!" As usual, Grace cut herself off in the middle of her goodbyes.

Sighing, Molly tucked her mobile into her pocket. "Appears we'll be draggin' this out another week."

Zachary looked away but she thought she detected a grin. Did he *want* to prolong this?

"They really want you back in Phoenix?" he asked.

"An ASAC called personally."

"I can see why."

Was he . . . complimenting her? Molly braced for the cut that would surely follow.

But it didn't. Molly allowed herself to enjoy the praise. A tiny tendril of hope wrapped its way around her heart. "Was that so difficult?"

He cocked his head. "What?"

"Complimentin' me—without turnin' it backhanded at best."

His eyebrows drew together in genuine confusion. "I've given you compliments. Hundreds."

"Sayin' I'm beautiful isn't the same as admittin' I'm a good FBI agent." Molly stared into his eyes until his gaze faltered. "Can you say that?"

Zachary stood up, pulling away. "Would you believe me?"

Could she, after the way he'd treated her?

He tapped her desk. "Let's get together next week to go over an action plan." He leaned in close enough to drop his voice to a murmur. "And you *are* beautiful."

Molly barely dared to meet his gaze. Did he think that was what she needed to hear? She wasn't a perfect agent, no, but Zachary couldn't even admit she was competent enough to work a case without his micromanagement.

He didn't want to be with her. He didn't respect her as an FBI agent. And *he* was the one who'd fallen in love with the wrong person?

"Good night, Zachary." She turned back to her computer as if her email was super urgent.

She wasn't even halfway home when her mobile rang. Grace? She hoped not. Molly pulled out her mobile: Mum. She hit the icon to turn on speakerphone. Molly sort of managed the small talk, but Mum wouldn't let her get away with that.

"Have you spoken to Nate?" Mum asked.

"Yesterday."

"How'd that go?"

Molly groaned in her heart and merged onto the freeway. "He leapt for joy and did a treble jig out the door. How d'you think?"

Mum chuckled. "What did you tell him?"

"That I'm not the person he wants to marry."

Mum sucked in a breath, as if hearing it cut to the quick. "Not that you had a lot to accomplish?"

"Already told him that."

"Hm." Mum was quiet, and Molly scanned the familiar exit signs. "Did you ever tell Zachary that?"

"We never discussed marriage." She'd told Lucy, but Lucy had always kept confidences.

"Hm," Mum said again. "But haven't you told every man you've dated that, in one way or another?"

"I don't know." Why did she need to sound so defensive? "It's true, anyway. I've to make up for all the time I lost these last six years."

"Lost, love? You earned a Master's and spent how many years runnin' an entire parish? That's not accomplishin' anythin'?"

"Mum." Molly let her tone convey her impatience with her

mother's logic.

"Molly, can I tell you somethin'?"

"Sure now."

"Are you sittin' down?"

Molly glanced around the car interior. "I'm drivin'."

"You might want to pull over."

She suspected Mum was being overly dramatic, but just in case she was about to reveal Molly was adopted or the like, Molly stopped on the freeway shoulder. "What is it?"

"Life doesn't end at marriage."

Molly half-laughed. "I know."

"Do you, love? Because I keep hearin' you say you've so much to accomplish, so much to do, but even you don't know what that is. 'Y'know, stuff.'" Mum delivered the last words lowering her voice and adding an American accent, imitating a teenage boy.

"I don't sound like that."

"No," Mum admitted. "But do you know what I 'accomplished' in the first five years after I married your da? I foiled three bombin' attempts, stopped six kneecappin's, and got seven IRA soldiers arrested. I survived a weekend in hostile police custody, went on countless clandestine missions and delivered more than one weapons cache to authorities. And honestly, havin' your da there with me was my greatest strength, to celebrate the good, and weather the bad together."

"Like when RUCs dragged him out and beat him? Like they did 'Seán Martin'?"

"Yes, exactly like that."

Molly took the opportunity to change the subject. "Mum, did Da write *The Blood-Dimmed Tide*?"

"Your father?" Mum hooted with laughter. "No! He hates to talk about it. You saw him try to play the Top Secret card for talkin' to you, didn't you?"

They both laughed.

Molly steered back onto the freeway, and Mum steered the conversation back to her topic. "Molly, your da and you girls showed me what was most important in life: love. When you find that, it doesn't matter what you need to 'accomplish.' You need to act on it, take that leap of faith, or you might lose it."

"You want me to ring Nate?"

"Who said anythin' about Nate?"

Molly fell silent. Obviously she meant Zachary.

If Molly was honest, she'd have to admit it: deep down, she knew seeing her future with Zachary hadn't meant dating him indefinitely. It'd meant marrying him.

"Mum, do you believe God has a plan for our lives?"

"Of course, love. God is always in control."

"What if . . . I've ruined mine?"

Mum's laugh was high and incredulous. "D'ye hear yourself, love? You're one of the most amazin', capable women I've ever known, but if you went up against God, who would win?"

She didn't have to go up against God. She was up against Zachary, and all they'd done to one another.

And when it came down to it, when she was ready to marry, she'd always wanted to marry Zachary.

That was precisely why seeing him again was hard, why she still hurt. Why some part of her still loved him. In the end, he was the one she'd wanted—still wanted—to have there for support, and to be there for him through those times, too, even up to a police beating. Knowing Zachary's penchant for antagonizing cops—like that time they'd been stopped for speeding in DC and he'd got his fine doubled—that was a possibility, though not as much as it had been for her parents.

"Wait a minute," Molly said, sitting up straighter. "Da's beatin' was 'exactly' like 'Seán Martin's'?"

"Did I say that?" Mum asked.

"Mum. Did *you* write *The Blood-Dimmed Tide*?"

"Oh, I have to go—my popcorn's ready!" And Mum clicked off.

Molly glanced at her mobile and the picture of her mum there. No. She'd sooner believe Mum had been abducted by aliens than written *The Blood-Dimmed Tide.* Although . . . they'd been extra cagey about their IRA involvement this go-round, but she'd dismissed that as trying to keep themselves and Bridie's family clear of the Canavans. Now their friends were in the book, along with Da's life.

On the other hand, alien abduction did seem the most likely

explanation if Mum had urged her to marry Zachary. That was all but impossible.

After all this time, she wanted to marry him. But how could she shackle herself to someone who would never respect her?

Wednesday night, Grace pressed herself into the alleyway's shadows as best she could. Every heartbeat pulsed in her stomach, a rhythm of nausea. Piecing together the components of this mission had taken four days. They didn't have time to start over.

She glanced up at Ed, but his balaclava brought back memories—not all of them reassuring. Grace shuffled farther into the building's shadows, willing herself not to remember.

That time he'd nearly got caught by the British Army at a weapons cache. She could taste the salt and metal of her own blood, biting through her lip to keep quiet.

Grace pressed the gun into Ed's gloves. Focus on this job.

Being shot at by Royal Ulster Constabularies. She could still smell the gunpowder and terror.

Grace shoved the memory aside, straining to hear the approaching footsteps.

The fistfight with Ulster Defense Force. She could never forget the sickening crack of the punch that left Ed unconscious for what felt like forever.

The footsteps continued, growing louder.

Time. Stooping to petty crime was one reason they'd abandoned IRA splinter groups, but once in a while, non-political violence was necessary for the cause.

Finally their target was close enough. Grace signaled, and Ed moved out of the shadows, gun at the ready.

"Give it," he said, his voice more gruff than usual with that American accent. "Everything."

"Hey, man, I don't have anything—"

"Watch, wallet. Keys. Now!"

Grace couldn't see the man, but she heard the wallet slap the ground. Then the jangle of the keys. She restrained the jolt of celebration. They still had to get out of here.

"Phone, too," Ed added.

"I–I need–" The man choked off. Heavy plastic clattered across the cement. "Not worth dying."

"That's right, buddy."

Grace watched Ed stoop to collect the haul. Once he had, he flicked the gun at the man. "Run."

Retreating footsteps echoed through the alleyway where Grace hid. Ed took off running past Grace, and she followed to where Pearse waited in his idling car. Grace and Ed piled into the backseat, and Pearse pulled away.

Grace held out a hand for the wallet, careful to handle it only with gloves. The license in its window read "Jimmy McCorkle." Next was his work ID: JIMMY MCCORKLE, FOREMAN, PRECISION DEMOLITION.

Ed passed the key ring to Pearse at the first red light. Pearse flipped through the keys until he found one and held it aloft. "This one."

Grace yanked the cash from the wallet and rolled down the window.

"Not takin' the bank cards, Mam?"

Amateur. Eejit. She tossed the wallet out the window, and the phone, too. "Too easy to trace."

"When do we hit the bunker?"

"Now, before he tells anyone at Precision he's lost his keys. We can be in and out before they get down there."

Pearse obeyed. Each mile, each minute that ticked by felt like a year. Had he alerted someone yet? Finally, miles outside of town, Pearse took a left into a tiny gravel parking lot. Grace climbed from the car, peering through the dark at the unmarked shipping container sheltered by a hill and a pile of sandbags. This was Precision Demolition's magazine bunker?

Pearse shut off the car. Grace and Ed trailed after him to the bunker. Pearse tapped a raised silver circle on a metal plate on the door. "Hockey puck locks."

"Gloves, ya spanner."

Pearse tugged on latex gloves. He stuck the key in the keyhole on the side and turned it. The silver hockey puck portion pulled free, and the metal plate swung open. He unlocked the lower lock as well and gave the puck to Ed.

"C-4's on the left, past the water-gels." A silent conversation passed between them. "Next time, Da," Pearse said with a nod. "I'll show you."

A smile stole across Ed's face. He clapped Pearse on the shoulder before heading into the storage container. Grace suppressed a groan. They wouldn't need explosives next time if they had enough snipers.

A siren wailed in the distance. "Ninety to the dozen," Grace called, though they didn't need the urging to go faster.

Pearse glanced over some paperwork while Ed's torch beam bounced around the back. Pearse clapped. "They left today's papers." He made a note on the top sheet. Grace shone her torch on the requisitions from the day. Her son had changed a 1 to a 4, accounting for the lot they were stealing.

"They won't notice the blastin' caps." He grabbed half a dozen from a shelf near the door. "Let's scarper."

Grace took the detonators and helped lock the shipping container. Now they were ready.

THURSDAY MORNING, Molly finished the last of her follow-up calls on their cold cases with nothing new to report. And nothing new on the Zachary front, either, since he hadn't called, texted or emailed with status updates or a confession that he'd always respected her on a professional level.

Probably because he hadn't.

The phone on Kent's desk rang. "Malone!" he called. "Can you take this? It's the Luxembourgish consul's office."

The phone rang again. Molly slowly turned her chair to him. "Isn't that your case?"

"Yeah, but—can't you?"

Ring.

Molly kept her gaze level. "Stand up and work this case yourself."

"But—but—"

Molly pointed at the phone on the next ring. "If you don't answer, you'll miss your chance. I'm not doin' it for you."

Kent looked at her and the phone, his eyes wide with panic. "I can't!"

"If you don't, no one else can, and the criminals will go unpunished."

Ring.

"Do it," Molly urged.

Kent yanked the receiver off the cradle. "Hello?" He straightened with a little gasp. "Mr. Consul, thank you so much for calling personally. . . . Yes, sir, one minute." He snatched up a pen and began writing furiously. "I think I can. Thank you—this is exactly what we were hoping for." Kent hung up his phone and stood, practically dancing from foot to foot.

"Well?" Molly asked.

"The consul said he appreciated your diligence and set up a meeting with the assistant director of the state intelligence service—he's in town this week."

"The *Service de Renseignement de l'État*?"

Kent pointed at her like she'd guessed the answer right in a board game. "Yeah, that. We're having lunch." He checked his watch. "In half an hour." He shoved into his jacket—and he was in such a hurry, he put it on upside down.

"There's no guarantee he'll give us what we need, Kent."

"The Consul said he would—said he'd talked to him about the case, and the guy said he'd bring the file." He took off his jacket and righted it. "How is the Luxembourgers' relationship to the Belgians?"

She dug up what she could remember from her research internship in Brussels. "Luxembourg's had an economic union with Belgium for nearly a century."

"You know that off the cuff?" Kent half-laughed, shaking his head. "Man, that's exactly why I like working with you."

"How's that?"

"You—you know everything: crime stats, languages, policing, tac-ops, international relations." Kent trailed off, his gaze drifting away. "I know I've been throwing a lot your way lately. Maybe I just got spoiled when we were at Quantico. All of us did. No matter what the question was, we always knew Malone had the answer."

"Um . . . thank you."

"Aren't you working on a cold case with a Belgian connection?"

He knew what cold cases she'd been working on—rather, not working on so she could help him? "I am."

"Krier, right? Can you give me a brief of anything you could use from them, and I'll ask the consul about it?"

Molly smiled and pulled up her case file. Hope for Kent yet indeed.

Kent hurried off with her notes, leaving Molly free to work on her own cases for the afternoon. Kent swooped back in, still bounding with enthusiasm, a few minutes before five, just as Molly finished up her last FD-302 and made the day's final email check.

Among the new messages was one vaguely familiar sender.

Raymond Hassan. Was that one of her cold cases, or—? Your man from Ireland's Independent Monitoring Commission. Had he found something on the Canavans after all? She hurried to open the email.

> Special Agent Malone,
>
> I received this email today. It may be a coincidence, but there's quite a bit of overlap between the case you described and the one below. Hope this helps.

After a break in the text and a series of assorted email headers, showing the message had made its rounds before reaching Hassan, a forwarded message followed.

A quick skim, and Molly grabbed her mobile and dialed Zachary.

Zach was on the elevator when his phone rang: Molly's number. He still didn't know how to answer her question from Tuesday—what did she want, a parade in her honor?—but this had to be about work. "Hey, Molly."

She didn't bother with a greeting. "I got an email from the Canavans' son. He said—"

"I'll be right there." Zachary ended the call. He jogged off the elevator at the next floor and then halfway up the stairs to Molly's cubicle before it registered that the case wasn't the reason he was running.

He'd pretend that was the reason until Molly gave him a better excuse to run to her side. Three minutes after she called, he was at her desk.

Kent was still there, looking the part of FBI agent filing paperwork instead of fan boy at loose ends. Did the audience make things less awkward for them, or more?

Molly glanced up and startled to see him. Too late to back out.

Zach nodded a greeting. "What's up?"

Molly gestured toward her monitor, and Zach leaned down to read.

> I wasn't sure who to turn to, but I've only just realized how involved my parents were in paramilitaries in the 1980s, and a few recent incidents have me worrying they're at it again.
>
> Earlier this week, they sent me an email saying they have "events" coming up, and I should be sure to watch the international news, especially in the next fortnight. My mam said I'd finally come to understand where Ireland stood on the world stage, as they had, and what a necessary sacrifice really was. She closed her email with her favorite quote, "Ireland unfree will never be at peace," and then she added, "and neither will the rest of the world."
>
> Normally, I'd dismiss this as her usual away-in-the-head ramblings, but something about this seemed more serious, so I gave her a ring to make sure she was all right. When she didn't answer, I sent a neighbor over to see her. He tried several times, but never caught anyone at home.
>
> I hate to do this to my parents, but I don't feel as though I've a choice.
>
> Donal Canavan

"The next fortnight," he repeated. He scrolled to the email headers. "Donal's email is dated a week ago."

"Somethin' in the next week."

Zach leaned against Molly's desk. They had to step up their efforts. "Grace invited us over, right?"

"Not for another week." After Donal's deadline.

"Reschedule for tomorrow night."

Molly's frown looked doubtful. "Tomorrow night?"

"You think they'd go for tonight?"

She shook her head. "I don't—it'll be hard enough to get in tomorrow."

"We have to. Let's say I have to go out of town. An on-site consult or something."

"In the middle of plannin' a weddin'?"

Kent cleared his throat. Before they could explain their wedding was all part of the assignment, he stood. "We'll pick this up tomorrow. Maybe we'll catch up with Brel."

"Sure." Molly beamed at him.

Zach waited until Kent was well away before he spoke. "What's gotten into him?"

"Can't say; not complainin'. He's been on fire since the Luxembourgish Consul rang us back today. He's even looked into *my* cold cases."

"Wow." He hadn't thought Kent had that in him. "Hope he keeps that up."

"Me too." She held up her cell phone. "So I'm convincin' the Canavans to let two undercover agents into their house while they're in the midst of executin' an attack."

He brushed aside her worry. "Piece of cake."

She nailed him with a skeptical frown but dialed, holding her phone so Zach could hear both sides of the conversation.

Getting this close to her was not wise, but he'd never had much sense when it came to Molly. Zach knelt next to her chair to hover at her shoulder. He could be here for support. Not just because he really, really wanted to be here.

"Molly," Grace answered. Terrorists shouldn't be allowed to sound cheery, ever. "How's about ye?"

"Hi, Grace."

"Tell me you have good news—did you get Jason to postpone the weddin'?"

Definitely hadn't discussed that. Zach checked her response; Molly rolled her eyes in an I-don't-want-to-talk-about-it message. "Not yet—but we've a kink in our schedule."

"Do you? What's this, so?"

"Jason's bein' called away on business."

He gave her arm an encouraging squeeze. She shrugged him off.

"How long is he leavin' you alone to plan your weddin'?"

She glanced at Zach, a flash of panic crossing her face. Before he could help her, she continued with the perfect mix of dread and heartache in her tone. "Three weeks."

Was that her tactic for getting him as far away as she could? Zach pushed the thought aside and grabbed a slip of paper to scribble a note—*leaving this weekend*?

"And he'll be leavin' this weekend," she added. "So we can't go to dinner next week."

"Pity. Where's he goin'?"

"On-site consult for a client in California." She sighed. "And Jason was so lookin' forward to your hospitality and authentic Irish cuisine." Molly smiled at Zach.

Man, she was beautiful. He returned her playful grin.

Grace was quiet a moment. "He's too kind. Perhaps youse could come to dinner Sunday night?"

"She'd choose the best time for her," Zach whispered in Molly's other ear. "By then it might be too late." He lingered there, close enough to smell that familiar scent of home.

Molly focused on her conversation. "Actually, Jason's leavin' Saturday mornin'." She paused a beat before making a suggestion. "We might be able to come tomorrow night, though."

"Oh, that's kind, but we couldn't take your last night with him."

She turned to Zach and stopped short. They were practically nose to nose, close enough for him to hear her draw in a sharp breath.

Molly pushed out of her chair, pacing away from him. "Grace, Jason knows he's leavin' us in the lurch. It'd mean a lot to him to come over and thank you for helpin' and for keepin' an eye on me while he's gone."

"Well," Grace drew out the syllable. "We couldn't take up your whole night. How's about six thirty? Then you can spend the rest of the evenin' together."

Molly again turned to Zach for guidance. Grace would pick a time convenient for her, but how pushy could they be? He urged Molly to finish up.

"Fantastic. Thank you so much, Grace. This means the world to Jason. And to me." They said their goodbyes, and Molly ended the call.

"Impressive." Zach held out his arms for a celebratory hug.

Molly seemed—or pretended—not to notice. "You'd better believe it."

He lowered his arms before it got awkward. Well, more awkward. He needed to defuse that. Humor was always a good choice. "At this rate, you'll be a real FBI agent in no time."

She flinched and slowly turned to him. Pain filled her eyes. "Zachary." Her voice held a hush of hurt, like he'd just slaughtered her puppy in front of her. "Can't you hear yourself?"

Wait, what did he do this time? "No, Molly." He took hold of her shoulder, but she jerked out of reach. He tried again. "I was teasing."

"Every time we talk about me as an agent?"

Had he done that before? "No, I just want to protect you."

That didn't help. "From what? My job?"

His mouth fell open. What was wrong with that? Did she want him to leave her hanging? Let her die?

Apparently. Molly snatched up her purse. "Don't worry about me, so. I'll be takin' that job in Phoenix." She marched away.

"Molly, wait." He started after her.

She turned back with a chopping gesture, cutting off his pursuit. "See you tomorrow night," she snapped.

He opened his mouth to protest again, but the only words that came to mind would surely make it worse: *you need me. I want to be there. You can't do it on your own.*

Zach watched her stride away. Even trying to compliment her was backfiring.

As slowly as possible, he headed for the elevator lobby, but Molly was still there, waiting. Knowing his luck, they'd end up stuck in the elevator together.

He took a detour for the water fountain. He hadn't even taken a sip when Kent walked out of the restroom.

"Oh, hey," Kent said, like he'd been meaning to talk to Zach.

"Yeah?"

"Molly's something, huh?"

"'Something'?"

"Yeah—she works all her cold cases and half of mine. She's only been here six weeks, and she's practically got a network set up. You know she has a bachelor's in applied policing and master's in international studies?"

She did? Oh, yeah, he knew that. Garda College and then DePaul. How had he forgotten that about someone he'd planned to marry? "You're pretty attached."

Kent held up two backing-off-now palms. "No worries, man. Definitely not stepping on your turf. Just trying to give a great agent her props."

Props? Was it 1997 day? "You know, most guys only geek out this hard over electronics and sports."

Kent snorted. "Even if I were geeking out, I'm not so insecure that I can't recognize when someone's awesome at their job."

Insecure?

Kent strolled away, and this time, Zach hung back to avoid taking an elevator with him. Waiting proved to be for the best when the doors to the next car opened, revealing President—SAC Evans. He nodded to Zach. "Saint."

"Agent Evans." He boarded the elevator.

The doors closed. "So, did you have fun with Tessa last weekend?"

"Yeah, she's great."

President Evans smiled. "She's always been a hit with our kids. We don't get to see her often enough. Such a drive from North Carolina."

"Yeah, definitely a trip."

"Though I'm sure she'd make it again if there was a good reason."

Zach resisted the urge to roll his eyes. SAC Evans couldn't think he was being subtle—tough to get anywhere in the FBI with that sense of nuance. "That what she told you?" He was careful to keep the skepticism in his tone to a minimum.

The elevator slowed for their stop. "Not in so many words, but she was pretty impressed by what you did for your sister."

Zach shrugged. "I wanted to make sure we all had a good time—Lucy's getting over a tough breakup." And as the end of the evening made obvious, so was he.

Molly was moving to Phoenix, and here was SAC Evans to

remind him it wasn't too late to go after Tessa.

Of course it was. Besides, she deserved better than a guy permanently on the rebound.

Evans stepped off the elevator with a goodbye nod.

Wait. Molly was moving to Phoenix because an *Assistant* Special Agent in Charge wanted her. What if Zach convinced a Special Agent in Charge to match the offer?

Zach followed the SAC. "Agent Evans?"

He turned back. "Yes?"

"I wanted to report on the case I'm working on."

The SAC furrowed his brow. "Afraid I'm not current with the details—"

Zach held up a hand to cut off the diplomatic version of *I don't keep tabs on every case.* "I mean the other agent I'm working with—Special Agent Mary Malone." Or did Molly use her nickname as her Bureau name? How could he have no idea what name used at work?

"Everything going okay?"

"Better than okay. I kind of inserted myself into this case, and she's had to go undercover and put up with me, while balancing a full case load in counterintel."

SAC Evans surveyed him sagely. "You make her sound good."

Like someone SAC Evans would personally beg to stay in Chicago?

Not yet, and he was running out of ammo. What else had Kent said? "She's going above and beyond on all her cases—she's been helping me with surveillance, working her squad's cold cases and cultivating good assets."

"Be sure to write this up. Even if it doesn't get her a commendation, it'll sound good in her file." He narrowed his eyes in a knowing expression. "Are you bringing this up just because you're impressed?"

Now what? Lay the whole pathetic story on the line? *Please, President Evans, beg her to stay in Chicago so I have a chance, because she won't listen to me?*

Yeah. Persuasive. "She's important. To the Bureau." Zach looked away. SAC Evans wouldn't be put off the trail with that act.

"Keep your personal feelings out of the case and the file."

"Yes, sir." Zach bid SAC Evans goodbye and headed for his car.

Maybe he still had time, if he got that write up in quick, and made sure SAC Evans saw it. Maybe Kent should write it up. Or he and Kent could both do it, and he'd say whatever he had to to make sure the Bureau was impressed whether Molly was the ex-girlfriend he was fighting for or just another agent.

Either way, they'd only work together until they finished this case. Which might mean tomorrow night was his last shot to change her mind.

And their last shot to stop the Canavans.

TWO DAYS. No, forty-three hours. Grace tried not to pace around the coffee table. Ed was only an hour late from work. The door crept open, and Grace reminded herself not to pounce on her husband. "What took you so long?"

Ed tapped his temple. As if he had anything in that empty head of his. "Workin' late, curryin' favor." He joined her on the sofa, sketching a map over the coffee table. "Patoka." He labeled the street running by the car park of the warehouse. "Riverbend." He drummed his pencil on the cross street.

"And DontRain." She touched the rectangle by the car park.

"Right. Here's the receivin' bay with a ramp—where you'd be wantin' your car."

"What security do they have in the warehouse?" Pearse interjected. "Is that bay door alarmed?"

"It's mildly surprised."

Grace stared at Ed a long moment. A pun? No Yeats quote?

Ed pressed on. "Infrared sensor, but I think from lookin' at it, the sensor could be compromised easily. Flip it upside down or loosen one screw. Doubt there's a secondary alarm."

Grace fired a glare at her husband. "Famous last words. Are there cameras? Remote access? Motion sensors?"

Ed floundered a moment.

"Time for Eddie Shore to worry about his 'job security.' You only have one day at work to do this, you know yourself."

"Of course I do. 'Hunger fiercely after truth.'"

They had to know everything about this warehouse before they went in. Nothing left to chance.

Molly pivoted to walk another round of her building's lobby, shifting the parcel of soda bread from hand to hand. She'd only taken the time to stop by her favorite bakery, load up her handbag with the emergency essentials and wrap the bread in a kitchen towel, so she was half an hour early.

This was it. All the other assignments, all the other meetings with Grace and Ed had led up to tonight. If Donal was to be believed, they had one final chance to avert whatever the Canavans were planning. Tonight was her chance to prove herself to Zachary and everyone else at the FBI.

Most of all, tonight was their last chance to get it right—and save dozens or even hundreds of lives. To stop another Omagh.

Molly checked the time again: quarter of six. Where was Zachary? Not that she was looking forward to an evening with him outside of work, not after the hames she'd made of everything between them.

With each step, she repeated her objectives: bring up Uncle Teague. Speak in Irish. Condemn Fine Gael. Get in on the plan.

After another circuit of the lobby, each goal was burned into her brain. She made sure she had her ring, the gaudy thing, and when she glanced up, Zachary was walking toward her. Under his jacket, he wore a navy sweater she'd given him—and looked every bit as good in it as she remembered.

Instantly, the tension building in her muscles relaxed a few ratchets. She released a sigh. Did it have to feel so good to see him?

He used to love her. Why couldn't he respect her?

Thinking like that wouldn't help either of them. He simply didn't. That was why she needed to cut her losses and tell ASAC Chin she'd accept the job in Phoenix. Soon.

She flashed Zachary a tight smile. "Ready?"

"Almost." Was it her, or was he standing very close to her?

"Everythin' all right?"

Zachary pondered her face for a moment. "I want . . ."

Molly searched his eyes, filled with yearning. Could he possibly want what she wanted?

What she wanted was to hear respect from him, the basic level of regard he'd give to anyone else in the Bureau. And that was never going to happen.

Zachary broke their gaze and started again. "I wanted to remind you how important tonight is."

Did he think she was such a rookie that she didn't know that? But work needed to come first. "I assure you, Agent Saint, I fully appreciate that."

"Good. So we're clear, we can't break cover until we have enough not just to arrest them, but to stop whatever they're planning."

"Understood. And if we don't find anythin' tonight?"

"We keep investigating."

Obviously. "Ready, so?"

Zachary checked his mobile. "You want to get there twenty minutes early?"

"I do. We'll catch them off-guard."

"Right. Good thinking." He stayed there, still closer than anyone else should've been, for another minute of silence. "Molly—"

His ringing phone interrupted him. Supreme frustration flickered to his face, and Zachary pulled out his mobile. "Sorry," he said to Molly. "This'll only take a minute." He answered, "Hello? . . . I guess." He mouthed, "Two minutes," and turned away to wander into the lounge off the entry. Xavier calling with details?

Before she could think of another excuse, the glass doors to the street swooped open again, and in walked Nate. Molly shifted the bread to her right hand and slid her left, with the impossible-to-miss engagement ring, into her pocket. "Hi, Nate," she said. Assuming he was here to see her.

He came to a stop between her and the stairs to the lounge. "Hey." His tone matched his expression: flat, resigned, but trying to make the best of this.

She tried for a sympathetic smile. "How're you doin'?"

"Hanging in there."

"Good to hear."

Nate nodded slowly. They stood there in uncomfortable silence for a few seconds. Molly checked over his shoulder. She could hear Zachary in the background, not close enough to make out the conversation, but she couldn't see much of the lounge. Nate had better make this quick.

Nate heaved a great sigh. "I just wanted to tell you," he began, but stopped haltingly.

She tried to maintain a sympathetic expression—but movement behind Nate caught her attention. Zachary. Coming up the lounge steps.

"I think I understand what you meant," Nate finished.

"And I think you're an idiot," Zachary's voice carried from behind Nate.

Nate spun toward him, as did Molly. Did he mean—oh. He was still on the phone. "But if you're happy," Zachary said. He met Molly's gaze, his face grim, before he spotted Nate. Something almost imperceptible shifted in his eyes and the corners of his mouth, but he seemed . . . angry. "Gotta go, Luce. Good luck." He put his mobile away. "How's it going, Nate?"

"Funny how we keep running into one another."

"When Molly's around." Zachary gestured in her direction. "She's helping me with some case files."

Nate raised an eyebrow. "You're with the FBI, too?"

"State Department." Zachary walked past Nate to stand by Molly, a step or two closer than a business acquaintance would. "Good thing you reintroduced us; we're making a lot of progress together."

Nate clenched his jaw. Silence settled awkwardly on them, with Molly between the two men she couldn't be with.

"Sorry to cut this short." But Zachary's grin was more like *sorry not sorry.*

Molly looked at the lobby clock. Nearly six. She didn't dare check Nate's reaction. "We do have work."

"Sure. Guess we're done anyway." Nate nodded to each of them. Zachary subtly took her elbow, but Molly tugged free.

She was sure Zachary was planning on driving, but she wasn't about to walk out of here with him in front of Nate. They'd take her car, then. She led the way to the elevators, without looking back to watch Nate. She couldn't.

As soon as the lift doors closed, Molly whirled on Zachary. "Why'd you do that?"

"What was I supposed to do? Announce our 'double date'?"

"That wasn't much better." The elevator reached the garage, and she strode off, toward her car.

Zachary followed to her green Jetta. "Sorry, I shouldn't have taken the call—just, Lucy . . ."

She would've answered for Lucy as well, with all she was going through. Molly gave him an *all right, all right* nod and got in the car.

Zachary restarted the conversation as soon as he was buckled. "She got back together with Paul."

No. "What?" How could that go better a second time around?

"Said it hurt too much to be apart." He rolled his eyes. He would. "Stupid."

Molly scowled at him. Apparently sympathy was too much to ask. "Hey, she's hurtin', and they still love each other."

"People do stupid things for love. Especially when they're hurting." They stopped for a red light, and Zachary's gaze locked on hers. "Prolonging it only hurts more. Trust me."

"I don't have to. You made sure of that."

Strained silence stole her breath—or was it Zachary's eyes, a mix of yearning and anger?

She looked away, realizing the light had turned green. She hit the gas, and they stared straight ahead in a silence as hard as stone.

She'd lost him. Again. Two weeks ago, he wanted to try again—or wanted to kiss her. Now, she was finally ready to admit the truth: she wanted to marry Zachary Saint.

But Zachary still saw her as a civilian he needed to protect. He didn't know who she really was any more than Nate had.

Molly parked outside the Canavans' building, and Zachary got out of the car first. He tried to get her door, but she was already standing by the time he offered his hand. "Are you ready to do this one more time?"

To do . . . what? To start over with Zachary? Molly studied his hand, then his expression.

Yes. She was ready. But he wasn't ready for her.

He folded his arms against the cold. "Sorry. I know. Boundaries."

Now *that* was something stupid she'd done because she was hurting. Molly fetched the soda bread, and they started for the Canavans'.

"Listen," Zachary said. "With our story tonight, and the deadline—there's a good chance this is our last shot together. If we don't find what we need, you'll be on your own."

"I know." Molly cautiously checked his eyes, but she couldn't see discouragement. Did he finally see she was just as capable as any other FBI agent?

"Sure you can handle this alone?" A double layer of doubt coated his question, slamming into those rising hopes like a lead weight.

"Meanin' you think I can't."

Zachary held up both hands defensively. "I just want to keep you safe. What is so wrong with that?"

Molly drew close enough to whisper. "You goin' to hover over me every day at work? I so wanted a nanny."

He gaped at her. How did he not understand that she deserved the basic respect he'd pay to any other agent? Molly shook her head and took the lead into the building. She'd show him, and then she'd let him go. Forever.

At precisely ten after six, Grace kissed Pearse on the cheek. Ed shook his hand. "Welcome to politics by other means."

"Whisht." Grace scoffed, then took her son by the shoulder. "Do *not* ruin this for me."

"'Course not, Mam."

"Right then." She brushed lint from his shoulders and straightened his overall. "Did you wash well, make sure you haven't any residue?"

"You're actin' like I'm a total amateur, here."

Grace fixed him with a look of *listen to your mother.* "Have to get this right. The first engagement sets the tone for the whole campaign."

Pearse rolled his eyes. "I got it, Mam."

"All right." She gave him a nod with military precision. "Don't ruin this."

"He won't—if you'll ever let him out of the flat." Ed yanked open the front door.

Grace gave her son one last pat and sent him out to begin the first effort of the final battle for Irish independence.

Nervy jitters vibrated through her as she shut the door behind Pearse. This time it would take. It had to.

She turned back to Ed. "Just have to get through dinner, and we'll follow."

"Can't believe you invited Molly and your man tonight."

At least he was using her name. Baby steps. "We'll have them out in plenty of time—probably before Pearse is in the warehouse. Besides, gives us an alibi."

He still muttered under his breath. "Better finish the dinner."

"Put away the schematics, and read through the letter while you're at it."

They both set about their work. But when the knock came less than five minutes later, Grace had only finished drying Pearse's dinnerware. Grace glanced back at the living room as she twisted the doorknob—and stopped short.

Ed was still poring over the latest draft of the letter and the schematics strewn across the coffee table. Had he not heard the knock? "Ed!" she whispered.

He looked up; Grace pointed to the door. Without another word, he hurriedly pushed the loose papers into a pile. Grace waited while Ed shoved the papers into a coffee table book and stowed the book and the planning notebook on the lower shelf of the table. There.

She opened the door to the couple beaming in the hall. "Ah, but you're early!"

"*Dia dhuit.*" Molly smiled with the standard Irish greeting.

"*Dia is Muire dhaoibh.*" Grace gave the reply and welcomed them in.

Next time, Molly would be on their side. But not tonight.

Zach hadn't realized he'd signed up for *The Molly Show*, but she was working the Canavans so well, it was hard not to sit back and applaud. By the time they finished the chicken, bacon and leek casserole—which went perfectly with Molly's soda bread—even Ed was returning Grace's *see? I told you* smirk with one of *all right, you win.*

Grace collected their empty plates.

"Mum always said that was Uncle Teague's favorite meal. *Go raibh maith agat,*" Molly said with her sincerest smile.

Zach opted for the English equivalent. "Thank you."

Grace cast Ed another look like *See? See?* Ed wrinkled his nose in reply, but it still carried that undercurrent of capitulation. In the last hour, Molly had spoken Irish, mentioned her parents and uncle, bemoaned the state of Irish politics and started a fantasy hurling team.

His main contribution was straight man, allowing Molly to show off her knowledge of everything Irish. Making him prop fiancé extraordinaire. Molly's hand landed on his knee. Zach drew in a silent breath, willing himself to act like that was totally normal.

For the last month, every time they'd been with the Canavans, they'd been in public. He hadn't realized how lucky he'd been: in public, they could pretend to be together without going for all-out PDA. But in private, they had to sell this relationship, and Molly had every little touch down pat.

Either he was way too aware of each contact, or she was way too good at this. Probably both. Zach scooped up her hand in his.

He only had one thing to bring to the table—or, really, under it: a paper sticking out from the large book on the rickety coffee table's bottom shelf. In plain sight, perfectly legal for even an undercover officer. He'd glimpsed Ed doing something with the table as Grace opened the door—arriving early was another good call by Molly—and Zach doubted Ed was simply straightening up for company.

Zach checked on Ed, who was staring at his and Molly's clasped hands like they should be flogged in the stocks. All night, he hadn't left them alone for a minute, chaperoning them like teenagers.

Or FBI agents waiting to get at whatever he'd hidden in that book.

Grace returned with a tray of fresh plates. "Sticky toffee puddings!" she announced. She passed out four chipped bowls filled with dark, sweet date cakes and toffee sauce.

Zach watched Molly for the first few bites of her dessert. If they finished at different times, maybe Ed and Grace would each take a round of dishes into the kitchen. Molly seemed to be savoring her dessert, so Zach stuffed the rest of his cake in his mouth and practically swallowed it whole.

"Ma'am, this is amazin'." He turned to Molly. "Maybe we should have this for our weddin' cake—you know, with the Irish theme."

"Massive, love." Neither of them dared to point out to the Canavans the dessert's English roots.

"Let me help you, love." Molly grabbed a paper napkin and leaned toward him. Oh, no, no—he tried to take it from her, but she maneuvered past him to wipe sauce off his lower lip. He held as still as he could until she finished. Then she stroked her thumb across his lip. For a long second, he stared into her eyes, and she looked back, just like she had in that bakery, in the parking garage, the night of their first kiss.

Then she turned back to her food.

The woman was giving new meaning to the word torture.

"Finished already?" Grace popped up to take Zach's empty bowl into the kitchen.

"Thank you so much, Grace," Molly called over the sound of running water. "This has all been just deadly." As if she sensed Zach's plan, she polished off her pudding as soon as Grace was busy in the kitchen.

Without a word, Ed took Molly's bowl from her hands.

"You're welcome. Just take me a minute to wash up. Ed, what're ye at, ya skiver?" Grace shouted. "Get the girl's delph!"

"I did." He dropped to a mutter: "Ya 'rough beast.'" He carried her dish out of the room.

And they were alone. Zach pushed through his suddenly racing pulse. He grabbed the book—a glossy hardback of misty Irish landscapes—and shook out the loose sheets.

"Were you needin' any help in the kitchen?" Molly dug her cell phone out of her purse, and Zach spread the papers ripped from a spiral notebook across the table.

"No, we're grand, thank you," Grace replied.

Zach scanned the pages while Molly snapped photos with her cell camera. One page was clearly a map, but they weren't so helpful as to label it with names or addresses. One of the streets running by the building, however, was named. He pushed the paper over to Molly. "You know it?"

She shook her head and took a picture.

"Send that to me and X."

"Can we get either of you a gargle?" Ed's voice carried from the kitchen. Molly and Zach glanced at one another.

"We're okay," Zach called back. They had to hurry.

"Oh, that's right, watchin' your girlish figure. How's about a nice ice water?" The derision in his tone was unmistakable.

"Could you make that two?" Molly called. Stalling. Good.

Zach looked back to the papers. The next sheet was a letter. He meant to skim, but by the end of the first paragraph, dread landed in his gut, thick and bitter.

> The Irish patriot Pádraig (Patrick Henry) Pearse famously wrote, "Ireland unfree shall never be at peace." He sealed that sentiment with his blood—and now so do the American people. If Ireland unfree shall never be at peace, then neither will anywhere in the world that supports England's continued tyranny.
>
> VIOLENCE WILL BE ANSWERED WITH VIOLENCE. TERROR WILL BE ANSWERED WITH TERROR. WE DECLARE WAR ON ANY COUNTRY THAT CONTINUES TO APPEASE ENGLAND'S OPPRESSION. THE PARADE WAS BUT THE OPENING VOLLEY. WAR ON ENGLAND AND ALL ITS ALLIES WILL CONTINUE UNTIL THE LAST

BRITISH TROOP IS DRIVEN FROM IRISH SHORES.

MERE ANARCHY IS LOOSED UPON THE WORLD,
THE BLOOD-DIMMED TIDE IS LOOSED, AND EVERYWHERE
THE CEREMONY OF INNOCENCE IS DROWNED.

"Bingo," Zach whispered. He tapped the word PARADE. Molly set aside a framed photo and snapped a picture of the letter, too. They only had another minute, tops. He glanced over the other papers: sketches, calculations, aerial photos.

"Enough to arrest them?" Molly asked.

"If the bomb's already in place, all they have to do is keep quiet until the parade."

"What do we do?"

"Find the bomb before they suspect anything, then arrest them. But they've got to lead us to it."

The background noise of running water stopped. Footsteps sounded in the short hall between the kitchen and living room.

Caught. His blood turned to ice. Zach shuffled the papers together, but the ragged edges torn from a notebook snagged, making a neat pile impossible. He stuffed the papers into the book, though their tampering was obvious.

They needed a better cover. Something. Anything.

Molly swept everything onto the floor. Before he could ask, she grabbed two fistfuls of his sweater and dragged him back onto the couch.

She threw herself backward and pulled him with her so fast Zach barely had time to catch himself on the back of the couch instead of landing on her.

Molly kicked one foot onto the table. "Zachary," she murmured.

He whipped around to look at her. Again, before he could ask about the plan, Molly slid her arms around his neck—and kissed him.

MOLLY HAD NO IDEA what she was doing.

Kissing Zachary was supposed to be a cover, but it didn't feel like either of them were pretending.

This couldn't just be part of his cover, not the way he was kissing her—just as he always had.

Could that mean—?

"What're ye at?" At Ed's gruff reproof, Molly's racing heart juddered to a stop. Zachary abruptly pulled back and Molly caught her breath. It couldn't have been ten seconds and she'd forgotten Ed was coming.

This plan was stupid. Dangerously stupid.

Zachary stared into her eyes for half of a stunned, breathless moment before he looked up to Ed. "Oh—oh, 'scuse us. Sorry, sir. We both are." He stood and helped Molly up from the worn sofa's orange velvet.

Appearing appropriately chagrined wasn't hard. Heat—more anger at herself than embarrassment—crept up her neck. She'd let herself get carried away, all wrapped up in her stupid feelings. What if the threat had been even greater?

"What're ye at?" Ed demanded again, doubling his volume. Molly tried not to flinch, but her pulse quickened. They had to get out of here.

Ed's weathered face grew red. That was more frightening than the shouting. Molly shifted in the silence. "Sorry," she repeated.

Ed gritted his teeth, gathering his fury for another blow.

This wasn't a storm to wait out. "We'll just be goin'," Molly said. She willed herself not to glance at the mess on the floor, looking at Zachary instead. He kept his eyes fast on Ed. His expression still carried traces of sheepishness, helped by the pink blush at the tips of his ears.

"We got carried away," Zachary acknowledged. "Guess we forgot where we were. We apologize."

Ed strode across the room and snatched up the large hardback book from the floor. "And what're you doin' with this? It was under the table, so."

Her lungs seemed to shrink, but she drew in a long, slow breath. They just had to play this cool and get out. Ed had no idea they were a threat.

"I must've kicked it," Molly said. "I'm sorry."

"It was under the table. How'd you manage that?" Ed ground out.

"I was lookin' at the pictures." Zachary glanced at Molly. "I was thinkin' of takin' Molly to Ireland for our honeymoon."

How else could she look innocent? She'd help clean it up. Molly bent to pick up the papers. "Hope I didn't hurt anythin'."

"Don't you move." Ed grabbed the loose leaves before Molly touched them. She straightened.

"Stay right there." Ed moved back to block their escape.

Molly's throat tensed, but she kept projecting the image of embarrassment, head bowed as she picked up her coat. "We should be headin'."

Ed barely budged. "Bit late for that, ya slapper."

She didn't react to the insult, simply brushing past. At the door, Molly reached for Zachary behind her—but he wasn't there.

He was jabbing a finger in Ed's chest, towering over the older man. "Don't you ever talk 'bout Molly that way." He didn't even flinch in his cover. "You ain't too old for a whuppin'."

Time to get out. Molly hurried to his side to tug his arm. "Let's go."

Grace walked into the room, still drying her hands on a dishcloth. "Headin' already?"

Silence fell, thick and awkward. Zachary lowered his hand and moved away from Ed.

"We are," Molly murmured. "Sorry. Thank you so much for havin' us."

Zachary picked up his coat, and they walked to the door, the

Canavans' eyes following them every step: Grace in bewilderment, Ed in indignant rage. Maybe suspicion? Molly barely dared to breathe until they slipped out of the shabby flat. As Zachary closed the door behind them, Molly glimpsed Ed's final mistrustful glare.

Molly's mind raced through the new intel: photos, maps, letter. Enough to find the exact target. A parade, yes, but which one?

Another thought fought its way to the forefront of her mind: she'd just thrown off her coronary Kevlar and dived into a firefight.

While they waited for the lift, Zachary sent the coded message to the surveillance crew to let them know the Canavans could be on the move. The derelict elevator finally arrived. Zachary waited until the lift doors scraped closed to speak. "Think they bought it?"

"Hope so." She looked to Zachary, and he turned to her.

Before she could think better of it, she closed the distance between them. Zachary twined his fingers into her hair, pulling her in to finish what they'd just started.

This kiss was everything the last one had been and more. His lips moved over hers with intense tenderness. She tried to return the sentiment, to convey the feelings she didn't dare put into words.

The elevator shuddered—or was that just in her mind? Molly drew back, drew a breath, drew her wits about her.

When she'd kissed him before, she'd done it on purpose. For a reason. This time, she'd done it on impulse—but what was she getting herself into? With someone who wouldn't respect her?

"You okay?" Zachary asked.

She pulled free from his grasp. "I need to think."

After an awkward silence, the lift screeched to a stop. Her last chance to say something. "It was only a cover," Molly said. She didn't dare meet his eyes. "Borrowin' a page from *Escape the Turkmen Prison.*"

A book he'd given her before they'd dated. Zachary searched her face.

She had to explain better. "I only did that because we needed to have made a mess."

His jaw dropped an inch. "Well, you definitely did that."

"I—" The doors finally screeched open and the words died in her throat. What could she do, proclaim her love to a man who'd take her kisses but not her heart, or who she really was?

No, she had to make sure she never forgot herself like that again. "Pleasure bein' engaged, but appears we're through with weddin' plannin'."

In silence, they walked out of the building. Molly itched to get at the photos on her mobile, but she wouldn't feel safe until they were in the car. They got in, and she started the car, then whipped out her mobile. She sent the photos she'd taken to Xavier. Once they were off, she pulled into traffic.

"What will you tell Nate?" Zachary finally broke the silence, but kept his gaze on the windshield.

Why would she do that? "Nothin'. Do I have to file notice with *you* every time I kiss someone?"

Zachary snorted. "What are you talking about?"

"Nate and I broke up."

"Is that what I interrupted tonight?"

"It was Sunday."

She watched his reaction—a smile tugged at the corner of his mouth.

Heat rose in her chest. "What are you grinnin' about? You had your chance, Special Agent Saint."

The smile instantly disappeared, and Zachary scoffed. "Like Nate O'Shaughnessy and Jason Tolliver did? You're on a roll, Malone."

"Jason Tolliver isn't real."

He turned to her. "No, but I am," he bit off. "You think this was nothing to me?"

"Of course. All your cover goin' to you head, didn't you say?"

"I'm not talking about the assignment." They stopped at a red light, and Zachary stared at Molly. "You never gave me a chance."

"I seem to remember *you* broke up with *me*, and as far as I can see, our lives are headin' the same directions they were last summer, whatever the devil that was supposed to mean."

"You tell me: did you break up with Nate because you had better things to do than marry him?"

The car's heater seemed to kick on full force, hot air pressing in on her. "What?"

"You have a lot to accomplish."

How did he know that? "We've never discussed—"

"That necklace."

She touched the emerald pendant he'd given her.

"Wasn't what I'd planned to give you. I had to pick it up at the last minute."

"Brilliant. You forgot my birthday, too?"

Every muscle in his face was carved from stone. "It went with something else—what I planned to give you before you got 'The Call.'"

"What, earrin's? A bracelet? Fan-freakin'-tastic, Zachary." What could her FBI offer possibly have to do with anything?

"No, Molly. Not earrings."

Raw pain shone in Zachary's eyes. What else could go with a necklace?

A car horn broke their silence. The light was green. She tore her gaze from his and started through the intersection, the streetlight glinting off her gaudy fake ring.

Wait. A chill of realization crawled down her back. Zachary couldn't mean . . .

Her head spun. He'd wanted to marry her. He'd transferred here—put his DC fast track on hold—and she'd said she had a lot to accomplish. Small wonder he'd dumped her. Different directions indeed. And her direction had been running away.

This should've been good news. Just as she'd finally accepted she did want to marry him, she'd find out he'd wanted to marry her? And yet somehow it felt like she'd been lied to. Betrayed.

He didn't give *her* a chance. "I don't understand. We never talked about this."

"Didn't have to. Once, when you were talking to Lucy, I . . . 'overheard' enough."

She probably didn't want to know what that meant, coming from a spy.

In her pocket, her mobile vibrated. She needed this distraction. At the next light, Molly glanced at the message: from Xavier. *Which parade?*

That was the right question. She needed to focus on anything but this disaster.

But she couldn't scroll through her photos now. She made the last few turns, checking for surveillance, before she pulled up beside Zachary's Subaru, parked down the block from her building.

"I'm sorry," Zachary said softly. "Just seemed like it wasn't enough to change your mind." He paused a heartbeat. "*I* wasn't enough."

The pain in his voice sliced through her again. But this was a pain she knew. "You know, you keep tellin' me *I'm* not enough."

"What?"

"You refuse see me as a peer, or a 'real FBI agent.' You never believed in me, that I could get this job. I saw your face when I told you I got 'The Call.'"

"Your parents were IRA." His volume rose, defensive. "The FBI would be crazy—"

She shook her head. "You didn't know that then."

"The Bureau told me when I was at St. Adelaide."

"All this time." Molly stared swords at him. "My parents were with Special Branch. With the Gardaí."

"Now I know."

"You're admittin' you never thought I could get the job."

Zachary held up his hands like that would help his argument. "No, that's not—"

"Do you think I'm a good FBI agent? Good enough to handle this assignment on my own?"

He opened and closed his mouth. Twice. And still no answer.

The final slap. "Exactly."

"You know, if I were anyone else, you'd roll your eyes and do it anyway instead of taking everything I say the wrong way."

"Well, I expect more from you. I expected you to care about who I am, my dreams, my capabilities." She fixed him with all the steel she could temper into her gaze and voice. "You've never bothered to see the real me. I'm not just a damsel in distress."

Zachary stared at her, stunned.

A car horn honked behind them. "Get out, Zach. Now."

"Wait, Moll—"

"I *have* waited. I've waited for you to get it through your thick head I can do this job without you constantly hanging over me." She turned to stare forward, gripping the steering wheel. "I'm done waitin'. Get. Out."

The horn sounded again, longer and louder. "Fine." Zach yanked his door open and slammed it behind him.

Molly hit the gas, turning into her garage faster than necessary. She parked in the closest spot, not caring whose slot she took.

Her mobile buzzed in her hand. A call from Zachary. She dismissed it without answering—and then she remembered Xavier's text.

Which parade? She paged through her pictures, then zoomed in on an aerial photo, a brown square with a green quatrefoil pattern in the center. She knew that block. Buckingham Fountain. Grant Park.

If that was their target, they were after the main city parade. A million people would attend. Tomorrow.

This could be the worst terrorist attack . . . ever.

And Molly had just kicked her partner out.

They should've been on the same team—in so many ways—but she could work as well alone. Especially when so many people were in danger in less than twenty-four hours.

His call rolled to voicemail—she must've seen his number. Zach sighed and hung up to try again.

What did she mean, he didn't see her as a real FBI agent? Just because he wanted to help—okay, more than help. But she needed him. She was barely out of the Academy. She couldn't handle this on her own.

Except she had. Memories paraded through his mind: Molly at lunch with the Canavans, trying on wedding dresses, getting in with Grace, coming up with a cover tonight when he blanked. He'd told SAC Evans he was impressed and written up the commendation, but even then he hadn't appreciated how much she'd done.

All this time he still thought of her as someone he needed to protect. Like Lucy. But Molly was the one protecting Lucy from

Grace.

He'd always loved that about her. How had he forgotten?

He'd really screwed this up.

Zach picked up his phone again. Even if he left a voicemail, what was he supposed to say? She hadn't said anything close to what he had. He'd admitted he bought an engagement ring and moved here for her, and she hadn't even said she cared.

But her expression—the shock, the horror at what she'd done. Or was it horror at what he was saying?

His phone vibrated. Before he dared to hope it was Molly calling, Xavier's name and photo popped up.

Right. They had a terrorist bombing to avert. As always, his personal life would have to wait. He'd waited last year for the transfer to Chicago. He'd waited when the Bureau gave him an assignment the weekend he'd planned to visit Molly to propose. He'd waited when Molly got "The Call." And tonight was no different.

Only Molly could afford the luxury of not waiting.

Zach answered his boss's call. "The Canavans gave their surveillance the slip," Xavier began immediately. "I got the pictures. We hunting for this building?"

"Yeah, I'll put in a request, and some clerk will find the address by Monday."

"Whoa, no, we don't have time for that." X sounded offended he'd even suggest standard operating procedure.

"St. Patrick's Day isn't until next Friday."

"Molly didn't tell you? Let me talk to her."

"Um . . . she's not here."

Xavier was silent. "Listen, man. I'm saying this as a friend: you're an idiot."

"Thanks." Like Zach needed another vote of no confidence after Molly's expression tonight. "What did she tell you?"

"She just texted. They're targeting the city parade. It's *tomorrow*, and a million people are supposed to be there."

"A million? An actual million?"

"Yeah. Including the mayor and the governor."

And Molly's little Irish dancers. Zach had never been to the Chicago parade. He tried to picture the route—by Grant Park? A million people along that street?

A recipe for disaster. No, for a massacre.

Tomorrow.

Zach checked the time. "Where do they keep the floats beforehand?"

"Probably in a warehouse."

"Hang on." Zach consulted the photos Xavier had forwarded him. The pencil sketch of a rectangle by a street—a building. On Patoka Avenue. He opened his GPS app. The street ran right through some industrial districts. He scrolled through the map. Patoka was almost three miles long, and the overhead map wouldn't cut it.

Could be worse. "Ready to drag the strip?"

"Yeah. I'll see what I can do for backup. You're lucky I'm in town this weekend, man."

Zach almost laughed as he pulled into traffic. He was anything but lucky. How long did they have to find this place?

Grace dialed Pearse as Ed pulled into the DontRain warehouse car park. Pearse had better have got this right. She noted the dark car park—no light above the side door—with satisfaction. The first phase of Pearse's job had gone off well. Nerves gnawed at her middle.

"'Round the back," Pearse answered the phone.

"'Tisn't alarmed, is it?" Grace didn't dare look at Ed, originator of the awful pun.

"Has an infrared sensor. I've fixed it."

"Motion sensors?"

"Only in the front offices."

Grace hesitated. Things went wrong when people took that attitude.

"I made sure, Mam."

Ed piped up. "Security code's six five one six. Then hit pound."

Grace gaped at him a moment. Why hadn't he told her this

sooner? She relayed the code to Pearse and waited.

Pearse crowed in triumph. "System's disabled."

"They'll think my supervisor's responsible." Ed almost cracked a smile. "Never liked him."

"'Round the back, then." Grace fell silent as they slid into the warehouse's shadow. "Boyo'd better be right."

"Learned from the best, didn't he?"

"We're the best because we've experience. He hasn't."

Ed pulled the car to the last bay of the back wall. The garage-type door at the top of the cement ramp slowly raised, and they rolled up into the warehouse bay, right up to a set of racks.

Almost too easy.

Pearse hit the switch to close the door against the snow blowing in. Ed and Grace got out of the car, moving with the stealth and efficiency from decades of clandestine attacks. Pearse and Ed retrieved the squib from its hiding place in the boot.

A banker's box sat in the trunk. A second bomb? "What's this, then?" Grace demanded.

"Sorry," Pearse said. "For your man, Allen; didn't know if I'd get another chance to get it down to the car."

She got her pistol and the tools before Pearse slammed the boot shut. "We can still be quiet." Grace scowled at her son as Ed passed around the torches. "We don't need any extra attention."

"Sorry, Mam. First time jitters." Pearse directed them to the target. "O'Connell Publishin's down this middle row."

He led the way, carrying the bomb between him and Ed, Grace bringing up the rear.

"Like the old days, yeah?" Pearse glanced from Grace to Ed.

"Complete with chatty novice," Ed grumbled.

Pearse took the hint. He said nothing further and led them down the aisle, past the empty floats. She could almost see the rightful paraders from Pádraig Pearse down to her own brother. They'd be proud of her, this ghostly procession.

They reached the chosen float. The flatbed was exactly what they'd expected after studying at the last three years' floats. Green fringe dragged along the bottom edge with more green frilled crepe decorating the sides of the risers. Fake grass covered the main surface and gold shamrocks festooned the white gazebo in the middle of the float.

But the ostentatious display of "Irish" pride had nothing to do with why they'd chosen that float. If that'd been their only criterion, they could've used any of the fleet. DontRain was singlehandedly keeping alive an entire industry of Irish kitsch.

No, they'd chosen O'Connell Publishing for this honor because of that book—another anonymous coward had come forward with a so-called exposé on the republican movement "from the inside," though he didn't have the bottle to sign his real name to it. Using the publisher behind the book would make the bomb all the more poignant—and attention-grabbing, after the headlines that book generated.

Grace took her place on the risers at the back of the float to hold the torches, one thing she'd been sure to invest in. She shone the light on the right spot, and Pearse and Ed set the bomb down gently. The fertilizer/diesel mix, and even the rest of it, the C-4 and the blasting caps, were stable enough that it didn't require much caution, but the glass jar they were sealed in was another story. Crack that, and they'd have bomb sniffing dogs swarming them.

Contrary to the impression Pearse had received, this wasn't like the old days, not really. In the old days, they could be bold. Sure, there was a lot of skulking around, a lot of care about keeping their identities unknown to police, but there was also the strength of their numbers that gave them license to do nearly anything. The one thing she missed about the organization.

Without a word, Ed and Pearse went to the tool kit for cable ties and electrical tools, then dragged the bomb with them under the flat-bed. Grace was alone with the muffled noise of the continued install. For several tense minutes, the occasional soft tearing of crepe paper was the only sound in the warehouse while they moved under the float and back out. Pearse fetched the trigger, a mobile phone with wires dangling from it. He carefully applied super glue gel, curled his hand under the float and held the mobile inside the plywood till it dried.

Ed gave a satisfied sigh. "Where's the electrical tape?"

"I thought you got it."

Ed frowned. "Wires might drag. Don't want anyone seein'."

"Should be somethin' around for that, yeah?" Pearse checked for his parents' approval. Ed nodded, and Pearse grabbed a torch from Grace. He pointed to the southwest. "That way?"

"Only the break room over there."

Pearse saluted, jogged to the north end of the row and turned east.

"Nothin' that way either," Ed muttered. He stalked off toward the south, turning east at the opposite end of the row to his son.

After waiting a reasonable amount of time without results, Grace grumbled to herself. Men. Couldn't find their nose with two hands and a map. She climbed down from her perch and started for the car. Even if she didn't find the tape first, she could still search the whole northwest quadrant of the warehouse before they returned.

Twelve hours until the floats left the warehouse. Plenty of time.

26

AFTER AN HOUR, Zach had scoured the north mile of Patoka Avenue block by block. The Canavans' overhead map of a warehouse and one street wasn't helping. Even an aerial photo wouldn't do them much good, since a rectangular warehouse could hardly be unique in an industrial district.

He'd found one building that seemed to match the sketch, with a parking lot between the cross street and the longer side of the building, but a nasal spray company was *not* the right place. Xavier's last text said he'd had the same luck at the other end of the street. With only one mile left between them, they were running out of possibilities.

Man, he wished Molly were here to help—but that was his own fault.

At least it'd stopped snowing. Zach pulled over on the next block and scanned the buildings at each corner. Nothing like the sketch. He puffed out a breath and drove on to the next intersection.

Once again, he pulled over and started with the building closest to him, the northwest corner of the intersection. No parking lot. Southwest corner: parking lot behind a chain-link fence, building facing Patoka. Southeast corner: dark parking lot with another chain-link fence. The building was hard to make out without a light on this side. Zach pulled back into the thin traffic and rolled through the intersection slowly, craning his neck for a view down Riverbend Drive.

A parking lot in front of the building, the long side of the warehouse facing Riverbend. Like the sketch.

His heart rate spiked a split second. Zach parked quickly, fighting off the surge of nervous energy. Grabbing his gear from the glove box—gun, creds, and lock picks, just in case—he glanced at the lot. No cars visible. No lights in the building.

He tucked his creds and picks into his pockets and his gun into his waistband holster, covering it with his sweater. With his head down, Zach walked across the street like he had somewhere to be, somewhere he went often. He didn't slow or look up until he was across the street from the building. Bricks showed through the building's faded logo: DONTRAIN PARADE FLOATS.

Bingo. Zach backtracked to the car and ran through his legal options. The map wasn't the strongest evidence, and without anything amiss here, not enough for exigent circumstances. Maybe enough probable cause. He just had to find a cooperative judge at—he checked his phone—ten o'clock on a Friday night.

Could be an easier route. He called X. "You there?" Xavier answered.

"Yeah—wait, where?"

"The address Molly sent."

How'd Molly find this place? "Didn't get it yet. What's the address?"

"Riverbend and Patoka. DontRain Parade Floats. Lame name."

"Yeah, I'm here. She say anything else?"

"She's hunting down the owner to get search consent. Unless you see a car in the lot?"

Zach checked again, in case one materialized. "Nope."

"Hear a baby crying?"

Zach didn't dignify the overused "exigent circumstances" pretext.

"Have you gotten any of her texts?"

"Not since we left the Canavans. My phone must be acting up."

X didn't respond at first. "What did you do?"

Zach leaned back against the headrest. "Didn't propose when I should've." Even if she would've said no.

Again Xavier was silent. "I didn't know—"

"You two can start a club. Text her about it." Bitterness snuck into his tone.

"Yeah, I'll just let you know when she's got consent."

"Great."

If she could get ahold of the guy. They could still try a warrant.

Zach paged through his contacts for the judges he usually called. Who might be available for a warrant?

He gave the building a once-over. He shouldn't think this way, but criminals didn't have a right to privacy in a crime scene they'd broken and entered. As long as an owner or employee wasn't responsible, the evidence would stand even if the search was bad. Probably.

What if they had a man on the inside at DontRain? A defense lawyer would throw out a search in a millisecond. Not worth the risk. Zach started with Judge Sanderson. Sanderson seemed to like him.

But fifteen minutes later, he hadn't reached even one judge programmed in his phone. He could try the clerk to see who was available, but you never knew whether you'd get Hang-'em-High Flye or Never-Met-a-Warrant-I-Liked Newton. But before he resorted to the clerk's number, his phone rang—X.

"Got it. On my way."

"Great." Zach tucked his phone in his pocket—then hesitated. Should he call in reinforcements? Molly?

She hadn't called back. She hadn't texted. She'd probably ignore a text from him, but he had to try. Zach sent her a quick *10-78.* Any backup beyond that was Xavier's call.

Zach couldn't risk bringing his phone in with him, even on silent. He tossed the phone under the driver's seat and crossed the street. X would be here soon, and they'd need all the time they could get to search for the bomb.

They could still cancel the parade—and they would if this didn't go well—but this might be their only chance to catch the Canavans.

Zach spotted a side door in the shadows. Good thing he'd practiced picking locks with his eyes closed—it was nearly that dark. The lock gave after only scrubbing the pins. Zach cracked the door, pocketed his picks and drew his gun.

He opened the door slowly until he had enough room to slip in, sweeping the room before he stepped all the way inside. He held the door latch to keep it silent as it closed.

He was alone in the warehouse, or so it seemed in the dim moon shining through the skylights. Should've grabbed his flashlight.

Just inside, Zach hesitated. He should wait for Xavier. X wouldn't be long, and he was more hesitant about picking a lock than Zach. Molly would do it, though. If she was coming.

They were on a deadline. The floats would leave the warehouse in less than ten hours. Even if they cancelled the parade, if this was a timed bomb and they had to get the bomb squad involved, every second would count. X would have to catch up.

Zach started a counter-clockwise circuit of the warehouse. The background noise from the street made his efforts at stealth moot. He rounded the southwest corner of the warehouse racks and saw the first row of parade floats, empty and silent.

He counted the floats in sight. At least ten. A million people would be there. They could kill thousands. Tens of thousands.

Zach continued along the wall until it turned away from him, making a corner. Zach followed around to a door. Seizing the element of surprise, he flung open the door and swept the room with his gun.

A bland, empty kitchenette greeted him. Another door on the far wall. With the same caution as before, he crossed the room and threw open that door, to a small bathroom. The single stall was also empty.

Maybe the Canavans had already finished. They could've even split town, for all he knew.

Zach headed out to the main warehouse, this time keeping his back to a rack parallel to the back wall. He'd only made it a few feet, scanning the second row of floats, when he saw it: a pile of clutter, unidentifiable at this distance, but obviously out of place in the pristine warehouse.

His heartbeat, deliberate and loud, filled his ears. This was his chance.

He should finish his sweep of the whole facility. But he was nearly half done without any signs of life. Maybe they'd left to get something—the bomb? Maybe they were done and merely careless.

If he checked it out and the bomb was there, he could have the bomb squad en route before he finished his sweep. Checking would take thirty seconds. The risk was minuscule. Right?

Zach pushed aside the nagging doubt. He was just too well-programmed with protocol; breaking from procedure a little bit hardly ever hurt.

He jogged down the row of parade floats to the clutter that had drawn his attention. Garbage bag, tool box, and a few tools lying about.

They were definitely coming back. He ducked down to glance under the float. A cheap flip phone was stuck to the plywood.

They'd started installing it. He'd just seen one of these. Where?

No time to think: time to get out and call the bomb squad. Zach turned to go. He'd barely taken a step toward the door when he heard the gasp behind him. Every muscle tensed. He spun to face the sound and raised his gun, but a super bright flashlight beam blinded him.

"Jason?"

Grace.

A less experienced agent would've broken cover and confessed all—definitely not what Zach needed. A better agent would play his cover harder. "Grace, what're you doin' here?"

The best agent would've cleared the whole warehouse before coming back to this. Idiot.

"I should be askin' you the same thing."

"My company's tasked with logistics on the parade. I'm makin' sure everythang's in order 'fore I leave tomorrow."

Grace finally lowered the flashlight from his face. "With a gun?"

"Cain't be too safe. This *is* Chicago."

"What's this?" A man's voice rang out behind him—Irish accent, familiar, *not* Ed.

Paddy?

This was bad.

Zach moved to see the newcomer without turning his back on Grace. Again, he was blinded by a flashlight.

"Allen?" Definitely Paddy.

The bomb trigger—exactly like Paddy's.

"What're ye at?" Ed's voice came from Grace's direction. Zach spun back again, maneuvering to keep everyone in sight. Ed didn't shine his flashlight in his eyes, allowing Zach to see every furious line etched into his brow. "Jason."

"Y'all, let's don't go jumpin'—" A blow to the back of his head cut Zach off. Pain exploded through his skull.

He stumbled forward, hoping to stop himself on the float. Instead, he landed on the floor on his back. The ceiling rafters' distant shadows flickered and reeled above him. Bursts of pain blossomed behind his eyes with every blink and heartbeat.

He had to get his bearings—he had to get his brain working—he had to get out.

But at that second, he couldn't do anything more than cling to the edge of consciousness.

This wasn't possible. Grace clenched her fists, barely containing her rage. Jason, here? Pearse strode to where Jason had fallen and raised his arm to strike again—but Grace seized his hand at the top of its arc.

"We're not bashin' his head in."

"We're not?" Ed wrenched Jason's gun from his fingers. "We caught him rapid. The gouger needs killin'."

Grace took the spanner from Pearse and tossed it toward the tool kit. "Get him up before he comes to. And watch the blood."

Ed and Pearse obeyed, roughly hauling Jason to his feet. He moaned and made a vague effort to escape, but Ed and Pearse held firm. Blood ran down Jason's neck. Grace checked the floor. He'd gone and left a mark. So much for a perfect job.

She mopped up the blood on the floor with a paper towel she'd packed, then retrieved the tools. "Where will we put him?"

"Kitchen. Over there." Ed gestured toward the building's southwest corner.

"That'll do." Before they started for the kitchen, though, Jason tried to pull free. Grace came up and slapped the back of his skull where Pearse had hit him. Jason cried out, but continued to struggle until Ed kicked his knee.

Since their captive was obviously recovering his wits, they hurried to the kitchen. Ed and Pearse shoved Jason into a metal folding chair, clamping a hand on each of his shoulders to hold him there.

Grace tossed the tool kit on the table. She gave Ed a handful of cable ties. "To the chair," she said, wiping his blood from her fingers. "Wrists and ankles."

Before he released Jason's shoulders, Ed gave the back of his head another slap. This time, he only winced and grunted.

Ed bound his wrists, then held up a billfold. "What do we have?"

"What's that?"

Ed flipped it open. "FBI. Zachary Saint, are we?"

He didn't respond beyond a bleary scowl. Pearse finished on his side and moved round to tie Jason's—Zachary's—other ankle.

"Right. Regroup." Grace led the trio to the main warehouse again, but left the door to the kitchen open, one ear on their prisoner.

"Where do we kill him?" Ed demanded. The torchlight coming from below hollowed out his cheeks and eyes, making him into a ghoul.

"Typical Ed." Grace chuckled. "Don't you recognize a golden opportunity on a silver platter?"

He scoffed. "Forgive me, Your Majesty. We can't keep him here. We can't let him go. We can't leave a mess. Where's the opportunity?"

"We'll use this to initiate Molly."

"Tonight?" Ed set his jaw. "No. Nearly made a hames of this already. We need to dispose of him, not pull in another unknown."

Grace turned to Pearse. "How d'you know him?"

Her son shifted from foot to foot. "He's your man wantin' to buy a squib. Called himself Allen. I know, I shouldn't have believed—"

"No time for that." Grace shook her head. "Workin' us from every angle. Time we repaid him the favor. I'll be ringin' Molly. Ed, you go find out if he's alone."

"What do I do?" Pearse looked from his mother to his father.

"Make sure the squib's set and camouflaged and go on home, Pearse. You'll have no part in this." She gave him the electrical tape she'd found.

He stuck out his chin. "I can help."

"He mightn't be alone, and if someone's comin' after him, one of us must get clear. Now leg it."

Pearse hung his head and started off, his torch beam moving

down the row of floats.

Ed frowned at her. "Why are you initiatin' her now? It can set."

"We'll never get a chance to galvanize her like this again."

"Wind your neck down, Grace. What're we goin' to tell her, shoot your fiancé for the chance to fight for the Republic?"

Grace returned fire for fire. "You wind your own neck down. Molly's engaged to Jason Tolliver, not Agent Zachary Saint. You think she knows who he really is?"

"What if she does? Or what if she balks at murder?"

She drew a breath, steeling herself against the emotions that would've been another woman's undoing. "They get the same. We shoot her too."

Then it really would be just like the old days.

It felt like his brain was sliding around his skull. Every time it hit the sides, he got another jolt of pain.

Zach forced his eyes open. The moonlight stabbed straight into his head, but he was mostly lucid by the time Ed came into the room. As long as Zach held very, very still, he could almost think clearly. Between blinks. He vaguely remembered being manhandled in the haze. Something had gone wrong if he was strapped to a chair in a dark, bland kitchenette.

"Awake, are we, *Zachary*?"

He shifted and pursed his lips in an air of defiance, careful not to open them and let out the cry of pain at the movement.

"Think you're smarter than us? Think we haven't known the whole time who you really were?"

Zach laughed, ignoring the pain. "I'm Jason Tolliver. I work for Arbor Haynes. Havin' that ID makes thangs run smoother for some of our clients."

"Not this time." Ed walked over and brought his face within inches of Zach's ear. Zach refused to flinch. "What about

Allen, orderin' a squib from Pearse?"

Paddy. Pearse?

His brain was definitely not firing on all cylinders.

Where was Paddy getting his stuff? Work? "We were hired to find the weak link in the supply chain. My boss thought I was a good fit, since I'm datin' Molly."

"Now you're a good fit for an unmarked grave, sleeveen." Ed straightened and folded his arms with a derisive chortle. "Nobody knows you're here, do they?"

The threat landed in the pit of his stomach like week-old soda bread. He hadn't exactly told X or Molly he'd gone in. "'Course they do. If I don't call in five minutes, the police'll be here."

Ed snorted. "Right. With their bomb sniffin' dogs, I'll bet. Because we don't know how to trick a stupid mutt."

They could defeat bomb sniffing dogs? How would they find the bomb? He had to get Ed to take him to it.

Yeah, that seemed likely.

Ed circled behind Zach. Zach tried not to let him out of his sight, but it was too painful to crane his neck.

Zach fell backwards, and his stomach plummeted.

His fall stopped short, jerking his head back. This time the moan escaped before he could stop it.

It took a minute to register that Ed was dragging his chair. Zach's head bounced with every step.

Ed finally threw him forward, the chair legs hitting the ground with a loud crack. Once the wave of pain subsided, Zach scanned his surroundings: that little bathroom off the kitchen. "Please tell me you don't want an audience."

Ed beamed like a sadist. Before Zach's half-functioning brain spun this into a horror film, Ed left the bathroom. Zach was pretty sure he'd left the kitchen, too.

Were X and Molly coming, or was he really on his own? Zach shifted to get a better idea of his restraints, but pain hit him like a wall of concrete.

After what felt like weeks with the way his head throbbed, Ed returned still wearing that wicked grin. "Does your *wan* know who you are?"

Molly. "I think she's even got my Social Security Number memorized."

"How's about we call her and find out?"

No. He could finally admit Molly was a perfectly capable FBI agent—but so was he, and look how he'd ended up. "I'll let you do your thing tomorrow, whatever it is. I'll go away. I'll do anythang, just leave her out of it."

Ed said nothing.

Zach leaned forward, straining against the restraints and the jackhammers on his brain in earnest. "Please. I'm beggin' you. Don't hurt her."

"Better you than her?"

Fear latched onto his rib cage this time. Ed had almost certainly killed before, but with bombs—distant, removed.

"You couldn't do it," Zach said.

"Couldn't I?"

Zach raised an eyebrow, sending a bolt of pain through his skull, but he fought off a wince. "You don't want to do this."

Ed rolled his eyes. "You don't know the first thing about me."

"Molly told me plenty. I was in Omagh when they placed the monument. Maybe you didn't mean to target all them women and children. Wasn't supposed to come to that."

He pulled a gun—a Glock—Zach's gun. "That what you think, ya bowsie?" He leaned down into Zach's face, his voice dangerously quiet. "You know the Internal Security Unit? The Nuttin' Squad?"

Zach tried to kick his mind into action, but nothing came up in his memory.

"The IRA's justice system. How do they say it on television—one behind the ear?" Ed cocked his chin, the black humor returning.

Zach glared back in silence.

Ed pressed the gun against Zach's skull, just behind his ear. Pain drilled into his brain. Ed leaned closer. "Think I couldn't pull one more trigger, add one more rat to the list?"

Zach fought to keep control through the pain and white hot fear.

"Why do you think you're in the jacks?" The pressure let up on Zach's brain, and Ed gestured around the bathroom with the gun. "Couldn't have your body where they'd find it, interferin' in our plans."

They'd thought this through. Ice seized his mind. Was this how he was going to die? Was he ready? Was his conscience clear?

Probably not. If this was the end, he'd definitely done something wrong.

He hadn't told Molly he still loved her.

"Ed," Grace rebuked. Zach could finally breathe again when Ed stepped back. He moved to reveal Grace holding a flashlight in the kitchenette. And Molly standing with her.

Had he been hit hard enough to hallucinate or was his life flashing before his eyes?

MOLLY GAPED AT ZACHARY, sure everyone could hear her heart drumming in her chest. When Grace had rung and asked after Jason, Molly hadn't imagined she'd find Zachary tied to a chair with a gun to his head, blood darkening one side of his neck.

Desperation clutched at her stomach like a drowning man. She had to get that gun from Ed. She had to save Zachary.

Molly took two steps toward him before Grace caught her arm. "What're you doin'?" Molly demanded. The shock in her voice was very real.

"You know what your parents did in the Troubles, don't you?"

Molly's heart dipped. Did Grace *really* know what they'd done? "Enough to know they're heroes."

"You bet your life. Not easy to tell you this, but your parents and their legacy, they're in jeopardy." Grace nodded at Zachary. "Because of him."

Ed didn't look at her, still standing at the door to the bathroom, his gun trained on Zachary. "Tell her who you are."

"Molly, run." Zachary's Southern accent remained intact.

"Or do you already know?" Ed turned his murderous glare on Molly.

Before she could respond, Zachary spoke. "Save yourself, darlin'." He was protecting her—or cuing her. She had to play her cover, too.

"Someone tell me what's happenin'!" Molly shouted.

"Don't worry 'bout that; you gotta get outta here. Don't you fret 'bout me." He met her gaze. Was the pleading there Jason or Zachary?

"He's not Jason Tolliver," Grace said. "His name is Zachary Saint.

He's with the FBI."

The blood drained from Molly's cheeks. They'd made him. Was she next? "That's not true."

Grace took her by the shoulders, pulling her away from the horror of the bathroom, and peered into her eyes. "Listen. I know this is killin' you, but bigger things are happenin' here. We're fightin' for Irish freedom again, and this time we'll win."

Molly searched for something to hold onto. How could she get that gun off Zachary?

Grace pressed on. "You can be part of it."

"Grace, I can't, I—" She gestured at Zachary. "I can't even think."

Grace nodded solemnly. "I know. You needed to know the truth—and you need to have the chance to hurt him like he's hurtin' you."

"What do you mean?"

Ed finally lowered the gun and walked away from the bathroom, to Molly and Grace. Somehow, she doubted they were giving up that easily.

Grace focused on her face. "You can make him pay for lyin' to you and leadin' you on all these years, sayin' he loves you."

"Don't listen to 'em, darlin'!" Zachary's voice echoed from the tiny bathroom.

Ed raised the gun again. "Hold your whisht."

"But, Grace." Molly shook her head. "He says—"

"He's said a lot of things, I'm sure. Can't you see, Molly? He's been after you this whole time to get at your parents and the movement. Us."

Ed passed her Zachary's FBI credentials. "Sorry you had to find out like this."

"I'm tellin' you," Zachary piped up, "the badge's fake, just for work."

Grace sneered. "That lie might've worked on Molly alone, but I've seen enough badges to recognize a real one. Have the decency to tell the woman the truth."

Molly focused on Zachary's badge. Feigning shock wasn't much of a stretch. She could take the gun, disarm them by pretending to jump at the chance to shoot a lying fiancé—but if she seemed too eager, they'd know something was up.

Grace tried again. "You have the chance here that no one else ever gets, the chance to make him pay for what he's done."

Ed held out the gun—Zachary's, too. She gripped her handbag straps tighter. How had they taken these away from him? It had to have something to do with the blood.

"Think, Molly—think of all he's told you, lyin' all along. Guff, every single time he told you he loved you. Tryin' to put your parents in prison. Usin' you to get to them."

Molly blinked several times before turning to the Glock in Ed's hand.

"Make him pay, for what he's done to you. Make him pay for tryin' to stop us, for upholdin' the English oppression even now."

She slowly raised her gaze to meet Zachary's. "It's not true," he said.

"And this badge is fake?" Ed scoffed.

"Do it, Molly." Grace's entire countenance burned with earnestness. "I know you're hurtin'—but you can make him hurt just as bad." She dropped to a whisper, as though Zachary couldn't hear her. "He deserves it. All that he's put you through. All the lies. Make him pay for all of it."

Molly wrapped her fingers around the grip as if she didn't quite know how one of these things worked.

"Point and shoot." Ed wrapped her fingers more securely around the gun. "Like on TV."

She strode deliberately toward the bathroom, and Zachary sitting there, pleading. She raised the gun with a shaking hand—not difficult, since aiming a loaded weapon at someone she had no intention of harming went against all her training.

For the first time, she hoped her training didn't show. Careful to keep her finger well away from the trigger, Molly took a deep breath through her nose, then sighed it out. Again. And again. She had to make this look real. Finally, she lowered the gun.

"Think of how he's hurt you," Grace pushed.

"I know, just—give us a minute?"

Grace eyed her warily. "Now, Molly—"

"I have to know."

"Talkin's never goin' to give you the same closure—"

Molly spun on Grace. "You're sayin' he's lied every second of the last two years. I have earned one minute!" She gestured with the gun to make her point, though she was careful not to aim it at anyone.

Grace pursed her lips, but nodded. She led Ed to the far side of the kitchenette. Obviously they couldn't leave them completely alone.

Molly edged into the small bathroom, maneuvering past Zachary's knees. In the shadows, she could just make out the black zip ties holding him to the chair.

She dug into her handbag for her Leatherman. They had to cover the noise. "The truth. All of it. Now."

"I'm tellin' you the truth."

Her fingers hit the Leatherman in her handbag and she pulled it out, opening the knife. Zachary cut his voice to the edge of a whisper, so soft even she barely heard. "Make them take you to the bomb."

Molly gaped at him. "No," she barely breathed.

Zachary nodded. "We have to stop them. Make sure they're not planning anything else."

She hesitated half a heartbeat. That was the oath they'd both taken, to protect people with their lives if necessary. But how could she sacrifice his life?

If she were in his situation, that was what she'd want, to have him protect the public and trust that she could take care of herself. She'd have to extend that same trust to him.

Maybe she could still help him. Molly pitched her voice for the Canavans to cover every other sound. She removed the magazine from Zachary's gun. "How can I believe you?"

"You'll believe them over me, Molly? C'mon, you know the truth."

She unloaded the bullets from the magazine with both hands. Zachary talked over the clacking as they dropped into her handbag. "The truth is I loved you since the minute we met in that little parish."

Wrong cover. Molly jerked, and the last bullet clattered onto the bathroom tile. She froze. She could forgive Zachary—obviously the man had a head injury—but had the Canavans heard his slip? Or hers? She waited another breathless second.

Nothing from the Canavans. She nudged the loose bullet out of sight with her toe. Where did his cover work? Arbor . . . something. "Is this why you never let me visit your work?"

"No, honey, security's a nightmare."

Molly drew the slide back just enough to eject the bullet from the chamber and replaced the empty magazine. She leaned down to Zachary, in sight of the kitchenette and the Canavans. "And if I ring your office number, will I find Jason Tolliver in the company directory?"

Zachary just stared at her. She took that moment of silence to shield her arm from sight of the door and slipped him her Leatherman, the knife still out. "Careful," she mouthed.

Footsteps sounded from the kitchenette. They'd been quiet too long. Their time was up.

Molly had to do one more thing. She scrambled in her handbag again. But she needed a cover—oh. Perfect.

She spotted the little box on the zip tie around his ankle. "How could you?" Molly lifted her boot and stomped on the zip tie lock. Zachary grunted—that probably wasn't pleasant, though hardly the worst thing he'd endured tonight—but the zip tie popped free. She finally found the right pocket in her handbag and her extra magazine. How could she give it to him? "Stall for me," she whispered.

"I love you, Molly." He was as quiet as her. The Canavans would never hear him that way. She met his gaze.

That wasn't for them. It was for her.

Molly raised her voice for the Canavans again. "You liar."

Ed and Grace reached the doorway, their shadows plunging the bathroom into near darkness. Molly leaned forward, again using her body to shield her arm from the Canavans' view.

She tucked her extra magazine under the hem of his sweater. "It's over, Jason."

"Molly," Grace said gently. "It's time."

Molly straightened. She lifted the empty gun again, but didn't let the muzzle track higher than Zachary's shoulders.

She stood there, hands shaking, to the count of five before she let her arms fall slack, careful not to jangle her bullet-filled handbag. Ed and Grace exchanged a grim nod and backed away. Molly trudged out of the bathroom and held out the gun at an awkward angle, praying that would keep Ed from detecting the weight difference. Ed took it without a word, and Grace slid an arm around Molly to walk her out. Molly cast one last glance back at Zachary.

If this didn't earn his respect for her as an agent, nothing would. But they had both had to get through it first.

He'd be all right. He had to be.

Grace ushered her to the bay door where she'd admitted Molly. She let go of Molly and moved to the door's control switches. Molly bowed her head, but watched Grace from the corner of her eye. How could she get Grace to take her to the bomb? "Wait," Molly said.

"I know, Molly. I can only imagine how you must feel—that kind of betrayal."

She let her shoulders fall. "I couldn't, Grace."

"But it would've been right."

"Anythin' else. You could ask anythin' else of me."

"That's enough for tonight."

Molly looked down again. What else could she try? "Grace, I want to help. Like my parents did."

"Not tonight, dearie. Sorry." Grace didn't reach for the control switches. Instead, she drew a gun.

Molly's heart crashed to a halt. Before Grace could even fully extend her arm, Molly leapt into action. She slammed Grace's wrist into the garage door. The impact's crash was swallowed by the roar of a close-range gunshot.

Grace fired? At her? Molly staggered away a step. Was she hit? She didn't feel anything. The shot must've gone wild.

Grace recovered first—and punched Molly in the face. Her forehead hit the garage door. Between the impact of her head, the muzzle flash and the ringing in her ears, Molly could barely register the screeching as Grace ran away.

"Kill him!"

A gunshot exploded and Zach flinched. It sounded farther away than he'd expected. He felt nothing, other than his head's continued pounding. Could he already be dead? Hadn't he watched Molly empty the gun?

"Kill him!" Grace screamed from the warehouse. "Kill him!"

Zach startled at the click of the dry fire inches from his ear. Ed hadn't fired the first time?

Zach looked up; Ed was frowning at the gun. Ed met his gaze, and Zach smiled back. As if by an unspoken signal, at the same time, Ed turned to run and Zach started from the chair.

Ignoring the surge of pain, Zach tackled Ed as hard and as fast as he could. They slammed to the floor, Zach on top of Ed. The jolt rocketed through Zach's brain, but it was the older man who cried out.

Zach pushed up to get a knee in Ed's back and pull his wrists behind him. Zach scanned the room for cable ties. Within reach on the table. He stretched to grab them, and Ed bucked.

"Whoa." Zach snatched the zip ties and shifted his weight back onto Ed.

The situation was better once Ed was tied to the table leg, though Ed's unintelligible bellows hurt his head almost as much as all that movement. Zach grabbed his empty gun from the floor where it fell. He dropped the empty mag and reloaded before running into the main warehouse.

Molly met him at the kitchen door, her own gun drawn. He pulled her close—it was over. She returned the hug halfway, but kept her weapon at the ready.

It wasn't over? Zach tried to check her expression in the shadows. "You have her, don't you?"

"I don't know where Grace is."

A soft footfall sounded behind them. Zach whipped around and aimed.

At Xavier. "X," Zach hissed and lowered his gun. "What took you so long?"

"Someone had to wait for the bomb squad," X said. "What happened to you?"

He ignored the question he couldn't answer. "We have backup?"

Xavier shook his head. "When I heard the gunshot, I was done waiting."

"You're lucky that gunshot wasn't in my head."

"How was I supposed to know? You should've waited."

"Boys," Molly interrupted in a sharp whisper. "She's armed and loose." Molly gestured for Xavier to guard the kitchenette and their prisoner. X nodded. Good call: Grace wouldn't leave without her husband.

Zach followed Molly's silent lead. He traced a door in the air and pointed behind him, where he'd come in. Molly gave him a thumbs up. She mimicked steering a car and jerked a thumb behind her.

Before he left her, Zach held up his loaded weapon and smiled his thanks. "Be careful."

Molly was already turning toward the Canavans' car. For once, he had no doubt she could do this.

After too many minutes, Molly's legs ached from crouching behind the Canavans' sedan just inside the warehouse's bay door. She only hoped she was as quiet as she thought. Barely able to hear Zachary and Xavier's discussion, she'd resorted to hand signals less for stealth and more to make sure she wasn't shouting.

She peered under the car to see Grace's loafers at the other end. Molly drew in a deep breath as Grace rounded the car and reached the driver's side door. She waited for a second set of shoes to appear.

Grace unlocked the car. Molly checked the undercarriage again. No Ed.

Did Molly risk revealing herself without knowing whether Grace had backup coming?

The car door opened.

Time to act. She stood, keeping her weapon ready but hidden. "Grace, what're you at?"

"What are *you* at?" Grace tossed a tool kit into the drivers' seat.

Ed was nowhere in sight.

She *was* making off without her husband. Pure class.

Molly calculated as fast as she could. She needed to know where the bomb was. Could she convince Grace to show her? "You shot at me, and you're tryin' to kill a man. What's worth murderin' someone for breakin' a girl's heart?"

Grace looked at her like it was her own heart that was broken. "This is bigger than you and your fella. Remember he's FBI; he's here to stop us, to stop the republican cause."

Something shifted in the shadows behind Grace. Molly kept her eyes on Grace, but hesitated until she recognized Zachary's form.

She had to keep Grace talking. "Bigger than Ed, too?"

"A small price to pay for the freedom of a nation! Of our people! I've got to get away. I'm the one who'll make this happen for all Ireland. Ed—" Grace dismissed her husband with a wave. "We don't need him. Have you nothin' you believe in enough to fight for?"

"Of course. But this would be Omagh ten thousand times over, slaughterin' innocents. We still have a chance to stop this. Where is the bomb?"

Grace's tone grew pleading. "Don't you understand?" She reached back—to her waistband. Drawing? Molly's gut tensed.

"Grace!" Zachary's bark was a decent imitation of Ed. Grace jumped and whirled around.

Behind her back, Grace's hand was on the grip of her gun.

Forget the bomb. While Grace was still distracted, Molly lunged for her. She knocked Grace to the floor and yanked the gun away from the older woman.

Molly restrained Grace with her weight on the older woman's back. Molly tucked both guns into her handbag and pulled out handcuffs. "Grace Canavan, you're under arrest." Continuing with the charges and *Miranda* warning, she ratcheted the cuffs onto Grace's wrists.

She'd just finished when shoes stepped into view at Grace's shoulder. Molly jerked her head up, reaching for her gun and fearing the worst. She couldn't hear threats coming.

Once again, it was Xavier. He helped Molly up. Together they hauled Grace to her feet.

Grace caught Molly's gaze and gave her a pitying head shake. "I was makin' the happiest day of your life perfect." She sounded as though she were whispering, or very far away. "I took you in as a daughter."

"If I were your daughter, Grace, I'd elope."

"And if I were marrying your daughter," Zachary said as he closed the last few feet, "I'd think twice." He beckoned them over, and Xavier and Molly pulled Grace with them, following Zachary into the kitchenette.

Molly couldn't hear the exchange with Xavier, but Zachary waved him off, and Xavier left.

Careful not to turn her back on the suspects, Molly joined Zachary at the door. "Where's he goin'?"

She couldn't hear the reply. She pointed to her ear. "Gun went off in my ear."

"Sorry." Zachary raised his voice. "Meeting the bomb squad."

"Good." Then it didn't matter if the Canavans hadn't shown them the bomb.

Zachary crossed to the table and snatched up his FBI credentials. "Thanks for hanging onto these for me, Ed."

Grace and Ed slowly looked up at him. "Your accent," Grace said.

"Oh, yeah." Still speaking loudly enough for Molly, he held out a hand as if to shake theirs. "Zach Saint."

For once, Grace was speechless. She and Ed gaped at Zachary for a full minute until Xavier returned with two uniformed police officers. They cut Ed free from the table and conducted the Canavans out of the room, X bringing up the rear.

Now it was over. Molly puffed out a breath, the excess energy already humming in her system without anywhere to go now that the danger was past.

"How'd you end up tied to a chair?" she asked.

"A chunk of my night's missing." Zachary ran his fingers through his hair and winced.

"A chunk of your head, too."

He lowered his hand, pausing for a double take at the blood there. "I'm bleeding?"

"You've nearly stopped." She grabbed a paper towel and applied it to the side of his skull. "Are you all right?"

Zachary shrugged, then winced. "Must've gotten hit on the head."

"You think?" Molly guided him forward and toned down the sarcasm. "How'd it happen?"

Fortunately, he spoke loudly enough for her to hear. "Can't remember. Maybe I was knocked out? Obviously something went wrong."

Molly stopped short. He couldn't remember? This could be serious.

Before she could voice her concern, a uniformed officer walked into the kitchen. "We need to clear the building for the bomb squad."

"That's what I'm forgetting." Zachary said. He and Molly tailed the policeman out.

Now it was over.

THE POLICEMAN SLAMMED the patrol car door, giving Grace and Ed privacy for a few seconds.

Grace leaned forward to hide her mouth from view of the window. "Squib's all set."

"Pearse got off grand."

Their son wasn't anywhere in sight. Pearse was free to trigger the bomb tomorrow and carry the plan into the next phase, she hoped. And if she'd only followed his escape route through the north door, she would've been free with him.

"Think they'll find it?" Ed asked.

The know-nothing. "I don't." They'd have to know precisely where to look. Wouldn't be any residue nearby, and even bomb sniffing dogs shouldn't be able to detect it. If anything, they'd find Pearse's client's bomb. "Don't let them see you talkin'."

Ed kept his expression impassive. "What do you know? All Pearse's talk of redundancy came to some use. 'Mere anarchy is loosed upon the world.'"

For once, Grace smiled at his Yeats quote. "'The blood-dimmed tide is loosed.'"

The policeman opened his door and got in, and they drove off in silence.

The bomb squad tech escorted Molly and Zachary from the

building. When they reached the car park, Zachary began to fall behind. Molly stopped to wait for him. She slid her arm around his waist and guided his arm to her shoulders.

He leaned on her more with every step. "Sure you're all right?" she asked.

He didn't answer.

Molly stopped. "Talk to me, Zachary."

He said something too quiet to make out. His eyes remained closed. She guided him to the nearest ambulance. A paramedic helped them into the back of the bus, seating him on the bench inside to extract the history of Zachary's injury. After the fourth time of admitting he didn't remember, Zachary glowered at the EMT. The medic turned to her. "Can you keep him talking?"

Molly scrambled for a conversation topic that she could broach with an audience.

The EMT moved away once Zachary started the conversation. "I guess I should either say 'Thank you' or 'I'm sorry.'"

"Oh?"

"You did kind of save my life." The medic handed Zachary an ice pack, and he applied it to his head.

"I doubt Ed would've—"

"He pulled the trigger." Zachary looked down. "If you hadn't unloaded the gun—"

"If we start playin' a 'what if' game, we'd both be dead how many times over?"

The medic returned with a wet towel and scrubbed at the dried blood on Zachary's neck. "Repeat this list after me: red, blue, car, bike, roses."

"Can you give us a minute?" Zachary responded.

The paramedic frowned at him, then Molly. "One minute." He passed the towel to Molly and hopped out of the ambulance.

"Was that 'I'm sorry' or 'Thank you'?"

"You'll know when it's 'I'm sorry.'"

Molly joined him on the bench. Zachary leaned back against the ambulance wall and closed his eyes again. She gingerly wiped at the blood in his hair. He winced.

"Should I get the medic?"

"Just—" Without opening his eyes, he reached for her. She took his hand with her free one.

"I'm sorry I gave out to you earlier." But had he actually changed his mind? She'd only saved his life in there.

He mumbled something unintelligible.

"Hilarious. You know I can't hear you."

His lips moved, but now she heard nothing. The hand holding his icepack drifted down to his side.

"Stop it." She nudged him with her elbow. Instead of absorbing the blow, he slid to the side. "Zachary?"

His eyes fluttered open, but he made no move to catch himself. Molly grabbed his sweater to stop his fall. "Say somethin'."

Zachary blinked slowly. He was speaking, but not loudly enough. His eyelids floated closed again.

Molly shook him. He moved a centimeter, then nothing. "Help! Medic!"

The paramedic vaulted into the ambulance, maneuvering past her. "What happened?"

"We were talkin', and he passed out."

The EMT paused long enough to cast her a wide-eyed stare. "How long since the injury? Did he lose consciousness before?"

"I don't know, maybe. Would've been a good thirty minutes ago, or more."

He turned back to Zachary, but Molly caught the concern in his expression. What had they said in first aid? This was . . . swelling on the brain?

Ice lanced through her. He wasn't safe from the Canavans yet. People died from that.

The paramedic called another man to assist him. The second medic half-helped, half-pulled Molly from the ambulance.

Xavier jogged up to her. "What's going on?"

"Zachary just passed out while we were talkin'."

Xavier fell silent, watching the EMTs work on Zachary. "So you two are . . . ?" He trailed off into a question.

"No idea." She was spared explaining further when one of the bomb technicians jogged over.

"Wasn't a car bomb after all—just a bomb in the trunk." He

sighed. "What you get with unis."

"Defused?" Xavier asked.

"Yep. Could've done it in our sleep—just a detonator and C-4. We'll analyze it and figure out where it came from. The dogs haven't found anything either, so it looks clear."

The ambulance door slammed shut, drawing Molly's attention. Worry invaded her stomach full force. "I'm goin' with him."

Xavier clapped a hand on her shoulder. "Listen. I didn't cover him once tonight. Hate to make it twice. I saw him the last time you broke up, and . . . don't mess with his head again."

Mess with *his* head? If his head survived this trauma. She nodded and forced her way back into the ambulance.

A sharp pain in his hand woke him. Zach tried to pull away, blinking through the haze and fluorescent light. Where—?

"Good, you're awake," Lucy said. He turned toward her voice—he was in a hospital bed, one tilting him into a sitting position. Snatches of last night came back: the Canavans, Molly, the arrest. Was the case closed? Didn't feel like it.

He looked back to Lucy sitting on the edge of his bed. She wouldn't know about the Canavans—and she was holding his hand.

The hand that was still stinging. He jerked it away and whacked her arm. "That hurt."

"The nurse said I could. Have to make sure you didn't pass out again."

He scowled at her. "I was sleeping."

Lucy flashed an evil grin. "Unconscious is unconscious."

Zach used a knee to shove her off the bed.

"Hey! I was up all night while you slept." This time, she was the one doing the hitting. "You scared me half to death."

"What happened?"

Lucy retold her night, starting after Paul left her place—which sounded like bad news to begin with, but he did remember that conversation. The hospital called her saying Zach was in and out of consciousness, and she'd sat through scans and hourly pain and reflex checks. Eventually they figured out it wasn't too serious: no broken arteries, swelling that responded to drugs, and no visible damage. He'd probably be hearing jokes about how hardheaded he was long after he finished the course of anti-inflammatories.

"Basically," Lucy concluded, "the doctors said, 'The brain is a mystery,' and yours reacted like a hysterical little girl."

Zach scowled. "Next time you get the brain injury."

"Like you'd come for me."

"Come to think of it, maybe you do have a brain injury. Why are you and Paul back together?"

Lucy looked away. "Hurts less to be together."

Before he fired back, a movement near the door drew his attention. He turned—too fast, sending pain crackling up through his head.

Molly stood at the door.

He couldn't let hope run away with him. His brain was sick enough already. "Lucy, am I seeing things?"

She checked the doorway. "Nothing there. Need a nurse?"

"Lucy." Molly sounded like their mom breaking up a fight.

Lucy didn't move. Alarm bells in his mind brought on a new layer of pain.

"Don't go messin' with his head."

Finally his sister turned to Molly. "But it's so easy," Lucy said. She studied Molly a minute. "You okay?"

Zach locked back at Molly. A bruise bloomed beneath one eye, her eyelids drooped, and her curls sprawled all over the place when she shook her head. "Slept in the waitin' room. Not well."

Lucy turned to Zach, with a look that could only be described as *oh-ho-ho?* "Guess I'm not the only one with news."

He cast a meaningful stare at the door.

"I'll . . . get your breakfast." She patted the rail of his hospital bed. "Good luck." The words carried a grim note, but Zach wasn't an idiot. He saw the little shoulder squeeze and eyebrow lift Lucy gave Molly.

And he saw the I'm-not-promising-anything-but-fingers-crossed smile for Molly's answer.

Kissing Molly, one second from the night before, replayed in his mind. Was that last night?

"Glad to see you conscious." Molly came to sit at the foot of his bed. "Gave us quite a scare."

He summarized Lucy's version of his medical history. When he finished, Molly shook her head in disbelief. "Someone's watchin' out for you."

"Seems like it."

"How much of last night do you remember?"

He wasn't about to throw that last memory out there. "We stopped the Canavans, right?"

She sighed, and her shoulders dropped like that was a major weight off them "We did."

"And they did that to you?" He tapped his own eye.

Molly carefully prodded her shiner, but nodded. "But my hearin's mostly back. That all you've got?"

"You did great."

"I saved your life," she pointed out, "and all you can give is a 'great'?"

He could definitely do better—because he could finally see she deserved it. "You were amazing. There's nobody I'd rather have my back. I'm writing up another commendation the minute I get into the office. Seriously."

"Another?" Molly tilted her chin to the side.

"Yeah, I wrote one yesterday. I didn't tell you that?"

"No."

He needed to make this right. Zachary met her eyes. "I've been a jerk. Obviously you're a great FBI agent, or we'd both be dead. It shouldn't have taken you saving my life for me to get my head on straight. I'm sorry."

A slow smile crept across her face. Man, she was beautiful, black eye, crazy curls and all.

Maybe it wasn't the case that felt off. It could definitely be something with Molly. He tried to replay the rest of last night, but his memories were a bad home movie on fast forward, juddery and out of focus. If Molly was here, something important was missing.

She plucked at his blanket. "I'm sorry I gave out to you last night. It was just that over the last four weeks, you've harped on any little mistake I've made and glossed over any successes."

Zach cringed. The argument—pieces of it—echoed in his memory. "Sorry. I know I can't hover over you every day of work. And you really were amazing last night. But I'm not going to apologize for wanting to protect—" He caught himself before he said *someone I love.* "—you," was the safest ending to that sentence. "It just means I care."

Molly fixed her deep blue eyes on his. "I love you, Zachary."

Was his mind playing tricks or—? He laughed. "What?"

"I love you?" Molly smiled, teasing. "This is when you say it back, and we live happily ever after."

Oh, he wanted to say it back. But still loving Molly—even her loving him—didn't mean anything had changed. No way had she crossed everything off her all-important to-do list in the last eight months. Zach pulled his knees to his chest and wrapped his arms around them. "Where does that leave us?"

"I'm fed up with weddin' plannin', I'll tell you that."

Zach allowed a soft chuckle. "Grace is definitely fired."

"That mass murder thing didn't go with the theme anyway."

She was letting him down easy. How soon could he get out of this situation? Considering it was his hospital room, it'd probably be a while.

"You were right." Molly focused on his hands, her voice soft. "That was how I felt last year." She paused, then corrected herself. "Last week."

And now? Zach barely dared to ask himself.

"But, once I finished everythin' I wanted to do, I imagined us together."

"I was your backup plan?"

"More like a final destination. But Mum says once you find love, you should act. Before you lose it." Molly focused on the pile of lint she'd collected. "I know how terrible that is."

He wanted to marry Molly, but more than that, he wanted her to *want* to marry him, not just settle because he asked her. "So you're willing to talk about marriage because breaking up sucks? I thought we were smarter, Lucy."

"Thank you, Paul." Molly leveled him with a sarcastic expression. "Can you not go spinnin' my words?"

"Sorry; probably the meds talking."

"Or the concussion."

"Sure, blame the traumatic brain injury." Zach smirked. "If you're going to take advantage of a man in my condition, I'd rather you kiss me than question me."

Molly allowed a reluctant laugh at his lame joke. Zach shifted closer, reaching across her to take her hand. He ran his other thumb along her unhurt cheek. "I do love you," he whispered as he leaned in. "I never stopped, and I've wanted to marry you for more than a year."

He held his breath. He'd finally admitted it, straight out. And this was her chance to run away screaming.

She studied his eyes, and one corner of her mouth lifted. "Then marry me, Zachary."

"Because you don't want to break up again?"

"Because I want you to be mine forever." Molly crossed that last inch between them and kissed him. He slid his arms around her waist, and she drew back just long enough for a soft sigh. He pulled her closer, and she brought her lips to his again.

This time, he'd never have to let her go. This kiss seemed to carry all the meaning of last night's kiss and more. Because this time it was real.

Until Lucy marched in. "Okay, Zach, we're—oh. Sorry."

Molly pulled back, covering her lips with her fingers, but she stayed curled up against his chest.

"I take it you guys have good news, too," Lucy said with a wry smile. "I talked to the nurse and you've got one more CT scan. If it's good, you could be out of here by nine."

"Can I drive?"

"No." Lucy folded her arms. "Doctor's orders."

Zach turned to Molly "Why don't you run home and get some sleep? We'll go to the parade later."

Molly hesitated until he gave her an I'll-be-fine nod. "Sure now." She bid Lucy goodbye and winked at him. "Love you," she mouthed from the door.

"Guess I'll be the one giving you a ride home," Lucy muttered.

He craned his neck to make sure Molly was gone—yep, that hurt. "Actually," he said. "Could you do me—us—a favor? A few of them?"

Lucy folded her arms. "Like what?"

"Number one, I need to see Molly's dad."

His sister squinted at him, not comprehending for a long second. Then the realization hit her, and she brightened with a gasp. "You *do* have good news. Wait, you're not supposed to make legally binding decisions for twenty-four hours."

"Don't worry. I made this decision a long time ago." Zach eased back against the bed. Everything was finally, perfectly *right*. So why did he feel like he was forgetting something, something more specific than "most of last night"?

With Lucy's help, Zach finished a CT scan, hospital paperwork, stopping by Molly's parents', and making arrangements for the rest of their afternoon by the time he arrived at Molly's at eleven.

Molly answered the door with a frown. "What're you doin' here, Zachary?"

"Aren't we going to the parade?" They'd decided that on the phone an hour ago . . . hadn't they?

"Are we? Jason's out of town. Can't let Grace see you."

Oh no. No, no, no. He had a brain injury, but could he have actually manufactured memories? Whole conversations? If the arrests hadn't happened, what else was he imagining—everything? When Molly said she loved him?

No, he couldn't have imagined everything—she had a black eye. Slowly, Molly's confused gloom melted into a smile. "You should see your face."

"You can't mess with a guy with a head injury." Zach didn't relax until she slid her arms around his waist and kissed him. Technically they'd only been dating a few hours, but she already felt perfect, comfy and familiar, in his arms. Like coming home after being away way too long. "We did say we were going to the parade, right?"

"We did."

He traced a finger over her bruised cheek and breathed in the relief. How had things fallen into place so fast?

Fast? He almost laughed at himself. He'd been waiting a year for this. Now just one piece was missing. "I got you something. But first, we've got a big day. Starting with the parade."

A grin danced in her eyes. "Let me get my jacket." Molly retrieved her green wool jacket, appropriate for a Saint Patrick's Day parade.

"Want to hit Navy Pier afterwards?" Zach called.

"Navy Pier?" Molly repeated, like she was pondering it.

"Or anything else out that way. Good thing it's all clear, right?"

"Suppose it's also a good thing you went in when you did—apparently the Canavans hadn't even got the bomb out of the boot yet."

That didn't feel right. "The bomb was still in the trunk? "

"It was. Xavier called with the analysis a few minutes ago, and it wasn't even real C-4." Molly paused, concern creasing between her eyebrows. "Navy Pier," she said again, as if something had just clicked into place.

"What is it?"

"Grace had a photo at Navy Pier on her coffee table—I think with her son."

"The guy that emailed?"

"They have *two* sons. Grace said they were both in Ireland, but would they put a picture of a stranger on their table?" She pulled out her cell and paged through the photos she'd snapped in their apartment. "I suppose Donal or Pearse could've come over for Christmas."

"Pearse?"

"After Pádraig Pearse." Molly finally found the photo and showed her phone to Zach. The Canavans stood in front of Navy Pier with Paddy. Pearse? Pádraig Pearse.

His heart plummeted and, finally, he remembered. Paddy at the warehouse. The bomb, not in the car. On a float.

Molly eyed Zachary warily. "You all right?"

"Get your gun."

She squinted, but opened her jacket and moved her sweater to show the badge and holster on her belt.

Good. "We need to get to the parade. And call the bomb squad."

Molly led the way out, all business. That was distractingly sexy, but with a million lives on the line, he could focus.

Chicago PD had to have known about this. Zach dialed Dice.

They made it to the elevator by the time Dice answered. "What's up?"

"Did you know Paddy was a Canavan?"

Dice took a very long time to think. "We thought he might be."

Molly pushed the button for the garage, and Zach scoffed into his phone. "You *knew*? Why didn't you—"

"It was in the endnotes."

"Are you kidding? What endnotes?"

"Weren't they attached?"

A software error put a million people in danger, and Dice was asking questions. "He's targeting the parade today. I'm headed there now."

Dice promised to meet them before Zach ended the call. He turned to Molly. "Chicago PD had me track an Irish guy stealing explosives from work. I gave him the fake C-4 they found—and the whole time, they knew he might be a Canavan."

"What?"

"They thought I knew, because they buried it in the report." Zach swallowed a groan. "The bomb I saw wasn't in a trunk. It was already on a float."

"You didn't say anythin' about that last night."

He pointed to his head, which throbbed in response. "Traumatic brain injury?"

"Right." The elevator slowed for the garage. They hurried to her green VW. "I'll ring Kent. He lives in the Loop." Depending on how close to Grant Park he lived—and how hard it was to find parking near the parade now—he should have a jump start on them.

"Which float was it on?" she asked as soon as she got off the phone with Kent.

Zach took a moment to think. "I don't know—all I can remember is the trigger under the float."

"Will we check every one?"

"Should've checked them all last night."

"They must've thought we were clear once they found the bomb in the car." She sighed.

Zach pressed his fingers to his temple to relieve the pressure beginning to build. "My fault; should've remembered—"

"Hey," Molly cut him off gently. "Beatin' yourself up won't

change anythin'. You've brain trauma, remember?"

"How do I keep forgetting that?" Zach pursed his lips. "Molly, I need you to be point."

She looked at him, a smile playing at one corner of her mouth. "You want me to be in charge?"

"I need you."

"Any time." She placed her hand on his knee. "Ring the bomb squad, will you?"

Zach did as he was told without a second thought.

THE CLOSER THEY GOT to the parade, the heavier traffic became. Molly was practically strangling her steering wheel by the time she found a parking spot in a 15-minute loading zone. They'd be faster on foot than trying to plow through the people.

"Never thought I'd want one of those ridiculous little police lights," Molly muttered, slamming her door shut.

"Too bad we don't have my car." Zachary climbed out, too. "But now I know what to get you for your birthday."

"Not one of those magnetic ones." She picked up her pace, weaving through foot traffic.

"No way. No less than LED dash strobes for you, deluxe model: thirty whole bucks."

"Wish that would help us now." She pushed past another family, startling a babe in arms. The father barked at her, but she didn't look back, running as fast as she could through the crowd.

Molly and Zachary found Kent arguing with a policeman guarding the gate to the parade staging area, waving his creds in the officer's face. "You've got to let me by!"

"Think I'm dumb? The FBI's going to send one guy down here?"

"It's true," Molly called as they ran up behind him. She and Zachary flashed their badges as well. The policeman turned to his radio, as if to cover his sheepish blush.

They didn't have time to wait while he checked. Molly read his nameplate. "Officer Welsh, we need your help." She waited until his eyes locked on hers, then angled her chin down, aiming for a mix of I'm-leveling-with-you-officer-to-officer and I'm-batting-my-eyelashes-so-you'll-help-me. "Can you direct the bomb squad right through to us when they get here?"

"Bomb—? Absolutely, ma'am."

"We're countin' on you, love."

Welsh saluted and waved the three of them through.

"*He's* your love?" Zachary muttered.

"Flattery gets you everywhere, Zachary." They huddled up behind the gate, where the floats and the trucks towing them were already lined up. Why were so many people milling about?

"What do we know about the bomb?" Kent asked.

Zachary's gaze fell as he searched his memory. Heavens, they were relying on the memory of a man just released from the hospital for a brain injury.

"Cell phone trigger," he said. "And maybe off-road diesel."

"Off-road diesel?" No, no, no. "That's what you'd use for fuel oil in an ANFO bomb. All they'd need is fertilizer."

She turned to Zachary the same time he turned to her. "The florist," they said in unison.

The crowd seemed to grow thicker by the minute. ANFO meant the toll would increase tenfold if they couldn't find it. Even if they tried to clear the area, thousands would die.

Molly looked to Kent. "You've got to find the triggerman."

"He'll have a phone," Zachary said.

People thronged the parade barriers. Lining a shooting gallery, practically. This time, the Canavans didn't need any decoy phone calls to herd victims to the bomb.

And they had to find one man holding a mobile phone.

They had to come at this from all angles. Molly moved closer to Zachary. "We'll find the bomb, in case we can't find him."

Kent rubbed his short hair, helpless and hopeless. "It'll take a bomb squad forty-five minutes to get here—the parade starts before that."

"Twenty minutes—we've already rung them."

"My boss is on his way to help, too." Zachary placed his hand on the small of her back. "With reinforcements."

Kent frowned at the crowd waiting along the parade course. "What's our guy look like?"

"Really Irish," Molly said.

"What, red hair, green eyes?"

Zachary snorted at the stereotype. "Young Pierce Brosnan who's lost a boxing match."

"Who?"

Molly and Zachary talked over one another to list the actor's most famous credits. "James Bond in *Die Another Day*—"

"*The World is Not Enough.*"

"*Tomorrow Never Dies.*"

"*GoldenEye*," they finished together.

Kent held up a hand to cut them off. "I get it. James Bond with a cell phone." He jogged off for the parade route.

"You forgot *Tailor of Panama*," Molly said.

"Not bad for a guy with a concussion," Zachary muttered. They turned back to the line of floats. Molly counted the floats stretching back through the huge field. Five, ten, twenty . . . So many people. "Seventy floats or more."

Zachary breathed out a groan. "It's a cheap flip phone, stuck just under the edge of the float. Frilly green paper."

Without another word they started for the first float, Zachary taking the west side of the street and Molly the east. She tried to act as though nothing was amiss as she ducked down to peer along the first float's platform. Where should she be searching? Wouldn't people notice and worry?

She straightened and spotted Zachary on his mobile. He lowered his mobile to shout to her. "Can you send Kent's number to Xavier?"

Molly sent the contact information, and Zachary leaned down to level his gaze along the bottom of the next float. She did the same, until her mobile rang. Zachary. "Yes?"

"Skip these flat ones. Not tall enough to fit it underneath."

"Grand. This next one's out, so?"

"Yep." They stayed on the phone and hurried down the line.

Ten minutes, eight floats cleared and ten skipped—nothing. Twenty minutes till the parade started, and more than fifty floats to check.

"Miss Molly!" a little voice called. She whirled around to find Olivia, one of her Irish dancers, grinning up at her in her bejeweled solo dress. "Are you marching with us?"

"Not today, lovey." She glanced at the milling marchers behind

Olivia. So many *children.*

There had to be a better way to find this bomb. She waved to Olivia and turned back to her search and her mobile. "Zachary, are they targetin' somethin' specific?"

"Maybe. Don't know if I saw what float it was on."

Brian injuries were never convenient, but his was putting all these people in jeopardy. They passed another flat float and looked at one another across the street. Her grim thought passed to him in silence.

They walked on, checking another two floats and skipping three more. Behind them, music blared to life—pipe bands.

The crowd cheered, a thin, high-pitched whine from here. The parade was starting.

Molly scanned the field, crowd, bigger floats for the parade finale, big sponsors: banks, the Irish American Heritage Center, department stores . . . and O'Connell Publishing.

The company that published *The Blood-Dimmed Tide.*

She lifted her mobile again. "Zachary, O'Connell Publishin'."

"Which float's theirs?"

"Double decker, gold shamrocks."

"Can you be more specific?"

"Gazebo, risers at the back?" They caught sight of one another through a gap in the floats again. Molly beckoned to him. "Over here."

They hung up and sprinted through the barely organized chaos to the last parade float. They split up on either side of the float, and both dropped to the ground to check underneath.

Even with her mobile's flashlight, the little she could see seemed the same as every other float she'd checked.

Behind her, a marching band drumline counted off. She looked back: high schoolers. Children.

They couldn't clear this field in time, let alone the parade route. Molly's chest ached. She was failing them.

She climbed to her feet again, her eyes stinging. They couldn't give up—they wouldn't—but they were too little and too late.

Molly dropped her shoulders and sighed. The float's frilly crepe fluttered in her gust of breath.

Frilly. Green. Paper. Molly dropped to the ground and ran her hand under the float to try again.

And hit something plastic. She tried to get a peek under the float again, and this time she spotted the flip phone.

"Zachary!"

He jogged around the float. When he saw it, he gave a sharp gasp. Zachary ripped the thin streamers away and reached underneath. He yanked out two wires, still covered with electrical tape.

"Scissors," he said.

"You can't be thinkin' of takin' care of it ourselves?" She pulled out her Leatherman, but didn't give it to him.

"He explained the detonator to me. I can do it."

Molly scanned the float riders above her. Laughing. Oblivious. What if they failed with all these people around? "Did he tell you how to disarm it?"

"Hey, what're you doing?" someone called down from the risers.

If they let on, they'd have a panic. So victims could have a choice of being trampled or blown up.

Zachary reached for his creds, but Molly stopped him. "Perfectly all right; we're authorized."

"'Authorized'?" Zachary said under his breath, raising an eyebrow.

"Sure now. We have authority, don't we?"

He fixed her with a look of *that doesn't cut it.*

"We can't clear the area in time." She lowered her voice. "How many people are we tryin' to kill?"

He gestured at the still-packed field. The only place the crowd had thinned was at the entrance to the parade route. "Where would you suggest we take it?"

Still frowning, Molly checked the time. "Quarter past."

Where was that bomb squad?

"I'll try to make room," she said. She handed Zachary her Leatherman and jogged over to a parade organizer. Much as she hated throwing her weight around by bullying people with a badge, today it was a requirement. "Special Agent Malone with the FBI. We need this float cleared. Quietly."

The woman with a headset and clipboard gaped at her, stunned. "Um, okay?"

"Come with me." Molly hurried back to the float with the organizer in tow. "All righ', everyone," Molly dialed up her Irish accent to shout at the float riders. They looked to her. "We're just after inspectin' this float, and I'm afraid we've a problem. We're goin' to have to ask you to be steppin' off the float. If you'll wait right over here—" She indicated an open area a good distance away, the opposite direction from the parade course. "—we'll let you know if we've fixed it. Otherwise, I'm afraid we won't be able to run the float. Apologies."

Although apparently disappointed, most of the float's riders began to shuffle off with only a low murmur of complaint.

"Nice," Zachary said.

"Better than nice." She crouched down next to him.

"Better than I could've done."

Molly allowed a quick grin. "You'd better believe it."

Zachary returned her smile and turned back to the trigger. They'd both had basic training in disarming a bomb—very basic. "If it's the same as Paddy showed me, there are no booby traps or backup circuits. I just have to disconnect the trigger."

Molly watched him. They'd cleared the area, but the crowd still seemed to press in around them. Potential victims.

Zachary wiped his palms on his jeans and gripped the Leatherman, carefully pulling the wires between the blades.

If the bare ends hit one another—she caught his wrist. "Those wires can't touch."

"Good call." He released one wire from the cutters and took a deep breath.

Molly placed a hand on his back. If this was their last moment—"I love you."

"And I love you." Zachary took another breath. His fingers tensed.

"Special Agent Malone?"

They both turned to face the person who'd called her—a man in a blue-and-black pocketed vest, complete with the FBI BOMB TECH tag. Finally.

Molly drew in air like she'd been drowning. "Just in time."

Zachary stepped aside, and they both gestured at the trigger.

The tech gave a low whistle. "Your girlfriend's brave to be here with you."

Zachary pointed at her. "*She's* Special Agent Malone. And she's point today."

The bomb tech looked away, embarrassed, but nodded. He signaled to the bomb truck. With that entourage, the news crews would be here before long, but not before the squad could clear the area, and take care of the bomb in peace.

The tech sent a remote-controlled robot under the float. After a minute, he held up a monitor to deliver the verdict. "Classic design. We got this."

Molly released her breath at the same time as Zachary. He wrapped an arm around her. "Ready?"'

To be done with the Canavans? "More than ready." She looked toward the parade route. "We haven't heard from Kent or X. Pearse must still be out there." He could even dial the trigger now.

"When he sees the float isn't coming, he'll be gone."

The end of the sentence went unsaid: to make another bomb.

For the second time that day, in unison they turned and broke into a run. A policeman at the start of the parade course tried to stop them. Zachary waited to shove his credentials in the cop's face; Molly ran straight by.

"I'm with her," Zachary tossed over his shoulder as he caught up with Molly again.

They ran the parade route alongside the floats, costumed marchers, pipe bands and Irish dance schools. "What is this," Zachary joked breathlessly, "*The Fugitive*?"

"With the villain from *Patriot Games*." Molly slowed to scan the area, and Zachary did the same, pressing two fingers to his head.

She realized how hard her own heart was pounding, between running and tension. That couldn't be good for Zachary. "You all right?" Molly asked.

"Yeah."

She wasn't entirely reassured, but Zachary walked on. "He wants a safe front-row seat."

Right. They needed to find him. Molly scanned the streets. This road ran through the middle of a park. Unless Pearse hid in the trees, there were no good perches to observe the aftermath from a safe distance. He couldn't have finagled his way onto the grandstand.

"Has to be somewhere." Molly closed her eyes. The viewing stand was by Buckingham Fountain but there was something else . . . She snapped her fingers. "The Art Institute."

The only buildings by Grant Park—and they had to be at the other end of the parade. Walking would take ten minutes without crowds. They pushed their way past a barrier to fight against the press.

Zachary grabbed his mobile, and Molly followed suit, dialing Kent. "Any luck?" she asked without greeting.

"Nothing on the east side of the street."

The buildings were on the west side. Molly scanned the street. "Where are you?"

"Columbus and Jackson."

The intersection before the Art Institute. "He might be in a perch at the Art Institute."

Kent groaned. "Not that new building—it's huge."

She covered the microphone and glanced at Zachary typing on his phone. "Think he's in the new wing?"

He maneuvered past a pair of rowdy teenagers and looked in that direction. "Good vantage point." He tapped his foot, thinking. "Go for it."

Molly relayed the conclusion to Kent. "Entrance on the west side, right?" he asked.

They'd have to run around the block, too. "It is. We'll be there soon as we can." Molly ended the call as they reached a less crowded spot on the sidewalk. She turned to Zachary.

"X is checking the Institute, too."

They looked at one another. Did they leave this up to Kent and X?

Those two could handle it. But after all this, could Molly and Zachary miss the final conclusion of the case?

Zachary held out a hand. "We can catch up if we hurry."

She smiled, took his hand, and started at a run.

They jogged around the block and badged the admission desk before the vast size of the space hit Molly. How would they ever find

Pearse? This wasn't any better than searching the street. She paused a moment, scanning the entry hall. The new wing was to the left.

Zachary reached her, panting heavily, holding his temple again.

"All right, love?"

"Sure, now *I'm* your love." He leaned against the wall. Molly stepped closer, but he held up a hand. "I'm good. Go get him. I'll catch up."

Could he? Zachary waved her on. "You got him."

She charged ahead to the Modern Wing, another high-ceilinged hall. Windows lined the north end and the east wall of the passage, facing the street.

Facing the parade.

From this level, she could only see the crowd outside. Pearse would need a better angle to see the floats. The galleries might have a decent view. No time for elevator traffic. Molly scanned the room again, her gaze finally settling on the suspended stairway with a landing by the windows, halfway between the floors.

She broke into a run again at the same time she spotted Kent running toward her. She pointed to the stairs, and they both curved for the target.

The gallerygoers on the stairs jerked out of the way. A couple spectators stood on the landing, unaware. Molly pivoted to dash up the rest of the stairs, but checked the landing's spectators again. Two seemed to be holding phones. One with black hair. In coveralls, a classic disguise.

"Pearse!"

He jumped and whirled around, his eyes the size of saucers. He lifted the mobile, his finger over a button. The trigger.

Time seemed to slow down. Kent lunged for him, and Pearse leapt sideways to escape. Molly seized the opportunity and Pearse's collar. She swept her foot behind his, tripping him to bring him to the floor. The mobile clattered across the floor.

By the time Zachary arrived to keep the onlookers back, a protesting Pearse was already in cuffs.

"Nice takedown, Molly. Got this under control," Zachary said between gasps.

She looked to Zachary. The poor man definitely needed medical attention. And a good workout. She hoped he was only winded because he was out of shape. "Someone needs a PFT."

He pursed his lips but not for long before he had to pant again. He obviously didn't want to endure the Bureau's rigorous physical fitness test. "I passed when I had to," he gasped.

"Do you need to go back to the hospital?"

"I'm not that out of shape." He shook his head. "Just gotta catch my breath." He panted. "And take it easy."

"And your meds." Molly turned to the resisting-but-restrained man she still held to the ground. "Pearse Canavan, you're under arrest." She continued with the charges and *Miranda* warning, then Kent and Molly hauled Pearse to his feet.

"You're *that* Molly," Pearse practically spat. "You traitor! How could you betray your people?"

Then he did spit.

"Way to add assaulting an officer to your charges," Zachary said under his breath, a threat behind his words.

Molly didn't flinch, wiping the spittle from her cheek and onto his shirt. "If you think mass murder makes you better Irish than me, you've no right to the name at all."

Pearse glared at her. "Anyone who oppresses her people deserves that and worse. I wish you'd been on the street when I pulled the trigger."

Molly looked to Zachary. "Did you hear that confession?" Before he responded, she turned back to Pearse. "You've the right to remain silent. Use it."

"We'll take it from here." Two Chicago cops strode past Zachary.

"Sure thing, Dice," Zachary said.

Xavier pushed through the spectators, and Molly was finally ready to hand over custody. Xavier and the cops marched Pearse off. They watched Pearse go. He glanced over his shoulder with a glower, and Molly returned a final smirk before the prisoner started down the stairs.

Now it was over. Molly dragged in a deep breath, jittery with all that excess energy and no release.

Zachary slipped an arm around her waist, and she released that breath, the adrenaline in her veins decrescendoing. She slid an arm around him in return and gave him a squeeze. She took a step toward the stairs down, but Zachary guided her around to the window to watch the rest of the parade. "The best vantage point, isn't it?"

She relaxed against him. "We're goin' to have so much paperwork Monday." But neither of them made a move to do anything but watch the parade pass. More than that, as her heart rate slowly returned to the normal range, Molly settled into Zachary's arms. Like she'd finally ended up where she'd wanted to be all along.

The pipe bands and floats, marching bands and just plain marchers passed. Molly spotted a group of dancers in green and purple. "My girls."

Kent strolled around to face them. "Looks like we need an FD-292."

Molly groaned. "You can do your own paperwork."

"Wait, that's . . . change in marital status?" Zachary guessed.

Molly shot him a lifted-eyebrow look. "Movin' a bit fast, aren't we?"

"I dunno," Zachary said. "We both loved wedding planning so much."

"You liar." She swatted his chest—then stopped short when she saw she was still wearing the fake engagement ring. "Would you look at this? You've dragged me down to your lyin' level!"

Zachary pulled out a ring box. "I'll make an honest woman out of you."

She gaped at him and reached for the box, but he tucked it into his coat pocket, trading it for two slips of paper—movie tickets for *The Woman from AUNTIE.*

Perfect.

"That's just the beginning," Zachary said.

Molly laughed and slipped her fingers between his. "Then I'll clear my to-do list."

Dear Reader,

Thank you so much for reading *Saints & Suspects*! Once again, this book is a labor of love: it took *eight years* to get it into shape to share with you. Now it's finally in your hands! I hope you enjoyed it as much as I enjoyed writing it and sharing it with you.

I've done all I can to make this book enjoyable for you. Can you do me a quick favor? If you'd be willing to review this book online, it would help me secure advertising spots and spread the word about this book. Additionally, if you send me a link to your review, I'll send you an invitation for a free review copy of my next novel. You can email me your link (or for any other reason! I love hearing from readers!) here: Jordan@JordanMcCollum.com.

Looking for more to read? There's one more novel in the Saints & Spies series, coming soon! In the meantime, check out my previous series, Spy Another Day, if you haven't already. If you join my reader's group, you'll get a free ebook to get you started in the series! You can join me here: http://jordanmccollum.com/read/

Thank you again, and I hope to entertain you again soon!

Jordan McCollum

P.S. **Want even more happily ever after?** Be sure to join my readers' group to get an extra bonus scene with a very important question! Join here: http://jordanmccollum.com/read/

I WAS SURE THE FIRST BOOK in the series would be the longest I'd ever take from writing a book until its final publication. And then this sequel threw me for a loop! After eight years and eight million changes, I'm so glad to finally get this novel out to you.

Publishing would be impossible without the love and support of so many people. My patient husband, Ryan, has gone above and beyond as I struggled and labored with this book for months on end. I cannot outline all the things he's done to support me and my writing—and you wouldn't believe me if I did. Our children, Hayden, Rebecca, Rachel, Hazel and Benjamin, have also been very patient, though I think we were all frustrated with the amount of work and time this book sucked up! My parents, Ben and Diana Franklin, taught me to love reading and writing from a young age, and they were my first (demanding!) editors. My sisters Jaime, Brooke and Jasmine, have cheered for me all along the way.

Once again, Sarah Anderson was invaluable as an alpha reader, the one and only time I've let someone read a work in progress. She encouraged and helped in the drafting process all those years ago. More recently, Raneé S. Clark again provided invaluable feedback, as did Heather Bairds, which led to another big rewrite. JoLyn Brown gave some great feedback to refine the next version, and Jaime Wilkins and Ben and Diana Franklin (AKA my parents) also gave final feedback. Naturally, Sarah Anderson gave it one last read-through before it was ready for you.

I want to again thank Sarah M. Eden for fantastic advice on writing an Irish character. Once again, Aisling Doonan of RubySasha Designs kindly read this book and offered excellent help on perfecting my Irish phraseology and culture from a native. Jenn Adams provided editorial feedback, but any errors here are not her fault. I swear, there are ghosts in the machine.

More research help came from Steven Kerry Brown, formerly of the FBI. He provided valuable information about how the FBI works—which led to more revisions. Joseph Francis Collins, a firefighter and paramedic with expertise in explosives, also helped with research facts on how a demolition company might store its explosives. Both of these men also understand the challenges of fact and fiction because they are authors themselves, and their help made this book stronger.

A special second round of thanks is due to Jaime Wilkins, Sarah Anderson and Ben Franklin, who gave extra feedback and an even bigger dose of encouragement at the last minute when I feared this book would never see the light of day. Without their help and feedback, I might've scrapped the whole thing. Instead, I was able to polish the book until it was not only ready to publish, but a work I was truly happy with.

Once again, the source of all inspiration, talent, time and effort is my Heavenly Father, and I'm eternally grateful to Him for these blessings. More than anything, this book became a very important part of a personal journey, and as such, despite the almost endless work this book required, I will always be grateful for the chance to tell this story.

About the Author

Photo by Jaren Wilkey

An award-winning author, Jordan McCollum can't resist a story where good defeats evil and true love conquers all. Her first four novels, the Spy Another Day series, were all voted as finalists for the Whitney Awards, a juried prize. In her day job, she coerces people to do things they don't want to, elicits information and generally manipulates the people she loves most—she's a mom.

Jordan holds a degree in American Studies and Linguistics from Brigham Young University. When she catches a spare minute, her hobbies include reading, knitting and music. She lives with her husband and five children in Utah.

www.ingramcontent.com/pod-product-compliance
Lightning Source LLC
Chambersburg PA
CBHW070833280626
47161CB00015B/560

9781940096209